PRAISE FOR AMY CLIPSTON

"A story of grief as well as new beginnings, this is a lovely Amish tale and the start of a great new series."

—*Parkersburg News and Sentinel* on *A Place at Our Table*

"Themes of family, forgiveness, love, and strength are woven throughout the story . . . a great choice for all readers of Amish fiction."

—*CBA Market Magazine* on *A Place at Our Table*

"This debut title in a new series offers an emotionally charged and engaging read headed by sympathetically drawn and believable protagonists. The meaty issues of trust and faith make this a solid book group choice."

—*Library Journal* on *A Place at Our Table*

"These sweet, tender novellas from one of the genre's best make the perfect sampler for new readers curious about Amish romances."

—*Library Journal* on *Amish Sweethearts*

"Clipston is as reliable as her character, giving Emily a difficult and intense romance worthy of Emily's ability to shine the light of Christ into the hearts of those she loves."

—*RT Book Reviews*, 4½ stars, TOP PICK! on *The Cherished Quilt*

"Clipston's heartfelt writing and engaging characters make her a fan favorite. Her latest Amish tale combines a spiritual message of accepting God's blessings as they are given with a sweet romance."

—*Library Journal* on *The Cherished Quilt*

"Clipston delivers another enchanting series starter with a tasty premise, family secrets, and sweet-as-pie romance, offering assurance that true love can happen more than once and second chances are worth fighting for."

—*RT Book Reviews*, 4½ stars, TOP PICK! on *The Forgotten Recipe*

ROOM ON THE PORCH SWING

OTHER BOOKS BY AMY CLIPSTON

ROOM ON THE PORCH SWING

AMY CLIPSTON

ZONDERVAN

Room on the Porch Swing
Copyright © 2018 by Amy Clipston

Requests for information should be addressed to:
Zondervan, *3900 Sparks Dr. SE, Grand Rapids, Michigan 49546*

ISBN 978-0-310-34905-1 (ebook)
ISBN 978-0-310-36295-1 (mass market)
ISBN 978-0-310-63656-4 (custom)

Library of Congress Cataloging-in-Publication
Names: Clipston, Amy, author.
Title: Room on the porch swing / Amy Clipston.
Description: Nashville : Zondervan, [2018] | Series: An Amish homestead
novel ; 2
Identifiers: LCCN 2017051646 | ISBN 9780310349075 (softcover)
Subjects: LCSH: Amish--Fiction. | Grief--Fiction. | GSAFD: Christian
fiction. | Love stories.
Classification: LCC PS3603.L58 R66 2018 | DDC 813/.6--dc23 LC record
available at https://lccn.loc.gov/2017051646

Printed in the United States of America

21 22 23 24 25 / LSC / 5 4 3 2 1

For my super awesome husband, Joe, with love and appreciation. Thank you for being my partner, my rock, and my best friend. And thank you most of all for putting up with my crazy for all these years. It's been a wild ride, and I wouldn't change it for the world. I love you!

GLOSSARY

ach: oh
aenti: aunt
appeditlich: delicious
Ausbund: Amish hymnal
bedauerlich: sad
boppli: baby
brot: bread
bruder: brother
bruderskind: niece/nephew
bruderskinner: nieces/nephews
bu: boy
buwe: boys
daadi: granddad
daed: dad
danki: thank you
dat: dad
Dietsch: Pennsylvania Dutch, the Amish language (a German dialect)
dochder: daughter
dochdern: daughters
Dummle!: Hurry!
Englisher: a non-Amish person

faul: lazy
faulenzer: lazy person
fraa: wife
freind: friend
freinden: friends
froh: happy
gegisch: silly
gern gschehne: you're welcome
grossdaadi: grandfather
grossdochder: granddaughter
grossdochdern: granddaughters
grossmammi: grandmother
Gude mariye: Good morning
gut: good
Gut nacht: Good night
haus: house
Ich liebe dich: I love you
kaffi: coffee
kapp: prayer covering or cap
kichli: cookie
kichlin: cookies
kind: child
kinner: children
krank: sick
kuche: cake
kumm: come
liewe: love, a term of endearment
maed: young women, girls
maedel: young woman
mamm: mom
mammi: grandma
mei: my

mutter: mother

naerfich: nervous

narrisch: crazy

onkel: uncle

Ordnung: The oral tradition of practices required and forbidden in the Amish faith.

schee: pretty

schmaert: smart

schtupp: family room

schweschder: sister

schweschdere: sisters

sohn: son

Was iss letz?: What's wrong?

willkumm: welcome

Wie geht's: How do you do? or Good day!

wunderbaar: wonderful

ya: yes

zwillingbopplin: twins

OTHER BOOKS BY AMY CLIPSTON

NOTE TO THE READER

WHILE THIS NOVEL IS SET AGAINST THE REAL BACK-drop of Lancaster County, Pennsylvania, the characters are fictional. There is no intended resemblance between the characters in this book and any real members of the Amish and Mennonite communities. As with any work of fiction, I've taken license in some areas of research as a means of creating the necessary circumstances for my characters. My research was thorough; however, it would be impossible to be completely accurate in details and description, since each and every community differs. Therefore, any inaccuracies in the Amish and Mennonite lifestyles portrayed in this book are due completely to fictional license.

ONE

"ALLEN!"

Allen Lambert rolled onto his side and yawned. His eyes blinked open, and his large but dark bedroom came into clear focus. The green numerals on his battery-operated digital clock read 2:12. What had awakened him so early?

He reached out his left arm and found nothing but cold sheets beside him. Savilla wasn't in bed. Had Mollie cried out in her sleep? He hadn't heard her.

"Allen!" His wife's voice was thin and shaky, as if she were calling to him through a thick door.

"*Ya?*" Allen sat up and shook off the remaining fog of sleep before leaping to his feet. He rushed to the hallway outside the master bedroom. When he heard Savilla's call again, he realized where she was.

His bare feet slid into the bathroom doorway, and what he saw alarmed him. Savilla sat on the floor, slumped against the far wall with strands of her golden-blond hair stuck to her pale face. Her honey-brown eyes were dull, and sweat beaded on her forehead as she reached for him.

He dropped to his knees in front of her and touched her forehead. It was blazing hot. A near panic clawed at his insides as his hands shook.

"You're burning up." He grabbed a washcloth from the towel rack above her and ran cold water over it. After wringing it out, he held it to her forehead. He felt guilty as he pushed the strands of hair away from her beautiful face. "How long have you been calling me?"

"I don't know." Her face contorted as she looked up at him. "I feel terrible." Her eyes widened. "*Ach*, no. I'm going to be sick again. You have to move."

He perched on the edge of the bathtub and gathered her thick, waist-length hair into one hand as she vomited into the commode. With his other hand, he rubbed her back and murmured reassurances.

When she finished retching, she covered her face with her hands and sobbed.

"Shh. This will pass."

Savilla made a guttural sound in her throat before being sick again. Then she collapsed onto the floor, leaning her head against his thigh, looking up at him.

"When did this start?" He wiped her mouth with the wet washcloth.

"I don't know. Maybe twenty minutes ago."

"Why didn't you call me to come sooner?"

"I thought it was going to stop, but it just kept going."

"I'm worried about you." He massaged the back of her head, and she closed her eyes.

"I'll be fine," she rasped. Then she lurched forward, slumping over the commode once again.

As he held back her hair, Allen cupped his other hand on the back of his neck. Confusion coiled through his insides. He needed to help his wife, but he didn't know how.

When she stopped vomiting again, tears spilled down her cheeks as she reached for his hand. "Would you please sit here with me?"

Pressure built in his chest as tears pricked his own eyes. "*Ya*, of course."

He dropped to the floor beside her and gathered her into his arms. He could feel her hot skin through the sleeves of her pink nightgown, yet she shivered against his chest. He kissed the top of her head.

"I must have the flu." She rested her head on his shoulder and sniffed. "Do you think that's it?"

"I don't know, but I'm really concerned."

"I'm sure I'll be fine tomorrow."

"I hope so." Once again he pushed Savilla's hair away from her face. His stomach churned. As her husband, it was his job to take care of her and protect her, and he hated that he didn't know what to do.

As she closed her eyes and continued to shiver, his worry increased. After several minutes, she gasped and then was sick again.

Nearly an hour later, Allen was trembling with anxiety as Savilla lay on a towel on the bathroom floor with her head in his lap, her body soaked with sweat and shuddering with chills. He'd gone for her robe to keep her warm, but she kept throwing it off no matter how many times he draped it over her.

God, please heal Savilla, he silently prayed as he held yet another wet washcloth to her forehead.

When her head suddenly turned to the right and her whole body went limp, he stiffened.

"Savilla?" He touched her shoulder, but she didn't respond. "Savilla!"

She remained silent, unmoving.

"Savilla!" His pulse galloped and his chest seized. "*Ach*, no. No, no, no." He rolled up two bath towels to make a pillow, placed them under her head, and then knelt beside her. "Savilla, please, answer me." He touched her cheek and then shook her arm. "Please answer me." He laid a hand on her chest and felt it move up and down. A tiny thread of hope took root.

"You're breathing," he whispered. "But you need help." He jumped to his feet, rushed into their bedroom, and pulled the quilt off their bed. After covering her with it, he stood for a moment in the bathroom doorway, his heart thumping against his rib cage. "I promise I'll be right back." She didn't respond or move a muscle.

He hurried back into their bedroom, pulled on a pair of trousers and a long-sleeved shirt, and ran down the stairs, taking two steps at a time. Then he ran through the kitchen and into the mudroom to push his bare feet into a pair of boots. Grabbing a Coleman lantern and the key to his shop, he launched himself out the back door and down the porch steps.

The cool mid-October air seeped through his shirt and trousers as his feet hit the ground.

When he reached the side door of his carriage shop, he unlocked the door and ran to the office. After calling nine-one-one and asking for an ambulance to hurry, he dialed Savilla's parents' number. He imagined it ringing in their phone shanty.

"Please answer," he whispered as the phone continued to ring. "Please, please answer." When their voice mail picked up, he waited for the greeting and beep as patiently as he could. "*Dat! Mamm!* It's Allen. Savilla is very ill, and I need your help." He ran his hand down his face and beard. "I've called for an ambulance, and it's on the way. Would you please meet me at the hospital? I need help caring for Mollie. *Danki.*"

After hanging up, Allen stood to run back to the house, but a fresh wave of panic drenched him. What if Milton and Irma Mae didn't receive the message in time? How could he take care of Mollie by himself when he was so worried about Savilla? His mind raced through a list of their closest friends. Laura Riehl,

Savilla's best friend, lived a couple of miles away and would help, but it was nearly three thirty in the morning. If he called their phone shanty, would anyone even hear it ringing?

Sirens blared in the distance, wrenching him from his thoughts. Help was almost here! He exited the shop, somehow remembering to lock the door, and stepped onto the rock driveway.

Moments later the ambulance arrived, its flashing lights casting eerie red shadows on his two-story brick home. The diesel engine rattled a noisy medley.

Allen's pulse pounded as he ran to the truck. Two EMTs leaped out of it.

"Please," he begged them. "Please help my wife."

Allen sipped from a water bottle as he walked down the long hallway toward Savilla's hospital room. He cupped his hand to his mouth to shield a yawn as he weaved past a woman in scrubs. She was delivering lunch trays. He'd been awake for nearly ten hours now, and his eyes were gritty with exhaustion.

Despite his fatigue, the time had flown by at lightning speed. Savilla was awake and talking when the ambulance arrived, and Allen and Mollie rode to the hospital with her. The doctor said Savilla's symptoms were similar to what he'd seen in other patients recently. She had the stomach flu, he said, and she'd passed out briefly only from dehydration.

While the medical staff treated Savilla with anti-nausea medicine and IVs for dehydration, Allen had tried to keep Mollie calm by walking her around the waiting area, thankful he'd remembered to grab the diaper bag Savilla always kept packed, as well as a bottle of formula from the refrigerator. Then Savilla's parents arrived around eight, and after they visited their daughter, they took Mollie home.

The medical staff had decided an hour ago to release Savilla, and Allen had just called his driver to ask for a ride. He couldn't wait to get his wife home. Perhaps Irma Mae would offer to stay and care for Mollie so he and Savilla could nap for a while. He longed to rest his weary eyes.

His shoulders tightened as he spotted a flurry of activity outside Savilla's room. A group of nurses stood by the doorway, their faces etched with something that resembled sorrow. One nurse covered her face with her hands as another patted her back.

Allen picked up his pace, and his heart thudded. "What's wrong?"

"Mr. Lambert," one nurse began. "I'm so sorry."

"What do you mean? Is something wrong with my wife?" He searched all their faces for answers.

Their doctor, a middle-aged man with a kind face, stepped out of the room, his head down. He looked startled when he realized Allen was there. "Mr. Lambert, may I please speak with you alone?" He gestured toward an empty room across the hallway.

"What's going on?" Allen gripped his bottle of water so hard it crackled in protest. He craned his neck, trying to see past the doctor and into Savilla's room.

The doctor hesitated.

"Just tell me," Allen insisted.

"I'm sorry, but your wife has passed away."

Allen froze as the words filtered through his mind. A choked sob sounded somewhere behind him. Had he heard the doctor correctly? "What did you say?"

The man rested his hand on Allen's shoulder. "Your wife passed away." His words were slow and deliberate.

Allen shook his head as it began to swim. "No, no. That can't be pos—"

"Mr. Lambert." The doctor leveled his gaze with Allen's. "Please listen to me. She's gone. We tried to save her, but we couldn't. I'm so sorry."

"Wha-what do you mean?" Allen's voice sounded strange to his own ears, higher pitched and wobbly. "I was only gone twenty minutes. I called her parents to tell them she was coming home, and then I called my driver to ask for a ride." His pulse pounded in his ears as he rambled on. "Then I went to buy a drink." He held up the bottle. "She was fine. In fact, we were talking about our daughter just before I—"

"Listen to me. Mrs. Lambert passed away approximately ten minutes ago."

"How is that possible?" Allen searched his eyes for any sign of a lie, but found none. "How could she have died? I had just spoken to her." He started to sway as everything around him went blurry. He had to be dreaming. This couldn't be real. None of this could be real.

"Her heart stopped." The doctor's words slammed into him.

"What?"

"I'm not a cardiologist, but I saw this with a patient a few years ago. It's called lymphocytic myocarditis, and it's extremely rare. To put it simply, an otherwise healthy person suddenly has heart failure caused by a virus." The doctor kept talking, but his words were only background noise to Allen's increasing disorientation.

Allen shook his head. None of this made sense. What was the doctor even saying?

"Your wife had flu-like symptoms, and the flu is a virus," the doctor continued, his words warm and gentle despite their chilling effect. "The virus attacked her heart, and her heart's immune response created the lymphocytic myocarditis condition. I'm so sorry, I didn't think—"

"No, no, no." Allen pushed past him and charged into the

hospital room as he tried to swallow against the terror crawling up his throat.

Savilla lay still on the bed, and her golden hair seemed almost brassy against her white skin. Her eyes were closed, and she looked well, peaceful, even beautiful. She was only sleeping. The doctor was wrong. He just had to be.

"Savilla?" Allen's voice came out in a strangled rasp. His body shook. "Savilla. Open your eyes, *mei liewe*."

He touched her cheek. It felt cool. He touched her arm, finding its warmth waning as well.

Allen's world tilted. The floor seemed to fall out from under him, and he nearly collapsed.

"Savilla. Please, open your eyes. Savilla. Don't leave me! I need you. Mollie needs you. I can't make it without you." Allen choked on a sob. "Savilla! Savilla! Please. Oh, please God. Don't take her." Bending at the waist, he dissolved in tears as he rested his cheek on her chest.

"Mr. Lambert." The doctor's voice was close to his ear. "I'm so sorry."

Allen closed his eyes and prayed he would wake up from this horrific nightmare.

TWO

LAURA RIEHL'S LUNGS SEIZED WITH GRIEF AS SHE stood between her boyfriend, Rudy Swarey, and her twin brother, Mark. They were at the graveside service for her best friend, Savilla. She tried to take a deep breath, but it seemed an impossible task.

The sky above her was infused with dark, threatening clouds, mirroring her emotions on this tragic, sad day. The heavy aroma of moist earth wafted over her, and she shuddered as her gaze moved to the coffin that held Savilla's body.

"Hold on, sis," Mark whispered in her ear as he rubbed her shoulder. "It will be all right."

"No," she whispered, her voice a little louder than she'd expected. "Nothing will ever be all right again."

Rudy covered her hand with his and gave it an encouraging squeeze. With her other hand she pulled a tissue from her coat pocket and wiped her nose and cheeks.

When her lower lip trembled, she took a shivery breath and willed herself to not cry. She'd cried so much during the past three days that she was surprised she had any tears left to shed.

She'd met Savilla, along with their mutual friend Priscilla Allgyer, on their very first day of school. The three of them became best friends, and they'd grown up together, sharing all

AMY CLIPSTON

their secrets and milestones like sisters. But then Priscilla unexpectedly left the community four years ago. Laura and Savilla had missed Priscilla terribly, but they still had each other. And now, in the blink of an eye, Savilla was gone, leaving behind a husband, a baby.

Another sob began to bubble up, and as if he could read her mind, Mark placed a hand on her arm.

"Shh," he whispered under his breath. "Be strong for Allen and Mollie. They need us."

Laura nodded and looked up at her twin's warm blue eyes. He always knew when she needed his endless encouragement.

The minister read a prayer, and her heart broke for Allen, Savilla's parents, and baby Mollie. Laura glanced at Allen's face. It was contorted with grief as he stared down at the ground, tears rolling down his cheeks and dripping onto his black coat. Irma Mae sobbed and hugged Mollie to her chest. Beside her, Milton wiped his eyes as he tightened his arm around his wife's shoulders.

When the minister's prayer ended, a murmur of conversations spread throughout the crowd. Laura began to make her way between the knots of mourners.

"Where are you going?" Rudy grabbed her arm and gently pulled her back.

"I need to talk to Allen." Laura shook her arm from his grasp.

"We spoke to him earlier today." Rudy's dark eyebrows drew together.

"I want to make sure he's okay."

"I know, but we've been at his *haus* for the past two days helping him through this. It's okay if we back off a little and let someone else help him now."

Laura sighed. "I know, but Savilla was my best *freind*. I need to remind Allen that I'm here if he needs me. I can't leave without talking to him again."

"I'm sorry, but I have to go." Rudy jammed his thumb toward the row of horses and buggies lining the cemetery. "I need to get back to *mei dat's* store. I promised him I'd be back in time for his lunch break."

Mark sidled up to Rudy. "You can go. I'll make sure she gets home."

Rudy divided a look between Laura and Mark and then gave Mark a curt nod. *"Danki.* I'll see you both later." Then he was swallowed up by the crowd as he left the cemetery.

"I don't understand how he can go back to work without talking to Allen," Laura muttered as Mark walked beside her. "I can't even think about leaving without talking to him one more time."

"Rudy is upset too. He just expresses his feelings differently than we do." Mark nodded toward her destination. "Go on."

Allen was shaking a church member's hand as Irma Mae stood next to him, still holding Mollie. Laura stepped in front of Allen when the man walked away.

"Laura. *Danki* for being here." Allen's voice shook. Dark purple circles rimmed his bloodshot eyes, evidence he hadn't slept in days. He cleared his throat and wiped tears from his face and beard with one hand. The pain and sorrow in his expression shattered her heart.

"Allen." She took his cold hands in hers. She was aware the intimacy could be considered forward, but Allen was like a brother to her. Surely everyone would understand their connection. "If you need anything at all, please call me."

"Danki. I—" A woman Laura didn't know nearly knocked her out of the way.

"Allen!" the woman said. "Oh, Allen. I'm so sorry. Savilla was so very young. Only twenty-two years old, and a new *mamm.* And she was Irma Mae's and Milton's only *kind.* You all must be simply crushed."

Allen winced at the words, and disgust rolled through Laura. She took a step toward the thoughtless woman and opened her mouth, ready to give her a piece of her mind.

As if he knew Laura was about to chastise the woman, Mark took her arm and steered her through the crowd. "Let's go now, sis. We can head over to Allen's *haus* and help serve the meal."

"Did you hear what she said?" Laura seethed as she turned to glare at the woman. "How cruel and thoughtless can you be? Did you see Allen's face?"

"Let it go," Mark warned. "Sometimes people don't think, and Allen doesn't need you to cause any more tension around him."

They walked in silence as they made their way across the cemetery.

"I can't believe she's gone," Laura finally said. "We just lost *Mamm* a few months ago. Why did God have to take Savilla from me too?"

"You know it's not our place to question God's will." Mark opened the passenger door of his buggy. He looked down the long line of horses and buggies and nodded. "*Dat* is riding back with Cindy, Jamie, and Kayla. They're going to meet us at Allen's and help serve the meal too."

"*Gut.*" Laura waved to *Dat*, their younger sister, older brother, and their brother's girlfriend.

As she climbed into Mark's buggy, her new reality hit her. Life would never be the same without Savilla. But she'd find a way to not only keep Savilla's memory alive, but be a support to Allen in any way he needed.

Savilla would do the same for her if circumstances were reversed.

Allen stared down at Mollie sleeping soundly in the baby swing in his family room. He scrubbed his hand down his face and beard and took a deep breath.

The days since the worst moment of his life had zipped by in a blur of tears, sorrow, and drowning anguish. His beautiful Savilla, the love of his life, was gone before he had a chance to say good-bye, and now he had to pick up the pieces of his life. The doctor told him the condition that killed her wasn't genetic or heredi-tary. It had just happened to Savilla without warning. He made it sound so simple, but Allen only understood his wife was gone.

Just days ago, his life was perfect. He had his thriving busi-ness, his beautiful wife, and their lovely baby girl. Now he was alone with more heartache and confusion than he ever could have imagined.

For three days, members of his community had paraded through his house, leaving casseroles, words of condolences, and promises of prayers in their wake. But now his home—his and Savilla's home—was silent. The only sound he heard was his heart shattering into a million pieces.

"I put whatever I could fit into the refrigerator."

Allen spun to face Irma Mae. She was standing in the door-way to the kitchen.

"There's still food on the counter. I don't know what you want me to do with it."

"Take it with you. I don't feel like eating anyway."

His mother-in-law stared at him.

"What?" he asked.

"I'd like to stay overnight so you can get some sleep." She crossed the room to stand beside him. "I'll feed Mollie Faith in the middle of the night so you can get up for work. I'm sure your buggy orders must be backed up by now."

"That's not necessary." He jammed his hands into the pockets of his trousers. "I can afford to hire a nanny. I don't expect you to take care of her."

"Don't be *gegisch*. She's *mei grossdochder*." She sniffed. "She's all I have left of Savilla, and I want to be here."

"Fine." He swallowed against his bone-dry throat.

"Besides, only family should care for her. I insist. I've already told Milton I'm going to be here as much as you need me."

"*Danki.*"

She stopped the swing, unbuckled Mollie, and lifted her into her arms. "I'll get her ready for bed. You should go to bed too." Then she headed up the stairs, holding Mollie against her chest.

As Irma Mae disappeared up the stairs, Allen sank onto the sofa and leaned his head back, smacking it on the wall as his thoughts roiled with a mixture of bereavement and despair. Today he'd put his beautiful wife into the cold, hard ground, but it seemed as if their life together had only just begun.

Tomorrow Allen would have to return to the business of life. How would he go on without her?

Closing his eyes, he began to pray.

God, please give me strength, because I don't know how to go on. I don't know how to be a daed *to Mollie Faith, and I don't know how to live without Savilla by my side. Help me, God. Guide me, please.*

THREE

ALLEN LEANED AGAINST HIS CURRENT BUGGY PROJECT and sighed. He swiped his hand over his sweaty brow as the sweltering July humidity hung over his three-bay shop like a dense fog. Glancing at the clock on the wall, he found it was only ten in the morning. It felt as if he'd been working for eight hours, not two. The days seemed to drag ever since he'd lost . . .

Shoving the thought away, he pushed off the side of the buggy and strolled through his shop. He wiped his hands on a red rag and dropped it on top of one of his toolboxes before pulling down the large garage door. Then he walked up the rock path to his house. He had three more buggies to repair and another one to rebuild, but he needed a break. A glass of ice-cold water would hit the spot right now, and then he'd get back to work.

As he climbed the back-porch steps, he stilled and held his breath. He was certain he'd heard a voice, someone yelling. But only his mother-in-law and baby were in the house. Why would Irma Mae yell?

Unless something was wrong.

Panic, swift and hot, shoved him up the steps and through the door into the mudroom.

"Allen! Allen, please help me!" Irma Mae screamed his name from the kitchen. She sounded desperate.

Blood roared in his ears as memories of the night Savilla had wakened him with a frightened call suddenly haunted him.

"*Mamm!*" Allen rushed into the kitchen. Irma Mae lay in a heap on the floor next to a step stool, her leg at an odd angle and tears spilling down her reddened cheeks.

Beside her, his daughter wailed in her high chair, reaching for Irma Mae. Sweat had matted Mollie's hair to her head, and her blue eyes sparkled as tears rolled down her cheeks. They were as bright red as Irma's.

"*Mamm!*" Allen crouched beside her on the floor, his body trembling with concern for his mother-in-law. "What happened?"

Sweat beaded on her brow and dampened the graying blond hair barely visible from under her prayer covering. Her eyes, the honey-brown color she'd passed on to Savilla, were wide with panic. "I was just trying to get a large mixing bowl off the top shelf, and my foot slipped. Next thing I knew, I was on the floor. I should have just asked you to come in, but—"

Her loud sob set Mollie screaming even louder.

"It's okay." He started to reach for Irma Mae's hand but then stopped, afraid of hurting her. "What hurts?"

"My leg." Her lower lip trembled and she gasped. "The pain is radiating up my leg and into my hip. I can't move it, and it hurts so badly I can hardly breathe."

"Ma-ma-ma," Mollie wailed between hiccups. "Mmmmm-ma-ma-ma."

Allen's heart twisted as he looked up at his daughter. "It's okay, Mollie. *Mammi* will be fine. I'm going to get her some help. Just calm down, sweetheart." He looked down at Irma Mae and patted her arm. "Don't move. I don't want you to do any more damage. I'm going to call an ambulance."

Irma Mae nodded. *"Dummle!* Please."

"I will." He rushed out the back door and down the steps to the side door of his shop. As he dialed nine-one-one in his office, he fought against the cruel, stinging memories still threatening to hijack his emotions.

"Nine-one-one. What's your emergency?" A steady feminine voice responded on the other end of the line.

"I need an ambulance. My mother-in-law fell off a step stool and she's hurt." Then he recited his address and gave his best description of her injuries.

"We'll have someone there to help you shortly," the woman promised.

"Thank you." Allen hung up the phone and dialed his in-laws' number. Again, memories of the night Savilla became ill taunted him, but he pushed on. He had to take care of Irma Mae.

"Hello?" Milton answered on the third ring, and Allen blew out a sigh of relief.

"Dat, it's Allen. I need you to come right away. *Mamm* fell off a step stool."

"Ach, no!"

"It's going to be okay." Allen held up his hand to calm him as if his father-in-law were standing in the office with him. "She hurt her leg and is in pain, but she's alert. The paramedics are on their way. Can you get here quickly?"

"Ya, ya. My driver is here. I'll be right over." Milton hung up before Allen could respond.

Allen replaced the receiver and ran back into the house. Mollie was still crying and smacking her hands on the high-chair tray.

"Give her some Cheerios." Irma Mae pointed to the counter.

"Oh. Right." Why hadn't he thought of that? He grabbed the box of cereal and placed a handful on the tray.

When Mollie arched her back and continued to howl, Allen removed the tray and lifted her into his arms. He bounced her and whispered in her ear until her wails were reduced to sniffs. Once she was calm, he returned her to the high chair, buckled her in, and replaced the tray.

"Why don't you eat some Cheerios?" He moved the cereal around on the tray.

With a loud sigh, Mollie picked up a piece of cereal and popped it into her mouth.

With his daughter soothed, Allen turned his attention back to Irma Mae. He crouched down, facing her. "Milton and the paramedics are on their way. Would you like a glass of water?"

"*Ya*, please."

He poured a glass of water and then knelt beside her, holding the glass as she took a few sips. Sirens sounded in the driveway.

"I'll be right back." Allen jumped up, set the glass on the counter, and rushed outside. A fire engine sat next to an ambulance.

He jogged down the back steps as Jamie Riehl, the eldest of the Riehl siblings as well as a volunteer firefighter, climbed out of the fire truck. Waves of relief flowed through Allen.

Jamie loped over to him. "What happened?"

"Irma Mae fell off a step stool. I think she may have broken her leg." Allen pointed toward the house. "She's in the kitchen."

"Where's Mollie?" Jamie asked.

"In her high chair. She's fine, but Irma Mae is in bad shape."

Jamie turned toward the EMTs. "We'll need a gurney."

In moments, the EMTs, both men who looked to be in their mid-twenties, rushed by, pushing a gurney. Leon King, another firefighter, and Brody Morgan, their volunteer firefighter chief, came to stand on either side of Jamie. He repeated what Allen said.

"Let's get inside and see how we can help." Brody nodded toward the back porch, and Leon followed him.

Jamie stayed behind. "Is Milton on his way?"

"*Ya.*"

Allen suddenly realized the EMTs might be scary for Mollie, so he sprinted into the house, made sure the team had no questions, and took Mollie outside. She'd stayed calmer than Allen had thought she would, but she seemed glad to see him.

He blew out a puff of air in frustration when he rejoined Jamie. "Irma Mae said she was trying to reach a large mixing bowl from the top shelf." Holding Mollie against his chest, he shook his head and kicked a stone with the toe of his boot. "I feel like I should go to the hospital with Irma Mae and Milton, but I can't take Mollie there. She'll get cranky, and that will just cause everyone more stress." Just being in the hospital at all would be stressful. The memories of Savilla's unexpected death there were still so fresh.

"There's an easy fix for that." Jamie started walking toward the shop.

"What's the easy fix?" Allen fell into step beside him as they moved up the path.

"I'll call *mei schweschdere.*" Jamie stepped into the shop through the side door, went to the office, and began dialing the phone. He held the receiver to his ear, and after a few moments, he began to speak. "Hey, Mark? It's Jamie. Could you ask Laura or Cindy to come to Allen's *haus*?"

As Jamie explained what happened to Irma Mae, Allen sat down on the edge of his desk, balanced Mollie on his lap, and held his breath. Mollie loved Laura and Cindy. If one of them came, she'd be all right and he could go to the hospital to lend his in-laws support.

Laura hefted her tote bag onto her shoulder and then headed up Allen's back porch steps.

As her shoe touched the top step, the door swung open, revealing Allen clad in black trousers and a dark blue shirt. At twenty-six, he stood at Mark's towering height. He had light-brown hair and, having been married, a beard. He also had a strong jaw and bright, intelligent baby-blue eyes.

His intense expression softened as he met her gaze. "*Danki* so much for coming on such short notice. I didn't know what to do with Mollie, and that's when Jamie suggested seeing if you or Cindy could come."

"*Gern gschehne.*" She stepped into the mudroom. "I'm always *froh* to help you, and my driver was able to come right away."

He held out his hand. "Let me take your bag."

"Oh, no. It's not heavy." She followed him into the kitchen and set the bag on a kitchen chair. Then she glanced around the room. "Where's Mollie?"

He nodded toward the family room. "She's asleep in her play yard in the *schtupp*." He shook his head. "As the EMTs were loading Irma Mae into the ambulance, she was shouting instructions to me. She said Mollie will nap until about noon, eat lunch, play for a while, and then nap again."

"Okay." Laura tilted her head with concern. "How is Irma Mae?"

He rested his arms on the back of the chair beside her. "I'm afraid her leg is broken. She was in a lot of pain."

Laura winced. "I'm so sorry."

He stood up straight. "*Ya,* I am too. She was trying to reach a mixing bowl. If she'd only called me in, I could've grabbed it for her."

She rested a hand on her hip and lifted an eyebrow. "What makes you think Irma Mae would've asked you for help? After all, she was barking orders at you as the EMTs were taking her to the hospital."

He nodded. "You've got a point."

"So after Mollie wakes up, I need to make her lunch." She crossed to the refrigerator. "Do I need to prepare anything special for her?"

"No, Mollie usually has something simple at noon." He pointed to two sippy cups and lids sitting in the drainboard. "Yesterday Irma Mae gave her half a cut-up grilled cheese sandwich, a couple of slices of banana, some yogurt in a bowl, and a cup of milk."

Then he pointed toward the family room. "Irma Mae has a diaper-changing station set up near the sofa. Diapers, cream, and wipes are all there. We've been using mostly disposable diapers lately, but cloth diapers are drying in the utility room if you want to use them. Irma Mae switches between the disposable and cloth ones. Mollie naps in the play yard since the upstairs is so hot this time of year."

"Okay. I can handle all that. Is there anything else I need to know?"

"She usually sleeps in the afternoon until about three." His eyebrows drew together. "Do you need to be home by a certain time?"

"No." Laura leaned back against the counter and pointed to her bag. "I brought clothes in case you decide to stay at the hospital and need me to be here overnight."

"I don't expect you to do that." He turned toward the window above the sink. "My ride is here." Then he looked back at her and clasped his hands together. "Can you think of anything else you might need?"

"No." She shook her head. "Do you need me to do any chores? I can make dinner or do some cleaning."

"I didn't ask you to be my housekeeper. Just watch over Mollie, okay?"

"That's an easy job." She waved him off. "Go. Give my love to Irma Mae and Milton."

"I will. *Danki*." He went through the mudroom and out the back door.

Laura walked to the sink and peered out the window as Allen climbed into the gray van. It steered down the driveway and out of sight, and then she leaned back against the counter. She glanced around the large kitchen, taking in the familiar long oak table with seating for six, the matching oak cabinets, and the golden granite countertops.

Her eyes stung with unshed tears at the realization that Savilla had been gone for as long as she had. She pressed her lips together as memories of the special times she'd spent in this kitchen with her best friend tumbled around her mind. It was here that Savilla shared she was expecting a baby, here that they cried together when Laura lost her mother, and here that they talked about their future plans. Never in her wildest dreams had she expected to lose her best friend before they turned twenty-three.

The aroma of fresh, moist air mixed with daffodils came through the window as her mind swirled with memories of how Savilla and Allen met. He was her cousin Lena's neighbor in Indiana, and he had just lost his grandmother, who raised him. Lena said he was a shy but kind man who could use a friend.

Lena suggested Savilla write to Allen, and a special friendship soon blossomed through their letters. At first Savilla called Laura when she received a letter from Allen and read it to her. But after a couple of months, Savilla only blushed when Laura asked if she'd heard from him. Laura realized Savilla was falling in love with her pen pal from Indiana.

When Allen came to visit Savilla for the first time, Laura rode with her to the bus station to pick him up. And as soon as Savilla saw Allen, Laura was certain she would marry him. When their eyes met, both Savilla and Allen grinned, and excitement radiated off the two of them. It was as if they'd known each other their whole lives, and Laura immediately felt like an intruder in their private moment.

Soon after that meeting, Allen sold his carriage business in Indiana and purchased a home and business in Bird-in-Hand. Savilla couldn't wait to be married and start a family. Their future seemed bright, but it had been snuffed out only months ago.

Laura's heart squeezed as she crossed the kitchen and stepped into the family room. Mollie slept on her stomach. Laura smiled as she crouched down and took in the baby's sweet little face and the shock of golden-blond curls covering her little head. Her left thumb was stuck in her mouth, the only sound coming from her soft snores.

Laura reached into the play yard and touched the back of Mollie's pink onesie and then her little hand. She enjoyed the softness of her skin. Oh, how her heart ached for Savilla, who wouldn't get to see her beautiful daughter grow up and become a woman.

"I'll be here for you, Mollie," she whispered. "If you ever need anything, you can talk to me. Don't ever forget that."

Mollie moaned and snuggled deeper into the play yard's cushion, her thumb never leaving her mouth.

Laura walked to the bookcase on one wall and ran her finger over the bindings of Savilla's collection of Christian novels. Savilla had always loved reading, and she read a book every week if she had the time.

She pulled one of the books from the shelf and opened it, finding a bookmark decorated with "John 3:16" and a rainbow stuck near the back. Was this the novel Savilla had been reading when she died? The thought caused her eyes to flood with tears, and Laura blinked them away.

She kicked off her shoes and curled up on the sofa next to the play yard, tucking her feet under her purple dress. Then she opened the book and began to read.

She was starting chapter three when Mollie began to rustle around. Mollie's eyes fluttered open and she stared up at Laura. While she had her father's baby-blue eyes, Mollie's golden hair resembled Savilla's. She also had a petite nose and a smile that could light up a room, just like her mother's.

Laura closed the book and set it on the end table, and then she leaned forward and smiled down at Mollie. "Hello, sleepyhead."

Mollie groaned and rubbed her hand over her nose as her eyebrows drew together.

"*Wie geht's?*" Laura stood over the play yard and held out her arms.

Mollie rolled onto her side and sat up. Then she grabbed the side of the play yard and pulled herself up, her stare never moving from Laura's face.

Laura clapped. "That's *wunderbaar!*"

"Mmmm-ma-ma-ma-ma," Mollie said with her little face contorted in a scowl.

Laura sighed. "You want your *mammi*, don't you? Your *mammi* had to see a doctor, but I'm going to take care of you. You know me. *Mei schweschder* Cindy and I stop by to visit you every week." When Mollie continued to frown, she added, "Can you say Laura?"

"Ma-ma-ma." Mollie's bottom lip quivered.

"Don't cry, little one. I promise we'll have fun together while we wait for your *dat* to get back." Laura scooped up Mollie and carried her to the sofa.

As she changed her diaper, Laura's thoughts turned to Irma Mae. She couldn't imagine the pain the older woman must be going through. She'd been through so much since Savilla's death.

They all had.

FOUR

Allen stepped into the kitchen and stilled as a sweet, melodic voice sounded from the family room.

"Jesus loves me, this I know, for the Bible tells me so . . ."

He quietly moved to the doorway leading to the family room, leaned his right shoulder against the doorframe, and peered at Laura and Mollie in the rocking chair. Laura was singing to his daughter as she sprawled across Laura's lap, staring up at her as she drank from a bottle.

Laura's dark-brown hair peeked out from under her prayer covering, and her blue eyes sparkled as she gazed into Mollie's. Allen had often marveled that Laura shared hair coloring with her older brother, not with Mark's. Her twin's hair was a lighter shade of brown than hers and Jamie's, but all three of the siblings shared the same bright-blue eyes.

"Little ones to him belong. They are weak, but he is strong." Laura smiled down at Mollie as she continued to rock. "Yes, Jesus loves me. Yes, Jesus loves me . . ."

His heart twisted as a vision of Savilla rocking Mollie in that same chair filled his mind.

Laura lifted Mollie to a sitting position and patted her back. "Yes, Jesus loves me. The Bible tells me—" She gasped when her eyes moved to the doorway, her gaze colliding with his. "I'm so sorry. I didn't see you there." Her cheeks blushed bright pink, and she looked down at Mollie. "Your *dat* is home. See?" She pointed to Allen.

Mollie let out a loud belch as she turned toward the doorway. Then she squealed and held out her arms.

"Hi, Mollie-girl." When he crossed the room and picked her up, she wrapped her arms around his neck.

"Aww." Laura smiled and stood. "You can have the rocking chair."

"No. Please sit." He sank onto the sofa as she sat back down.

"I was giving her formula." She handed him the bottle. "I remembered Irma Mae telling me when I visited last week that Mollie still has two bottles a day. I hope that's okay."

"It's perfect. *Danki.*" He looked down at Mollie when she swiped the bottle from his hand and began to drink again.

"I guess I didn't need to feed her like a *boppli.*" Laura folded her hands in her lap. "She was a little fussy earlier, but she stopped when I sang to her."

"You have a *schee* voice."

"*Danki.*" She rocked the chair back and forth. "I think Mollie misses Irma Mae. How is she?"

Allen shook his head. "She not only broke her right leg in two places, but her hip as well. No wonder she was in such pain. She had surgery today, and she'll need more this week."

"*Ach,* no!" Laura cupped her hand over her mouth.

"She's still in a lot of pain. I was going to stay longer to keep Milton company, but he sent me home. He said he could handle everything."

Regret settled over him. *If only—*

"But how are you, Allen?"

His eyes snapped to hers in confusion. Why would Laura ask

how he was when Irma Mae was the one who was in pain and facing multiple surgeries?

Her expression softened. "You look upset."

"I am upset." He frowned.

"It's not your fault."

"It happened in *mei haus*. I can't help but feel responsible." He rubbed Mollie's back. "Irma Mae's going to be in the hospital for a while and then go into a rehabilitation center to learn how to walk again. I can't work and take care of Mollie, so I'll have to hire a nanny."

"No, you won't."

He looked into her eyes, surprised she'd think so. "What do you mean?"

"I'll take care of Mollie."

He lifted an eyebrow. "But you have chores to do at your *dat's* farm."

"I'm sure Cindy will handle my chores while I'm here." She placed her hands on the armrests as she continued to rock back and forth.

"Are you sure?"

She stopped rocking and leaned forward. "You and Mollie are like family. I want to help you. Besides, Irma Mae has done so much for my family. She stopped by to check on us, brought us food, and helped with chores for weeks after *mei mamm* passed away. She's like my second mother. This gives me a chance to repay her. She normally takes care of Mollie while you work, right?"

He nodded slowly as appreciation replaced his worry. "*Ya*, you're right."

"It's settled, then."

"Should you check with your *dat* first?"

"I will, but I'm sure he'll agree to it. We all want to help you."

Allen pressed his lips together. He didn't want anyone's pity.

But this was Laura Riehl, Savilla's dearest friend. She was like family, and when Savilla died, Irma Mae said only family should care for Mollie. This was his best option.

Laura stood. "Let me take Mollie so you can go back to your shop and get some work done."

He shook his head. "It's after four. I think I'll just call it a day."

"Do you need me to give her a bath?" She held out her hands.

"No, *danki*. I can take care of that too."

"Oh." Laura folded her arms over her black apron.

"You can go home."

"Okay." She hesitated as if unsure if she should go or insist on staying. "What time would you like me to be here tomorrow?"

Allen scratched his head as Mollie finished the formula and then burped. "That's really up to you." He took the bottle from Mollie, and she grumbled before arching her back. He stood, and as he bounced her, she blew bubbles at him.

Laura touched Mollie's arm while she paused to think. "How about eight? Is that early enough for you to get to work in your shop?"

"*Ya*, that's perfect."

"Great. I'll talk to my family tonight and then call you to confirm I'll be here at eight."

"*Danki*."

Laura leaned forward and kissed Mollie on the cheek. "Be *gut* for *Dat*."

Mollie reached for Laura, and Laura grinned.

Then Laura looked up at him. "I'll see you tomorrow."

"*Danki* again for helping me today on such short notice."

"Stop thanking me." She headed to the kitchen, and he followed her. "Oh." She turned to face him. "Do you want me to make supper before I leave? I can throw a casserole together for you. I found some ingredients in the refrigerator."

"I think I've had enough casseroles to last me a lifetime." The words slipped from his lips without forethought, and he cringed when Laura's eyes widened.

"I'm so sorry. I didn't mean to insult you or the rest of the women in our community." His apology came in a rush. "I've appreciated all the meals everyone has provided for me during the past months."

She laughed, and his shoulders loosened with relief.

"Well, Allen." She lifted her chin in mock irritation. "Remind me to never make you another casserole." She smiled. "Do you want me to make you something else?"

"No, *danki*. I'll just make myself a sandwich."

"Okay. I need to call my driver."

He nodded toward the mudroom. "Let me put Mollie in her play yard with some toys and I'll walk you out to the shop."

As they headed out the back door together, he silently prayed Vernon would allow Laura to care for Mollie until Irma Mae recovered. He needed the help.

"Irma Mae broke her leg *and* her hip?" Cindy shook her head, and her light-blue eyes widened. "That's *bedauerlich*."

"I know." Laura scooped up a spoonful of mashed potatoes, and then she glanced at her sister. Cindy's light-brown hair always turned a golden hue in the summer sun, reminding Laura for a moment of Savilla's and Mollie's hair. But she shoved that thought aside, noting last year her seventeen-year-old sister had grown taller than she was.

"That's why I offered to care for Mollie while Irma Mae is in the hospital and then the rehabilitation center. She's going to have to learn how to walk again." Laura glanced at her father at the head of the table. "Is it okay with you if I take over as Mollie's full-time nanny for now?"

Dat smiled as he gestured toward Cindy. "I think you need to ask your *schweschder* that question." In his mid-fifties, *Dat*'s graying light-brown hair and beard had once been the same color as Mark's hair, but his bright-blue eyes still reminded Laura of her twin's eyes.

Laura looked back at Cindy. "Would you please handle my chores while I help Allen out? I'll do double the chores on Saturdays and in the evenings."

Cindy rolled her eyes. "Of course you can help Allen. It's the right thing to do, and you don't need to make up anything. I'm sure I can keep pace. After all, I'll have to handle all the chores once you and Rudy are married."

Before Laura even had a chance to digest what Cindy said, her sister shot Mark a cheeky grin across the table. "Everything will be fine as long as your twin picks up after himself."

"Hey." Mark gave her a palms up. "I'm not the one who leaves his dishes on the table. That would be Jamie." He waggled his eyebrows and smirked as he pointed at their eldest brother beside him.

"Oh, no, no, no!" Jamie shook his head. "Why are you blaming me for your messes? We all know Laura picks up behind Mark."

"That's not true." Mark forked a piece of pot roast and shoved it into his mouth.

"*Ya*, it is." Jamie turned to face him. "It's that whole twin thing."

"I don't pick up after him all the time," Laura said as she chimed in, even though it was a fib. She did pick up after Mark. Sometimes she felt more like his mother than his sister.

"All right. That's enough." *Dat* gestured around the table. "We'll all pitch in with the household chores so Laura can help Allen and so Cindy won't feel overwhelmed. One of us will even dry the dishes tonight before we go outside to do our evening chores."

"*Danki.*" Laura breathed a sigh of relief. "I'm going to be at

Allen's *haus* by eight tomorrow so he can get caught up on his buggy projects. He didn't get much work done today since he spent so much time at the hospital."

They were all silent for a moment, the scraping of utensils on plates the only sound in the kitchen. Laura's mind spun with thoughts of Irma Mae, Allen, and Mollie. She hoped she would be an adequate replacement for Irma Mae.

Bringing her thoughts back to her family, she turned to Cindy. "Did you finish that log cabin quilt today like you planned?"

Cindy nodded as she finished chewing and swallowing. "Mary came and picked it up."

"I bet she loved it." Laura smiled at her younger sister when she gave a half-shrug. "You'll never admit just how talented you are. Are you going to start another one now?"

"*Ya*, I am. Sara Glick asked if I'd make one as a gift for her *sohn*. She said I could suggest a color scheme and pattern. I started looking through my fabric and drawing patterns this afternoon, but I haven't decided yet."

"That's *wunderbaar*. You'll have to show me what you choose." Laura looked across the table at Jamie. "How is the construction going on your *haus*?"

"Not as quickly as I'd hoped, but it's coming along." Jamie ran his fingers through the condensation on his glass as a smile turned up the corner of his lips. "I still have to finish the floors, and then I need to order the appliances. But it's starting to look like a *haus* on the inside. I picked out a kitchen set, and that will be delivered soon."

"So it sounds like you might be moving out before you know it," Mark said.

Jamie lifted his glass of water. "*Ya*, it looks that way."

"When you do, Laura will get your room." Mark pointed his fork at her.

Laura nodded. "*Ya*, I guess so."

Cindy cleared her throat and said, "Jamie, why haven't you asked Kayla to marry you yet?"

Although her question was simple, Jamie stilled, his glass suspended in the air as he stared wide-eyed at his youngest sister.

Mark snickered and punched Jamie in the shoulder. "Did Cindy scare you?"

"No." Jamie shot Mark a glare.

Laura covered her mouth as she laughed. Soon *Dat*, Mark, and Cindy joined in.

"I've been thinking about asking her." Jamie stared down at his plate.

"What are you waiting for?" Mark asked.

Jamie pursed his lips. "Why are you so worried about when I'm going to get married when you can't settle on only one *maedel*?" He pointed toward the back door. "Didn't you tell me Ruthann, Franey, and Sally all left you messages today on voice mail? You said every one of them wanted to know if you'd like to come over for supper this week."

"Looks like I'm going to eat well, then." Mark leaned back in his chair and rubbed his flat abdomen. "Cindy, you won't need to worry about my dishes for a while."

"You're missing my point, Mark." Jamie scowled. "You've been pressuring me about Kayla ever since I met her, but you can't even date just one *maedel*. They all chase after you like you're some great prize, and you like it that way."

"I am a great prize." Mark forked another piece of pot roast.

"Is that so?" Jamie lifted an eyebrow. "And you're modest too." He aimed his fork at Mark. "Maybe you need to concentrate more on your own love life and stop worrying about mine."

"My love life is just fine the way it is." Mark smirked at him. "You're the one who's approaching thirty."

"Are we really back to this again?" Jamie massaged his forehead as if a headache brewed there. "I'm only twenty-six."

"True." Mark's smile widened. "But I'm only twenty-three. I have plenty of time before I need to worry about settling down."

"Can we please change the subject?" Jamie's voice held a hint of a whine, and Mark chuckled.

"Did you notice if I had messages?" Laura blurted the question and then took a sip of water.

Jamie shook his head. "No, there weren't. Were you expecting any?"

"No." Laura stared down at her plate and remembered Cindy's earlier comment, the one about her and Rudy getting married. She hadn't spoken to Rudy since he came for supper last Wednesday, and she'd expected to hear from him since yesterday was an off Sunday without a church service. It wasn't unusual that she and Rudy would go a few days without talking, but thoughts of him always lingered in the back of her mind when Jamie mentioned Kayla.

Her brother and Kayla had been dating for a year now, he had already built a house on their farm, and he was probably going to get married soon. She and Rudy had been dating for four years, but the subject of marriage rarely entered their conversations. If Laura even mentioned someone's upcoming marriage, Rudy changed the subject. Did he ever think about marrying her?

Did her family wonder why Rudy hadn't asked her to marry him yet?

Suddenly her mother's voice filled her mind.

Rudy is a gut, honest man, but he's a bit immature. You need to have patience with him. Give him time to grow up and realize how important your relationship is to him.

Mamm said that a little over a year ago when Laura complained that Rudy sometimes chose to see his friends instead of her. And Laura soon realized *Mamm* was right about him. Their relationship was comfortable and easy. There wasn't any pressure, but there weren't any promises for a future either.

How long should she wait for Rudy to grow up and want marriage and a family? Was he the man God wanted for her, obligating her to wait? But what if he never wanted those things?

Laura swallowed back the questions buzzing through her mind. When she looked up, she found Mark watching her from across the table. With his eyes trained on hers, Mark lifted his eyebrows in question. She shook her head, telling him everything was fine before she set to finishing her supper.

After she and Cindy had washed the dishes, with Mark assigned drying duty, Laura walked out to the phone shanty. She breathed in the humid air as the cicadas serenaded her. She looked out over the pasture to Jamie's new two-story, three-bedroom white clapboard house on the other side, and she smiled. Kayla and Jamie would be married someday soon, and then she would see Kayla every day. She looked forward to welcoming her into their family and calling Kayla her sister.

When she stepped into the phone shanty, she dialed Allen's number and waited for his voice mail. Her mind whirled with memories of the thousands of times she'd dialed this number to speak to Savilla, and her chest tightened. Oh, how she missed Savilla's voice, her smile, her sage advice, and her patient ear.

After six rings, Allen's voice rang through the phone. "You've reached the Bird-in-Hand Carriage Shop. We restore, repair, and sell buggies. The shop is open Monday through Friday, eight to five, and Saturdays, eight to noon. Please leave a message, and I will call you back as soon as I can. Thank you."

"Allen," Laura began after the beep, "this is Laura. I'll be there at eight in the morning. My family is very supportive, so you can depend on me to take care of Mollie until Irma Mae is back. Have a *gut* evening. See you tomorrow."

She hung up and stepped out of the phone shanty, almost colliding with Mark's chest. "I'm sorry. I didn't hear you."

"I was looking for you." Mark leaned back against the side of the shanty and wagged a finger at her. "You seemed preoccupied at supper. What's bugging you?"

"Nothing is bugging me." She picked at a loose piece of wood on the phone shanty doorframe. "Well, that's not entirely true. I'm worried about Irma Mae. She has extensive injuries."

"That's not it." He touched her arm. "I'm your twin. We've always been able to sense each other's moods, and I can tell when you're not telling me the whole truth."

He paused for a moment, and she held her breath and continued to fiddle with the piece of wood. She knew Mark was assessing her silence. At times, he could see right through her façade, but other times, he mistook her moods. Still, Mark always knew when something was bothering her, and she could sense his distress as well. Her finger worked the piece of wood loose, and she tossed it to the ground.

"Do you feel obligated to take care of Mollie?"

Her gaze snapped to his. "Why would you say that?"

"I don't know." He shrugged. "Maybe because Savilla was your best friend. It's just a big commitment to become Mollie's full-time nanny. It's going to take away from your time at home."

"I'd do anything to help Savilla's family. Besides, Irma Mae has been a tremendous help to us since we lost *Mamm*."

"I understand that, but Allen runs a successful business." He gestured wide. "He can afford to hire one of the teenagers in our church district to be a full-time nanny. Or maybe a widow who needs the income."

She scrunched her nose. "Why would he hire someone when

I'm willing to help him? I've known Mollie since she was born, and I'm like family to them. Cindy and I go to see her at least once a week so we can still be part of her life."

"But you're not family. It's not your job to drop everything and run to his rescue."

"Run to his rescue?" Frustration washed over her. "He lost his *fraa*, and now his mother-in-law is injured. It's not like he decided to be stuck in this situation."

"You're right. I'm sorry." He held up his hands as if to calm her.

"Besides, it's our way to help one another. I'm just doing what others did for us when we lost *Mamm*."

Mark was silent for a beat, but she could almost hear his thoughts. He wasn't done analyzing her. She looked toward the house and searched for an excuse to walk away from him.

"Have you discussed it with Rudy?"

She stared at him as confusion replaced her annoyance. "Why would I discuss it with Rudy? It's my decision where I work. Besides, we're not married. I only need *Dat*'s permission to work for Allen. Rudy won't care."

He tilted his head and rubbed his clean-shaven chin. "There's something up with you. Did you have an argument with Rudy?"

Laura threw her arms up in the air. "No, everything is fine with Rudy."

"*Gut.*" He looked past her toward the barn, and a grin overtook his lips. "Did you see Jamie's face when Cindy asked him why he hadn't proposed to Kayla yet?"

She looked to where Jamie stood talking with *Dat*. "*Ya*, I did. You should stop hassling him about Kayla."

"Why would I do that? It's fun."

"You really know how to get under his skin."

"That's my job. I'm his younger *bruder*." He spread his arms wide. "It's all in fun, and he knows that."

Laura watched Jamie for a moment. "Do you think he'll marry her this year?"

"I think it's a possibility. He has a *haus* now, and they seem to be *froh* together. Why wouldn't they get married?"

"It will be strange having a wedding without *Mamm*."

His smile drooped. "*Ya*, it sure will." He pointed toward the house. "Let's get inside before we get eaten up by mosquitos."

She fell into step with him as they walked toward the back porch.

"So, Laura, I have a really important question to ask you."

"What is it?"

"Whose *haus* should I go to first for supper this week? Should I go to Franey's, Ruthann's, or Sally's? Ruthann makes the best steak you could ever eat, but Franey's beef stroganoff is out of this world. *Mmm*." He grinned. "Then again, Sally sure knows how to make the most *appeditlich* fried chicken. My mouth is watering just thinking about it."

As he droned on about his choices, Laura again considered her relationship with Rudy. Where were they heading?

FIVE

A LIGHT BREEZE MOVED OVER ALLEN'S SKIN AS HE stared up at the ceiling and replayed the events of the day. Worry had been his only companion for hours. He couldn't stop thinking of Irma Mae and hoping she was doing well after her surgery earlier today. He prayed she would have a smooth recovery, but he knew it would also be a long one.

After he'd put Mollie to bed three hours ago, he'd checked his voice mail and was relieved when he found Laura's message confirming she would start coming tomorrow. His daughter would be safe in Laura's care while he worked. Now he just needed to get some rest. But first he had to turn off his swirling thoughts.

He rolled onto his side, facing the wall next to Savilla's side of the bed. He reached out and touched the cold sheets as memories took over his thoughts. He remembered their first night together in this house, the night of their wedding. It seemed as if that had been last month, not nearly two years ago.

When he'd married Savilla, he'd been certain they'd grow old together. He'd imagined sitting on the back porch and holding hands while watching their grandchildren play on a swing set in their backyard. It wasn't fair that her life had been snuffed out when she was only twenty-two, barely a year after they'd married.

Why had God chosen to take her away when they'd just begun their life together?

Closing his eyes, he tried in vain to push away the memories. It was a sin to question God's will. Besides, he needed sleep so he could tackle his projects in the shop with fresh eyes tomorrow.

Just as he started to drift off, a piercing sound split through the dark room. He sat up and spun toward the door.

"Ma-ma-ma-ma! Maaaaaaa!" Mollie shrieked.

Allen grabbed a lantern off his nightstand, flipped it on, and rushed down the hallway to the nursery. He crossed the floor to Mollie's crib, where she stood holding on to the rails and screaming. Her little face was red as fat tears streamed down her cheeks.

"Ach, mei liewe." His heart twisted as he set the lantern on the floor and lifted her into his arms. "Shh, baby girl." He walked backward to the rocker and sank into it. "It's okay, Mollie Faith. Your daddy is here now."

He rocked her in a gentle motion as she buried her face into his shoulder and the tears continued to flow. He sighed and patted her little bottom as his thoughts turned to Savilla and how she would rock Mollie back to sleep. Even Irma Mae seemed to have the gift of calming Mollie when she was upset. She usually didn't spend the night anymore, but if only Irma Mae were here now.

Closing his eyes, Allen rocked until Mollie was asleep. When he stood and laid her back in the crib, her eyes flew open.

"Maaaaaa! Ma-ma-ma-ma!" Her wail tore through the room, and she again stood, grabbed the rails, and started jumping up and down.

"Okay, okay. I won't leave you, Mollie." Allen picked her up and returned to the chair, and they rocked back and forth. Perhaps he wouldn't get any sleep tonight.

As he leaned his head against Mollie, he breathed in her

scent—baby wash combined with diaper cream—and he closed his eyes. It was going to be a long night.

⌒ᘓᖆᘓ⌒

"*Gude mariye*," Laura sang as she stepped into Allen's mudroom the following morning. "*Wie geht's?*"

"I'm all right. How are you?" He reached for her large tote bag, and she handed it to him.

"I'm fine. *Danki*." She followed him into the kitchen, where Mollie sat in her high-chair eating Cheerios. "*Wie geht's*, Mollie?" She crossed the floor and touched Mollie's shock of blond curls. "How are you, sweetheart?"

Mollie looked up at her and sputtered.

"I guess that means you're well." Laura laughed and then turned to Allen as he removed the four portable Pyrex containers from her tote bag and put them on the counter. "I brought meals for lunch and dinner. And don't worry—they aren't casseroles."

His shoulders hunched and he frowned. "I really didn't mean that."

"I'm just teasing you." She chuckled, and his face relaxed a fraction. She idly wondered when she'd seen him smile last. Was it before Savilla died? She walked to the counter and picked up the containers. "Do you mind if I put them in the refrigerator?"

"Go right ahead." He gestured toward the appliance. "Let me help you."

"No, I can do it." She piled the containers on the top shelf of the refrigerator and closed its door.

Allen leaned back against the sink and cupped his hand over his mouth to stifle a yawn. Then he rubbed his eyes with the heels of his hands. She'd already taken in the dark purple rings under his tired blue orbs.

"You're exhausted." She stepped closer to him, worried.

He snorted. "*Ya*, I am."

"Did you sleep at all last night?"

He shook his head. "Not much."

"What happened?"

He rubbed the back of his head with one hand and then looked past her toward Mollie. "I couldn't sleep because I had too much on my mind. Just as I was about to drift off, she started crying. I rocked her for most of the night. I slept maybe an hour."

"*Ach*, no. Why don't you go take a nap?"

He shook his head as he covered his mouth to stifle another yawn. "I have too much to do out in the shop. I need to get three buggies done by Friday."

He pushed off the counter and then nodded toward Mollie. "She ate a piece of *brot* and a scrambled egg, so she should be full. I'm going to take care of my horse, and then I'll be in the shop if you need me." He waved at Mollie and left.

Allen stepped into the house at noon and sat down on the mud-room bench to remove his work boots.

In the kitchen, he found Laura sitting beside Mollie's high chair as she broke some cheese into pieces. "I'm Laura. Say Laura. Come on, now. You can say it. Say Laura." She pronounced the word slowly as she handed Mollie a piece of cheese.

"Ma-ma-ma," Mollie responded before shoving the cheese into her mouth.

"No, that's not it." Laura chuckled. "Try again. Laura." She drew out the name. "You can do it. Laura."

Warmth, sudden and unexpected, hummed through Allen.

Mollie met Allen's gaze and squealed. "Da! Da! *Dat*!"

Laura turned toward him, and her face lit up with a wide smile. "That's right! That's your *dat.*"

Mollie squealed again and clapped her hands against the high chair's tray.

"I didn't hear you come in." Laura placed another piece of cheese in front of Mollie.

"I just got here." He moved to the sink to wash his hands. "So you're giving her a speech lesson." He looked over his shoulder at Laura.

"I wanted to see if she could say my name."

Her cheeks flushed pink. Was she embarrassed?

"I think she's calling Irma Mae." Allen ripped off a paper towel, dried his hands, and then tossed the paper towel into the trash can.

"I do too." She gestured toward the table, where a tray of assorted lunch meats and cheese slices, a basket of rolls, and a bowl of macaroni salad sat. Two places were set with placemats, plates, utensils, and glasses of water. "I hope you like lunch meat."

"Wow. Were you expecting company?" He sat down in the chair across from her.

"I didn't know what you like, so I wanted to make sure I had a variety."

Appreciation rolled over him. "This is amazing. *Danki.*"

"*Gern gschehne.*" She gave Mollie another piece of cheese and then turned to face the table before bowing her head.

After a silent prayer, they built their sandwiches and then ate in silence for a few minutes. In between bites, Mollie babbled and tapped the high chair tray with her fingers.

"I'd like to do a few chores this afternoon." Laura's offer broke through the silence. "After cleaning the kitchen, I can do your laundry."

"No." He scooped a mound of macaroni salad onto his plate.

"I already told you. I don't expect you to be my housekeeper. I just appreciate your taking care of Mollie for me."

"I don't mind doing it. I need something to do while she naps this afternoon." She placed a piece of macaroni on Mollie's tray. The baby stuck it into her mouth, swallowed, and then held out her hand for more.

"I guess you liked that," Laura said. She placed a small pile of macaroni on the tray and then looked at Allen. "I'm not going to sit all afternoon while Mollie naps. If I don't do the laundry, I'll do something else for you."

"All right." Then the issue of payment resurfaced in his mind. "You need to let me know how much you want me to pay you."

After swallowing the bite in her mouth, she said, "What do you mean?"

"I want to pay you for your time. I would pay a nanny if you weren't here, so it's only fair to pay you as well."

Her bright-blue eyes narrowed. "I won't accept money for caring for Mollie. She's like *mei bruderskind.*"

"I at least need to pay you for the food you brought today." He gestured toward the bounty.

She shook her head as she chewed and then swallowed. "I don't want any money from you. I just want to help."

He was too tired to argue. "Fine. *Danki.*"

"So you'll let me do the laundry?" Her face lit up with a smile.

He bit back a smile at her enthusiasm. "*Ya,* you can do the laundry."

"Great." She pointed to the utility room off the kitchen. "Baskets are in there, and hampers are in the corner in your bedroom and Mollie's room, right?"

He nodded. "*Ya.*"

She placed another spoonful of macaroni salad onto the high chair's tray. "How are your projects going?"

"I've made some good headway with the one buggy." He

explained the damage he was repairing while they finished lunch. Then he helped her carry dishes to the sink.

"You can go." She waved him off. "I'll clean this up."

"*Danki* again for lunch." He touched Mollie's head and then walked back out to the shop.

After Laura cleaned the kitchen, she set Mollie in her play yard with a couple of toys. Then she found a large plastic laundry basket in the utility room and went upstairs to gather the dirty laundry.

When she reached the landing, she stopped at the master bedroom, the first door on the left. As she stood in the doorway and scanned the room, memories of the last time she was there formed.

Savilla had invited her over for lunch, and when the baby spit up on her dress, Savilla asked Laura to run upstairs to fetch a clean dress for her and a clean onesie for Mollie. The large bedroom looked exactly the same with the king-size bed in the center of the nearest wall and two dressers on the far wall. One of the dressers had a tall hutch with a large mirror, shelves, and six drawers below that. The other dresser was also tall with six drawers.

She set the basket on the floor next to the hamper and walked over to the dresser with the hutch. She swallowed hard when she found Savilla's favorite things on it—her comb and brush, a small trinket box, a vanilla-scented candle, and a picture of a rose with Savilla's favorite Scripture passage engraved on it.

Laura picked up the picture frame and ran her fingers over it while letting the verses soak through her. They were from 1 Thessalonians 5:16–18: *Rejoice always, pray continually, give thanks in all circumstances; for this is God's will for you in Christ Jesus.* The words touched her deep in her soul.

Then she set the frame back on the dresser and lifted the

brush, turning it over in her hand. Strands of Savilla's gorgeous, thick golden hair were stuck in the bristles. Her eyes stung as she imagined Allen looking at Savilla's belongings and recalling all their special memories together.

She returned the brush to its place on the dresser and then touched the brass knob on the top drawer. She hesitated, but then, unable to tame a suspicion, she pulled the drawer open. It was full of Savilla's underwear and stockings. She pushed it closed and opened the drawer beside it. It was full of her nightgowns and slips. The bottom two drawers contained more of her clothes.

Laura opened the closet door and found Savilla's dresses and aprons tucked in the back of the closet beyond Allen's shirts and trousers. She reached into the back and ran her hand over a rose-colored dress, which always brought out Savilla's pink cheeks and beautiful brown eyes. Grief rolled over her. Allen hadn't disposed of any of Savilla's clothes. He was still holding fast to her memory.

So was she.

She gently closed the closet door and returned to the hamper. It was stuffed, and she piled Allen's clothes into the basket. Then she moved toward the doorway, but stopped and turned back toward the bed. It was unmade. The dark-blue sheets were a twisted knot in the center, evidence of Allen's restless night. She paused. Should she wash his sheets? Or was touching them too invasive, too personal? Even more personal than washing his clothes?

She shook off the thought. She'd changed her brothers' sheets and remade their beds for years without a second thought. Why would touching Allen's sheets be any different?

Because he's not your bruder. He's not family. He's Savilla's husband.

She stood up straighter.

No, he's Savilla's widower, and he needs my help.

As she began pulling the sheets off the bed, her gaze moved to the floor. She spotted something metal sitting in the cramped space between the bed and the nightstand. Bending down, she picked up a small, square box. Engraved on the top was "S.L. + A.L."

Laura ran her fingers over the engraving. "Savilla Lambert plus Allen Lambert." She opened the box and found a handful of bobby pins. Closing its lid, she turned it over in her hands. She didn't recall Savilla ever mentioning the box to her. It had to be a gift from Allen. Had it been an engagement gift? Or a wedding or anniversary gift? Laura was certain it was special.

How had it wound up on the floor? Had it been lost during the chaos the night Savilla became ill? Allen would want to know she'd found it. She slipped it into the pocket of her apron and made a mental note to give it to him.

After she finished stripping the sheets from the bed, she stuffed them into the basket before adding Mollie's dirty clothes. Then she went back downstairs and found Mollie sleeping in the play yard. After making sure she was all right, Laura went into the utility room and began the wash.

Allen yawned and glanced up at the clock. It was only three. He didn't always take a midafternoon break, but with the blanket of exhaustion wrapping around him today, he needed one—and a bottle of water. He stood up from the buggy he'd been repairing and stretched.

He set his tools on the bench and left through the side door of his shop. As he made his way up the path, he saw Laura hanging laundry on the back porch. The line was filling up with his sheets and both his and Mollie's clothes.

He climbed the steps and joined her by the line. "You've been busy."

"It needed to be done." She gave him a half-smile before hanging a pair of his trousers. "Mollie is still fast asleep in her play yard. I just checked on her a few minutes ago. I think she was really full after eating all that macaroni salad at lunch."

He bent down, picked up another of his trousers, and handed them to her.

"*Danki.*" She hung them on the line, and he handed her two more pairs before she turned toward him.

"Don't you have something better to do?"

"I needed a break, so I thought I'd get a bottle of water." He handed her one of his shirts.

"Oh." She set the shirt back into the basket and headed for the back door. "I'll get you one."

"Wait." He grabbed her arm and tugged her back. "I didn't mean for you to get the bottle of water. I can get it." When she faced him, he released her arm.

"Oh. Okay." Her forehead puckered. "I don't mind getting it for you. You look exhausted." She pointed to the glider. "Why don't you have a seat?"

"You don't need to take care of me. I can get things for myself. You just looked like you needed some help." He gestured toward the basket. "That's a lot of laundry. Irma Mae was going to take care of it yesterday." Guilt twisted through him as he glanced back toward the clothesline. "You really need to let me pay you."

Her face twisted into a scowl as she lifted her chin and slammed her hands onto her small hips. "If you offer to pay me once more, I won't come back."

He bit back a grin as a comment Savilla once made echoed through his mind. "All those Riehl siblings are stubborn," she'd said. Yes, indeed that was true.

Her expression softened. "Have you heard from Milton?"

"*Ya.*" He leaned back against the porch railing. "He called earlier and said Irma Mae's first surgery went well. Her leg is in a cast now. She's going to have surgery on her hip tomorrow."

Laura cringed. "I'm so sorry she has to have more surgery, but I'm glad the first one was successful."

"Milton said her spirits are *gut*, and she's already talking about what she has to do at the *haus* when she gets home."

She chuckled. "That sounds like Irma Mae."

They studied each other for a moment, and he noticed her powder-blue dress somehow made her eyes even bluer. Was it the bright afternoon sun making them even more striking?

She opened her mouth as if to say something, but then she closed it and looked away.

Curiosity pushed him away from the railing, and he stood up straight. "What did you want to say?"

"Nothing, nothing." She waved off the question, and the ties of her prayer covering bounced off her slight shoulders as she retrieved two clothespins from the pouch hanging next to the line.

He waited a moment and then pulled open the screen door. A thought occurred to him. Did Rudy approve of Laura's working for him? Rudy had become his first friend in Bird-in-Hand, and Allen considered him a good friend. They'd spent so much time together on double dates, as Savilla called them.

But everything changed after Savilla passed away. He only interacted with Rudy at church, and they rarely talked beyond discussing the weather. It was as if Rudy didn't know what to say to him after he lost Savilla. But Rudy wasn't the only one who didn't seem to know what to say to him now that Savilla was gone. No one really talked to him at church, except to ask how his business was doing or to comment about how big Mollie had grown since the last time they'd seen her.

"Have you spoken to Rudy?" he asked.

Laura faced him, her brow furrowed again. "Not since last Wednesday."

He blinked. This was Tuesday. Rudy hadn't talked to her for . . . six days? When he was dating Savilla, they spoke to each other at least three times a week and wrote letters daily. How could Rudy go so long without seeing her or checking to see if she was okay?

"You haven't spoken to him for nearly a week?"

She shrugged. "Sometimes we don't talk for a few days, but I'm sure I'll hear from him soon. Do you need something from him?" She pointed to the shop. "I can call his *daed*'s hardware store for you if you want."

"No, that's not it." He paused. "I was wondering if he approved of your working here."

Something unreadable flickered in her eyes as her lips pressed together before she responded. "Rudy doesn't need to approve where I work."

"Oh." Savilla's words about the stubborn Riehl children sounded in his mind once again. "I didn't want to upset him by having you over here all the time."

"He won't mind." Her expression brightened. "What time would you like to eat supper?"

"You don't have to—"

"I think we need to set some ground rules." Her hands were back on her hips. "You need to stop telling me what I don't need to do. If I want to make you supper, then I will. You look worn-out, and you don't need to worry about making a meal after working all day in your shop. Besides, I enjoy cooking, and trying new recipes is one of my favorite pastimes."

He bit his lower lip to prevent a chuckle from escaping. How long had it been since he'd laughed at anything but his daughter's antics? Since Savilla died, of course.

He nodded. "You're right."

"Also, when I ask you what time you want me to have your supper ready, you must give me a specific time. The last thing I need is for you to come in at five thirty looking for supper when I have it planned for six. I think that's a fair request, don't you?" She lifted her eyebrows.

"*Ya*, I agree. How about five thirty, then?"

"That's perfect." Her smile was back. "I'll go home after the kitchen is clean and Mollie has had her bath." He opened his mouth to protest, and she held up a finger. "What did we just discuss?"

He sighed. "Fine. *Danki*."

"*Gern gschehne*." She grinned. "And I promise it won't be a casserole."

He groaned as she laughed. "You're never going to forget that, are you?"

"Nope." She opened her mouth to say something more, but she was interrupted when a wail exploded from inside the house. "Someone is awake." She started for the door.

"I'll finish the laundry and you get Mollie," he offered as she stepped past him into the house.

"Don't be *gegisch*. I can handle everything. You just get your water and then go back out to your shop. I'll see you at five thirty."

As she disappeared through the screen door, Allen felt his shoulders relax. He continued to hang the clothes on the line anyway, and after several minutes, he heard the door open and then click shut. He pivoted as Laura walked toward him, balancing Mollie on her small hip.

"Hi, baby." He reached for Mollie and took her from Laura. "How was your nap?"

Mollie yawned and then burrowed her head into his shoulder.

He kissed the top of her head as she sighed.

"I just remembered something," Laura said as she dug into her apron pocket. "I found this when I was stripping your bed." She held out a small metal box.

Allen balanced Mollie with one arm and took the box in his free hand. He gasped as he turned the box over in his hand. "I've been looking for this. Where did you find it?"

"It was on the floor between the bed and the nightstand."

Tears stung Allen's eyes as he stared at it. He'd given Savilla the special box engraved with their initials the night before their wedding. It was a symbol of their impending union and their new life together, a life cut short after little more than a year. An ache opened in his chest and quickly spread.

"When did you give it to her?" Laura's question was quiet, as if she were afraid of the answer.

"The night before our wedding." He cleared his throat and pushed the box into his pocket. "*Danki* for finding it." He looked down at Mollie to avoid Laura's sympathetic eyes.

"If you take her, I'll finish hanging the laundry," she offered.

"Okay." Allen moved past her into the house and plopped Mollie into her play yard. "I'll be right back," he promised before loping up the stairs and into his bedroom.

He crossed the room to his dresser and recalled Savilla's gorgeous smile when he'd first handed her the gift. She'd cried tears of joy and then kissed him. The moment was forever etched in his mind as if it had happened yesterday. His lungs tightened as a tear trailed down his cheek.

Although he'd given Savilla many gifts during their short time together, she told him this small memento meant the world to her. Every night she'd stood at her mirror and removed the bobby pins from her hair before storing them safely in the box. After she died, he searched for it, tearing his room apart to find it.

He looked over at the bed. How had the box wound up on the floor?

Now that he'd found it, he wouldn't risk losing it again. He pulled open the top drawer of his dresser, moved aside his clothes, and set the box at the back. Then he covered it with his clothes. He would guard the box and keep it safe, as if it were his heart.

SIX

THE BACK DOOR CLICKED SHUT AS LAURA PLACED A platter of baked pork chops in the center of the table and took in her work.

She'd set two places, including two glasses of water. A bowl of green beans, a bowl of mashed potatoes, and a basket of bread surrounded the pork chops. A plate of oatmeal raisin cookies sat on the counter for dessert.

She rubbed her palms over her apron and turned toward the doorway to the mudroom. Allen stood staring at her, his eyes wide.

She frowned. "Let me guess. You dislike pork even more than you dislike casseroles." She groaned as she pointed to the table. "I suppose I should have asked if you—"

"No, no, no." He shook his head and crossed the room, coming to a halt at his chair. "I'm just a little surprised you had all of that in your tote bag."

"Not all of it." She gestured to the green beans. "I found those in the refrigerator and the rolls in the *brot* box."

Mollie crawled across the kitchen floor, sat up, and reached for Allen. *"Dat! Dat! Dat!"*

"Hi there. I'll pick you up in one second," he told Mollie before moving to the sink to wash his hands. Then he lifted his daughter, who squealed and held up a teething necklace. "Everything looks *appeditlich.*"

Laura stood a little taller. "Aren't you *froh* you let me stay for supper?"

"Let you?" His eyebrows shot up. "You make it sound like I had a choice."

She laughed and leaned on the back of the chair where her place was set. "I'm ready to eat when you are." She reached for Mollie. "Would you like to get in your high chair?" Mollie didn't answer, but Laura took her from Allen, buckled her in, locked in the tray, wiped her hands with a clean cloth, and handed her a roll. "Can you say *brot*?"

Mollie squealed again and then took a bite.

"That's close enough." Laura shook her head and then looked over at Allen as he folded himself into his chair across from her. She sat down and bowed her head for the prayer.

After they ate in silence for several minutes, Laura shifted in her seat. "Did you finish any of your projects?" she asked while buttering a roll.

He nodded as he cut a pork chop into neat pieces. "I finished the one and called the customer. He's supposed to come for it tomorrow."

"That's *gut.*" She lifted the roll to her lips.

"You've been busy today too."

"*Ya,* I have. I changed your sheets and put away your clean laundry. I also swept the *schtupp* and started dusting, but I ran out of time."

He frowned, and she hurriedly chewed and swallowed the bite she'd just taken.

"Don't say it." She pointed her fork at him. "I wanted to. I know I didn't have to."

His expression relaxed, and he shook his head and took a bite of pork chop. "This is amazing."

"I'm glad you like it. I used *mei mamm's* favorite recipe. I brought her cookbook with me in case I needed it. *Mamm* and I used to cook together every day. I miss that." She cut up her own pork chop while trying to think of something else to say. She'd shared many meals with Allen after he moved there from Indiana, but she'd never shared a meal alone with him. She didn't remember ever being alone with him before the last couple of days. She racked her brain for something to discuss.

"Do you miss Indiana?" she finally asked.

"I guess so." He shrugged. "Sometimes I miss *freinden*, but I don't really think about it much."

"Did you leave any family behind?"

He shook his head. "No."

She tilted her head. "You don't have any cousins or *aentis* and *onkels*?"

"Not that I know of."

She stared at him, trying to comprehend his response.

He picked up his glass. "You look confused."

"I am. What do you mean by 'not that I know of'?"

"I guess Savilla never told you about my parents?" he asked. She shook her head. "*Mei mamm* wasn't really Amish. She was raised in an Amish home, but she left when she was twenty. She came home when she was pregnant, had me, and then left again. I don't know anything about *mei dat* or his family. I don't even know his last name. My grandparents were the only family I've ever known. *Mei daadi* died when I was eighteen, and *mei mammi* died when I was twenty-one."

"You never met your *mamm*?"

"I met her once when I was six. She came to visit, but she didn't stay long."

"Do you remember meeting her?"

"*Ya.*" He forked some green beans. "I remember her arguing with *mei mammi*, and then she left."

"I'm so sorry."

"It's okay, really. My grandparents were my parents. My biological *mamm* gave birth to me, but that's it. I had a *gut* childhood. *Mei daadi* had a carriage repair business that he passed on to me." His expression was warm. "I miss them, but I was *froh* to move here to be a part of Savilla's family and her community." Something flitted across his face—sadness or maybe grief—and then it was gone.

Laura nodded as she contemplated his story.

Mollie grunted, and Laura turned toward her. The roll was gone except for a few crumbs.

"You like *brot*, huh?" Laura cut two tiny pieces of pork chop and dropped them on the tray. "You need some protein. Try that."

Mollie picked up a piece and ate it before smiling up at Laura with her blue eyes sparkling.

"You like pork?" Laura leaned down and grinned at her. "Can you say Laura? Come on, now. Laura."

Mollie sputtered at her and then ate the other piece of pork.

"One of these days she's going to say my name." She looked over at Allen and found him watching her with intensity in his expression. She swallowed. "Did I do something wrong? Do you not want her to eat pork?"

"That's fine." He wiped his mouth and beard with a paper napkin. "I'm just surprised by how *gut* you are with Mollie. You really have a talent with *boppli*."

"Not really." She cut up more pork and placed it on Mollie's tray. "I helped our neighbors with their *kinner* when they were young. I've always loved taking care of *kinner*, and I guess you just never forget how to handle them. And even at five, I liked helping *Mamm* take care of my baby sister Cindy."

"Your childhood was different from mine. You had siblings."

"*Ya*." Laura laughed a little. "And I got a twin as a bonus."

"You and Mark are close."

"*Ya*, we are. Contrary to popular belief, we can't read each other's minds, but we can sense each other's feelings. Sometimes I long for some space, but he means well. He's protective, and I do appreciate that. Well, most of the time." She ate some potatoes and then turned to Mollie. "You're doing well with your green beans." After giving Mollie some mashed potatoes, she turned back to Allen. "Are you refurbishing any buggies to sell?"

"*Ya*, I picked up two."

"What's wrong with them?"

During the rest of supper, she and Allen talked about his buggy projects, and Laura was relieved to avoid awkward silence.

When they were full, she carried the dirty dishes to the sink, scraped them, and then turned on the faucet. Allen brought the leftovers to the counter and pointed to her empty Pyrex dishes. "Do you want me to put these in the containers for you?"

"*Ya*." She nodded toward the refrigerator. "You can keep them."

He raised an eyebrow. "Are you certain?"

"*Ya*." She set the dirty dishes in the sink. "You can go sit down if you'd like. I'll take care of the dishes."

He hesitated and then held up a hand. "I have a suggestion. Why don't you give Mollie a bath, and I'll do the dishes?"

Laura was about to tell him he didn't have to keep helping her, but then she looked at Mollie. The little girl was smashing potatoes on her tray, and they were caked in her curls and stuck to the side of her face. Laura grinned. "Do you really think she needs a bath?"

"*Ya*, I really do."

Laura looked up at him, still smiling. "I think that's a *gut* idea."

"Whew." He cupped his hand to his forehead with feigned dramatics. "I thought you were going to yell at me for suggesting you not complete one of your self-imposed chores."

She chuckled. "Am I that bad?"

"I don't want to answer that question. You might yell at me." He turned toward the sink. "I'll get started on the dishes."

With a clean, wet washcloth, Laura wiped off what food she could from Mollie's face and hands, unhooked the tray to the high chair, and lifted her into her arms. She kissed her messy forehead and smiled. She was going to enjoy caring for Mollie.

As she walked out of the kitchen, she thought she could feel Allen's stare burning into her back. Was he concerned she wouldn't be the best caregiver for his daughter? She certainly wasn't Savilla, or even Irma Mae, but she'd do everything she could to reassure him.

—⟨∞⟩—

Laura yawned as she climbed out of her driver's van two hours later. After giving Mollie a bath, she helped Allen finish cleaning the kitchen and then offered to watch Mollie while he showered. But he insisted she go home.

The weight of her exhaustion pressed down onto her shoulders. It had been a long day, but she'd enjoyed every moment with Mollie.

"You're finally home."

Laura looked up at the back porch. Rudy sat there, pushing the glider back and forth with his toe. He leaned forward, resting his elbows on his thighs as he studied her.

"*Wie geht's?*" She stopped at the top of the steps and let her tote bag drop to the porch floor with a loud *thunk*. "I didn't expect to see you tonight."

Suddenly Allen's confused expression and his words from earlier filled her mind. *You haven't spoken to him for nearly a week?*

As she took in Rudy's dark eyes and handsome face, doubt confronted her. They'd always had a relaxed relationship, but the realization that they hadn't spoken in days suddenly struck her as odd. Maybe Allen's suggestion was correct. Maybe it was unusual for a boyfriend not to contact his girlfriend for so long.

"Well, I wanted to see you. But when I got here, Cindy told me you started helping Allen because Irma Mae is injured. But why were you there so late?" he asked, oblivious to her inner turmoil. "Cindy said you'd be home soon and I could wait for you, but that was nearly an hour ago."

"I needed to help Allen." She rested her hand on the railing as she stood in front of him.

"Help him with what? Weren't you there all day?"

"Yes, but his *boppli* and household chores don't run on a time clock. I spent the day doing laundry and taking care of Mollie, but then they needed supper, and Mollie needed a bath." She folded her arms over her chest. "Didn't you hear Irma Mae will probably be in rehabilitation for quite a while?"

"I heard she'd fallen and been hurt, but I hadn't realized it was that bad. Or that Allen would need someone like you there." He settled against the back of the glider. "That's really kind of you to help him. I'm sure he appreciates it. Now that I think about it, I realize he can't run a business and care for Mollie and his *haus* by himself." He patted the seat beside him. "You must be tired."

"I am." She dropped down next to him.

"How's Allen coping with Irma Mae gone?"

"He seems exhausted, like he's burning the candle at both ends. Mollie didn't sleep well last night, so he was worn-out today."

"That's tough."

"*Ya*. That's why he needs my help. How was your day?"

Rudy rested his arm on the back of the glider as he turned toward her. "Busy. We had customers all day long. I was thankful for my lunch break."

"That's *gut*, right? It's always *gut* when the store stays busy?"

"*Ya*, but my feet hurt." He chuckled, and then paused for a moment, as if contemplating something. "I just realized I haven't seen you since last week."

"Oh, so you *have* noticed."

"Noticed what?" His forehead wrinkled as his eyes moved over her. Did he think she was annoyed he hadn't noted a new dress or apron? Was Rudy truly that dense?

"Never mind."

"How have you been—I mean, even before you started helping with Mollie?" His words seemed genuine despite his weeklong absence.

"I don't know. I'm too tired to remember."

"I'm tired too."

They stared at each other as an awkward silence stretched between them like a great chasm. When had they started to run out of things to talk about? They'd known each other since they were children, and their relationship had always been full of fun. But lately the relationship felt different, like a favorite sweater she'd suddenly started to outgrow.

"Rudy!" Mark exclaimed as he and Jamie came from the barn. "I didn't realize you were here. How are you?"

"Fine." Rudy nodded at Mark.

Laura shifted on the glider and folded her hands in her lap as new doubt swirled through her mind. She hoped Mark couldn't read her expression. If Mark discerned how disappointed she was with Rudy, he'd harass her until she shared her feelings. She was too exhausted for an emotional discussion tonight.

"How are you?" Rudy asked her twin.

"*Gut, gut.*" Mark sat down on the rocking chair next to the glider, beside Laura.

In her peripheral vision, Laura could see her twin was watching her face, but she kept her focus on Jamie.

"How's your *dat's* store doing?" Jamie leaned against the railing across from the glider.

"Fine. Staying busy, as always." Rudy gestured toward the pasture as he looked at Jamie. "Your *haus* looks like it's done."

"*Ya*, it's close." Jamie's expression revealed how pleased he was. "I'm hoping to move in soon."

"Let me know when you're ready. I can ask *mei dat* if I can leave work early that day." Rudy once again rested his arm across the back of the glider. When his hand touched her shoulder, she jumped, but he didn't seem to notice how awkward she felt beside him. She'd never shied away from his chaste expressions of intimacy, but tonight she was too disappointed in his lack of attention to accept any gesture of love.

"*Danki*. That's thoughtful of you. I'll let you know." Jamie stood up straight. "I'm going to head inside. It was great seeing you. *Gut nacht*."

"*Gut nacht*," Rudy echoed as Jamie disappeared into the house.

Mark angled his body toward Laura. "So how's Allen?"

"He's fine." She shrugged. "Tired. Mollie didn't sleep well last night."

"*Ach*, that's tough." Mark shook his head. "She probably misses Irma Mae."

"*Ya*, that's what I think too."

"How's Mollie otherwise?" Mark moved the rocking chair back and forth.

"She's fantastic." A smile overtook Laura's lips. "She's gotten so big, even since I saw her last week. I noticed her onesies are a bit snug. I had a tough time snapping one over her diaper when I changed her. I might pick up a couple for her as a birthday gift. I thought about making her a few dresses too."

"Her birthday is in a couple of weeks, isn't it?" Mark asked.

"*Ya*, it is." Laura grinned, impressed her brother remembered the date Mollie was born.

"They grow so fast."

She smiled to herself. Mark said that as though he were a parent, not a happy bachelor. But he did seem to be reflective as he stared toward the pasture. What was that about?

The sun had begun to set, staining the sky with vivid streaks of pink, orange, purple, and yellow.

An awkwardness descended over the porch like an itchy blanket. Laura looked toward Jamie's house as questions filled her mind. Did she and Rudy have a bright future like Jamie and Kayla? She realized she had no real idea. How could she have been assuming they would for so long?

"Well, it's getting late." Rudy stood. "You and I are both tired, Laura, so I think I should get home."

She looked up at him. "*Danki* for coming to see me. Have a safe trip home."

"*Gut nacht.*" Mark gave him a little wave.

"*Gut nacht.*" Rudy lingered for a moment as his eyes fixed on Laura, and then he descended the porch steps and strode to his waiting horse and buggy.

"Why didn't you walk him to his buggy?" Mark asked.

"I'm too tired." Laura slumped back against the glider and cupped her mouth as a yawn overtook her. "Mollie kept me hopping all day long."

"Or did you have an argument?"

She blew out a deep sigh. This conversation was unavoidable.

"From the sounds of that sigh, you did have an argument."

"We didn't have an argument." She covered her mouth to shield another yawn. "I'm just really tired."

"Are you sure that's it?" He touched his chest. "It feels like more than that."

"We didn't argue, but I'm just a little bit annoyed with him. We haven't spoken since he came for supper last week." She pointed to the glider seat. "He didn't realize he hadn't seen me since then until he was sitting here. So I said, 'Oh, so you *have* noticed.' And his response was, 'Noticed what?'"

Mark grinned. "You're kidding, right?"

She shook her head. "I wish I were. Sometimes I feel like Rudy doesn't even notice *me*." She pointed to her chest. "That's *gegisch*, right? After all, we've been together for four years now."

She waited for Mark to share his opinion of her relationship with Rudy, but to her surprise, he was silent. He turned to look out over the pasture.

"Mark?" She nudged his arm. "Do you have laryngitis? Or did you fall asleep?"

"I'm not sure what to say."

A bark of laughter exploded from her throat. "You don't know what to say? Are you *krank*?"

He met her gaze with a wry grin. "Sometimes I know when to shut up."

She sat up straighter. For the first time in a long time, she didn't want her twin to be quiet. She wanted to read his mind, like some people believed twins could.

His smile faded. "Why are you looking at me like I hold all the answers? I'm the last person who should give relationship advice." He held up his hand. "Don't tell Jamie I said that."

"What are you hesitating to tell me?"

He looked down at one arm of the rocker. "Rudy is a *gut* man, but he's sometimes a little selfish and self-centered." He looked up again. "I do think he cares about you. He's just a little stuck on himself sometimes. Yet I don't think he means to be thoughtless."

She nodded slowly. "*Ya*, that makes sense."

"Don't give up on him. Just give him a little time, and he'll eventually realize he tends to take you for granted."

Relief fluttered through Laura. "*Danki*." She squeezed his arm. "Sometimes you know exactly what I need to hear."

Mark's grin was back. "If only Jamie appreciated my wisdom as much as you do."

SEVEN

ALLEN SLOWLY MOVED THE ROCKING CHAIR BACK AND forth as Mollie's soft snores sounded in his ear. This had become his nightly ritual for the past two weeks. He patted her back and fought to stay awake in the dark room. The only light came from the sliver of moonlight spilling in between the edge of the green shade and the window casing.

He felt as if he'd been rocking Mollie for hours. He'd fallen asleep around one o'clock, but then she woke him up screaming, just as she had for the past fourteen consecutive nights. After changing her diaper, he managed to calm her down by rocking her, but she'd started screaming as soon as he tried to place her back in her crib. He tried to put her there two more times before giving up and succumbing to her need for his affection.

Now she slept with her head tucked under his chin, and her warm little body stretched across his chest. His eyes fluttered shut as an image of Savilla filled his lonely mind.

He recalled the day she told him she was pregnant with Mollie. He'd come into the house at lunchtime and found Savilla grinning as she stood by the kitchen table. Her cheeks were rosy, and her beautiful honey-brown eyes sparkled in the light of the afternoon sun streaming in through the windows.

"You look like you're going to burst," he quipped as he walked over to her.

"I think I might." Her smile grew even wider as she looked up at him. "I have some news."

He touched her arm. "What is it?"

"We're going to be parents."

He gasped. "What? You're . . . ?"

She nodded. "Uh-huh."

"Yes!" He picked her up and spun her around as she squealed. "I'm so *froh*."

She wrapped her arms around his neck and he kissed her.

"*Ich liebe dich*," she whispered as she stared into his eyes.

"I love you too. *Danki* for making me the happiest man on the planet."

"*Gern gschehne*." She cupped her hand to his cheek. "I can't wait to be a *mamm*. Let's have a big family. Maybe six or seven *kinner*. You and I have both longed for siblings. Our *kinner* will grow up together and always have each other." She pointed toward the back door. "The *buwe* can work in the shop and barn with you while the *maed* help me in the kitchen and garden. Our *haus* will always be busy and loud and full of laughter and love. What do you think?"

"If that makes you *froh*, then *ya*." He pushed an errant lock of her golden hair behind her ear. "I want whatever you want."

She beamed as she placed his hand on her flat abdomen. "I can't wait to meet our *boppli*."

"Neither can I."

Mollie's sudden whimper brought him back to the present.

"*Ach, mei liewe*," he whispered against her warm head. "Daddy is here."

Mollie shifted, nuzzling her nose against his neck, and Allen bit back a sad sigh. He'd never imagined he'd raise Mollie alone. Mollie needed her mother, but God had taken her away. How could he give Mollie everything she needed? How could he make it by himself?

———— ✿ ————

"*Gude mariye*," Laura sang as she stepped into Allen's kitchen later that morning. "*Wie geht's?*"

"I'm fine." Allen sat at the kitchen table with his chin in his hand, and Mollie squealed in her high chair beside him. She was holding a handful of Cheerios. He had a mug in front of him, with no steam coming out of it.

"How are *you*?" Allen yawned and covered his mouth with his hand. Dark circles outlined his eyes.

She crossed the kitchen to stand in front of him. "You look terrible."

"*Danki.*" He frowned, his blue eyes dull.

"Did you get any sleep?"

He rubbed his beard as if considering the question. "I think I finally got her to sleep in her crib around five thirty. She was awake again at seven, and I gave up."

"*Ach*, I'm so sorry. You've been struggling with this for a couple of weeks now. I was hoping she'd get out of the habit of waking up in the middle of the night." She shook her head with concern. "Have you eaten?"

He shook his head as another yawn barred any verbal response.

"I'll make you breakfast. And some fresh *kaffi*." She filled the percolator and then pulled supplies out of the refrigerator, including eggs and bacon.

"Just a couple of eggs would be *wunderbaar*." He stood and pulled the large frying pan from the cabinet.

"You need your strength. I'll make you bacon too." She pointed to a cabinet. "Would you get me another pan?"

He set a second pan on the stove and then pointed to the bacon. "I can put the bacon on."

"No, you can sit and relax." She pointed to his chair. "Has Mollie had something to eat beside Cheerios?"

"She had some yogurt." He yawned again as he sank into the chair beside his daughter.

"I'll make her an egg too." She unwrapped the bacon and tossed several pieces into a large skillet. Then she broke and scrambled three eggs.

When the eggs and bacon were done, she slipped two of the eggs and most of the bacon onto a large plate and turned toward the table. Allen was slumped over, his head resting on his folded arms on the table's surface. She walked over and heard faint, muffled snoring. She held the plate in the air, debating if she should wake him or let him sleep.

Mollie squealed, and Allen jumped, sitting up and rubbing his eyes. He looked up at her, and a sheepish expression overtook his face. "Did you say something?"

Laura frowned. "You were asleep on the table."

"I'm sorry." He pointed to the plate. "Is that for me?"

"*Ya.*" She set it in front of him. "You need to get some sleep."

"I'm fine." He swallowed back a yawn. "I just need something to eat."

"No." She handed him a set of utensils and a napkin. "You need a nap. Eat your breakfast and then go take one." She headed back to the counter and poured them both coffee.

"No, I have two buggies to finish, and I'm already late getting out to the shop." He shook his head as he shoveled a fork full of egg into his mouth.

"The buggies can wait," she said when she put his mug on the table. Before she said more, she cut up the third egg, making sure it wasn't too hot, and then set it on the high-chair tray. Mollie pushed it around with one finger before picking up a morsel and shoving it into her mouth. "You haven't had a decent night of sleep since before Irma Mae's accident, right?"

He nodded as he yawned again.

"Wasn't Mollie sleeping through the night before Irma Mae was hurt?"

"*Ya*, she was. She only started waking up after Irma Mae left."

"That's what I thought. You're too tired to think clearly, and that's when accidents happen. You shouldn't handle tools right now. I'll put a sign on the door of your shop that says you're closed today. You can respond to your voice mail messages this evening or tomorrow."

He kept his eyes focused on his plate as he ate. "Fine," he finally said. "You're right."

She broke up a piece of bacon and gave it to Mollie. Then she leaned down. "Can you say Laura?" she whispered as Mollie grinned at her. "Come on, now. Laura." She pointed to her chest. "Laura."

Mollie laughed and then pointed to Allen. *"Dat! Dat!"* She kicked her feet against the high chair's legs.

"That's right." Laura turned toward Allen. "She knows your name."

"*Ya*, she does. If only she was that agreeable at two in the morning."

She took in the exhaustion etched on his face. "I'll stay tonight."

"What?" His eyes locked on hers.

"I said I'll stay tonight. Overnight. You can't function like this." She pointed at him. "You're a mess right now. You can't run your shop on an hour of sleep. I'll stay in her room and rock her if she's awake at night."

"And when will you sleep?" His expression challenged her.

"When most women taking care of *boppli* full-time do. I'll nap when she naps during the day. I can manage."

His shoulders slouched. "Fine."

"It's settled, then." She put away the eggs and bacon and then washed the skillets. When Allen had cleaned his plate, she picked it up and carried it to the sink.

"*Danki* for breakfast," he said as he stood.

"*Gern gschehne.*" She pointed toward the stairs. "Now, go get some sleep."

He tilted his head as he studied her. "Are you always this bossy?"

"Only with my family and the people I care about." Fire scorched her cheeks when she realized what she'd said.

"Mollie and I are glad you're here." He looked at his daughter. "Right, girl?"

Mollie held up a piece of egg and laughed.

He kissed Mollie's head and then looked back at Laura. "*Danki*, Laura."

"*Gern gschehne.*" She watched him leave the kitchen and then returned to the dishes.

She wished it hadn't taken her so long to realize Allen needed help with Mollie at night—at least for a while. But she was determined to help him now.

Allen was certain his legs each weighed five hundred pounds as he climbed the steep steps. He closed his bedroom door, stripped down to his boxers, pulled on a white undershirt, and climbed into bed.

A warm breeze filtered through his two open windows as birds sang in nearby trees. When he snuggled against his pillow and closed his eyes, a vision of Laura scolding him in the kitchen came to mind. He smiled, remembering her determined expression when she insisted he take a nap.

Savilla would be happy to know Laura was taking good care of Mollie and him. Her friendship was a blessing.

His body relaxed, and soon he felt himself drifting off as the birds serenaded him.

⸻

When she was done in the kitchen, Laura ran outside and hung a sign on the door of Allen's shop that read, "The shop is closed today. Please come back tomorrow. Thank you."

Then she went back inside and put Mollie in her play yard for her morning nap. The baby fell right to sleep, and Laura swept the kitchen floor before dusting the family room. She'd sweep that room later, when she wouldn't risk waking Mollie. Then she swept the front and back porches.

She was looking through the freezer for something to make for supper when a knock sounded on the back door. She hurried to open it, expecting to find a customer inquiring about the shop. She blinked as her eyes met Rudy's.

"Hi." He gave her a little wave.

"Hi." She opened the screen door. "What are you doing here?"

"I was wondering if we could talk."

"*Ya*, of course." She gestured toward the inside of the house. "Mollie is sleeping in the *schtupp* and Allen is sleeping upstairs. I think it would be better if we talked on the porch."

"Oh." He pointed toward the shop. "Is he *krank*?"

"He's exhausted. He was up all night with Mollie. He hasn't had a decent night's sleep for two weeks. I told him to take a nap."

"Oh." He pulled the door open wide, and she stepped out onto the porch, where they sat down on the glider together.

"Why aren't you at work?" she asked.

"*Mei dat* asked me to run an errand, so I thought I'd stop by on my way back to town. I haven't seen you since you invited me over for supper last week."

"Oh." She fingered the hem of her black apron. "What did you want to discuss?"

He turned toward her, his expression serious. "Nothing. I just missed you. It seems like lately we see each other only once a week unless we have church, and then only twice a week. I figured I'd stop by and surprise you."

"Oh." Her eyes widened. *"Danki."*

"I was wondering if you'd come over for supper tonight. *Mei mamm* is making roast beef, and she baked a couple of lemon meringue pies." His expression turned hopeful. "I can pick you up at five. Allen's *haus* is on the way to mine, so it's not a problem to stop here."

"I appreciate the invitation, but I can't tonight. Maybe another night?"

"Why can't you come tonight?" His eyes searched hers.

"I promised Allen I'd stay overnight so he can get some sleep."

"You're staying overnight *here*?" He pointed to the porch floor.

"Ya." Her shoulders tensed as his expression clouded with a frown.

"Why?"

"I told you. Allen hasn't had much sleep for the past two weeks. Mollie has been up screaming every night. He rocks her for hours, but she won't let him put her back into her crib."

"What do you mean she won't let him put her back into the crib?"

"She cries inconsolably when he tries, so he has to rock her all night. I offered to stay over." When his lips flattened into a thin line, words tumbled out of her mouth at a quick clip. "I can sleep in her room with her, and I'll rock her if she gets upset." She

71

pointed to the shop. "He can't possibly work on an hour of sleep. He could get hurt if he slips with a tool."

Rudy's jaw tensed. "How many nights are you going to stay here?"

"I don't know." She shrugged. "It depends on how long she keeps waking up in the night. Right now I'm just focused on helping them. Irma Mae was a tremendous help to my family when we lost *mei mamm*, and I want to do the same for her and her family. Besides, Mollie is like *mei bruderskind*, and I'll do anything for her."

"So when will I get to spend time with you?"

"I don't know." She forced a smile. "How about Sunday? We can visit after church."

He nodded, but his expression remained clouded. Maybe he was angry that he had to wait until Sunday to see her. But if so, what was the source of this sudden need to spend more time with her?

"Today is Wednesday, so that's only a few days away. Will that work for you?"

"Sure." He shrugged, but his expression hardened.

When a cry sounded from inside the house, she jumped up. "I need to get Mollie. She's going to wake up Allen."

She hurried into the house before Rudy could respond. Mollie was standing up in the play yard, jumping up and down and crying.

"Hi, Mollie. I'm here." She lifted the baby into her arms, and when she instantly calmed down, Laura deposited her on the sofa and began changing her diaper.

"Laura, I really was hoping we could get together tonight." Rudy sidled up beside her. "You're working long hours for Allen, and I want to be sure I see you."

"You'll still see me," she said as she fastened a diaper on Mollie.

"I'm just really surprised you're inviting me over for supper. Lately it seems like a week goes by before you even think about me. If I hadn't invited you over for supper last week, I probably wouldn't have even seen you."

"That's not true. We're both just busy. *Mei dat* has given me more responsibility at the hardware store. He says he wants me to take over the store when he eventually retires, so he wants me to know every side of the business. He has me working with suppliers and handling inventory. I'm under a lot of pressure. And you're working here, so we both have a lot going on. But you're still my girlfriend. We just have to make time for each other."

Laura snapped Mollie's onesie and looked at Rudy as irritation nipped at her. Was he really that dense? "Sometimes I feel like you don't make time for me, so it's really not fair for you to try to make me feel guilty because I'm here helping Allen. I told you, helping him is very important to me, and I need you to understand—"

Allen was standing at the bottom of the stairs. His eyes were bright and alert, and they were focused on her. While his expression was unreadable, it was also intense, sending an unfamiliar tremor through her body.

"Allen." She breathed his name as she adjusted Mollie on her shoulder. "You look much more rested. How do you feel?"

"I feel better. *Danki.*" His eyes moved to Rudy, and his expression relaxed slightly. "Hi, Rudy. It's nice to see you. It's been awhile."

"Hi, Allen." Rudy stepped over to Allen and shook his hand, but his jaw remained set.

"When do you want lunch?" Laura asked Allen.

Allen shrugged. "Maybe in an hour or so?"

"Just let me know when you're hungry, then." She tried to smile, but her frustration pressed her lips together. How could

Rudy blame their lack of time together on their schedules? They used to make time for each other when they were younger. What had changed between them?

Embarrassment heated her cheeks as she looked at Allen. How much had he heard? She'd never planned on airing her problems in front of him. He had enough on his mind. She longed to ask Rudy to leave. Now was not the time to discuss their relationship issues.

"Okay. I'll let you know when I'm ready," Allen told her. "I'm going to get to work." He looked at Rudy before heading into the kitchen.

"Laura." Rudy held up his hands. "I didn't mean to upset you."

Guilt chewed on her as she studied his brown eyes. How could she be angry with Rudy for wanting to see more of her? She needed to try harder if their relationship was going to work.

"I'm sorry I'm busy tonight, but we can see each other another day." When Mollie shifted, she placed her on the floor and handed her a couple of toys from her play yard. "Let's plan on visiting Sunday after church."

Rudy's expression softened. Perhaps he was beginning to understand her point of view. "That sounds *gut*. I need to get back to work. We'll talk more soon, okay?"

"Of course." She hugged her arms to her chest.

"*Gut.* Take care." He started for the kitchen but then turned and faced her one last time. "I do care about you."

"I know." She nodded. "Tell your family hello."

As Rudy walked into the kitchen, Laura looked down at Mollie. "No matter what, I won't abandon you."

EIGHT

GUILT COILED IN ALLEN'S GUT AS HE LINGERED IN
the kitchen and listened to Laura and Rudy's conversation. He
didn't want to eavesdrop, but he couldn't push himself toward the
back door.

He had awakened from his nap refreshed and ready to take
on the rest of the day. After dressing and washing his face, he'd
stepped into the hallway, and their voices had carried up the stairwell. He walked slowly down the stairs, taking in what Rudy and
Laura were saying.

Allen's concern had come true—the time Laura spent helping him was interfering in her life and the time she could spend
with Rudy.

Once Allen had reached the bottom step and Laura saw him,
her expression registered both shock and embarrassment. But
what shone in Rudy's formal greeting was disapproval.

Allen longed to tell Rudy he never intended to cause problems
in their relationship, but the little voice in his head insisted he stay
out of their business. Now he stood near the doorway and listened
to their discussion.

When Rudy announced it was time for him to leave, Allen
slipped quickly into the mudroom, pushed his feet into his boots,
and headed out the back door and down the porch steps to his

shop. He didn't want to get caught eavesdropping, and he also didn't want to be forced into a conversation with Rudy.

As Allen opened the bay doors and gathered his tools, a whisper of guilt intruded. He needed to tell Laura she could quit. It would be better if he hired a nanny. He didn't want to be the reason Rudy and Laura encountered problems in their relationship.

As he turned toward his current buggy project, he saw movement out of the corner of his eye. He spun to face the driveway, where Rudy strode toward his waiting horse and buggy. He froze, hoping Rudy wouldn't walk over and say something to him. But he climbed into the buggy and guided his horse down toward the road.

Shoving away frustration, Allen set to repairing the waiting buggy.

An hour later, the sound of footsteps on the concrete floor of his shop pulled Allen's attention away from the buggy he'd been restoring. He set his tools on the floor and stood while wiping his hands on a red shop rag.

"Are you hungry yet?" Laura stood a few feet away from him, smoothing her apron.

He noticed she wore a light-blue dress that complemented her eyes. She seemed somehow different from usual—nervous or unsure of herself. Had her discussion with Rudy caused her to feel uncomfortable around Allen? That feeling of irritation from earlier resurfaced as he studied her.

"I'm still not very hungry," he told her.

Her eyebrows lifted. "You know, along with proper sleep, you also need proper nourishment to stay healthy. You can't run a shop if you're not healthy."

His lips turned up in a smile. "You're right. I'll be in soon."

Her expression brightened.

"What?" he asked.

"You smiled. Again." She pointed at him. "That's one of only a few smiles I've seen since—well, since we lost Savilla."

"Is it?" His smile widened. "I suppose it is."

"You should smile more."

"I'll try."

They stared at each other for an awkward moment, and then he gestured toward the buggy behind him. "I'll be in soon. I just want to finish fixing the suspension on this buggy. It will only take me a few minutes."

"Okay." She hesitated. "Do you like chicken salad?"

"*Ya*, I do. *Danki*."

"*Gut*." She paused again. "Mollie has been calling for you."

His heart tugged at her words. "I promise I won't be long."

"*Gut*," she said once more and then nodded and started for the door.

"Laura."

She spun to face him, her eyes wide. "*Ya?*"

"I feel like I owe you an apology." He stepped closer to her.

She stared up at him. "Why would you say that?"

"I overheard your conversation with Rudy in the *schtupp*."

"Oh." Her cheeks glowed from what he assumed was embarrassment. "What did you hear?"

"I got the impression that he's upset you're working here so much. He can't see you as often as he wants to." He cringed. "I never wanted to cause problems between you and Rudy. I appreciate all you're doing, but this is too hard on you. You've been together a long time, and my situation is temporary. It's not worth risking your relationship."

"You're not causing any problems for me."

He raised his eyebrows. "That's not the impression I got

earlier. Look, Laura, I appreciate your dedication to Mollie, but I can hire a twenty-four-hour nanny without any repercussions."

"No. I want to do this for Irma Mae and for Savilla. We're family." Her lower lip quivered and her eyes glimmered. "Savilla would want it this way, and Rudy needs to understand that."

Was she going to cry? His throat dried. "I agree. She would want it this way. But I still don't want to cause problems between you and Rudy."

"I told you. You won't cause any problems." She pointed toward the house. "Come in for lunch, okay?"

Before he could respond, she was out the door and marching up the path toward the house.

❧

"Have you heard from Milton?" Laura asked as she handed Allen a bowl of chicken salad. "I was wondering how everything is going for Irma Mae at the rehabilitation center."

Rudy's frustrating words had haunted her all morning. But instead of worrying, she'd tried her best to concentrate on taking care of Mollie and Allen.

"*Ya.*" Allen's response pulled her back to reality. "He left me a message. Her physical therapy is going well, and she's making *gut* progress. She's getting stronger."

"That's great news." She turned toward Mollie, who hummed as she ate a handful of chicken salad. "We should take Mollie to see her." She stilled, realizing she'd just given Allen instructions as if they were a couple.

"That's a great idea." Allen's face brightened. "I think seeing Mollie would be therapeutic for Irma Mae." He looked at his daughter.

"*Ya*, I agree." She swallowed a sigh of relief, grateful he hadn't been offended by her bossiness.

They ate in silence for a few minutes, and her mind moved to her plans for the evening. A friend of Irma Mae's had offered to shop for groceries the week before, beating Laura to it. And today, when Laura had chosen a recipe from her mother's favorite cookbook, she found all the ingredients she needed in the well-stocked refrigerator and cabinets. She'd start on supper once Mollie was down for her afternoon nap.

Her thoughts turned to sleeping there tonight, and she realized she didn't have any pajamas or clothes to wear tomorrow.

"What's on your mind?"

She lifted her head to find Allen shooting her a laser-like look. He lifted a potato chip and bit into it.

"I was wondering if I could borrow one of Savilla's nightgowns for tonight."

"Sure." He shrugged, but some emotion flashed over his face as he looked down at his plate. "I haven't gotten around to packing up her clothes. Would you like them?"

"*Ya*, I can take them." She gave him a little smile. "I would have to hem her dresses since she was taller than I am. Her dresses and aprons would fit Cindy better than me."

He turned his gaze on his plate.

"And could we move a bed into Mollie's room so I can sleep in there with her? That way she won't wake you up if she cries. I'll keep the door closed and just stay in there with her. I know it would probably be easier to move her crib into your spare room, but all her supplies are in the nursery, and I think she'll feel more comfortable in familiar surroundings."

"Of course. I can move the single bed from the sewing room after lunch." He lifted another chip.

"I'll have to call my family and tell them I'm staying tonight. Can I use your phone?"

He paused and studied her as he lifted an eyebrow. "Are you serious, Laura? Do you really feel like you have to ask permission to use my phone?"

She gave a nervous laugh. "I guess I knew I didn't have to ask."

"You should feel as comfortable here as you did when Savilla was here, okay? Like you said earlier, we're family."

"Right."

"But there is something else I want to discuss." They both glanced at Mollie, but she seemed to be entertaining herself.

"Okay." She braced herself, praying he wouldn't bring up the subject of Rudy again. She didn't want to analyze her relationship with Rudy. She only felt comfortable discussing personal subjects with Mark. She didn't even share as much with Cindy as she did with her twin.

"I've been thinking about something all morning." He folded his hands on the table. "If you're going to stay overnight and then work all day, I want to pay you. I'm taking you away from your family and your chores at home." He pointed to the table. "I'm not going to take no for an answer, so don't even try arguing with me."

Laura opened her mouth to protest but then closed it. Allen was right. It was only proper to take payment for her time. "Okay."

His expression relaxed as he leaned back in the chair. "That was much easier than I expected."

"I'm sorry to disappoint you."

"I can't say you've ever disappointed me." He shook his head. "So I was thinking about your salary while I was working outside. Let me tell you what I think sounds right."

They had agreed on a salary amount by the time they finished lunch.

Allen helped her carry their dishes to the sink.

"You can go work," she said, waving him off.

"Nope." He shook his head. "I want to help you. I used to help Savilla wash dishes at times, so I can help you." He nodded toward the back door. "Why don't you go leave a message for your family?"

"All right." She hesitated as he carried the bowl of leftover chicken salad and utensils to the counter.

He swiveled toward her. "What are you waiting for? Do I need to get bossy like you do?"

"No." She grinned. "*Danki* for helping. I'll be right back."

Once in Allen's office, she sat down at the desk and dialed the number for her father's phone shanty. As the phone rang, she imagined her family sitting at the kitchen table for lunch. After the fourth ring, her own voice sounded through the phone.

"You've reached the Riehls' farm. To leave a message for Vernon, please press one. For Jamie, press two. For Laura, press three. For Mark, press four. And for Cindy, press five."

She pressed one and then began to speak after the beep. "Hi, *Dat*. It's Laura. I want to let you know I'm going to stay at Allen's overnight. He hasn't had any sleep in two weeks because Mollie cries and wants to be rocked all night long. I'm going to stay in her room so Allen can get some sleep and feel rested enough to work. Please call his shop if you need me. I'll check in with you tomorrow. Bye now."

When Laura reentered the kitchen, Allen was drying dishes. He glanced at her and smiled. "Did you leave a message for your *dat*?"

"*Ya*, I did." She leaned against the counter beside him. "You can go back to work now."

"I'll go move the bed into Mollie's room first." He handed her the dish towel. "Here you go." He touched his daughter's head as he walked out of the kitchen.

—⚬×⚬—

Laura laid Mollie in the crib and then held her breath, hoping she wouldn't start crying again. An hour earlier, Mollie had awakened, crying, and Laura had sung to her and rocked her until she was snoring on her shoulder. It was now one o'clock, and Laura was hoping to get some more sleep. The soft glow of the Coleman lantern on the nightstand beside her bed was her only light as she looked down into the crib.

After several moments, Mollie pulled her right thumb into her mouth, sighed, and then began to suck on it in her sleep.

Laura smiled as she gazed down at the beautiful baby. She waited a few more moments and then padded out to the hallway to use the bathroom with a lantern in hand. When she came out, she glanced down the hallway. Allen's bedroom door was open. She took a step toward the stairwell and spotted a light downstairs. It moved, as if someone carried a lantern. A level of alarm buzzed through her. Was Allen okay?

She stepped into Mollie's room, pulled on Savilla's pink terry cloth robe, and covered her hair with a matching scarf before walking down the stairs.

When her feet hit the bottom step, she glanced toward the front door. It was open, leaving the screen door as her only protection from the dark night. As she looked around the family room, she felt a sudden, razor-sharp edge of unease. It tasted like panic.

"Allen?" she called, her voice trembling. "Allen? Are you there?"

"*Ya.*" His voice sounded from the front porch. "I'm out here."

She blew out a trembling puff of air as she stepped outside. Allen sat on the porch swing clad in a pair of trousers and a white undershirt. A lantern by his bare feet cast a soft yellow glow on his face, and the humid air held a faint scent of rain.

He gave her an embarrassed smile as he looked up at her. "Did I wake you?"

"No, I was up with Mollie, but I got her back to sleep. Are you okay?"

"*Ya.* I just needed some air."

"Oh." She shifted her weight from one bare foot to the other as she held on to the door handle. Should she go back inside and give him his privacy?

"Would you like to sit?" He patted the seat beside him. "There's room on the porch swing for you."

"Okay." She gently closed the door and then sat down beside him, turning off her lantern and setting it on the floor. "Are you okay?"

"*Ya.* Sometimes I just can't turn off my thoughts."

She turned toward him. "Do you want to talk about it?"

He lifted his eyebrows as he faced her. "You really want to know?"

"Why would I ask if I didn't want to know?"

He paused, and she held her breath, regretting asking such a personal question.

"Sometimes I'm numb, and other times I'm drowning in grief, wondering if I can take another breath without her." His voice shook and his eyes misted.

She swallowed against what felt like sandpaper in her throat. An overwhelming urge to comfort him grabbed her by her shoulders. "Do you think talking to *mei dat* would help you?"

"I don't know." He turned toward the front lawn, which led out to the main road. "Maybe."

They sat in silence for several moments, and she fiddled with the belt tied around her waist. A mixture of grief and exhaustion emanated from this man, and she longed to take away his pain.

As the silence stretched between them, she searched her

mind for something to say. When nothing special came to her, she just started talking. "Jamie's *haus* is done."

"Really?" His expression brightened. "I didn't realize he was that close to finishing it."

"I know. It seems like he just broke ground, but it went fast. He's going to get the appliances this week and then move the furniture in on Saturday." She stared down at the tie to the robe as she went on. "I'm going to move into his old room, which seems so strange. I've always shared a room with Cindy. I guess I never really considered this day would come so quickly, but he's been with Kayla for a year now. Mark thinks Jamie is going to propose to Kayla soon. The wedding could even be this fall. I guess it makes sense since they're *froh* together, and now he has a *haus*. Why wouldn't they get married, right? But it will be so strange having a wedding without *Mamm* here."

She took a quick breath and went on.

"I'm really glad Jamie found Kayla. He's been alone for so long. Mark always teases him that he's almost thirty, when he's only twenty-six, but I think he met Kayla at the perfect time. God's timing is always perfect, right?"

When she realized she was babbling, she looked up and found him looking at her. She'd expected she was boring him, but his expression was full of interest. To avoid his stare, she looked out toward the road as a warm mist of rain kissed her face.

"How did you meet Rudy?" he suddenly asked.

"We've always known each other. We went to school together, and we've been in the same church district and youth group. We were *freinden*, and he asked me to be his girlfriend after I was baptized."

"And you've been together four years?"

She nodded. "*Ya.*"

"Have you discussed marriage?"

Without thinking, she snorted. Then she clapped her hand over her nose and mouth.

"I'm sorry. I had no right to ask you that. That's much too personal."

"It's okay." Laura paused while considering how to respond to the question. A part of her wanted to confess her doubts about Rudy, and even longed to ask Allen his opinion about how Rudy avoided the subject of a future with her. But discussing something so personal would be inappropriate. Allen wasn't her best friend, but she suddenly felt so comfortable with him. Perhaps it was because they both missed Savilla so much?

Taking a deep breath, she confessed the thoughts that had haunted her for months, but had come to the surface in the last couple of weeks. "We've never discussed the future. In fact, the few times I've brought it up, Rudy has changed the subject. Sometimes I feel like he's too afraid to even consider a future with me." When she finished speaking, an invisible weight lifted from her shoulders.

Allen shook his head and then looked away. A staggering desire to read his thoughts burned through her.

"What are you thinking?"

He leaned back on the swing, and his leg brushed hers. "I knew I wanted to marry Savilla the moment I met her in person. We'd been writing letters for about a year."

"I remember that."

His expression softened. "I don't understand stringing someone along for four years, especially someone as sweet, kind, generous, and *schee* as you are."

She sniffed as tears stung her eyes.

His face contorted. "I'm sorry. I didn't want to hurt your feelings or make you feel bad." He started to reach for her hand, but then stopped. "It's not my place to interfere in your relationship."

"You're not interfering." Her voice sounded thick even to her own ears. "You just confirmed what I've been thinking but have been too afraid to say out loud."

He frowned. "The last thing I want to do is hurt you. I should have kept my opinion to myself."

"No, you did what I wanted you to do. You told me the truth. That's what *freinden* do, right?"

"*Ya.*" He nodded, but sadness and regret seemed to fill his eyes.

"You should get some sleep. I stayed over so you could rest." She took up her lantern and stood. "How about I make you some warm milk?"

"It won't help. I can't turn off my brain at night."

"Why?"

"Nothing for you to worry about." He gave her a smile that seemed more forced than genuine.

"Okay." She respected his need for privacy, but worry continued to thread through her. She hoped someday he'd open up, ready to tell her what was burdening his heart and his thoughts.

Without thinking, she held out her hand. "Come upstairs. You need your rest."

He stared at her hand and then took it before standing. They stared at each other for a moment, and Laura felt something pass between them. Their friendship felt deeper, more meaningful, and an unexpected tremor, like the one she'd felt this morning, shivered through her.

She released his hand and pulled open the front door, desperate to put some space between them.

He's Savilla's widower, and you're Rudy's girlfriend. Don't get too close to him!

She entered the house and Allen closed and locked the front door behind them. She started up the steps, and soon his footsteps echoed behind her. When they reached the second floor, she swiveled toward him.

"*Gut nacht*," she said.

"*Gut nacht*," he echoed before stepping into the master bedroom and closing the door.

She tiptoed into Mollie's bedroom and peeked into the crib. Mollie was still asleep. As she climbed into bed, Laura whispered a prayer, asking God to help Allen sleep too.

NINE

ON FRIDAY MORNING, ALLEN HUNG HIS HAT ON A WALL peg in the mudroom and smiled as a sweet voice filtered in from somewhere inside the house.

"This little light of mine, I'm gonna let it shine . . ."

He walked through the kitchen and came to a stop in the doorway to the family room. Laura was singing and rocking Mollie.

"This little light of mine, I'm gonna let it shine . . ." Her eyes were closed as she held Mollie against her chest and rocked back and forth. "Let it shine, let it shine, let it shine."

Her beautiful voice filled his ears and curled through him, settling deep in his soul. Leaning against the doorframe, he took in the serene scene as his chest ached with a mixture of appreciation and fondness for Laura.

For the first time since Irma Mae's fall, he was rested and relaxed. Laura had stayed overnight again last night, and he had slept for almost seven hours. He woke up once, but then he managed to go back to sleep. Laura told him Mollie had only awakened her once during the night, but she was able to calm her and get her back to sleep. Laura had a gift when it came to caring for Mollie, and Allen was grateful for her help.

Today Laura wore a purple dress and black apron. Cindy

had stopped by yesterday to drop off clothes for her. Cindy had also taken Savilla's dresses and aprons since they were the perfect length for her. And with his permission, the two women had discreetly packed away Savilla's shoes, purse, and other garments. He trusted Laura to know what to do with them. He also appreciated her offer to determine if Mollie might want an article of her mother's clothing as a keepsake.

Allen, of course, would keep items that meant the most to him, like the framed picture of a rose, believing they would one day be meaningful for his daughter too.

Laura's eyes fluttered open, and she gasped when she turned and saw Allen. "I didn't know you were standing there." She stopped rocking and swiveled toward the clock on the wall. "*Ach,* no. It's almost twelve. I haven't even started your lunch. I'm so sorry."

Mollie stirred, and Laura sat her on her lap. When Mollie whimpered, Laura handed her a bottle, and his daughter immediately began to drink from it.

"It's fine." He held up his hands to reassure her as he stepped into the room. "I just wanted to tell you Milton called to tell me Irma Mae is feeling stronger and has been asking about Mollie. I want to take her to see Irma Mae this afternoon. I already closed my shop and hung a sign telling customers I'm closed for the rest of the day. Since you've been stuck here since Wednesday, you're welcome to have the afternoon off."

"Oh." Laura paused. "Would you mind if I went with you to see Irma Mae?"

"You're welcome to come, but you don't have to. I can handle Mollie."

"I know you can, but I'd love to see Irma Mae. She's been like my second mother since Savilla and I were *kinner.*" Her face seemed hopeful. "Would it be okay if I tagged along?"

"Of course it would."

"Great. I'll make our lunch." She started to stand.

"You sit and relax. I'll make lunch for us."

She studied him. "Are you sure?"

He raised his eyebrows. "I can make sandwiches."

"I bet you could make a casserole too." She grinned.

He snickered. "You're still enjoying taunting me about that."

"I think I always will. And it's *gut* to hear you laugh."

The gleam in her eye sent a strange sensation racing through his veins. He stilled as confusion washed over him. No, he was mistaking his feelings. She was his friend, his very good friend, and that was all.

Laura rubbed Mollie's back as his daughter drained the bottle.

He pointed toward the kitchen. "Lunch is coming up."

The aroma of bleach overwhelmed Laura's senses as she pushed Mollie's stroller toward Irma Mae's small room at the end of a long hallway in the rehabilitation center. Mollie had taken a short nap on the way there, but she was awake now.

"Dat?" Allen called as they entered and saw an empty hospital bed. The whole space looked unoccupied. *"Mamm?"*

"We're over here. By the window," Milton responded on the other side of a curtain.

Allen gestured for Laura to go first, and she pushed the stroller past the curtain to where Irma Mae sat in a recliner beside another bed. Milton was next to her in a chair, a newspaper in his hands.

"Mollie!" Irma Mae smiled, and Mollie squealed in response. "I've missed you."

Mollie reached for her. "Mmmmmmm-Ma! Ma!"

"How are you feeling?" Laura unsnapped the stroller belt and lifted Mollie into her arms.

"It's been painful, but I'll make it through." Irma Mae sighed.

"*Mei fraa* is tough." Milton gave her a smile full of pride and adoration. "She can handle it, and she'll come out stronger."

"Oh, Milton." Irma Mae waved off his comment.

Laura's heart warmed at the love and respect Milton and Irma Mae held for each other. Would she ever have that kind of deep relationship with Rudy?

Mollie whined again and reached for Irma Mae. "Mmmmmmm. Ma-ma-ma!"

"She's been calling for you ever since you got hurt." Allen stepped over to Mollie.

"Ma-ma-ma!" Mollie squealed.

"Do you want to hold her?" Laura moved closer to Irma Mae and then hesitated. "I don't want her to hurt you."

"Why don't I hold her on my lap, and you can talk to her?" Milton suggested as he folded the newspaper and set it on the window ledge beside him.

"That's a *gut* idea." Allen took Mollie from Laura and handed her to Milton.

"How are you, Mollie?" Milton asked before kissing her on her head. "*Ach,* she reminds me so much of Savilla at this age."

"*Ya,* I know." Irma Mae sniffed as she touched Mollie's leg, her eyes brimming with tears.

Laura turned toward Allen. Leaning his shoulder against the wall, he stared down at the floor and wiped at his own eyes. Beneath lowered eyelashes, they seemed to sparkle with grief. She fought the urge to comfort him, but instead she gripped the stroller's handle.

"Laura, why don't you sit on the bed?" Milton suggested.

"*Danki.*" She sat down on its edge. "How is your physical therapy going?"

"It's been hard, but they insist I'm getting stronger." Irma Mae touched Mollie's hand. "They said my leg and hip seem to be healing well, but I can't tell a difference. I just know they hurt."

"Is there anything I can do for you, *Dat*?" Allen offered.

"No, *danki*." He spoke while keeping his eyes on his grand-daughter. "I'm doing fine. I care for the animals in the morning and then when I get home from visiting Irma Mae." Milton pivoted toward Allen. "How are you doing with Irma Mae out of commission?"

"Laura is taking *gut* care of both of us." Allen nodded toward Laura. "She's making sure I'm sleeping and eating right, and she's doing a great job with Mollie."

"Oh *ya*?" Irma Mae raised her eyebrows as her gaze bounced between Laura and Allen. "Am I out of a job?"

"No, no." Laura shook her head as her cheeks warmed. "Mollie misses you terribly. I know she'll be thrilled when you're back. But please take your time healing. My family is supportive of my working for Allen for as long as he needs me."

"I think I'm going to be here awhile." Irma Mae frowned. "I have to learn to walk again, and it will be a couple of months before I can even lift her."

"There's no hurry," Allen said. "Laura will make sure Mollie and I have what we need."

They visited with Irma Mae and Milton for an hour, and then Mollie started whining and rubbing her eyes.

"I think she's ready for a nap," Irma Mae said. "You should get her home."

Allen picked up Mollie, set her in the stroller, and fastened the belt. Mollie leaned back in the seat and stuck her thumb into her mouth.

"*Danki* for bringing her here to visit." Irma Mae sighed. "I've missed her so much."

"We'll bring her back before too long," Allen promised. "Take *gut* care of yourself." He shook Milton's hand and then Irma Mae's.

"I hope you feel better soon," Laura said before she pushed the stroller out of the room, following Allen into the hallway. "She looks well."

"*Ya*, she does." Allen nodded as they moved past an aide pushing a man in a wheelchair. "I think she has a long way to go before she'll be herself, though."

"I do too, but I think Mollie really brightened her day."

"She did." Allen gave her a sideways glance as they turned down another hallway and walked toward the entrance.

Allen held the door open for Laura and then made a sweeping gesture for her to walk through it. "Mollie looks worn-out. Let's get her home before she has a tantrum."

"Okay."

Laura rode in the back of the van with Mollie while Allen sat up front and chatted with his driver. When they reached the house, Allen paid for the ride and then carried a sleeping Mollie into the house. Laura hefted the diaper bag over her shoulder and lifted the stroller up the back porch steps.

She left the stroller in the mudroom and the diaper bag in the kitchen, and then she stood in the doorway to the family room as Allen placed Mollie in the play yard. He stared at his daughter as she snuggled down and sucked on her thumb.

He smiled when he joined her in the kitchen.

"She's fast asleep. I thought she might wake up, but she's comfortable."

"*Ya*, she is." She smiled up at him as he rubbed at his beard. "Do you want me to come tomorrow?"

"No, I'll be fine."

"But you have Saturday hours at your shop." She pointed

toward the back door. "You missed part of Wednesday and part of today."

"It's okay." He shrugged. "I'll put a note on the door explaining customers can knock if they want to buy a buggy. I think I need the weekend to rest a little."

"I really don't mind staying over tonight if you need me tomorrow."

His expression warmed. "You've been here helping me all week. I'm sure your family would like to see you. Jamie probably needs you to help him move furniture tomorrow, right?"

"Oh, right. I'd forgotten he's moving out tomorrow." An unexpected sadness came over her. She should be happy about finally having her own room, but she wasn't excited about that either. She'd miss her middle-of-the-night talks with her younger sister. Why did things have to change?

"Where did you go just now?" His eyes were locked on hers, and their intensity sent goose bumps dancing up her arms.

A shiver of awareness rolled through her despite the humid August air that filtered through the open kitchen window.

"Did I say something wrong?" he asked.

"No, you haven't said anything wrong." She moved to the kitchen table and began unpacking Mollie's diaper bag to avoid Allen's stare.

When a sudden urge to confide in him overwhelmed her, she dropped into a kitchen chair and looked up at him. "I'm just confused."

"About what?" He sat down beside her.

She drew circles on the table with her index finger as she tried to make sense of her emotions. Then she rested the side of her face on one palm. "I just don't know how I feel about Jamie moving out. It feels sudden, but it shouldn't. I mean, he's twenty-six and a grown man. But I'm going to miss him."

She looked up into his eyes and found patience and under-standing there. "I also don't know how I feel about moving out of the only bedroom I've ever known. Mark made it sound like a big deal that I'll have my own room, but I'm going to miss Cindy. After we lost *Mamm* last year, we stayed awake for hours some nights, crying and talking about how much we missed her. If I wake up in the middle of the night now, I'll be all alone."

She covered her face with both hands as embarrassment crawled up her neck to her cheeks. "Things are just changing too quickly. I'm still adjusting to not having *mei mamm* around, and now I feel like I'm going to lose my siblings. I'm not ready for this." Her voice was muffled by her palms. "That sounds so immature and stupid."

"No, it doesn't." He pulled her hands away from her face. "Change can be scary, especially when it's unexpected. You and I both know that really well."

She nodded, any further words she might say stuck in her throat.

"I'm sure everything will be just fine for Jamie." He grinned. "You'll see him all the time, especially if he doesn't have anyone else to cook for him. I imagine it will seem like he never moved out, and in a couple of weeks you'll find yourself asking him when he's going to start acting like a man who has his own place."

She laughed. "You're probably right."

"I'm also sure you and Cindy will keep having your middle-of-the-night talks. You'll just have to visit in each other's rooms." His smile faded. "You don't ever have to feel like you can't talk to me."

"*Danki.*"

They studied each other for a moment, and then something she couldn't decipher flashed across his face. He pushed back his chair and stood.

"I should get to work." He started for the mudroom. But when he'd almost reached it, he turned back. "*Danki* for going with me today to see Irma Mae."

"*Gern gschehne.* I enjoyed it."

As he turned to go, she suddenly remembered what she wanted to ask him.

"Allen," she called. He turned around. "Would you like to have supper with my family tonight? They would all love to see you and Mollie."

"Oh, no thanks." He shook his head. "You go home for supper, and Mollie and I will figure something out on our own."

"Oh." Her shoulders sagged. "I'd love for you to come."

"*Danki*, but it's fine. I'll see you and your family on Sunday at church."

"That's right." She stood. "I'll make you supper before I leave tonight."

He shook his head. "You don't need to do that. Just give me a couple of hours to work, and then you can go home. I was going to take the whole afternoon off, but I think I better get a few things done in the shop."

"That would be fine."

As he headed out the door, Laura tried to brush away sudden guilt. But how could she feel good about leaving Allen and Mollie without preparing their supper? Yet she had to abide by Allen's wishes, no matter how keenly she felt Savilla would want her to stay.

TEN

CURIOSITY FILLED LAURA AS SHE CLIMBED THE BACK-porch steps and heard loud voices floating out of the windows. While her family was naturally loud, it sounded as if half of their church district was in her house tonight.

She entered through the mudroom and stopped in the door-way to the kitchen as she took in the crowd seated around the table—Kayla, her brothers, her sister, and her father. And to her surprise, Rudy.

Although the group wasn't large, they were loud and festive as they talked and laughed. Platters of fried chicken, a bowl of corn, and a basket of rolls cluttered the center of the table, and the delicious aromas filled her senses.

"Laura!" *Dat* sang out when he saw her. "I'm so *froh* you're home. Have a seat. Jamie has some news." He gestured toward the only empty chair at the table, across from Mark and between Rudy and Cindy.

Laura let her tote bag drop to the floor, and then she sat down beside Rudy, who gave her a tentative nod. "Hi," she said, keeping her voice low. "It's *gut* to see you."

"Mark called and invited me over."

"I'm glad you came." She studied his dark eyes, searching for any sign of irritation. She hoped he wasn't still annoyed with her after their discussion on Wednesday.

"Laura." Mark's voice sliced through her thoughts. "You need to hear Jamie's news."

"Oh." Laura looked over at Jamie, who was smiling at Kayla. "What's your news?"

"I asked Kayla to marry me today," Jamie announced with a wide grin.

"We're celebrating," Kayla said. Her grin was even wider.

"Really?" Laura glanced around the table as disappointment knocked the smile off her face. "I missed your engagement celebration? I should have come home sooner. I'm sorry."

"The celebration is still going on. You haven't missed a thing," Kayla said. Laura knew she was just being nice, but she smiled anyway. "I'm so *froh* for you both!" She clapped her hands. "When is the big day?"

"The first Thursday in December." Kayla beamed as she turned toward Jamie.

"Oh my goodness. That will be here soon." Laura leaned forward. "How did he ask you?"

"He surprised me at work today." Kayla bumped her shoulder against Jamie's. "He told me he needed to talk to me, so we went into the back room. He was so *naerfich* I was afraid he was going to break up with me."

Everyone laughed as Jamie shook his head.

"And then he asked me to marry him." Kayla's cornflower-blue eyes shimmered as Jamie threaded his fingers in hers. "And I said yes."

"I'm so grateful you did," Jamie said, and they looked as if they were having a private conversation with their eyes.

"That's amazing." Laura took a deep breath. While she was overjoyed for Jamie and Kayla, she also was aware of the anxiety creeping into her chest. Jamie was getting married. Her family was morphing and growing, and they didn't have *Mamm* to guide them through all the challenges coming at them at full speed.

"You should eat." Rudy pointed to Laura's empty plate.

"Oh, right." Laura had been so immersed in Jamie's news she'd forgotten it was suppertime. She bowed her head in silent prayer and then put some of everything on her plate.

"Jamie, do you have enough help for tomorrow?" Rudy asked. "Mark mentioned on the phone that tomorrow is the day, but I can't get off work. I was hoping to help you, but we're short-staffed at the store right now. One of my cousins went to Florida for a week, and I have to cover his shift. I'm sorry I can't be here."

"Oh, that's fine. *Danki* for trying to get the day off, but I've got it covered. Noah, Leon, Mark, and I can handle it." Jamie took a drink from his glass of water.

"I haven't committed to actually helping you yet," Mark teased. "I might be busy washing my hair."

Jamie rolled his eyes, and Rudy snickered.

"I had really hoped to help you," Rudy said.

"Don't feel bad about it," Jamie told him. "I don't have that much to move."

"Laura." Kayla leaned forward and gestured to her and Cindy. "I told Cindy I'd like to have you both as attendants in my wedding. Jamie is going to have Mark, Noah, and Nathan, and it would mean a lot to me if you, Cindy, and Eva would be my attendants."

Tears pricked at Laura's eyes. "I'd be honored. *Danki*, Kayla."

"*Ya*, I'd love to," Cindy said, her blue eyes glistening. "*Danki* for asking us."

"Of course I want you to be in the wedding. We're going to be *schweschdere*." Kayla served herself a slice of ham. "I have a lot to do. This was so unexpected. I'd hoped he'd ask soon, but I didn't think it would be this summer."

"I'm not surprised," Cindy commented.

"Really?" Kayla turned toward her.

Cindy nodded. "It just seemed like a natural progression since you're both so *froh*. If you need help making the dresses, just let us know. I can pitch in."

"Danki."

"Cindy, are you still busy with that quilt you were going to make for Sara Glick?" Laura asked.

"I finished last night. Sara picked it up this afternoon," Cindy said.

"You finished the quilt?" Laura set down her fork. "I didn't get to see it before you gave it to her. When I left Wednesday morning, you were still working on it."

"It's okay. It came out pretty well."

"It was *wunderbaar*, Cindy," *Dat* chimed in from the other end of the table. "Tell the truth."

Cindy shrugged and looked down at her plate.

Laura frowned as disappointment crowded her pride in Cindy's work. "I'm so sorry I didn't get to see it."

"Don't worry about it," Cindy insisted. "I'll make sure you see the next one."

"How's Irma Mae doing, Laura?" Kayla asked. "Jamie told me she's been in a rehabilitation center for a couple of weeks now."

"She's doing better. Allen and I took Mollie to visit her today." Laura was almost certain she sensed Rudy's body go rigid when she mentioned Allen's name. So he was still upset with her. She dreaded what more he might have to say to her later.

"Did you say Irma Mae is doing well?" *Dat* asked.

"*Ya*, she is. Allen and I took Mollie to see her today. She has a long way to go. She has to heal and build her strength, but her spirits are *gut*." Laura took a bite of ham.

"That's great news," Mark commented.

"How's Mollie?" Kayla asked.

"She's *wunderbaar.*" Laura couldn't stop a smile. "I'm really enjoying taking care of her."

When they were done eating, the men went outside to talk on the porch while the three women cleaned the kitchen.

"How did your family take the news?" Laura asked as she scrubbed a sticky platter.

"The news about my engagement?" Kayla looked up from sweeping the floor.

Laura laughed. "*Ya,* the news about your engagement. What else would I ask about?"

Cindy snickered as she finished drying a dish and then set it in a cabinet.

"Right." Kayla laughed as she turned toward the mudroom, where a window beside the screen door was opened to the porch. "They were really, really *froh.* They all love Jamie and your family." She looked back at Laura and Cindy. "I was thinking about blue dresses for the wedding. What do you think?"

Cindy nodded. "That would be *schee* with your eyes."

"And your eyes too."

"But it's your day," Cindy insisted. "We're just grateful to be a part of it."

"Are you going to come over tomorrow to help Jamie move?"

"I have to work at the restaurant, but I'll try to get off early. I'm going to go to church with you on Sunday, though."

"That's *gut.*" Laura rinsed the platter and set it in the drainboard. "I'd love to spend time with you. I don't see you much anymore. I miss you."

"I miss you too," Kayla said as she swept crumbs into her dustpan.

Once done, they went out to the porch. Kayla sat down beside Jamie on the glider when Mark stood and hopped up on the porch railing. While *Dat* stood beside Mark, Cindy slipped into a rocking chair on one end of the porch, and Laura dropped into a rocking chair next to Rudy's straight-back chair.

Laura folded her hands in her lap as she listened to the men discuss their farms and businesses. She glanced at Rudy and took in his rigid demeanor. He was staring at Mark, and his back and shoulders looked as if someone had poured steel down his spine. The slight smile on his handsome face seemed disingenuous.

She pressed her lips together and looked down at her hands as her mind filled with images of Allen and Mollie. Would Allen get any sleep tonight without her there to care for Mollie if she cried during the night? She worried at the thought of Mollie missing her, screaming for her.

"Right, Laura?"

"What?" Her head snapped up, and she sensed every set of eyes trained on her face.

"I said you're probably going to work for Allen tomorrow," *Dat* said.

"Oh, no, I'm not." Laura shook her head.

"You're not?" Rudy's eyes were focused on hers now.

"No, he's going to close his shop tomorrow. He said he didn't need my help until Monday." Laura gripped the arms of the rocking chair as she moved it back and forth.

"How is he doing?" Jamie asked.

"He's fine. Mollie is still a little out of sorts, but I think she misses Irma Mae. Even little ones can sense stress and change, but I'm trying to help. She likes it when I rock her and sing to her. It seems to be the only way to calm her down."

Rudy continued to watch her, his intense gaze burrowing into hers when she looked his way.

"That's really sweet," Kayla chimed in. "Junior likes it when Eva sings to him too," she said referring to her sister-in-law and nephew. "I love watching her sing to him. It's adorable how he cuddles up to her."

"Mollie does that too. She snuggles right up to my neck." Laura grinned. "She's the sweetest *boppli*."

The conversation turned to other topics, and soon the sun began to set.

After a while, Kayla stood and held out her hand to Jamie. "It's getting late. I think you should take me home."

"*Ya*, you're right." Jamie jumped up and stretched.

"*Gut nacht.*" Kayla gave *Dat*, Mark, and Rudy a little wave.

Laura stood and hugged her. "I'm so *froh* for you. I can't wait for you to be *mei schweschder*."

"*Danki.*" Kayla squeezed her tight. "I can't wait either. I'll see you Sunday."

After giving Cindy a hug, Kayla took Jamie's hand, and they walked side by side down the porch steps and toward his horse and buggy.

"I'm going to go to bed. *Gut nacht*," Cindy announced before heading into the house.

"I'll go check on the animals." Mark grabbed a lantern.

"I'll come with you," *Dat* said as they started down the steps.

Laura took a deep breath when she realized she and Rudy were the only two left on the porch. When he turned toward her, she hoped their conversation would at least be less tense than it was on Wednesday. "I didn't expect to see you tonight."

"I couldn't wait until Sunday to see you, so when Mark called..."

She smiled. "That's really sweet."

"So things at Allen's *haus* are going well?"

"*Ya*. Fine."

"I'm assuming you stayed there the last two nights."

She nodded. "I did. I slept in a spare bed in Mollie's room, and I was up with her both nights."

"Who else knows you're staying overnight at his *haus*?"

"No one. Why?" She searched his eyes, wishing she could read his thoughts. "What are you worried about?"

A muscle flexed in his jaw, and he turned his attention to her father's pasture.

"Talk to me, Rudy," she said, nearly begging. "What's bothering you?"

He continued to stare out toward the darkness.

"Please look at me. We need to talk this out." She held up her hand as her body quaked with billowing tension. "We've been together for a long time. Let's work this out and not let it come between us."

"Fine. I'll tell you what's bothering me. I'm not comfortable with my girlfriend spending the night at another man's *haus*. It gives people the wrong impression about you."

"It gives people the wrong impression? What do you mean?"

He gave her an arrogant smirk. "You know what I mean."

She was stunned silent as she stared at him. "You can't be serious."

"I am."

"But this is Allen we're talking about. When Savilla was alive, the four of us spent a lot of time together. You know him. He's one of your *gut freinden*."

"That doesn't matter. If word gets back to the bishop that you're staying over at Allen's *haus*, you could get into trouble."

"No." She shook her head as wetness overtook her eyes. "I don't believe that. The bishop will understand the situation. Irma Mae is hurt, and Allen needs help. No one has any reason to believe there's anything inappropriate going on between us. Allen isn't even permitted to date until a year after Savilla has been gone, and I'm already your girlfriend."

They sat in a tense silence as the sound of the cicadas filled the porch. Her mind raced with disappointment and anger as Rudy's words echoed through her mind.

"You have no reason not to trust me," she finally said, her voice hoarse with frustration. "I'm only helping Allen until Irma Mae is better. No one will doubt the reason I'm at his *haus*."

She turned toward Rudy as he stared down at the porch floor. "Let's not argue, okay? I want things to go back to the way they were. Everything is changing so fast that I feel like my head is spinning." She sniffed and wiped her eyes with the back of her hand.

He leaned back in his chair and stared toward the barn.

Reticence stretched between them like a giant crater. She craved his understanding and sympathy when it came to her fear of change. She needed his reassurance their relationship would be okay, and his warm words of encouragement. But he gave her nothing but rock-hard silence. Did Rudy even sense what she needed after all the years they'd spent as friends and then as a couple? Or was he completely oblivious to her needs?

After several frustrating moments, she stood. "I'm really tired. I'm going to bed."

"Wait." He took her hand and pulled her back into the rocker. "I'm sorry for upsetting you. I don't want to argue. I just don't know how I'm supposed to accept that you're staying over at Allen's *haus*."

"The only way to do that is to have faith in Allen and me. You have to trust us."

He gave her a curt nod. "I'll try."

"Danki." Relief flooded her, loosening the painful muscles in her neck and back.

"Will you walk me to my buggy?" An unsure smile spread across his lips.

"Ya, of course."

Rudy took her hand and led her down the steps to the rock

driveway where his horse and buggy awaited him. When they reached the buggy door, he touched her cheek. "I'm sorry I can't come tomorrow to help Jamie move. *Mei dat* needs me at the store."

"I understand."

"I'll see you at church, then. *Gut nacht.*" He leaned down and brushed his lips across her cheek.

While the gesture was tender and sweet, she felt nothing—no spark, no excitement, no heat. Had they really grown so much apart? Renewed concern swirled inside.

"Gut nacht." She did her best to curve her lips into a smile as he was leaving, and she waited until the taillights of his buggy disappeared at the end of the driveway before walking back to the house.

Dat met her at the porch steps. "That was nice that Rudy could join us for supper tonight."

"It was," she agreed. "I'm excited for Jamie and Kayla."

"Ya, I am too." They walked up the porch steps together, and he set his lantern on the porch railing and looked at her. "We'll have something more to celebrate in December."

"Were you surprised?"

"No, not really." *Dat* looked toward the pasture. "Jamie has changed so much since he met Kayla. He finally found a balance between work and his family life, and then he built the *haus* he'd talked about for years. God blessed him when he brought Kayla into Jamie's life."

A faraway look overtook his eyes. "Your *mamm* would be so thrilled Jamie is finally going to settle down. She really liked Kayla and her family."

Laura's lower lip trembled. *"Ya,* she would be so *froh.* The wedding will be bittersweet without her, though."

"It will." He turned toward her. "But I know in my heart she's celebrating with us."

"*Ya.*" She wiped the back of her hand across her teary eyes as her thoughts turned to Allen and Mollie. "I was wondering if you would consider talking to Allen. He's dealing with a lot of emotions after losing Savilla. I thought you might be able to give him some encouragement."

"I'd be *froh* to talk to him." *Dat* fingered his beard as if he were deep in thought. "It has to be so difficult for Allen to face this alone. Losing your *mamm* was devastating, and it still is difficult, but I have *mei kinner* for support. When I couldn't bring myself to walk outside to work in the barn, *mei buwe* carried the load for me."

Then he looked at Laura and smiled. "But Allen has you. You're a blessing to him."

"Uh, no, I'm not really a support to him. I just take care of Mollie."

Dat touched her arm. "You're more than just a nanny. You're a special *freind*, and that's very important right now."

She swallowed as doubt came calling again, this time about Allen. Was she truly a support to him? She pushed the thought away. "I was thinking you might be able to talk to him after church on Sunday."

"That's a *wunderbaar* idea." *Dat* looped his arm around her shoulders. "Let's go inside. Tomorrow will be busy as we move Jamie into his new *haus*. And with preparations for the wedding, it's going to be a hectic fall."

ELEVEN

ALLEN RAN HIS HAND DOWN HIS FACE AS HE MOVED back and forth in the rocking chair and swallowed a sigh. He had been rocking Mollie for nearly two hours, and she hadn't stopped sobbing for more than a few minutes at a time. His body was so tired that every bone ached.

The undercurrent of worries that had been rippling around surfaced and grabbed his attention. He'd considered leaving a message on Laura's voice mail, begging her to come over and help him, but it was now Sunday afternoon. She and her family would be resting. Mollie was his daughter and his responsibility. Plus, Laura deserved to rest after working for him twenty-four hours a day.

Mollie shrieked, and he tried again to feed her a bottle.

"Are you hungry?" He handed her the formula, but she smacked it away.

"Ma-ma-ma-ma!" she hollered, her face beet red.

"*Ach, mei liewe.* If I only knew how to make you *froh.*" Total despair rained down on him. He was a failure as a father and didn't deserve to have Mollie as a daughter. A good father would know how to care for his child and give her what she needed.

Maybe she's ill.

The thought caught him by surprise, sending a chill cascading up his spine. He placed the back of his hand on her forehead to check for a fever, but he couldn't tell if the warmth he felt was from illness or her constant sobbing and screaming.

A noise sounded from the back of the house, and Allen stopped rocking. When he heard it again, he stood. Was it a knock on the door? Or was he only imagining a visitor had come who could help him calm Mollie?

She's your daughter. It's your responsibility to care for her!

He set her in the play yard, but she stood up, still sobbing and reaching for him.

"I'll be right back." He touched her hair. "I'll bring you a piece of cheese. Maybe that will calm you?"

His shoulders stiffened as she screamed, and he walked into the kitchen.

The knock sounded louder as he stepped into the mudroom. He pushed open the back door and gaped at the crowd gathered on his porch. Laura stood there, surrounded by her whole family, plus Kayla and Rudy.

"Allen!" Laura's face brightened. "We were so worried about you and Mollie when you didn't come to church." Her eyes widened as she took a step toward him. "Is she crying?"

Allen snorted. "She hasn't stopped crying for more than a few minutes at a time since five this morning. We both only slept about an hour overnight."

Laura reached for the screen door handle. "May I try to calm her?"

"Please. I was going to call—" Before he could finish his sentence, she slipped past him and rushed through the kitchen to the family room. He blew out a deep sigh of relief, looked up at the bright blue sky, and sent up a silent prayer.

Thank you for sending Laura to Mollie and me.

"Rough night, huh?" Mark patted Allen's shoulder.

"The roughest." Allen rubbed his eyes with his knuckles. "I don't know how Mollie and I can function without Laura."

Rudy's stony face glared at Allen.

"We brought you food." Kayla held up a covered dish.

Cindy also held up a dish. "Are you hungry? Have you had any lunch?"

"*Ya,* I am hungry. And no, I didn't have lunch. *Danki.*" He opened the screen door wider. "Please come in."

They filed into the kitchen, Cindy turned on the oven, and Kayla began gathering plates from the cabinets. The men stood by the table, and Vernon seemed as though he was about to say something. But when Mollie's crying suddenly stopped, Allen hurried to the family room and halted in the doorway. His eyes widened when he saw Laura was rocking Mollie and quietly speaking to her. His daughter was draped across Laura's lap like a large doll, and she stared up at her, sucking on a pacifier.

He pulled a footstool over to the rocker and dropped onto it. Then he looked up at Laura and tilted his head. "How did you do that?"

"I just picked her up, told her it would be okay, and started rocking her." She pointed to Mollie's mouth. "I found the pacifier in the diaper bag on the sofa and thought I'd give it a try."

He groaned, cupping his hand to his forehead. "Why didn't I think of that?"

"Because you're strung out from not getting any sleep." She gave him a warm smile. "Why didn't you call me?"

"I thought about it a million times, but I didn't want to bother you. I kept you tied up all last week. Besides, today is Sunday. I'm sure you'd rather be at church than with Mollie and me."

"I would have come." She touched his arm. "I worried about you last night. I almost called to see how things were going." She pulled her hand away and quickly looked down at Mollie. Was she embarrassed?

"She didn't sleep at all last night?" She touched Mollie's curls as she spoke. Was she avoiding his gaze?

"Not much." He gripped the back of his neck. "She woke me up at one and then cried on and off for hours. Every time she fell asleep, I would try to put her in the crib, but then she'd start all over again. I finally got her in around five. I was just falling asleep when she started again around seven. I gave up at that point."

"I convinced *mei dat* we should come over here to check on you right after the church service." She kept her eyes focused on Mollie. "Everyone else decided to come too, and we stopped at home for the food. We were all worried about you."

"Danki." When Allen sensed someone watching him, he turned toward the doorway.

Rudy stood with folded arms while dividing a look between Allen and Laura. When his gaze came to a rest on Allen, he gave him a tentative smile. "The other men went out to check on your horse and barn. How are you doing?"

Allen blew out a deep sigh. "I'm better now that Laura is here." When Rudy's expression hardened, Allen did a mental head slap. Why had he said that? "I mean, she's the only one who can soothe Mollie," he added, but Rudy's expression didn't change.

Great job, Allen. Now he's upset with Laura.

"What I meant to say," Allen began, keeping his words cautious, "is I appreciate Laura's ability to calm Mollie down. I'm grateful. She cried most of last night, and she's been cranky all day. I'm so exhausted I can't think straight. I'm also grateful you're all here."

"I see. Well, then, it's *gut* Laura insisted we all come check on you and Mollie." A look passed between Rudy and Laura that Allen couldn't quite comprehend. Then, with a scowl, Rudy walked back into the kitchen.

Allen leaned in close to Laura. "Is Rudy still upset with you for helping me? And did you really insist he come?"

"Don't worry about him," she responded, her voice low. "And no, I did not insist Rudy come. He just did."

"Laura, if you want to quit, I can find a nan—"

"I don't want to quit." Her blue eyes turned almost fierce. "I want to help you and Mollie."

"All right." He nodded, but guilt and anxiety thrashed in his gut and tightened the muscles in his shoulders. He would have to ask her about the situation with Rudy when they were alone.

"Allen?" Kayla appeared in the doorway. "We have the tuna casserole and hamburger pie casserole all warmed up."

Allen gave Laura a sideways glance. She bit her lower lip as if trying to prevent a laugh from escaping her mouth, and she kept her focus on Mollie. Laura's suppressed smile made the knots in his shoulders loosen. She wasn't upset with him or Rudy.

Turning back to Kayla, he forced a smile. "That sounds fantastic." He did his best to keep his voice chipper. "Thank you so much."

Kayla beckoned him toward the kitchen. "Come eat with us, then."

He nodded. "I'll be right there."

Kayla disappeared into the kitchen.

Allen leaned in close to Laura once again. "Did you tell them to bring casseroles as some sort of punishment for me?"

"Allen Lambert, is that how you respond to a gift?" Her eyes widened with mock disappointment. "I'm offended that you aren't grateful for the meal we generously brought you."

He grinned as he took in her expression. "So it *was* your idea."

"No, it wasn't." She leaned over toward him and lowered her voice. "It was Cindy's idea. She really appreciates the dresses and aprons you gave her, and she wanted to do something nice for you.

The casseroles were left over from yesterday when Jamie's *frein-den* helped him move into his *haus*, and Cindy wanted to share them with you." She looked toward the doorway and then back at him. "Be sure to thank her. She's very sensitive."

"I know, and I will thank her. I was just teasing you."

"I know." She gazed down at Mollie, who hadn't moved a muscle except to keep her pacifier between her lips. "You just wanted your binky, didn't you?" She ran her fingers through Mollie's curls. "I'll have to remind your *dat* to give it to you when you get upset."

"I'm so glad you're here," Allen told her.

"I am too." She bent down and kissed Mollie's head. "I missed you last night, little girl." She looked up at Allen and shook her head. "Is that *gegisch* that I missed her?"

"No, it's not silly. We missed you too." His words caught him by surprise as some emotional response crossed her face. But he had no idea what it was.

Mollie reached up and grabbed one of the ties from Laura's prayer covering. She yanked at it as Laura looked down at her and laughed. The tenderness between Laura and Mollie tugged at his heart, and he felt an invisible magnet pulling him to Laura. She seemed somehow different, and their relationship was stronger. Almost intimate.

The sudden rush of emotion knocked him off-balance for a moment. Why would he feel such a strong connection to Laura? She was Savilla's best friend and Rudy's girlfriend. He was confusing his friendship with Laura with his love for his daughter. It had to be the haze of exhaustion that made his feelings fuzzy. He needed something to eat, and perhaps a cup of coffee too.

He stood. "I'd better go have some casserole."

"Be nice to Cindy and Kayla." She grinned up at him and then looked down at Mollie again. "Are you ready for a nap? You look really tired, Mollie Faith. Would you please fall asleep for me?"

Allen mentally shook himself as he walked into the kitchen. Everyone else sat at the table, already eating casserole and talking. The delicious aroma of coffee permeated the room as the percolator hissed and belched on the stove.

Cindy popped up from her chair, picked up a mug from the counter, and faced him. "Would you like some *kaffi*?"

"*Ya*, please," Allen said. Had Cindy read his mind?

"Have a seat," Kayla instructed, pointing to the empty chair between her and Vernon. "Would you like some casserole? I'll scoop it up for you." She picked up an empty plate.

"*Ya. Danki*." Allen sat down in the chair as she filled his plate with some of each of the casseroles. He worked to suppress his grin as Laura's warning to be nice rang in his ears.

Kayla rose and began helping Cindy deliver mugs of coffee to everyone at the table.

Cindy handed Allen one. "*Danki* for the dresses and aprons." She gestured toward her green dress and black apron. "I just had to take them in a little, but the length was perfect." Her cheeks blushed bright pink. "It's a special way for me to remember Savilla."

"*Gern gschehne*. I'm glad you can use them. Savilla would be *froh*." Allen took a sip of coffee and then turned toward Jamie, who sat at the end of the table. "How did the move go yesterday?"

"It went well." Jamie smiled up at Kayla as she handed him a mug of coffee. "I'm all moved into the *haus*. Laura moved into my room yesterday too."

"Really?" Allen's thoughts turned to Laura's earlier comment about missing Mollie last night. Did she sleep well in her new room or did she have trouble adjusting to being alone? He made a mental note to ask her about that too.

"Allen, did Laura tell you our news?" Kayla asked as she gave Vernon a mug.

"No, she didn't." Allen shook his head.

"Jamie and I are getting married in December." Kayla's face lit up as she said the words.

"That's fantastic." Allen turned to Jamie and lifted his mug as if to toast him. "Congratulations."

"And we thought he'd never find someone to marry him," Mark quipped before pouring milk into his coffee.

Jamie sighed and shook his head.

"I'm just teasing," Mark added, his smirk fading. "We're really *froh.*"

"*Ya,* we are," Vernon chimed in.

"*Danki.*" Kayla glowed as she handed coffee to Rudy. "We're excited."

Allen glanced across the table to where Rudy stared down at his mug, and shame like a geyser swamped him. He had to apologize for what he said earlier about needing Laura there.

He closed his eyes for a silent prayer and then forked some of the tuna casserole.

"How is your family doing, Kayla?" Allen asked.

"They're doing well. *Danki* for asking." Kayla scooped a pile of tuna casserole onto her plate. "The restaurant has been very busy since it's still tourist season. Junior has gotten so big. He's almost two now, and he's into everything."

"They grow so fast," Vernon said.

About thirty minutes later, Laura entered the kitchen and sat down next to Rudy. She met Allen's gaze and smiled before bowing her head for prayer. Then she put some of the hamburger casserole onto her plate as Cindy brought her a mug of coffee.

"She's sleeping?" Allen asked when she'd had a bite or two.

Laura nodded and wiped her mouth with a napkin. "She didn't want me to put her down at first, but I managed to get her to stay asleep once she drifted off again."

"*Danki,*" Allen said.

"You seem to have the special touch with Mollie," Kayla said. "She calmed right down when you picked her up."

Laura shrugged and stared down at her plate as her cheeks reddened. "I just tried what I thought would work. I'm thankful it did." She looked up at Kayla. "Did you tell Allen your news?"

"*Ya*, I did." Kayla beamed. "We have so much to do. December will be here before we know it. *Mei dat* is concerned our barn is too small for the guests. He said he should have built a larger barn after our old barn burned down last summer."

Allen kept his gaze trained on Laura as Kayla talked about wedding plans. She had deflected the attention Kayla had brought to her by mentioning Jamie and Kayla's wedding, and now she was staring at her plate as she ate.

When he felt someone watching him, Allen looked at Rudy and found him frowning at him. Allen looked away and continued to eat.

When they were finished, the women began gathering the dishes, and Allen stepped to the doorway to check on Mollie. She was still sleeping in her play yard, and her pacifier was still in her mouth.

"Allen." Vernon clapped him on the shoulder. "Would you walk outside with me? I'd like to talk to you alone."

"*Ya*, of course." An uneasiness gripped Allen. "We can go out to my shop."

"*Gut.*"

As Allen followed Vernon toward the back door, he glanced at Laura. She stood with her back to the sink, and she gave him a shy smile. Did she know why her father wanted to speak to him? If so, why hadn't she warned him?

"Please have a seat." Allen gestured toward the desk chair once they were in his office.

"*Danki.*" Vernon sat down, and Allen pulled over a nearby stool.

"What do you want to discuss?" His stomach tightened as he sat down on the stool. Would Vernon tell him he no longer wanted Laura to work for him? But then how would Allen cope without her help with Mollie?

"Laura is worried about you, and she asked me to talk with you to see how you're doing."

Allen blinked. "She's worried about me?"

"*Ya.* She said you're struggling with grief, and she thought I might be able to offer some support since I've struggled with the loss of a spouse as well. There were days when I couldn't get out of bed because I was drowning in not only grief, but guilt and regret." Vernon's expression clouded. "I blamed myself for a long time after I lost Dorothy. I believed if I had repaired the basement banister, she wouldn't have fallen. I also wrestled with all the broken promises, and how I never gave her the things she longed for."

Vernon leaned back in the chair, and it creaked under his weight. "Dorothy wanted to travel. She wanted to see Niagara Falls and the Grand Canyon. She also wanted to go to Florida, but I always told her I couldn't leave the farm. In reality, Jamie and Mark were capable of taking care of this place, but I was too prideful to let go and trust them."

Allen folded his arms over his chest as Vernon's words took hold.

"I've realized it's not healthy to hold on to those regrets," Vernon continued. "All I can do is try to teach *mei kinner* to never take anything for granted. I know it was God's will that Dorothy passed away, and I can't punish myself for it."

Allen nodded as his own regret and grief pummeled his heart.

Vernon lifted an eyebrow. "You look like you want to say something, but you're hesitating."

"I don't even know where to begin." Allen's shoulders hunched. "I regret not telling Savilla how much I loved her one last time. It tears me to pieces that Mollie will grow up without knowing first-hand how special and loving her mother was." His voice was thick, and his hurt ran so deep he thought he might drown in it. "Most of all, I'm crushed that she's not here."

"Savilla knows exactly how much you love her because you showed her every day. Mollie will feel Savilla's love and know all about her because you will tell her." Vernon leaned forward and gripped Allen's shoulder. "You need to let all your regrets and self-blame go. Pray about it. Ask God to heal your heart, and learn to accept it was all his plan. None of it was your fault." He squeezed his shoulder.

Allen nodded and tried to clear his throat past the swelling lump of emotion stuck there as Vernon went on.

"We can't allow ourselves to question God's plans for us or blame ourselves for what's not in our control. We all know God is in control. He has the best plan for our lives because it's his plan." He squeezed Allen's shoulder once again and then released it. "Mollie will be fine. She has you."

Allen blew out a deep gust of air he hadn't realized he'd been holding. *"Danki."*

"I know how you feel because I lost Dorothy suddenly too." Vernon's face was full of warmth and understanding. "The difference is that you have Mollie, who depends on you, to keep you moving forward. You need to get out of bed and keep going for her."

"Ya, that's true." Allen swiped the back of his hand over his eyes to fend off threatening tears. "The *haus* just feels so different without her. Sometimes it feels cold and empty. It's too quiet without her voice and her laugh. I miss the smell of her favorite vanilla lotion and seeing her smile. Something is missing without her there. It even feels foreign to me, like it's not *mei haus* anymore."

"I understand. I promise you it does get easier, and you'll get through it. Just ask God to give you the strength you need."

Silence fell between them, and Allen's thoughts turned to Laura and his concern about her helping him.

"Vernon, do you support Laura's decision to help me with Mollie?"

Vernon tilted his head. "*Ya,* of course I do. What gave you the impression I didn't?"

"I just wanted to be sure."

"My family and I will do anything we can to help you. Savilla was like *mei* third *dochder,* and Irma Mae helped us for weeks after I lost my Dorothy. Laura will help you for as long as you need her. And if you need anything else from us, please let us know."

Once again, Allen was thankful for the Riehl family and their endless support and generosity. If only he could convince Rudy to share that understanding.

TWELVE

"DID YOU HEAR WHAT I SAID?" CINDY ASKED LAURA as they stood at the sink.

"What?" Laura spun toward her younger sister. Her cheeks burned as she folded her arms across her apron. Her eyes had been focused on Allen and *Dat* as they walked out together, and she'd missed her sister's question.

Cindy lifted a light-brown eyebrow. "I said I'll wash and you can dry and put away the dishes since you know where they go. Okay?"

"Oh, *ya*. Right. That makes sense." She retrieved a dish towel from the bottom drawer by the sink and readied herself to begin drying.

"I'll help too." Kayla placed two coffee mugs on the counter and retrieved another dish towel. "Just tell me where the dishes go."

"Should we sit outside and wait for *Dat* and Allen to join us?" Mark asked.

"*Ya*, that's a *gut* idea." Jamie stood and touched Kayla's arm. "We'll leave you ladies to your work."

"Oh, how kind of you," Kayla said, teasing him. "Enjoy the porch."

"We will." Jamie started toward the mudroom with Mark in tow.

Laura glanced over at Rudy, and he frowned at her. She smiled, but his expression remained somber as he followed her brothers. After a couple of beats, the screen door clicked shut and silence filled the kitchen.

Laura's shoulders hunched as she worked in silence for several minutes alongside Cindy and Kayla.

"Is everything all right between you and Rudy?" Kayla's question sliced through the heavy silence.

Laura turned toward her. Her mouth worked, but her words were stuck in her throat.

Cindy glanced over her shoulder at Laura, her eyebrows lifting.

"*Ya*," Laura finally said. She leaned her hip against the counter as the question rolled around in her mind. She looked toward the open window in the mudroom. The interior door was open too, and they could hear the men's voices through both the window and screen door. "Rudy isn't *froh* I'm spending so much time over here helping Allen."

"I don't understand." Kayla scrunched her nose. "Why would Rudy be upset?"

"He doesn't want you to help Allen?" Cindy's eyebrows drew together as she scrubbed a casserole dish.

Laura took a deep breath. "A few days ago he told me he was concerned I'm spending too much time here. Then on Friday night he said he was worried about how it will look to other members of the community that I'm staying overnight to take care of Mollie when she wakes up and cries."

Cindy stopped washing the dish and turned toward Laura. "But Rudy is Allen's *freind*. He should be supportive."

"Shh." Laura pointed toward the back porch. "I don't want him to hear."

Kayla shook her head. "Doesn't Rudy understand Allen needs your help right now?"

Laura shrugged. "I think he's more worried about how it could look to the community than concerned about how much Allen and Mollie need me."

Cindy frowned as she returned to washing the dish. "That's awfully selfish. I'm disappointed in Rudy."

Laura nodded as she plucked another dish from the drainboard. *I am too.* "I'm really worried about Allen, so I asked *Dat* to speak to him."

"Oh?" Cindy looked over her shoulder at Laura. *"Was iss letz?"*

Laura kept her eyes focused on the dish she was drying. "He's struggling with his grief. I thought *Dat* might be able to help him."

"That's very thoughtful of you. You're a *wunderbaar freind* to Allen." Kayla touched Laura's shoulder. "Rudy should be a *gut freind* too."

"I know." Laura sighed. "I keep trying to make him understand that."

"Do you want Jamie to talk to him?" Kayla offered as she took a dish out of the drainboard. "I can ask Jamie to do it."

"No, but *danki.*" Laura picked up the last dish Cindy set in the drainboard. "I think it's best to just let it go for now. Hopefully Rudy will come around." She looked over at Kayla. "Are you *froh* with the *haus*?"

Kayla's pretty face lit up with a bright smile. "Oh, *ya.* I love it so much! My family is going to come for supper at the *haus* one night next week to talk about decorating it. I can't wait for Eva to see it."

Later they were sitting at the table when Mollie cried out. Laura rushed into the family room with the other two women right behind her. Mollie was standing in the play yard, holding up her arms. Tears flowed in rivulets down her pink cheeks.

"Ach, mei liewe." Laura held out her arms and Mollie reached for her. "Don't cry."

Mollie snuggled into Laura's shoulder as Cindy picked up her pacifier from the bottom of the play yard.

"Do you want this?" Cindy held out the pacifier, and Mollie took it from her and put it in her mouth. Then Cindy stepped over to the sofa and checked the diapering station. The diaper bag was empty too. "I don't see any diapers here."

Laura nodded toward the stairs. "Why don't we change her upstairs?"

"Ya." Kayla picked up the diaper bag. "We can restock."

Laura led them up the stairs and into Mollie's room. She placed Mollie on the changing table and began to remove her clothes as Cindy started filling the bag with diapers.

"Is this where you sleep?" Cindy pointed to the bed by the crib.

"Ya." Laura nodded toward the rocking chair by the crib. "I rock her when she cries and then put her back in her bed as soon as she'll let me." She looked over at Kayla. "Kayla, would you please get a onesie and a dress from the dresser next to you? The onesies are in the top drawer, and the dresses are in the bottom drawer."

"Sure." Kayla opened the top drawer and started rooting through its contents.

"Hi, Mollie." Cindy came to stand next to Laura.

"Mollie," Laura began, "can you say Cindy?"

Mollie reached for Cindy, and Cindy took her hand and laughed. When Cindy released her hand, Mollie reached for Laura and said, "Ma-ma-ma."

"No, I'm Laura," Laura corrected her. "Say Laura." She turned to Cindy. "We've been working on this."

"Has she tried to walk yet?" Kayla asked as she sidled up to Laura with a dress and onesie in her hand. "Junior walked on his first birthday."

"We haven't tried," Laura said. "Why don't we try after I dress her?"

"That's a great idea," Kayla said, agreeing to the plan.

After changing Mollie's diaper, Laura pulled on the onesie and then the purple dress Kayla selected.

"That dress is a little tight," Cindy observed.

"It is." Laura stood Mollie up on the changing table. "I found some fabric in Savilla's sewing room, and I'm going to make her a few new dresses and nightgowns."

"Let me know if you want some help," Cindy offered.

"Danki." Laura smiled at her sister and then set Mollie on the floor.

Kayla sat down on the rocker and held out her hands. "Have her walk to me."

"Okay." Holding Mollie's little hands over her head, Laura turned the little girl toward Kayla. "Can you walk to Kayla?"

"Kumm, Mollie." Kayla held her hands out to her.

Mollie sputtered and then squealed as she took a step, all while holding on to Laura's hands.

"Yay!" Kayla clapped. *"Kumm,* Mollie!"

Mollie squealed again and kept walking. When she reached her, she took Kayla's hands.

"Gut job, Mollie!" Tears filled Laura's eyes as she clapped. Savilla would be so thrilled.

"Walk to me now, Mollie." Cindy stood by the doorway and held out her hands.

Laura took Mollie's hands, and Mollie started walking toward her. When she reached Cindy, she squealed, and they all clapped.

"Walk back to me now," Kayla said from the rocking chair.

For the next several minutes, Laura helped Mollie walk back and forth from Cindy to Kayla. They all cheered after each journey Mollie made across the room. When she walked back to Kayla one last time, Cindy joined them by the rocker.

"You're such a big girl," Laura told Mollie, and Mollie squealed and stamped her foot.

"What's going on in here?"

Laura spun to the door, where Allen stood with his forearm leaning on the doorframe. "Mollie is walking."

"Really?" His eyes brightened as he stepped into the room.

"*Ya.*" Laura took Mollie's hands and turned her toward Allen. "Can you walk to *Dat*?"

"Da! Da! *Dat!*" Mollie repeated as she walked toward Allen. "*Dat! Dat!*"

"Look at that!" Allen squatted, and his eyes sparkled. He held out his hands as Mollie came close. "You're doing great, Mollie."

When Mollie squealed and reached for his hands, he scooped her up and hugged her. "Great job." He kissed the top of her head and then looked at Laura. "I can't believe it."

Laura laughed, feeling pure joy.

Cindy stepped over to Laura. "She's doing so great."

"*Ya*, she is." Kayla joined them. "She'll be walking by herself in no time."

"Walking by herself?" Allen grinned down at Mollie. "I'm not sure I'm ready for that." He looked over at Laura. "She's been crawling for a while, but now I'm envisioning her running everywhere."

"*Ya*, she will." Laura touched Mollie's foot. "You're going to be unstoppable."

"Kayla!" Jamie's voice sounded from downstairs. "Are you ready to leave? Your parents are expecting us."

"Oh. I didn't realize how late it is." Kayla's eyes widened as she stepped into the hallway. "I'll be right down," she called toward the stairs. She turned to Laura and hugged her. "It was so *gut* seeing you." Then she hugged Cindy. "Good-bye."

"*Danki* for coming, Kayla," Laura told her.

"*Gern gschehne.*" Kayla shook Allen's hand. "It was nice seeing you." She touched Mollie's cheek, and Mollie smiled at her. "Bye, Mollie." She waved before disappearing through the doorway.

Cindy looked from Laura to Allen and then back to Laura before pointing to the doorway. "I'm going to see if Mark and *Dat* are ready to go. I'll need to make supper for *Dat.*" She said good-bye to Allen and stepped into the hallway.

"Would you please tell Rudy I'll be down in a minute?" Laura called after her.

"*Ya,* of course." Cindy disappeared, her footsteps echoing in the stairwell.

Laura stepped over to the changing table and picked up Mollie's dirty clothes.

"I'll take care of that," Allen said.

Laura tossed the clothes into the hamper, which was half full. "I was just putting them away. I can do all the laundry tomorrow."

"That's fine, but please don't push yourself."

She faced him, and his expression warmed as he looked at her.

"*Danki* for coming by today." He leaned against the wall and rubbed Mollie's back as she snuggled into his shoulder.

"*Gern gschehne.*" She folded her arms across her chest as concern blossomed in the pit of her stomach. "Are you upset with me because I asked *mei dat* to talk to you?"

He raised a light-brown eyebrow. "Why would I be? No, I'm not upset at all." He shifted Mollie in his arms and then looked down at her. He touched his daughter's cheek and kept his focus on her as he spoke. "I had a really *gut* talk with your *dat.* I appreciate your asking him to talk to me."

"Oh *gut.*" She breathed a sigh of relief.

He looked up at her. "You honestly thought I'd be upset about that?"

She shrugged. "I don't know. I guess I was afraid I had overstepped my bounds."

"No, I don't think you could do that. Quite frankly, I'd be lost without your help." He glanced back down at Mollie as she babbled, telling him some story he couldn't understand. "Wouldn't we be a mess without Laura to help us?"

Mollie gurgled in response.

"*Ya*, I think that about sums it up." Allen grinned as he looked at Laura again.

Laura laughed. "Do you need me to stay tonight so you can get some sleep?"

"No, that's okay. We'll be fine." He stepped over to the changing table and retrieved a pacifier from the top drawer. "I have a secret weapon now."

Mollie reached for the pacifier and popped it into her mouth.

"See?" he asked.

"*Ya*." She started toward the door and then hesitated, facing him once again. "You look exhausted. I don't mind staying so you can get some real sleep." She pointed to the closet. "I left a few things here to wear, so I can just tell Rudy I'm going to stay here tonight."

"*Danki*, but I think both Mollie and I will sleep just fine." He looked past her, and his smile faded. He stood up straight and shifted Mollie in his arms again. "Hi, Rudy."

She spun toward her boyfriend. He was hovering in the doorway. "Rudy. Are you ready to go?"

"*Ya*." Rudy pointed toward the stairs. "Your *dat* and *bruders* already left. It's almost five. My parents are going to wonder where I am if we don't leave now."

"I'm sorry." She looked at Allen again. "I'll see you tomorrow." She touched Mollie's arm. "Be *gut* tonight, and let your *dat* sleep, all right?" She kissed Mollie's head and then looked up at

Allen. "Have a *gut* night. Cindy put the leftover casserole in a dish in the refrigerator."

"*Danki.*" His mouth twitched, and she bit her lip to stop a threatening grin.

"Laura, we need to go." Rudy's voice held a thread of annoyance.

She turned to him. "I'm sorry. I just wanted to make sure Allen had everything he needed tonight."

Rudy pursed his lips. "Allen is a grown man. I think he can take care of himself."

Laura swallowed back frustrated words, sure a frown had overtaken her face. She turned toward Allen, who was scowling at Rudy. "*Gut nacht.*"

"*Gut nacht,*" Allen told her before looking at Rudy again. "It was nice seeing you. *Danki* for coming to visit." His kind words contradicted his flat tone.

"It was great seeing you too." Rudy's response echoed Allen's tone. He turned to Laura. "Let's go." Then he stalked out of the room and down the stairs.

Laura hesitated in the doorway and looked back at Allen. "I'm really sorry for his attitude."

"Please don't apologize for him." Allen made a sweeping gesture toward the door. "Go before I cause more problems."

"It's not you."

"It *is* me, and I don't want to make things worse for you." His expression warmed. "Please go. We'll be fine."

"I'll see you in the morning." As she hurried down the stairs, Laura couldn't shake the feeling that Allen needed her more than he was admitting. And deep down, she longed to stay.

THIRTEEN

"You didn't have to be so rude to Allen." Laura folded her hands on her lap as she sat with her back ramrod straight in Rudy's buggy.

Rudy was guiding the horse down Allen's driveway and toward the main road, but he gave her a sideways glance. "I wasn't rude to him. It was time to go, and you were stalling."

"I wasn't stalling." Hot frustration surged through her veins. "I was just trying to help Allen care for Mollie." She looked at him as a thought occurred to her. "Why haven't you tried to help him since Savilla died?"

"What do you mean?" His forehead creased.

"You're supposed to be Allen's *freind*, but you haven't even really spoken to him since he lost Savilla. Why is that?"

"What are you talking about? I talk to Allen all the time. We've spoken at church plenty of times since Savilla died."

"No, you don't really talk to him. You say hello and ask about his carriage shop, but that's about it."

He halted the horse at a red light and turned toward her, his expression suddenly warmer. "What am I supposed to say to him?"

"You're supposed to ask how he is and then listen."

Rudy nodded and then turned toward the windshield as a strained silence permeated the buggy. Irritation emanated from him, and Laura's back and shoulders stiffened. Why was conversing with Allen so easy, but talking to Rudy, her boyfriend of four years, so cumbersome and tense?

The light turned green, and Rudy guided the horse through the intersection.

"You're upset with me," she finally said.

He sighed.

"Just tell me what's bothering you."

"Are you serious?" He raised an eyebrow. "You honestly don't know why I'm upset?"

"No, I don't. Tell me."

"First of all, you said you wanted to spend time with me today after church, and I assumed you meant visiting at either *mei haus* or yours, or possibly even going to the youth group. Instead we spent all afternoon at Allen's *haus*. That's not exactly what I had in mind when you said we'd spend time together."

"But we were together," she insisted.

"When did we actually have time to talk alone?"

She opened her mouth to argue and then closed it. "I'm sorry," she finally said. "You're right."

"And also, today was embarrassing."

"Embarrassing how?" She turned toward him.

"Weren't you there at Allen's *haus*?" He gestured with one hand while keeping the other on the reins. "You walked into his *haus* and took over with Mollie like you were her *mamm*."

"What do you mean?" Her voice pitched higher. "Allen said she'd been crying all morning. He needed my help. What was I supposed to do—let her cry?"

"That's not what I meant." He scowled, his handsome face twisting. "You don't have to walk in there and act like it's your *haus*."

"I don't act like it's *mei haus*."

"*Ya,* you do." His frown deepened. "You behave as if you're Mollie's *mamm* and Allen's *fraa*. You take over with Mollie and you know where everything is in the kitchen. You and Allen talk like a married couple. It's like you're playing *haus*."

"Playing *haus*?" Anger warmed her from the inside, hot and explosive as tears stung her eyes. "You can't really mean that."

He squared his jaw and kept his stony eyes trained on the road ahead.

"I'm not trying to be his *fraa* or Mollie's *mamm*. I just want to help them. If I don't help them, who will?" She wiped away her tears and sniffed.

"He could hire someone to work as Mollie's nanny. Plenty of teenaged *maed* in our church district would jump at the chance for a job like that."

She turned toward the windshield and folded her arms over her chest. They rode in silence for several minutes. When her farm came into view, she took a shaky breath and then looked at him once again.

"What's happened to us?" Her voice shook.

Rudy halted the horse by the back porch, and then his shoulders slumped. "I don't know. Everything was fine until you started working for Allen." He paused. "Or maybe until your *mamm* and then Savilla died. I know their deaths have been a blow, but a strain between us has only grown worse the last few weeks."

"I don't understand. I'm still the same person I was before Savilla died and *mei mamm* had her accident." She sniffed again.

"Maybe so, but I get the feeling you'd rather be with Allen than with me." His voice was soft and sounded unsure as he stared down at his lap.

Laura gasped.

"Is that how you feel?" He looked at her, his dark eyes seeming as hesitant as his question.

"No." She shook her head.

"So then where do we go from here?"

"If you don't trust me, maybe we shouldn't be together." She held her breath, praying he wouldn't break up with her. She'd already lost her mother and Savilla, and she couldn't bear the thought of losing Rudy too.

He placed his hand on top of hers. "I don't want to break up with you. I just want to feel like you're still my girlfriend."

"I am still your girlfriend, and I would never do anything to break your trust. I'm sorry if I gave you the wrong impression. And I'm sorry for not truly spending time with you today." She searched his brown eyes for solace but found none. Was their relationship really falling apart? Alarm gripped her. She had to find a way to fix whatever had broken between them. "Maybe if you talked to Allen more, you'd see he needs us both to help him through this tough time."

"*Ya.* Maybe I'll give that a try." His eyes seemed unconvinced. "*Gut nacht.*"

"*Gut nacht.*" She paused, waiting for him to lean over and kiss her, but he remained cemented on his side of the bench seat. "Tell your parents hello for me." She pushed open the buggy door and climbed out.

As soon as she closed the buggy door, Rudy guided the horse down the driveway. Laura stared as he disappeared, and a sense of foreboding came over her. She felt rooted to the ground.

"Are you okay?"

She spun toward her twin. He was standing on the path with hands shoved into his trouser pockets. "How long have you been standing there watching me, Mark?"

"I don't know. Maybe five minutes? As long as you've been

standing there, staring, I guess." Mark walked over to her. *"Was iss letz?"*

"Nothing." She squared her shoulders. "I was just thinking about what a *wunderbaar* day it's been." She pointed up. "There isn't a cloud in the sky, and it was a *schee* summer day."

He raised an eyebrow. "You know you can't lie to me, right?"

"I'm not lying. It's been a fantastic day."

"So then why are your eyes red and puffy?" He pointed to her face. "Why do I have a feeling you're coming apart at the seams?" He touched his chest. "I can feel what you're feeling. Remember?" He gestured between them. "We're *zwillingbopplin*."

She blew out a deep breath. She'd been caught, and it was time to confess the truth.

"Rudy is upset with me." She summarized her painful conversation with him in the buggy. "I feel like I'm losing him, and I can't stand the thought of losing someone else." She swiped the back of her hand across her eyes. "I don't understand why Rudy isn't as worried about Allen as I am. I thought they were *gut freinden*. Why doesn't Rudy see I'm doing this for Mollie? For Savilla? Why doesn't he trust me? I've never given him any reason to doubt my feelings for him."

Mark looked toward the street, and worry pricked the back of Laura's neck.

"Why aren't you answering me?"

He fingered his suspenders and turned toward her. "I don't think you're going to like what I have to say."

"Just say it." She held her breath.

"I think Rudy has a point."

"What do you mean?" Her voice rose, but she couldn't seem to help it.

"I think you're getting too attached to Mollie."

She gasped. "How could you—"

"Hold on," he said, interrupting and holding up his hands as if to silence her. "Before you yell at me, just listen, sis. I'm worried you're going to be heartbroken when Irma Mae returns to care for Mollie." She saw the concern in his eyes. "You're going to miss that little girl."

"*Ya*, I am, but I'll still be a part of her life. I won't see her every day, but Cindy and I will visit her once a week like we used to do. I'll be fine."

Mark nodded, but he seemed unconvinced.

"Laura?" *Dat*'s voice sounded from the porch. "Are you home?"

"*Ya, Dat.*" She waved at him. "I'm coming."

"Cindy made supper." *Dat* gestured for them to come into the house. "Let's eat." He disappeared through the screen door.

She started toward the porch, and Mark grabbed her arm. "What?"

"Just make me one promise, okay?" Mark's blue eyes pleaded with her.

"Okay."

"Promise me you'll be careful." He released her arm. "You're so focused on Allen and Mollie that you don't see how it's affecting Rudy. Just take a step back and think about how he feels."

"I will."

"*Gut.*" Mark rubbed his hands together. "Let's go eat."

As she followed her brother into the house, his words sunk in. Maybe he was right. Maybe she did need to put Rudy first. She would consider his feelings and do her best to be a better girlfriend.

But she'd continue helping Allen any way she could. It felt right.

Later that night Laura climbed the stairs to her room, and her thoughts turned again to Allen and Mollie. She hoped they were sleeping well. As she headed down the hallway to her bedroom, she suddenly realized Friday was Mollie's first birthday, and she got excited. She had to plan a party!

She rushed into her bedroom, found a notepad and pen from her desk, jumped onto her bed, and began to write down the things she'd have to buy and do. Soon she had a long list with everything from a menu to gifts. She couldn't wait to share it with Allen.

Leaning back on her pillow, Laura smiled as she imagined hugging Mollie tomorrow morning. Surely Rudy wouldn't mind her making a little girl's first birthday special.

The rain beat a steady cadence on the roof as Allen rocked Mollie in the chair beside her bed. She'd wakened an hour ago, crying, but then finally had settled down. Mollie rubbed her nose against his shoulder and sucked her pacifier while he watched rivulets of rain trickle down her bedroom window. The green numerals on the battery-operated clock on her dresser glowed 2:17.

Allen caressed Mollie's back as the sound of the rain and the creaking of the rocking chair echoed in the large, dark room. The house was quiet—too quiet. He missed his one true companion, the love of his life. He missed Savilla's gorgeous smile, her beautiful brown eyes, her golden hair the color of the afternoon sun, and her sweet voice. His heart ached for her. Today would be the ten-month anniversary of the day she left them.

His heart and his soul cried for her to come back to them. Mollie needed her mother, and Allen needed his partner. Friday was Mollie's first birthday, and Savilla should be here to celebrate this momentous occasion with them. It wouldn't be right to sing "Happy Birthday" to her without his wife by his side.

"I miss you, Savilla," he whispered.

His words echoed around the room. He was lonely. He needed someone to talk to, someone to soothe the cracks in his heart, someone to tell him he was a good father.

Maybe he should have asked Laura to stay tonight.

His eyes widened at the unexpected thought. It wasn't Laura's job to listen to him, offer him solace, or calm his worries about his lack of skill as a father. Laura was only a friend, and she would care for Mollie until Irma Mae had recovered enough to come back. She wasn't his companion, and he needed to stop imagining her as one.

Mollie hummed in her sleep, and he patted her back as his thoughts wandered. After finishing their conversation in his shop, Allen and Vernon had joined the rest of the men on the porch, where they talked about the weather and upcoming harvest season. Rudy had been quiet during most of the conversation, only responding to questions directed to him. His expression remained bleak, and Allen could feel his resentment despite Mark's repeated jokes and amusing stories about friends in the community.

Sitting next to him, Allen had tried to apologize to Rudy for what he'd said about needing Laura, but Rudy had simply grunted a response. Allen missed when he and Savilla would spend evenings talking and laughing with Rudy and Laura, but his friendship with Rudy seemed to have died with Savilla.

No, it had been crippled when Savilla left them, but it died when Laura became Mollie's temporary nanny. Would Allen find a way to regain his friendship with Rudy when Irma Mae came back? Or had he lost his good friend forever?

Mollie snorted and shifted in his arms, and he stood and laid her in the crib. He held his breath as she settled onto her belly and snuggled into the sheet. To his relief, she sighed and slept on.

He sank into the rocking chair and looked out the window as

the remainder of the afternoon filtered through his mind. When he and the men had come into the house from the porch, he'd followed the sound of claps and cheers up the stairs to Mollie's room. Laura, Cindy, and Kayla were teaching his daughter how to walk.

As soon as he'd stepped into the doorway of Mollie's room, he'd been struck by the happiness and excitement on Laura's face as she helped Mollie move across the floor to greet him. Laura's striking blue eyes had been bright, and a pretty smile curled her lips. She'd been radiant. She loved his daughter, truly loved her, as much as a blood relative would. And that love had struck a chord in his heart.

But Laura wasn't family. She was a friend. More accurately, she was Savilla's best friend, but not his. Yet she certainly felt more and more like a special friend every day. In fact, she felt like his one and only true friend. She was the only one who cared enough to ask how he was coping.

That wasn't true, though. Irma Mae and Milton cared about him, and often asked how he was doing. And Vernon had taken an interest in him today. But that was because of Laura's suggestion. Once again, Laura was the one looking out for him and Mollie, in a way no one else did.

Allen rocked back and forth in the chair as Vernon's words filled his mind. He needed to pray.

He yawned but then closed his eyes and opened his heart for a silent prayer.

God, please guide me. Make me strong, especially today. Help me be a better man, a better father. Please help me be the father Mollie needs. And thank you for my special friend Laura and her family.

FOURTEEN

"Gude mariye!" Laura sang as she entered Allen's kitchen and set her bag on a kitchen chair.

"Gude mariye," Allen echoed her words through a yawn as he covered his mouth.

Mollie squealed in her high chair.

"Mollie!" Laura strolled over, leaned down, and kissed her head. "I missed you last night. How are you?"

Mollie grabbed a handful of Cheerios, dropped them, and giggled.

"I see you're doing well." Laura laughed. "I brought you some cheese. Let me get it for you." She turned toward her bag, but stopped when her eyes met Allen's. Guilt washed over her as she took in the dark circles under his eyes. "You look so tired." She clicked her tongue. "I'm sorry. I should have stayed over last night, no matter what you said."

"You shouldn't be sorry." He shook his head as he carried his mug to the percolator. "It's not your job to babysit me." He lifted the percolator. *"Kaffi?"*

"Ya, danki." She retrieved the cheese from her bag and set it on the high chair's tray. "Here you go."

Mollie squealed and began to eat the treat.

Laura stepped over to the counter as Allen handed her a mug

of coffee. *"Danki."* She set the mug on the table and then pivoted toward him. "Did you eat breakfast?"

"Ya. I had some toast." He poured himself coffee and then set his mug on the table.

"That's all?"

He nodded as he sat down.

"Let me make you some eggs." She started toward the stove.

"No." He placed his hand on her arm. "Please sit with me."

She hesitated.

"Please?" He raised his eyebrows. "I'm really not that hungry."

"What about Mollie?" She pointed to the baby. "Should I make her an egg?"

"She's had cut-up bananas and grapes, a piece of toast, a roll, and Cheerios." He counted the items off on his fingers. "And now she has cheese."

"Oh." She sank onto the chair beside him. "I guess she's had enough, then."

"Ya, I think so." He sipped his coffee.

She studied the dark shadows under his eyes. "Did you get any sleep at all?"

He rubbed the back of his neck. "A little bit, but the rocking chair wasn't very comfortable."

"You slept in the rocking chair?" She turned toward Mollie. "Did she cry all night?"

"No, she only cried for about an hour, but I had a lot on my mind last night."

"I did too." Her gaze collided with his, and they stared at each other for a beat. She bit back the urge to tell him everything that had haunted her last night. She longed to share the details of what Rudy said to her in the buggy and what Mark told her as they stood in the driveway.

But Allen wasn't her best friend. He wasn't Savilla. Yet he felt like her closest confidant other than her twin. He hadn't laughed at her when she shared she was nervous about having her own bedroom for the first time in her life. He hadn't mocked her when she admitted she was afraid she'd lose Jamie when he moved into his new house.

If she felt that close to Allen, did that mean he'd replaced Savilla in her life? But shouldn't she feel this way about Rudy, not Allen?

She swallowed.

"Laura?" He raised an eyebrow. "You look as if you're going to burst if you don't tell me what you're thinking."

She blinked. *Oh no!* She'd been caught, just like she'd been with Mark. Heat burned her cheeks as a smile tugged at the corners of his mouth.

"The party!" she blurted before reaching for her bag. "I made a list of things we need for Mollie's birthday party on Friday." She yanked the list from her tote bag and set it on the table.

"Oh dear." She looked up at him as her cheeks warmed. "I should ask your permission before I plan something. After all, you're her *dat*. Would you mind if I plan a birthday party for Mollie?"

"That would be *wunderbaar*. *Danki* for offering to do it. I remembered last night that her birthday is Friday, but I have no idea how to even begin to plan for it." He peered down at the list. "You've even come up with a menu?" He looked up at her. "You're amazing. You've thought of everything."

"Um, *danki*." Suddenly self-conscious, she touched her apron to see if it was straight. "I guess it's just part of being a *maedel*. I've planned quite a few parties, so I know what to put on a list."

"Let me know how much money you need for the supplies."

"I will."

He finished his coffee, pushed back his chair, and stood. "I better get started. A couple of customers said they'd stop by today to look at my rebuilt buggies." He yawned as he set his mug on the counter. "I'll see you at lunchtime."

Concern filtered through her veins. "Are you certain you feel alert enough to work with tools?"

"*Ya*, I'll be fine." He stepped over to the high chair and touched Mollie's cheek. "See you in a bit. Behave for Laura." Then he started for the mudroom.

"Wait." Laura popped up from her chair, and he spun toward her. "Why don't you take a thermos of *kaffi* with you?"

He shook his head. "I'll be fine."

She pressed her lips together. "You could cut yourself. You really should take a nap. You can put up a sign telling the customers to knock on the back door of the *haus*, and I'll instruct them to come back later."

"I promise you I'm alert enough to work, but I appreciate your concern."

She frowned. "You can't get hurt. Mollie needs you."

"I know she does, and she needs me to work so I can pay for her party supplies."

"No, I can—"

"Uh-uh." He held up his finger and shook it. "You will not pay for her party supplies."

She jammed her hands on her hips. "You knew what I was going to say."

"I knew *exactly* what you were going to say." He frowned. "If we keep bickering like this, it will be lunchtime and I won't have gotten anything done."

"That's a *gut* idea. If you stand here and argue with me, you can't get hurt."

He shook his finger at her again. "Nice try, but I really need to leave."

Then he disappeared into the mudroom, the screen door clicking shut moments later.

She stared after him as she considered the exhaustion lining his face. He seemed as if something more than fatigue was plaguing him today. He hadn't laughed or smiled when she'd tried to convince him to rest. He looked as if the weight of the world were on his shoulders. If only she could put her finger on what was bothering him. But if he'd wanted to tell her, he would have. She had to respect his distance and wait for him to open up.

She turned to Mollie. "Why don't we get you cleaned up, and then we can practice your walking before I start some chores."

—⚬⚬⚬—

"*Danki!*" Allen called after Henry, his second customer of the day.

Henry waved in response as he guided his horse from the rebuilt buggy he'd just purchased from Allen.

Allen folded a stack of bills in his hand and turned toward the shop. He stilled when he found Laura standing in the bay doorway with a sheepish smile. He wanted to smile in return, but he couldn't bring himself to form the gesture on his lips. Not today.

Today is the ten-month anniversary of Savilla's death. How dare I even think about smiling today?

The realization nearly knocked the wind out of him as he walked over to her.

She fiddled with one of the ties on her prayer covering. "I'm sorry to bother you."

"You're not bothering me." He slipped the money into his trouser pocket. "Is everything okay?"

"*Ya.*" She gestured toward the house. "Mollie woke up from her morning nap and she's been playing with some toys in her play yard." She bit her lower lip. "I got some housework done, and I was going to clean the upstairs and get the dirty laundry, but then I remembered I wanted to make a shopping list for the party. When I started looking through your pantry and cabinets, I realized you're running low on a few things. So I was wondering if I could go grocery shopping."

She held up her hand as if to stop him from speaking. "I know you're very busy, so I'll take Mollie with me. I just wanted to see if it's okay and if we could call your driver."

"I have a better idea." The words flew out of his mouth without any forethought, and he pulled the wad of bills out of his pocket and held it up. "I just sold my second buggy of the morning. How about I take you to lunch and then we can do the grocery shopping together?"

"You don't need to buy me lunch."

"*Ya*, I do need to buy you lunch."

Her dark eyebrows cinched together. "Why?"

"Because the salary I convinced you to allow me to pay you isn't nearly enough to compensate for keeping you away from your family for such lengthy periods of time."

"I can buy my own lunch."

"Laura Riehl." He folded his arms over his chest and gave her a mock scowl. "Are we going to argue for the second time today? If so, why don't we have a seat in my office? It's more comfortable in there, and I can get each of us a couple of bottles of water to keep our throats wet while we impale each other with our biting retorts."

To his surprise, she laughed. "Fine, fine. You win. I'll get Mollie ready, and you hitch up the horse."

"Great." He rubbed his hands together. "I've been craving Dienner's meat loaf."

"That's Mark's favorite too." She started toward the house but then stopped and swiveled toward him. "Oh. Congratulations on the sales."

"*Danki*."

Laura flashed another smile and then jogged to the house.

FIFTEEN

"Laura! Allen!" Kayla reached over the podium in her family's restaurant and touched Mollie's head as Allen held his daughter in his arms. "How are you, Mollie? What a *wunderbaar* surprise. I'm so *froh* you came in today."

"It's great to see you too." Laura smiled. "Allen suggested we get out for lunch today, so here we are."

"The truth is Laura informed me *mei haus* is running low on supplies." Allen looked chagrined. "If it wasn't for Laura, Mollie and I would starve."

"Stop it." Laura waved him off and turned back to Kayla. Her friend's eyebrows had raised, and she wondered why. "Do you possibly have a table available for us?"

"*Ya*, of course." Kayla picked up two menus. "Follow me." She led them to a table in the corner of the large room and then pointed toward the other end of the restaurant. "I'll grab a high chair for you."

"No, no. I'll get it." Allen handed Mollie to Laura. "I'll be right back."

Laura shifted Mollie in her arms as the baby grabbed for the ties to her prayer covering. She turned toward Kayla and found her looking in the direction Allen had gone. Now her brow was furrowed. "What's that look for?"

"Is he okay?"

"What do you mean?" Laura moved closer to her.

"He's a different person than he was yesterday. Yesterday he seemed more open and social, but today he looks even more worn-out and maybe even melancholy." Kayla set the menus down on the table.

"I thought that too, but I can't seem to get him to open up to me. I think something is bothering him."

"Don't worry." Kayla touched her shoulder. "You're a blessing to him. You'll help him through whatever it is."

"I don't know if I can—" Laura began, but she stopped speaking when Kayla's gaze moved behind Laura and she smiled.

"Here's the high chair." Allen appeared beside Laura and set the high chair down. Then he reached for Mollie. "Let me get her settled. I'm looking forward to your meat loaf, Kayla."

Once Mollie was strapped in her seat, Allen sat down and tapped the table. "Are you going to stand through our whole meal, Laura? Or are you going to get comfortable?"

Without comment, Laura sat down, and Kayla recited the day's specials. Then she took their drink order and headed to the kitchen.

"It looks like the Dienners have some new employees." Allen nodded toward two young Amish girls who spoke to customers at nearby tables.

"I had no idea they were hiring." Laura glanced around the dining area. "I wonder where Eva is." She opened the diaper bag, pulled out a bottle, and handed it to Mollie, who wasted no time drinking it.

"Maybe she's in the back?" Allen suggested.

Kayla set a glass of water in front of each of them. "Here are your drinks."

"*Danki.*" Laura nodded toward the new girls. "You have new employees?"

"*Ya*. They're both in Nathan's youth group." Kayla pulled her notepad from the pocket in her apron and then gestured toward the young girl with dark hair. "That's Lorraine." She grinned. "I think she has a crush on Nathan, and he seems to like her too. They're so cute together. I have a feeling they'll date after they're both baptized." Then she nodded to the girl with blond hair. "And that's Kathy. They're both really sweet and hard workers. My parents are very *froh* with them."

"Where's Eva?" Laura asked.

Kayla retrieved a pencil from her pocket. "She's home with Junior."

"How old is he now?" Allen asked.

"He's eighteen months, and he's a handful." Kayla's smile widened as she talked about her nephew. "He's too much to handle at work now, so she has to keep him at home. And since Eva is home, Nathan is training with the fire station one day every week, and I'm getting married, *mei mamm* suggested we hire two new *maed* to help. It's a relief since I'll most likely go part-time after I'm married. I'll have a lot to do at the *haus* and on the farm."

Laura looked around the restaurant. "Wow. A lot of changes."

"*Ya*, that's true. Life doesn't slow down." Kayla poised her pencil on the notepad. "Do you know what you want today?"

"Oh." Laura opened the menu. "I hadn't even looked at the selections." She glanced over at Allen. "Go ahead if you know what you'd like."

"I don't need to look at the menu," he said. "I'd like the meat loaf with egg noodles and green beans."

Laura closed her menu. "I'll have the same." She looked at Mollie. "She can share my meal." She turned toward Allen. "Are you okay with that?"

"*Ya*, of course I am." He lifted his glass of water.

"*Gut.*" Kayla wrote on the notepad. "I'll put that in right away." She took the menus from them and left.

Laura dug in the diaper bag and pulled out a container of Cheerios. "Would you like a snack while we wait for our lunch?" She gave Mollie a handful of cereal. "I was thinking of making a chocolate *kuche* with frosting for the party. Would that be okay?"

"*Ya.* That would be fantastic." Allen looked down at the table as he ran his fingers over the wood grain.

"Is everything all right?" She leaned toward him as concern wafted over her. Did he regret taking her and Mollie to lunch?

Allen looked up at her, and his face clouded with a frown. "*Ya.* I just—"

"Laura! Allen!" Nathan, Kayla's younger brother, approached the table. "How are you doing?"

"Hi, Nathan." Laura shook his hand. "It's *gut* to see you."

"Hi, Nathan." Allen shook the teenager's hand as well. "How are things?"

"They're great." Nathan folded his hands over his white apron. "*Mei dat* is teaching me more and more of the recipes. I'm helping him cook instead of busing the tables." He pointed toward the kitchen. "Kay mentioned you both were here, and *mei dat* said he'd love to see you. Would you like to come back into the kitchen to see my parents?"

Allen nodded at Laura. "You can go and visit. I'll stay with Mollie."

"No, no." Laura shook her head. "You go. I'll stay here."

Allen raised an eyebrow. "Are you sure?"

"*Ya*, go. I'll say hello before we leave." Laura gestured in the direction of the kitchen. "Go on."

"All right." Allen stood and followed Nathan.

Laura leaned over to Mollie. "How are those Cheerios? Are they *appeditlich*?"

Mollie giggled and handed one to Laura.

"*Danki.*" Laura popped the Cheerio into her mouth and then touched Mollie's little nose. "That was *gut.*" She rubbed her abdomen. "Yum, yum!"

Mollie looked past Laura and squealed as she waved at someone.

"Hi, Mollie!" Kayla waved back as she sat down in the chair across from Laura. "I thought I'd take a break and see how you're doing." She jammed her thumb toward the kitchen. "Allen is talking to my parents and Nathan."

"I offered to stay with Mollie so he could go." Laura touched the high-chair tray. "Mollie, can you give Kayla a Cheerio too?" She pointed to Kayla.

Mollie picked up a Cheerio and held it out to Kayla.

"Very *gut!*" Kayla grinned as she took the piece of cereal. "*Danki*, Mollie."

Laura clapped. "*Wunderbaar!*"

Kayla ate the Cheerio. "What are your plans after lunch? Are you just going grocery shopping?"

"*Ya*, we have a lot to get. His pantry really is empty." Laura folded her hands on the table. "I need to get supplies for Friday too." She touched Mollie's arm. "We're going to have a birthday party for Mollie. I hope you and Jamie can come."

"Absolutely!" Kayla said. "What can we bring?"

"Oh, you don't need to bring anything. I was thinking of having finger sandwiches, chips, and pretzels. And I'll make a couple of *kuches.*" Laura pulled her list from her pocket. "Let's see. What else?"

"Let me bring the sandwiches."

"What?" Laura looked up from the list.

"I'll bring the sandwiches." Kayla pointed to the kitchen. "I can bring the pretzels and chips too."

"No." Laura shook her head. "I can't let you do that."

"Why not?" Kayla shrugged. "We're family, right?"

"*Ya*, but Allen has a list of customers and *freinden* from church he wants to invite." She started listing all his friends. "I imagine Mark might bring a date or two. I don't expect you to feed all those people."

"We run a restaurant. I can make the sandwiches." Kayla pulled out her notepad. "So you said your family and possibly Mark's *freinden*. Tell me how many you think will come, and I'll make sure to have more than enough food." When Laura did, she added, "Okay. We'll have a variety of sandwiches, plus chips and pretzels."

Laura hesitated. "Let me know how much I owe you."

"You don't owe me anything."

"No, I can't accept it for free. That's a lot of food."

"Stop it." Kayla frowned. "This will be my gift to Mollie and Allen. Does that work?"

Laura scrunched her nose and shook her head. "I don't know how Allen will feel about that."

"How will I feel about what?" Allen appeared beside her and sat down.

"Laura was just telling me about Mollie's party on Friday, and I offered to cater it." Kayla nodded toward Laura. "I can bring sandwiches, chips, and pretzels, and Laura said she'll make the *kuches*."

"That would be fantastic." Allen turned to Laura and tilted his head. "I thought you mentioned you'd be making the sandwiches."

"I did, but Kayla wants to make them, and she doesn't want to charge us." Laura swallowed when she realized she'd spoken as if they were a couple. She held her breath to keep her blush at bay and hoped he hadn't noticed her use of the word *us*.

Allen looked at Kayla. "Oh, I'm *froh* to pay you. How much will it cost?"

Kayla looked at Laura, who lifted her chin as if to say *I told you so*.

Kayla laughed. "You two drive a hard bargain, but, no, neither of you will pay. It's a gift, and it's rude to not accept a gift, right?"

Allen pulled at his beard and looked down at Mollie. "What do you think?"

Mollie squealed and then laughed before popping another piece of cereal into her mouth.

"I guess it's settled, then." Allen nodded without smiling. *"Danki."*

"So what time is the party?" Kayla asked as she wrote something else on her notepad.

Allen turned to Laura. "What time do you think?"

Laura shrugged. "I don't know. Is five too early for you, Kayla?"

"That's perfect." Kayla wrote on her notepad again. "Jamie isn't on duty at the firehouse on Friday, so he can pick me up." She looked toward the kitchen. "Oh, there's your food. Lorraine is bringing it."

Kayla jumped up from the chair as the young girl with dark hair approached with a tray. Lorraine looked to be about fifteen, and she had bright, hazel eyes.

"Danki, Lorraine. I'd like you to meet *mei freinden."* Kayla took one of the plates and placed it in front of Laura. "This is my future sister-in-law, Laura. She's Jamie's *schweschder."*

"Hi." Lorraine smiled at Laura.

"It's nice to meet you," Laura said.

Kayla set Allen's plate in front of him. "And this is Allen and Mollie."

"It's great to meet all of you." Lorraine set the tray on the table and then touched Mollie's hand. "She's adorable. How old is she?"

"She'll be a year on Friday," Allen said.

Lorraine studied Mollie, and then she looked from Laura to Allen. "She looks like both of you." She pointed to Laura. "She has your eyes and Allen's nose. What a cutie."

Laura's cheeks burned as she shifted in her chair. She was almost certain she saw Kayla cringe out of the corner of her eye.

"*Danki.*" Allen's expression appeared pleasant, but Laura was aware of his tight jaw and stiff nod. "It's very nice to meet you."

"You too." As Lorraine picked up her tray, she turned toward the front of the restaurant, where four *Englisher* women were walking toward the podium. "I'll seat them," she told Kayla before heading there.

"*Danki.*" Kayla turned to the table. "I'm sorry about that. I'll straighten her out later. Do you need anything else?"

"Not for me, *danki.*" Allen looked at Laura, and she shook her head.

"All right." Kayla smiled brightly. "I better go check on my other orders. Enjoy your lunch."

As soon as Kayla walked away, Laura bowed her head for a silent prayer, aware her cheeks still blazed hot. She had to get her emotions under control. It wasn't Lorraine's fault she didn't know Laura and Allen weren't a married couple.

When Laura opened her eyes, she and Allen both began to cut up their meat loaf, and Laura placed two small pieces on Mollie's high chair.

"Are you all right?" Allen asked before taking a second bite.

"*Ya.* How's your meat loaf?" She stabbed a piece of her own meat loaf and forked it into her mouth.

Allen wiped his mouth with a paper napkin as he studied her. "I made you feel uncomfortable, and I'm sorry."

She set her fork on her plate as she stared at him. "What are you talking about?"

His lips pressed into a thin line. "I thought by allowing Lorraine to believe you and I were married and Mollie was our *boppli*, it would minimize the awkwardness. But instead it embarrassed and humiliated you. I've become so accustomed to people making inappropriate comments to me since Savilla died that it doesn't bother me anymore. I didn't consider how it would make you feel, and I'm truly sorry."

"What have people said to you?"

He glanced down at his plate and then up at her. "I took Mollie out alone a few times soon after Savilla died. Irma Mae had a doctor's appointment or needed to run an errand, and I felt confident enough to take Mollie with me to the market and the hardware store. No matter where I went, people made unsolicited comments to me." He moved the food around on his plate as he spoke. "I had to change her diaper in the men's room at the hardware store, and an *Englisher* asked me if I'd given *mei fraa* the day off."

"No!"

Allen nodded as he met her gaze. "Another time a woman in line at the market asked me if *mei fraa* was sleeping in and I was 'playing mommy today.'" He made air quotes with his fingers.

"That's terrible." She shook her head. "How could people say such thoughtless things?"

"I think that's it exactly." He jammed his finger on the table. "They're thoughtless. But I don't think there's any malice behind the words, so I've learned to brush them off." He frowned. "That's why I let Lorraine think you were *mei fraa* today. I thought it would be easier to just agree with her than to explain our relationship and your relationship with Mollie."

"It's okay."

"No, it's not." He blew out a deep sigh. "It was disrespectful to you and to Rudy, and I'm very sorry. I hope you know I would never intentionally hurt you. Your friendship is precious to me."

Laura sucked in a breath as she took in the regret in his eyes. "*Danki.*"

"I hope you'll forgive me." He said the words as if his life depended on them.

"I was never angry. I was only embarrassed for your sake."

"For my sake?"

"*Ya.* I was embarrassed people would give me credit for Mollie. She doesn't look like me at all. She's your *schee boppli.*" She touched Mollie's soft cheek. "She's the spitting image of Savilla and you."

Something flickered across his face, and his eyes seemed to glisten in the sunlight pouring through the skylights above them. Sadness came off him in waves, and it nearly crushed Laura's heart. His grief was tangible, and she longed to soothe his soul.

He pointed to her plate. "Please eat before your food gets cold."

The pain in Allen's eyes penetrated Laura as she put a bite of noodles into her mouth. She fought the urge to beg him to talk to her, but she forced herself to respect his privacy. Instead she sent a silent prayer to God, asking him to show her how to help Allen find peace.

SIXTEEN

"ALLEN! ALLEN, HELP ME!" SAVILLA'S VOICE ECHOED *around Allen as he stood at the top of the stairs.*

"Savilla! Where are you?" He spun into the bathroom doorway, but the room was empty. "Savilla? Answer me!" His body trembled. "Savilla! Where are you?"

"Allen! Please help me. You're the only one who can help me!" Her voice was more distant, as if it were fading away.

His heart pounded against his rib cage as he rushed into Mollie's room, but only Mollie was there, sleeping in her crib. He hustled out to the hallway.

"Savilla! Please tell me where you are!" he called, his voice thin and shaky.

"Allen! I need you!" Savilla's voice was softer.

"Savilla!" His footsteps echoed as he checked the sewing room and then the spare bedroom before running into their bedroom. All the rooms were empty. "Where are you? Savilla? Savilla!"

He stood at the top of the stairs and screamed her name over and over, but she didn't answer. Sinking onto his knees on the cold, hard linoleum, he sobbed.

Allen's eyes flew open, and in one swift motion he sat up and scooted back until his spine slammed against the headboard, sending pain spiraling up his back to his shoulders. His body was drenched in sweat despite the breeze filtering through his open bedroom windows.

Amid the gentle tapping of raindrops hitting the roof, he gasped, filling his lungs with air as he worked to calm his pounding heart and frayed nerves.

It was just a dream. It was just a dream. It was just a dream.

No, it was a nightmare.

He rubbed his wet eyes. He'd been crying. He glanced at the digital clock beside his bed. It read 2:18. Covering his face with his hands, he breathed in a gulp of air and then stilled when he heard a noise. No, it wasn't a noise. It was singing. Laura was singing to Mollie again.

Allen stood, pulled a pair of trousers over his boxers, and then put on a white undershirt. He retrieved the lantern from his nightstand, and without turning it on, he padded into the hallway. Laura's beautiful voice grew louder as she finished singing "Jesus Loves Me."

Mollie's door was partly open, letting the glow of a lantern shine through. He leaned his shoulder against the doorframe and looked in, and his body shuddered with the remnants of the vivid nightmare. And yet the scene before him had a calming effect.

Laura wore a plain white nightgown, and her thick dark-brown hair draped over one of her slight shoulders and hung to her waist. It was uncovered. As she moved the rocking chair back and forth, she held a sleeping Mollie against her chest.

Her tenderness and gentleness for his child warmed his cold and lonely heart, and a knot of emotion choked his throat as fresh tears stung his eyes.

When Laura leaned down and kissed Mollie's head, she saw him. And when her bright, intelligent eyes locked on him, a sweet smile spread across her lips. She stood and set Mollie in the crib and then paused as if waiting for his daughter to cry. But Mollie snuggled down and then sighed.

Laura pulled on a white robe and tied it at her waist. She turned off her lantern as he turned his on, and then she crossed the room and slipped past him into the hallway before motioning for him to follow her. "Did I wake you? I didn't mean to leave the door open."

"No." His voice croaked as he ran his hand down his face.

Her eyes widened. *"Was iss letz?"*

He shook his head, his words stuck in his arid throat.

She hesitated and then motioned for him to follow her down the stairs, out the front door, and onto the covered porch. The raindrops continued to tap on the roof, and the aroma of wet grass filled his nostrils.

She pointed to the swing where they'd sat together the week before. "Please sit."

He sat down, slid over to the far side, and set his lantern on the floor.

She sank down beside him and angled her body toward his. "Please talk to me."

He swallowed and tried to form the words that would explain all the emotions whirling through him like a tornado—grief, regret, guilt, confusion, and anxiety. He looked out on the lawn as the rain picked up, no doubt leaving puddles in its wake.

"I can't help if you won't tell me what's wrong." Her words throbbed with anxiety. "I could tell all day that something was wrong. You've seemed so *bedauerlich* and distracted ever since I arrived this morning. It's been killing me that I couldn't help you, but I didn't know how to ask what was bothering you without sounding like I was prying."

He turned toward her. "You could never pry. You're *mei freind*, and I trust you completely."

Surprise flashed in her eyes, and her expression warmed. "I want to help you."

He trailed his fingers over the arm of the swing and stared

down at the porch floor, working to gather his thoughts. "I asked you to go to lunch with me today because I wanted to thank you for all you've done, but I also felt like I needed to get out of the *haus* and the shop. I've been antsy and emotional. I felt like I was on the verge of having a breakdown."

He kept his gaze trained on the wood beneath his feet as his chest tightened. "I came into Mollie's room because I'd had a nightmare about Savilla, and then I heard you singing."

"What did you dream?"

"She was calling me, begging me to help her, but I couldn't find her." He closed his eyes as the dream filled his mind. "I was searching the upstairs rooms, but her voice faded away from me. Then I was left alone at the top of the stairs." He swallowed back threatening emotions. "I woke up alone in my bed."

"I'm so sorry," she whispered, her voice quavering.

"It's not your fault." He opened his eyes. "It was just a tough day." His lips turned up in a wry smile. "But I had been expecting it."

"What do you mean?"

He turned toward her. "It's been ten months since I lost her."

Laura made a strangled sound in her throat as her eyes shimmered. Her pretty face crumpled and tears streamed down her cheeks. She covered her face with her hands, and a sob escaped her lips.

His lungs seized, and he felt the urge to pull her into his arms and comfort her. But it would be too forward to hold her, even though watching her sob was tearing him apart.

"Oh, Laura. I didn't mean to upset you." He touched her shoulder. "Please don't cry. I'm so sorry."

She pulled a tissue from the pocket of her robe and wiped her eyes and nose before shaking her head. "I'm the one who should be sorry."

"Why should you be sorry?"

"I should have known it was the ten-month anniversary. When I looked at the calendar in your kitchen, the significance of the date never occurred to me. I was only thinking about Mollie's birthday." She looked up at him, and her lower lip trembled. "I'm so sorry for being such a terrible *freind*."

He couldn't stop a smile. "That's where you're wrong."

"What?" Her eyebrows cinched together as the rain picked up, splattering the edge of the porch with large drops.

"You're a dear *freind*." He spoke louder to be heard over the rain. "You're the only one who wants to hear how I'm truly feeling, and you're the only one I trust with my feelings." Without any forethought, he reached over and wiped a tear from her cheek. He expected her to shirk away from his touch, but she stilled, her bright eyes focused on his. "When Savilla died, I lost my closest *freinden*. I used to be able to talk to Rudy, *mei gut freind*. But now it feels like no one knows what to say to me, not even him."

She scowled. "I told Rudy he should try to talk to you more. He said he doesn't know what to say to you. I guess it's because he's never lost anyone close to him, and he doesn't know how that feels. But I also believe he's immature and selfish."

Allen shifted away from her. What would Rudy say if he witnessed Allen's behavior—sitting close to her, touching her, and telling her she was a dear friend? Allen was out of line, and he needed to back off now before he went too far and ruined his friendship with Laura, Rudy, and maybe their whole community. Guilt, hot and searing, cut through him.

She shook her head, oblivious to his inner turmoil. "I'm so sorry I wasn't aware of the anniversary. No wonder you've been so upset all day."

"I appreciate that you care so much."

"Of course I care." She looked out toward the rain and sniffed. "I can't believe it's been ten months."

"I know. Some days it feels like two years, but other days it feels like it's only been a few weeks. All I know is that she's gone, and I have a hole in my life."

"I know." She looked at him, and her eyes sparkled in the low light of the lantern. "I miss Savilla all the time too. We grew up together, and we went through everything together. She was there when I had my first crush, and she defended me on the playground when one of the other girls made fun of me. We celebrated our birthdays together and exchanged gifts. We were there for the happy milestones. I was in your wedding, and I was one of your first visitors when Mollie was born. We were there for each other during the *bedauerlich* times too. She stood with me at the funeral for *mei mamm*." She wiped away a tear and sniffed. "But now she's gone."

She paused and took a deep, shuddering breath. "Sometimes I think about *mei mamm* and Savilla, and I feel like I can't breathe." Fresh tears poured down her cheeks, and she wiped them away with the back of her hands. "It just hurts so much when you lose someone you love."

An ache spread inside his chest, and once again he shoved away the urge to pull her into his arms, to hold her close and attempt to take away some of her pain. "It hurts, but we have each other, right?"

"*Ya*, we do." She gave him a watery smile. "And I'm so thankful for you."

An image of Laura holding hands with Rudy after church flashed through Allen's mind, followed by a vision of Rudy glaring at him yesterday. Allen had overstepped his bounds with Laura. He frowned. He had to keep his distance.

He picked up the lantern and stood. "I've kept you up too late already." He gestured toward the front door. "We should try to get some sleep before Mollie wakes up again."

Laura looked up at Allen and blinked at his sudden change in demeanor. Minutes earlier, he'd told her she was the only person with whom he could share his true feelings. Yet when she told him she was thankful for him, he stood and headed for the door.

Oh no. I said too much and scared him away. Laura swallowed a groan as hot humiliation crawled up her neck to her cheeks. She'd crossed a line with him.

She berated herself. She sounded like a girl who was desperate for Allen's affection and attention. She'd behaved like one of the many young women in her youth group who followed her twin around like puppies, hoping to gain Mark's offer of a real relationship.

Laura's shoulders hunched. How could she be so immature? *Mamm* would be so disappointed in her!

Behind Allen, the rain increased, and a mist of cool water kissed her flaming cheeks.

Allen wrenched the door open with one hand and held up the lantern with the other. "You need to get in before you're soaked."

She jumped up from the swing and scooted past him into the house. She reached up and touched her head and felt her cheeks spark even more. She'd hurried out of Mollie's room without pulling on a scarf.

She cringed. Yes, her mother would be disappointed in her tonight. Not only had she been brazen with a young man, but her head had been uncovered. And to make matters even worse, she'd been bold with Allen, her best friend's widower! What would Rudy say if he saw her now?

She hugged her arms to her chest as she stood in the family room and waited for Allen to lock the front door. As soon as the lock clicked, she started up the stairs. He followed close behind her, the warm yellow glow of the lantern guiding their steps.

When they reached the landing, Laura turned toward him and forced a smile. *"Gut nacht."*

"Gut nacht," he echoed.

She spun down the hall toward Mollie's room.

"Wait," he said.

With her back to Allen, she closed her eyes and held her breath. *Please don't make this even more embarrassing!* She looked over her shoulder at him. *"Ya?"*

"Danki for talking with me." He had a hand on each hip, looking down at the lantern he'd set on the floor outside his room. "Today was really tough for me, but you made it bearable. I just wanted you to know I appreciate you."

He looked up, and she nodded. "That's what *freinden* are for. I'll see you in the morning."

Before he could respond, she slipped into Mollie's room, shucked her robe, and climbed into bed. Then she stared up at the ceiling as her conversation with Allen churned through her thoughts.

She rolled to her side and faced the crib. Mollie snored softly, but her brother's warning echoed loud in her mind. Perhaps she was getting too attached to Mollie. And then she heard his words about Rudy.

You're so focused on Allen and Mollie that you don't see how it's affecting Rudy. Just take a step back and think about how he feels.

Mark was right when he said that. She needed to think of Rudy. Maybe she should ask for an evening off to make time for him. If she reconnected with Rudy and repaired her relationship with him, she could clear her head.

Yes, that was what she needed to do. She needed to make time for Rudy and be the girlfriend he deserved. That would fix all their problems. She would ask for the evening off and keep a safe distance from Allen. That would solve everything.

SEVENTEEN

LAURA SAT DOWN AT THE TABLE ACROSS FROM ALLEN the following morning and bowed her head in prayer. Then she pushed the oatmeal in her bowl around as she recalled their awkward conversation hours before, as well as her decision to ask for the evening off. Her eyes moved to Mollie, sitting in her high chair, humming as she picked up globs of oatmeal and popped them into her mouth.

Would Mollie miss her if she took a weeknight off?

Mark's warning echoed in her head once again, and her mind was made up. Allen and Mollie would be okay without her one evening. After all, they had survived the weekends.

"Breakfast is *appeditlich*," Allen said as he lifted his glass of orange juice.

"*Danki.*" She set down her fork and looked at him. "I was wondering if I could take tonight off."

Allen blinked. "Sure. I didn't realize you had plans."

"Well, I don't exactly. At least not yet. But I'd like to make some."

"Okay." He nodded slowly. "May I ask what your plans are?"

"Of course you can. Don't be *gegisch*. I was thinking I would ask Rudy if he wants to get together since we haven't spent much time together lately. Maybe it would ease his mind about my working here." She held her breath as if waiting for Allen's approval. What was wrong with her?

"I think that's a great idea." Allen chose a roll from the basket in the center of the table and cut it open. Was he avoiding her gaze? "Enjoy yourself."

"Are you sure?"

"Of course. Mollie and I will be just fine." Allen turned to his daughter. "Right, Mollie?"

Mollie sputtered and reached for Allen's hand.

"I think she wants your food," Laura said with a laugh.

"*Ya*, I do too. You have a *schmaert* stomach, Mollie."

After the breakfast dishes were washed and put away, Laura plopped Mollie in her play yard and walked out to Allen's shop. At breakfast, he mentioned he'd be working on a buggy that had been in an accident, and that's how she found him. He lifted his chin and smiled.

She pointed toward the office. "I was wondering if I could use your phone."

He grabbed a red shop towel and began to wipe his hands. "I've told you before that you don't have to ask."

"*Danki.*" She stepped into the office, sat down at Allen's desk, and dialed the number for Rudy's father's store. She wound the cord around her finger as the phone rang.

"Lancaster Hardware Supply." Rudy's voice sounded through the phone. "This is Rudy. How may I help you?"

"Rudy, hi. It's Laura." She grinned as if he could see her.

"Laura, hi. *Was iss letz?*" The noise behind him faded as if he'd stepped away from the cashier desk.

"Nothing is wrong. I was wondering if you were busy tonight."

"Uh, no." He paused. "Why?"

"Because I want to ask you out on a date."

The line went dead for a few beats.

"Rudy?" she asked. "Did we get disconnected? Are you still there?"

"*Ya*, I'm here."

"So what's your answer?" She frowned as an uneasiness teased her. Was he going to turn her down?

"That sounds nice. What did you have in mind?"

"What if we went to that pizza place we used to visit after spending the day at Cascade Lake with our youth group? They have the best pizza and breadsticks. That way we can talk and not be interrupted."

"That sounds like fun. Do you want me to pick you up?"

"*Ya*. How does five sound?"

"Perfect. I'm sure I can get off work early. See you then."

As Laura hung up the phone, she smiled. She was excited at the prospect of spending the evening with Rudy. She missed him! Yes, this was a great idea. This date would go a long way toward fixing the problems they'd encountered lately. They just needed some time together without any other distractions. Everything was going to be just fine.

"How was your day?" Laura asked as she and Rudy sat across from each other in a booth at their favorite pizzeria. The aroma of cheeses, tomato sauce, and spices permeated her senses and caused her stomach to growl.

"Busy." Rudy sipped his glass of Coke. "A man came in and bought all our chicken wire. I had to help him load it into his truck." He held up his hand, displaying two bandaged fingers.

She gasped and reached for his hand. "Are you going to be okay?"

"It's nothing. It's part of the job." He took another sip of his drink. "How was your day?"

"*Gut.*" She smiled. "I did a few chores this morning while Mollie napped, and then I slept during Mollie's afternoon nap. Since she has me up every night, I nap with her. I started doing that last week, and it helps me get through the day. Last night she had me up at two and then again at four, but I think the rain woke her up. Did you hear that storm last night? It was pretty bad."

Rudy's expression darkened. He sat back in his seat and studied her. "Why did you ask me out tonight?"

She blinked. "I wanted to see you since we haven't talked much lately."

"Is that all?" He crossed his arms over his wide chest.

"*Ya*, that's all. I don't have an ulterior motive, Rudy." She leaned forward and placed her hands flat on the table. "I miss you. I miss *us* and the way things used to be before life got so complicated that we seemed to have lost touch with our relationship."

He studied her, his expression grim and his jaw set.

Her stomach twisted and she chewed her lower lip, waiting for him to tell her he missed her too. When he remained silent, new doubt crept in, strangling her hope for their future.

"I was surprised when you called me," he finally said. "After our conversation on Sunday I thought you'd given up on us."

"No." She shook her head. "I haven't given up. In fact, I realized I haven't been trying hard enough. I'm sorry for being a bad girlfriend."

"It's not just you." He sighed. "I haven't been patient enough."

"Here's your pizza." The waitress appeared with their large pepperoni pie and placed it on a stand in the center of their table. "Enjoy."

They bowed their heads for a prayer, and then they each took a slice. They ate in silence for a few minutes, and Laura racked her brain for something to say. Why was conversation with Rudy such a chore lately?

"How are your parents doing?" she finally asked.

He nodded as he finished chewing and then swallowed. "*Gut. Mei mamm* has been busy with her quilting circle. They're getting a lot of orders for Christmas gifts."

"Oh. That's *wunderbaar*. How long does it take for her to make one quilt?"

While they finished the pizza, they made small talk about their families and the weather. After sharing an ice cream sundae Rudy said he'd been craving, they walked back to the buggy.

Rudy climbed into the driver's side and turned toward her. "I hope our getting dessert doesn't get you home later than you wanted."

"Oh, I need to go back to Allen's *haus*."

He scowled. "I thought you had the night off."

"Well, the evening. I need to stay overnight so I can take care of Mollie if she wakes up crying. Then I can make breakfast in the morning too. Allen's often too tired to make a *gut* breakfast for himself."

"Fine," he muttered before guiding the horse toward the main road.

The painful silence that had drifted over their supper filled the buggy, and her blood ran cold. What was happening to them? Were they headed toward a breakup?

After several minutes, Laura was certain the silence might choke her. She had to get him to talk to her before she exploded.

"Rudy, you know I'm not going to work for Allen forever. Irma Mae is going to come back."

"Have you accepted that fact?"

"What does that mean?"

"You act as if this is your permanent job."

"You mean I'm playing *haus*, right?" she snapped.

Rudy gave her a sideways glance, and she went on. "I'm here with you now, aren't I?"

"You had supper with me, but you're going home to him."

"I'm not going home to him." Determined for him to listen to her, she kept her words slow and measured. "I'm going back to his *haus* to take care of Mollie, which is the main part of my job. I earn a salary to take care of her."

Rudy gripped the reins with such force that his knuckles turned white.

They rode in silence until both the sign for Allen's business and his house came into view. Rudy guided the horse up the rock driveway and halted near the back porch.

Then he turned toward her, his dark eyes assessing her. "How long are you going to stay here overnight?"

"I've already told you I don't know. It all depends on when Mollie sleeps through the night again." She gripped the door handle as disappointment coursed through her. "I asked you out tonight because I thought some time alone would help us figure out what's going wrong between us."

He sighed and stared out the windshield.

"Rudy, if you really tried to talk to Allen and be his *freind*, then you'd see why this is so important to me. Allen doesn't just need my help. He also needs his *freinden* to support him. Irma Mae is going to recover, and then things can go back to the way they were. I just need you to be patient with me."

Rudy nodded while keeping his attention focused straight ahead.

"You have nothing to say?" She hated the thread of desperation she heard in her voice.

"I'm sorry." The words sounded weak.

She glanced toward the house and spotted a light glowing in the kitchen. She thought Allen, as exhausted as he'd been, would have been asleep by now. He'd given her a key to the back door in case she ever needed it.

Focus on Rudy, not Allen!

She turned toward her boyfriend and found him still studying his horse. It was time to give up and let him go home. She was tired, and Mollie would probably have her up during the night.

"Well, *gut nacht.*" She pushed the door open.

"Wait." He reached out and touched her shoulder. "When will I see you again?"

"Allen is having a birthday party for Mollie on Friday at five. I'd like it if you came."

He gave her a curt nod. "I'll try."

"You'll try?" She frowned.

"*Mei dat* said something about staying late on Friday to do inventory. I'll call you and let you know."

"Okay." A tiny flame of hope ignited in her chest.

"*Gut nacht,*" he said.

"*Gut nacht.* Be safe going home."

When he'd left, she climbed the back steps and knocked on the door. It didn't seem right to use the key if Allen was up.

Footsteps echoed from the kitchen, and then the door swung open, revealing Allen dressed in trousers and a white T-shirt. His eyes widened. "I thought you were taking the night off."

"The evening, not the night. I'm sorry if I failed to be specific about my intention. Rudy just dropped me off." She slipped past him and through the mudroom as he locked the back door.

"How did it go?"

"Great. *Danki* for giving me the evening off." She hoped her smile was convincing. "I'm going to bed. I'll see you in the morning."

Before he could question her further, Laura hurried up the steps to Mollie's bedroom. As she quietly changed and climbed into bed, she fought the urge to pour out her heart to Allen. She closed her eyes and swallowed back the pain and disappointment the evening had brought her. She had believed tonight would be a chance to start mending the tear plaguing her relationship with Rudy.

But the evening only brought to light what she had suspected— their problems were deeper than any pizza dinner could repair.

EIGHTEEN

"TODAY IS YOUR BIG DAY!" LAURA SANG AS SHE STOOD Mollie on the changing table and pulled on the new pink dress she'd made her for the party. "All your party guests will be here soon, and we're going to sing 'Happy Birthday' to you."

Mollie giggled and clapped her hands.

"People are going to bring you presents, and they're going to wish you a happy birthday. Aren't you excited?" Laura adjusted the dress and smiled.

The remainder of the week had flown by quickly as Laura kept busy cleaning the house in preparation for the party. She'd also taken care of the laundry, helped Mollie practice walking, and sewed two new dresses for the little girl.

Now it was Friday, and the party guests would arrive within the hour. Laura had baked two cakes earlier today—a large one for the guests and a small one Mollie would have on her high chair.

Laura set Mollie in her crib and closed the bedroom door before changing into a fresh blue dress and arranging her hair and prayer covering.

The shower in the hallway bathroom hummed as Allen bathed in preparation for the party. He'd closed his shop early to help get ready for their guests.

Laura had done her best to keep a distance between her and Allen since she'd arrived at his house after her failed date with Rudy Tuesday night. While they spoke about Mollie and their chores, she avoided personal or intimate discussions. He also had kept their discussions more mundane, which further convinced Laura she had taken their conversation on the porch swing too far. But she was careful to keep a smile on her face, even though it was painful for her to pretend the distance didn't hurt.

Once her hair, dress, and apron were straight, Laura scooped Mollie from the crib. "I think we're ready."

Mollie giggled and held on to Laura's shoulder as Laura carried her downstairs, where she deposited her into her play yard.

In the kitchen, Laura began gathering plastic utensils, serving trays, and disposable cups for the party. She was setting out paper plates when a knock sounded on the back door.

"I've got it." Allen smiled as he moved past her into the mudroom, and then she heard him open the door. "Hello! *Danki* for coming."

Laura followed him and found Jamie, Kayla, Nathan, and Lorraine burdened with loaded serving trays, bags of chips and pretzels, and three large drink containers.

"*Danki* for bringing so much food," Allen said as he reached for one of the trays in Nathan's hands. "I'll carry this for you."

"This is fantastic!" Laura reached for the tray in Kayla's hands. "Let me help you."

"Oh, no." Kayla shook her head. "I've got it."

"I'll get the door." Laura held the screen door open wide, and the others carried the food into the kitchen, where they deposited it on the long table. The trays held a variety of sandwiches.

When another knock sounded on the door, Allen scurried off to greet more guests.

Laura folded her hands together as she surveyed the food. "This is *wunderbaar. Danki* so much."

"*Gern gschehne.*" Kayla removed a tote bag from her shoulder and set it on a chair. She leaned in close. "I hope it's okay that I brought Nathan. He wanted to come, and Lorraine offered to tag along and help serve the food."

"That's fine. I'm glad they could come."

"*Danki.*" Kayla looked past her. "Where's the birthday girl?"

Laura pointed toward the doorway. "She's in the *schtupp.* I put her in her play yard so she wouldn't wander out the door or get stepped on."

"I want to go see her." Kayla rushed out of the kitchen with Lorraine and Nathan in tow. "There she is!" Kayla gushed from the family room. "Happy birthday, Mollie!"

Jamie sidled up to Laura. "How are you?"

"I'm fine." Laura removed the plastic covers on the sandwich serving trays. "Have you been on duty at the fire station at all this week? Kayla said you'd have today off."

"I was on duty Wednesday, and it was quiet. We had one medical call and one car accident, but the people were fine. No bad injuries." Jamie leaned on the back of a kitchen chair. "I haven't seen you since Sunday. How are things here?"

"They're great." Laura smiled as she took a stack of paper napkins from the pantry. "When will *Dat,* Cindy, and Mark be here?"

He glanced at the clock above the sink. "They should be here soon. *Dat* and Mark were going to come after finishing a couple of things at the farm. Cindy was finishing a project. I think she made something to give to Mollie." He looked toward the doorway, where Allen stood talking to a couple of his friends from church.

Laura set the napkins in the center of the table.

"Is Rudy here?" Jamie asked.

She looked at him. "No, but I assume he's coming."

"You assume?" He raised a dark eyebrow. "You haven't talked to him?"

She shook her head. "No, I haven't spoken to him since Tuesday night, but I invited him to come. He was supposed to call me and tell me if he could make it, but I haven't heard from him."

"He hasn't called you since Tuesday?" His words were careful, as if he were attempting to comprehend their meaning.

"*Ya*, but that's not unusual for us." She shrugged despite her tightening stomach. "Sometimes we don't talk for a few days."

He stood up straight and motioned toward the doorway. "I'm sure you remember I took Kayla for granted when we first started seeing each other last year, but I quickly learned my lesson."

"Rudy doesn't take me for granted. He's just busy."

"We're all busy, but Kayla and I talk at least every other day. I try to see her at least twice during the week and then on the weekend. I can't imagine not talking to her, because I think about her all the time. I wonder how she is, and I want to hear how her week is going. I can't fathom going more than a day without talking to her and checking on her."

"That's nice, but Rudy and I aren't like you and Kayla."

"Uh-huh." Jamie rubbed his chin as he studied her.

She began to arrange the trays of sandwiches on the table to avoid his concerned gaze. She hated the fist-size ball of unease forming under her ribs. After she'd moved the sandwich trays around, she placed the pile of plates at one end of the table. "These sandwiches look *appeditlich*. It was so generous of Kayla to bring them."

"Oh my goodness!" Kayla came in holding Mollie. "She's getting so big!" She carried Mollie over to Jamie. "Can you say hi to Jamie?"

Lorraine walked over to Kayla while Nathan lingered in the doorway to the family room. "Is there anything I can help you do?"

Laura glanced around the table and then snapped her fingers. "We need ice. Let me get the ice bucket down, and maybe you can fill it with ice from the freezer?"

"*Ya.*" Lorraine followed Laura to the cabinet.

Laura opened it and then groaned when she spotted the ice bucket on the top shelf. How she despised being the shortest in her family.

"Let me get it." Nathan, who seemed to have sprouted at least two inches during the past year, appeared beside her. He retrieved the ice bucket, and then he and Lorraine set to filling it with ice.

When a knock sounded on the back door, Laura turned toward the family room. Allen was still talking to friends. Instead of interrupting his conversation, she hurried to the back door, where she found Rudy, Cindy, Mark, and *Dat.*

"Hi." She opened the screen door, and relief flooded her when Rudy smiled. *Jamie is wrong. Rudy and I are just fine. We're just working a few things out.*

"Hey, sis." Mark grinned. "Long time, no see."

"Come in." Laura opened the door wider, and they filed in.

Cindy held up a large gift bag as she stepped into the mudroom. "I have to show you what I made for Mollie."

"I can't wait to see it." Laura stepped back as her father and twin followed Cindy into the kitchen. When Rudy stepped over to her, she smiled. "I'm glad you came."

"Did you think I wouldn't?" Rudy's face clouded with a frown.

"I didn't know if—" Laura began.

"Laura!" Kayla called.

"*Ya?*" Laura moved into the kitchen.

Kayla scrunched her nose. "I think Mollie needs a diaper change. Is it okay if I take her upstairs and change her?"

"*Ya,* that's fine. *Danki.*" Laura stepped toward her. "But do you want me to do it?"

"No, no." Kayla shifted Mollie in her arms. "I can handle it."

"I'll come with you." Cindy walked over to her.

"Great." Kayla grinned at Laura before they left the room to disappear up the stairs.

"Laura." Lorraine frowned. "I spilled some iced tea. Where's a mop?"

"It's in the utility room." Laura crossed the kitchen and opened the door to retrieve the mop. "I'll clean it up."

"No, I'll do it. I'm so sorry." Lorraine blushed.

Another knock sounded on the back door, and Laura started toward the mudroom. But a hand on her shoulder startled her, and she stopped.

"I've got it." Allen's voice was close to her ear, sending a chill dancing up her spine.

Whoa. Where did that reaction come from?

Laura looked up at him and nodded. "Okay. *Danki.*"

"It's the least I can do." Allen motioned toward the table. "You've practically planned and run this party by yourself. *Danki.*"

Before she could respond, he headed for the door. When she felt a hand on her other shoulder, she spun toward Rudy.

"Can we talk?" His dark eyes seemed hopeful.

"Um, well . . ." She took in the chaos in the large kitchen. "I need to get ready for everyone to eat, and I—"

"Allen can handle it." He nodded toward where Allen now spoke with a few people she knew were his customers turned friends. "Please."

The desperation in his eyes shoved away her anxiety about the party.

"Of course. Let's talk on the front porch." She took his hand and guided him through the family room and out the front door.

When they stepped onto the porch, her gaze landed on the swing where she and Allen had so recently sat and poured out their souls. What would Rudy say if he knew she and Allen had shared such an intimate discussion?

Pushing away her guilt, she leaned back against the railing and faced him. "What do you want to talk about?"

Frowning, he stared down at the wood floor and fingered his suspenders. "I don't know how to say this."

Her eyes widened as her chest seized. "Are you breaking up with me?"

"What?" His brow furrowed as he looked up at her. "No, I'm not breaking up with you. I just wanted to apologize, and I didn't know how to begin."

"Oh." Her shoulders relaxed.

"I thought about what you've been trying to tell me, and you're right."

"What are you talking about?" Her mind swam with all their recent discussions.

"I need to be a better *freind* to Allen." He lifted his hand and then let it drop. "I'm sorry for not thinking about what Allen is going through. I was only thinking of myself, which is prideful and sinful. I'll talk to him tonight and see how he is. I'll make an effort to be a better *freind*."

Laura blinked.

"You look stunned." He snickered. "I'm sorry for being unsupportive. I'm going to try to do better."

"Does that mean you approve of my staying here at night to take care of Mollie?"

When his smile faded, she gripped the railing behind her, awaiting his explosion.

"No, I don't approve of that, but all of this will end when Irma Mae is well, right?"

She nodded.

"Then I suppose I can tolerate it since it's temporary."

"*Danki.*" She smiled.

"*Gern gschehne.*" He stepped forward and threaded his fingers through hers. "We should probably get back inside." He led her toward the door.

Jamie's words from earlier echoed through her mind, and she stopped him, pulling on his arm. "Wait."

"What?" He looked down at her, his eyebrows lifting.

"When I last spoke to you Tuesday night, you promised you'd call me to confirm that you could make it tonight. Why didn't you?"

"I don't know." He shrugged. "I've been busy."

Her shoulders stiffened. "Too busy to call me and let me know you were coming?"

"I would have called you if I couldn't come."

"But why don't you ever call me just to talk?"

"What do you mean?"

She released his hand and gestured around the porch. "Why don't you call to say hi and check on me? Maybe to see how my week is going."

He paused as if processing her question. "I guess I just sort of assume you're fine and you'll call me if you need something from me."

"So you're telling me you never just want to hear my voice and make sure I'm okay?"

His eyebrows drew together. "Why are you asking me all these questions?"

"Do you think of me during the week? Or am I more of an afterthought?" She dreaded his reaction to the hint of anguish she heard creeping into her voice. She couldn't allow Rudy to see how much his nonchalance hurt her. Still, didn't she have a right to know?

"I thought you accepted my apology."

"I do accept your apology, but I need you to answer my question." She dug her fingers into the railing. "Do you think about me during the week? Do you wonder how I am and if I'm having a *gut* day?"

"*Ya*, I guess so." His expression hardened. "Where's this coming from?"

"I just want to know how you feel about me." *I want your reassurance that we're going to get through this, and that Jamie is wrong about you. Tell me you don't take me for granted! Ease my muddled heart!*

"You know I care about you, Laura. I always have." He sighed as if the words were painful to say. "I don't know what else I can do to show you you're important to me." He gestured toward the house. "This is somehow about Allen, isn't it?"

"No, it has nothing to do with Allen. Forget it, Rudy." She waved him off, defeat weighing heavily on her heart. "I need to get inside." Her stomach felt hollow. She shook her head and started toward the door, her body trembling despite the humid evening.

Laura wrenched open the front door and was greeted by a flurry of conversations. Party guests were seated throughout the family room and in the kitchen, eating and drinking iced tea.

Laughter floated through the air as Laura squared her shoulders and plastered a smile on her face. She looked across the room, and her gaze locked with Allen's. He stood between her father and Milton. A smile turned up the corners of his mouth, and he nodded a greeting to her. His eyes were warm and comforting, and the tension in her back and shoulders eased as she basked in his gaze. She returned the gesture as the front door clicked shut behind her, signaling that Rudy had also entered the house.

"Laura!" Lorraine and Nathan appeared in front of her, blocking her view of Allen. "Is this your boyfriend, Rudy?" Lorraine asked.

"*Ya*." Laura gestured between them. "Lorraine, this is Rudy. Rudy, this is Lorraine. She works at Dienner's restaurant."

"It's so nice to meet you." Lorraine shook his hand and then turned toward Laura. "I'm so sorry about Monday at the restaurant."

Panic gripped Laura's spine. *Please don't bring this up now!* She had to redirect the conversation. "Oh, it was nothing." She pointed toward the kitchen. "I should go make sure we have enough iced tea. I might have to make some more."

"Oh, we have plenty." Lorraine dismissed the concern.

"What happened on Monday?" Nathan asked.

Laura cringed. *Oh no. Not now!*

"I thought I told you." Lorraine looked at Nathan. "When I brought out Laura's and Allen's orders, Kayla introduced me to them, and I thought Allen and Laura were married." She chuckled a little. "I told Laura Mollie looked like her and Allen. I said Mollie had her eyes and Allen's nose."

Her cheeks reddened as she turned to Laura. "I was so embarrassed when Kayla explained you're helping Allen care for Mollie while his mother-in-law recovers from an accident. I'm so sorry for my mistake."

"It's no problem at all." Laura could feel Rudy's resentment radiating from him in furious waves. "*Danki* for coming today. I'm going to go check on the drinks just to be sure."

Laura was certain of Rudy's angry stare as she stepped toward the kitchen.

NINETEEN

"Is it time to sing to the birthday girl?" Kayla asked as she stood in the doorway to the kitchen. She had Mollie in her arms.

Allen studied his beautiful daughter as she grinned up at Kayla. She was a year old today. How was that possible when it seemed like she had been born only a few months ago? If only Savilla were here to celebrate this momentous occasion . . .

A pang of grief sliced through him.

But he wasn't alone. His house was bustling with people who had come to mark the occasion with him. Allen scanned the sea of faces surrounding him in his family room, and affection overwhelmed him. Although Irma Mae was still recovering in the rehabilitation center, Milton had come to celebrate the special day, along with friends from church and special customers, and Laura was the reason they'd all come. She had planned the party down to every last detail.

Allen's gaze tracked to the kitchen where Laura scurried around, holding a birthday candle shaped like a number one. She looked beautiful tonight—happy as she moved among the guests. He bit back a groan. He had to stop thinking about how attractive and special she was. She was someone else's girlfriend. She was forbidden!

He had spent the last few days trying to dodge any personal discussions. He wanted to avoid another intimate conversation like the one they'd shared on the porch swing earlier in the week. But it seemed impossible since he felt the invisible magnet between them growing stronger every day. He yearned to get to know her better, to learn everything about her. He longed to read her mind and find out how she felt about him. But all those thoughts were inappropriate when he was only her friend and her heart belonged to someone else.

Allen glanced over his shoulder at Rudy, who stood scowling beside Mark. He'd approached Rudy after Laura came in from the front porch with him. But when Allen tried to pull Rudy into a conversation, the man had given him one-word responses and then turned to Mark and asked him about his farm. So much for trying to mend their estranged relationship.

"Let's sing to Mollie!" Laura called as she gestured for everyone to come into the kitchen.

Allen followed the knot of people into the room, and Laura beckoned him over to Mollie in the high chair. His daughter was wearing a bib with a pocket over her diaper.

Allen leaned down to Laura. "Where is her dress?"

"I took it off since I'm going to give her a small *kuche* to eat by herself." She smiled. "I'm sure she's going to wind up wearing most of it."

Allen grinned. "I suppose you're right."

She held up her hand as if to stop his next thought. "Don't worry. I'll give her a bath before I leave tonight."

An unexpected twinge of disappointment nipped at him. It was Friday night, and Laura would go home to her family after the party was over. He would miss her. He shook off the thought.

"You don't need to bathe her," he said. "I can handle it."

"We'll argue about that later," she whispered before turning toward the crowd. "Let's sing," she called. "Happy Birthday to you," she began.

Everyone sang to Mollie as Kayla carried the small chocolate cake over to the high chair. Mollie squealed and banged her hand on the tray as they finished the song. Then Kayla set the cake on the tray, and Mollie smashed her hands into it. Allen laughed as Mollie lifted her fingers to her mouth and licked off the icing.

"She's very *schmaert*," Laura quipped with a grin.

"*Ya*, she is," he agreed.

Mollie grabbed two handfuls of cake and shoved them into her mouth, and everyone laughed.

Laura began to cut pieces of the larger cake, and Lorraine and Kayla distributed them to the crowd. Cindy had made coffee in the percolator and Lorraine helped pour it into Styrofoam cups. Soon everyone was seated throughout the family room and kitchen while they ate cake and drank coffee.

"Would you like a piece?" Kayla offered him a plate with a large hunk of cake.

"*Ya. Danki.*" He took it and then grabbed a fork from the pile on the table.

"*Kaffi?*" Cindy appeared next to him and held out a cup of the steaming liquid.

"*Danki.*" He took the cup and then turned toward the table, where Laura still stood by the cake. "Are you going to have a piece?"

"*Ya.*" She smiled up at him, but her smile didn't meet her eyes.

He longed to take her arm, pull her into the utility room, and ask her what was wrong. Had Rudy hurt her feelings when they spoke alone on the porch? His jaw tightened at the thought of Rudy once again hurting her, but it was none of his business.

He leaned in closer. "*Was iss letz?*"

"Nothing." She placed a piece of cake on her plate and then

licked her fingers. "Did you try the *kuche*?" She pointed to the large piece of cake on his plate.

"Not yet."

"Well? What are you waiting for?" She jammed a hand on her hip and lifted her chin. She was adorable. "You realize I slaved over these two *kuches*." She looked over at Mollie, who had already demolished her cake. Her face was covered in chocolate icing and sprinkles, and pieces of cake peppered her blond curls. "You can't tell I made two, but I did."

"She definitely enjoyed that *kuche*."

"Are you going to try your piece?"

Allen set his cup on the table and then forked a piece of the moist, sweet cake into his mouth. He groaned as he nodded. "Superb."

"Superb?" Her eyes sparkled.

"Outstanding." He took another bite.

"Allen." Vernon sidled up to him and tapped his shoulder. "I meant to ask you earlier. How are you feeling? Are you doing better?"

Allen nodded as he swallowed another piece of cake. "I am. *Danki* for asking. Our talk helped."

Laura sat down in a chair beside Kayla and began talking to one of their friends from church.

"How are you doing?" Allen asked Vernon.

"I'm doing fine." Vernon set his cup on the table beside Allen's. "The farm is always busy, but Jamie and Mark have made me take a little bit of a step back. They want to handle more. I think they're pushing me into retirement, but I keep telling them I'm not as old as I look." He chuckled.

Allen smiled, but a niggle of worry remained at the base of his neck. He would try to get Laura alone later to ask if she was okay. Surely, because they were friends, her well-being was his business.

Kayla touched Laura's shoulder. "Lorraine and I are going to start cleaning up."

"Oh. Is it time?" Laura looked up at the clock on the wall and found it was after seven. "I didn't realize how late it was."

"That's because we were having too much fun talking." Sadie Byler, a friend from church, put her hand on Laura's arm. "It was so *gut* seeing you. *Danki* for inviting us to come celebrate Mollie's birthday."

"I'm so *froh* you could." Laura stood and began gathering plates and cups.

"I can do this." Kayla took the stack from her and then nodded at Mollie in the high chair. "Why don't you clean up the birthday girl?"

"*Danki.*" Laura wet a paper towel and began wiping the cake and icing off Mollie's face.

Mollie squirmed, arched her back, and grimaced in protest.

"I'm sorry, *mei liewe*, but you're a mess." Laura struggled to wipe Mollie's hands, too, and then started on her curls. They were matted with a mixture of cake and icing.

"I don't think you can wipe off that icing." Cindy stood beside Laura while leaning on a broom. "I think you should put her right into the bathtub."

"*Ya*, you're right." Laura pulled the tray off the high chair and unbuckled Mollie's safety belt. "You need a bath, little one."

"I put Mollie's gifts in her room. I'm going to sweep up the kitchen and then see if anything else needs to be picked up in the *schtupp*."

"*Danki* so much for helping," Laura said.

"*Gern gschehne.*" Cindy tackled the kitchen floor with her broom.

Mollie held up her arms, and Laura scooped her up. She looked toward where Lorraine was washing trays and Kayla was drying. What would she do without her friends' help?

Laura said good-bye to the remaining guests in the kitchen before she carried Mollie toward the stairs. She stepped into the family room, where Allen sat on the sofa. Jamie sat across from him in a wing chair.

Allen jumped up and approached her. "Do you need help?"

"No. I'm going to give her a bath before I go home." She glanced around the room. "Where are Rudy, Mark, and *mei dat*?"

Jamie pointed toward the front door. "They went to sit outside."

"Why are you two in here?" Laura shifted Mollie in her arms as the messy baby rested her head on her shoulder, no doubt making her own dress a mess. But she didn't mind.

Jamie shrugged. "We just didn't want to go outside. We were talking about Allen's buggy projects."

"I was boring him to tears." Allen smirked. "He's just being nice."

"No, not really." Jamie shook his head. "I like hearing about your projects. It's much more interesting than my cows."

"I doubt that." Allen gave her a sheepish smile.

Laura's heart warmed. Perhaps Jamie would be the friend Allen needed since Rudy wasn't making any effort to reach out to him.

She nodded toward the stairs. "I'm going to get Mollie in the tub."

"Call me if you need me," Allen said as she ascended the steps.

"I will," she promised.

When she reached the top of the stairs, she walked into Mollie's room, flipped on the lantern, and set Mollie in her crib. Then she entered the bathroom, turned on the lantern there, and began filling the tub. While the water ran, she stepped back into Mollie's room and spotted the gift bags piled on her bed. She opened the one from Cindy and pulled out a crib-size quilt stitched with a pink and purple lone star pattern in the center. Laura gasped as she ran her fingers over the intricate stitching. It was gorgeous! Her sister was so very talented.

Then she opened a large shopping bag from Kayla and Jamie and found a baby doll and a pink corn popper toy.

Laura laughed and turned to Mollie, who stood in the crib, holding on to the railing. "Look at what Kayla got you." She held up the corn popper. "What do you think?"

Mollie squealed and reached for it.

"You need to walk if you want to use it." She set the corn popper in the crib, and Mollie touched it. "We'll have to practice again next week."

Laura checked the other gift bags. She found board books and a teddy bear from Allen's friends and a dog pull-toy from her father and Mark. One of Allen's customers had given her more books and a set of plastic blocks.

"You got some nice gifts." She smiled as she lifted Mollie into her arms. "Let's get you cleaned up so you can go to bed."

She carried Mollie into the bathroom and undressed her. Then she set her in the bath seat before kneeling next to the tub. Mollie squealed and giggled as she splashed. Laura laughed as she gathered a washcloth and baby wash.

"Did you have a *gut* birthday party? Did you enjoy the *kuche*?" As she continued to ask Mollie questions as she bathed her, Mollie babbled, squealed, and splashed in response.

Laura was washing Mollie's hair when footsteps sounded on the stairs. She grinned and leaned down to Mollie. "Is that your *dat* coming up the stairs? Do you think your daddy is coming to see if I got all the icing and *kuche* out of your *schee* curls?"

Mollie squealed, and her blue eyes widened. *"Dat! Dat! Dat!"*

The footsteps grew louder, and Laura grinned as she turned toward the doorway. When Rudy appeared, Laura's smile dissolved.

"Hi, Rudy." She sat back on her heels and wiped her hands down her apron, which was damp from Mollie's splashing. She turned to Mollie. "This is Rudy. Can you say Rudy?"

Mollie laughed and splashed again, creating a small tsunami in the tub.

"Are you almost done?" Rudy gestured toward the tub.

"*Ya.* I just have to finish washing her hair, and then I need to rinse her, dry her, and dress her for bed."

"Why can't Allen do that?"

"I offered to do it to help him."

His mouth pressed into a hard line. "I thought you and I would have some time to spend together tonight. That's why I came."

She blinked. "You didn't want to come to a party?"

"I wanted to see you. Is that a bad thing?"

"No, it's not bad, but I thought you'd want to see everyone else too." She pointed at Mollie, who was still happy in the water. "I thought you'd want to help celebrate her special day."

A muscle ticked in his jaw. "I wanted to see you, Laura, and now it's almost eight o'clock. I don't think your *dat* will be *froh* if I keep you out too late."

"He'll understand." She pointed toward the stairs. "Why don't you go tell him it's going to take me another thirty minutes or so to get Mollie into bed, so I won't be home until later."

"Your family is already gone," he snapped, his voice echoing through the bathroom. "We're the only ones left here."

"They're gone?" She stood and sat down on the lid of the commode. "But Cindy, Kayla, and Lorraine were cleaning up the kitchen. They're all done?"

"They all just left."

"Oh." She looked toward the tub where Mollie bobbed a

plastic toy beneath the surface of the bathwater and sang to herself. "I didn't realize we'd been playing in the tub for that long." She frowned as guilt seeped under her skin. "I'm sorry. I must have lost track of time. We were having too much fun in the tub."

"Why can't Allen finish getting her ready for bed so we can go? I'd like to be home before ten."

Frustration gripped her. "If you want to go, then go."

"And how will you get home?" His voice challenged her.

"I'll see if Allen's driver can come and get me, or I'll just stay here tonight." She gestured toward Mollie's room down the hall. "I already have clothes here."

"So you'll just stay here like Allen's *fraa*?" He sneered, his words steeped with sarcasm.

She stood, her back ramrod straight as she glared up at him. "How dare you say that!"

"Even Lorraine thought you were Allen's *fraa* and Mollie's *mamm*!" He nearly spat the words at her. "And why were you out to eat with Allen? Did you go on a date with him before you asked me out on a date? Are you dating both of us now?"

Laura tried to speak, but no words passed her lips. Her eyes stung with furious tears. "How could you even say that to me?"

"I think it's a valid question." He folded his arms over his wide chest. "Why would Lorraine think you and Allen were a couple unless you acted like it? Were you holding hands in the restaurant? Maybe whispering to each other?" He pointed to Mollie. "Maybe you were cutting up Mollie's food and feeding it to her like her *mamm* would?"

His words shot across her nerves like shards of glass, cutting and fraying them. "Do you even have a heart at all, Rudy?" she said sternly. "Do you remember how *mei dat* grieved when *mei mamm* died? Do you remember how I grieved—how I'm still grieving for her every day?" She jammed a finger into her chest. When he didn't respond, she added, "Do you?"

His eyes widened as he held up his hands. "Calm down. I wasn't talking about your *mamm*."

"*Ya*, you are. When you accuse Allen of trying to steal me away from you, then you're also disrespecting other widowers, like *mei dat*. Allen lost his *fraa*, the love of his life. He's mourning, and he's hurting."

She made a sweeping gesture toward Mollie and lowered her voice. "She lost her *mamm*. Allen and Mollie need me, and that's why I'm here. If you can't get that through your head, then maybe you should leave. I don't need your accusations and criticisms in my life. You're not the man I thought you were when I agreed to be your girlfriend, and it's breaking my heart." Her voice broke as tears streamed down her face and a sob choked back her words. She yanked a handful of tissues from the box on the counter and wiped her eyes and nose before tossing the tissues into the trash.

Swallowing a deep breath, she sank onto her knees in front of Mollie, grabbed the little plastic bucket from the edge of the tub, and began to rinse her off. She worked in silence for a few moments, waiting for Rudy's footsteps to echo in the stairwell as he left her. Instead he remained in the doorway, his eyes no doubt boring into her back.

"Laura, I'm sorry." Rudy's voice was soft and gentle as it broke through the heavy tension hovering over them.

She kept her back to him as she released the stopper in the tub, sending the water gurgling down the drain. She grabbed a towel from the rack on the wall.

"Please look at me," he said.

Standing, she lifted Mollie from the tub and wrapped her in the towel. Then she faced him.

His eyes pleaded with her. "I'm sorry. I was out of line once again. Will you ride home with me?"

She paused, taking in his hunched posture and contrite expression. It was their culture to forgive, and she and Rudy had a long history together. Regret diminished her frustration. "*Ya*, I will. You can wait downstairs. I promise I'll only be a few minutes."

He nodded and then stepped out of the bathroom. She could hear him going down the stairs.

As she carried Mollie into her bedroom, an ache overtook her. If she was meant to be with Rudy, why did they argue every time they spoke? They were supposed to be in love, but he hadn't told her he loved her in months. Had they fallen out of love?

Were we ever in love?

The ache morphed into a block of ice as she set Mollie on the changing table and began to dress her. She dismissed the sobering thoughts and smiled down at her charge. All that mattered right now was taking care of this little girl. Laura would sort through her problems with Rudy later.

TWENTY

WHITE-HOT FURY BOILED THROUGH ALLEN'S VEINS as he stood at the bottom of the stairs and leaned on the banister.

Laura's angry and frustrated words echoed in the stairwell as she spoke to Rudy. "*Ya*, you are. When you accuse Allen of trying to steal me away from you, then you're also disrespecting other widowers, like *mei dat*. Allen lost his *fraa*, the love of his life. He's grieving, and he's hurting. She lost her *mamm*. Allen and Mollie need me, and that's why I'm here. If you can't get that through your head, then maybe you should leave. I don't need your constant accusations and criticisms in my life. You're not the man I thought you were when I agreed to be your girlfriend, and it's breaking my heart."

Allen closed his eyes and pinched the bridge of his nose. His chest constricted as if a rubber band were wrapped around it, biting into his skin and robbing him of air in his lungs. He longed to march upstairs and instruct Rudy to leave his house and stay away from Laura.

But Laura was the one to tell Rudy to leave and stay away from her.

Allen clenched his fists. Why did Laura allow Rudy to disrespect her? She was beautiful, kind, loving, and loyal, and she deserved so much better than a man who castigated her and accused her of cheating on him. She deserved a man who would cherish and protect her, not make her cry.

Allen gritted his teeth and stared up toward the second floor as he waited for Rudy to reply, but they both must have lowered their voices. He thought he heard the sound of bathwater gurgling down through the pipes, and he held his breath, hoping Rudy would come to his senses and realize how cruel he'd been to Laura.

After several moments, footsteps echoed in the hallway, and Allen moved away from the stairs. He folded his arms over his chest and lifted his chin as Rudy descended.

When Rudy reached the bottom step, he gave Allen a sheepish smile. "Do you need help with anything down here?"

"No, *danki*." Allen motioned toward the kitchen. "The *maed* cleaned up the kitchen, and Mark and Jamie helped me straighten up in here. It's all done."

"Oh." Rudy rubbed his clean-shaven chin. "Laura asked me to wait down here for her. I'm going to take her home."

Allen frowned as disappointment lanced through him. *So she forgave him.* "You can have a seat." He pointed to the wing chair.

"*Danki.*" Rudy crossed the room and sat down.

Allen started toward the kitchen but then stopped and faced Rudy. "I hope you realize Laura and I are only *gut freinden*, like you and I used to be before Savilla died and you stopped really talking to me." He took a step toward him. "You were my first *freind* when I moved here, and I appreciated how you reached out to me and helped me adjust and blend into the community."

Rudy's mouth dropped open.

"Right now I need Laura's help, but it's not going to last forever. This will all come to an end when Irma Mae is well and ready to help me again." He pointed at Rudy as his body shook.

"So why don't you do us both a favor and stop practically accusing Laura of having an affair with me? Our relationship is strictly platonic, and I would never risk Laura's reputation or your friendship by allowing people to assume we were behaving inappropriately."

A vision of Savilla filled Allen's mind and he cleared his throat. "Besides that, Savilla has only been gone ten months. You know we're not permitted to date until a year after a spouse dies, but that's irrelevant. I'm not ready to have another relationship, and I could never disrespect Savilla's precious memory."

"I'm sorry." Rudy stood. "I've been selfish and prideful, and I'll do better. I miss your friendship, and I'll do my best to be a better *freind* to you."

"Don't worry about me." Allen kept his voice low so Laura wouldn't hear him. "The person you should worry about is Laura." He pointed toward the stairs. "She deserves someone who cherishes her, not someone who cuts her down." He wagged his finger at Rudy. "You need to be a better boyfriend before you break her heart and lose her forever."

To his surprise, Rudy nodded. "You're right."

"Allen!" Laura called down the stairs. "Mollie is ready for bed. Do you want me to tuck her in?"

"I'll be right there." Allen looked back at Rudy once more and then climbed the stairs.

He stepped into Mollie's room, where his daughter stood in the crib, clad in a pink onesie as she held on to the railing.

"Did you see her presents?" Laura turned toward him and gestured toward the bed. "Cindy carried them up here for me. Did you see the quilt she made for Mollie?"

"I did see it. It's *schee*." He stepped over to her and touched the quilt. "She's talented."

"She is. She inherited *Mamm*'s talent for sewing." She snapped her fingers. "That's what I forgot to tell you. I made Mollie a few dresses this week. I found Savilla's fabric in the sewing room, and after taking a short nap, I worked on them a little each afternoon while Mollie finished sleeping. I wanted to make her five for her birthday, but I only completed two." She pointed to the closet. "I hung them up. I also mended two of your shirts that had holes in them. I put them in your dresser. I hope that's okay."

"That's really generous of you." He searched her eyes but found no sign of sadness or anger. Was she hiding her resentment toward Rudy? Or had she truly forgiven him?

She gave him a shy smile. "Why are you staring at me like that?"

"Nothing." He shook his head.

"I was going to carry the toys downstairs and put them in the *schtupp*, but I got sidetracked with her bath."

"It's fine." He motioned toward her crib. "I'll take care of her. I can't tell you how much I appreciate all you've done to make Mollie *froh*."

Her pretty face lit up in a smile. *"Gern gschehne."*

"Go spend some time with Rudy. Enjoy what's left of the evening." His stomach soured as he said Rudy's name.

Laura waved at Mollie. *"Gut nacht, mei liewe.* Happy birthday. *Ich liebe dich."*

Mollie reached for him. He took her in his arms, and she touched his chest and looked up at him. *"Dat."*

"That's right," he whispered, his voice thick.

Mollie touched Laura's shoulder and looked up at her. "Lala."

Laura gasped and her eyes shimmered. She touched Mollie's cheek.

When Laura looked up at Allen, their gazes locked. His breath hitched in his chest, and the air around them shifted. He nearly gasped as something electric passed between them. Had she felt it too? His heart thumped, and he stared into her striking eyes, losing himself in her gorgeous pools of blue. Once again, he felt the invisible magnet pulling him to her.

What does this mean? Laura belongs to Rudy.

"Are you ready to go?" Rudy's voice crashed through Allen's trance.

He took a step back and turned toward the doorway.

"*Ya,*" Laura said. "I was just saying good night. I'm sorry for taking so long." She kissed Mollie's head. "I'll see you Monday." Then she looked up at Allen. "*Gut nacht.*"

"*Gut nacht,*" he echoed.

"Have a *gut* night." Rudy gave him a half-hearted wave.

"You too," Allen said. "Be safe going home."

Laura smiled before following Rudy out of the bedroom and down the stairs.

Allen held Mollie against his chest and swallowed the urge to ask Laura to stay so they could discuss these confusing feelings.

He sank into the rocking chair and closed his eyes. He was losing his mind. He had to stop these crazy notions about Laura before they ruined his friendship with Rudy, Laura, and her family. The only way to cleanse his mind was to ask God for help.

As he began to rock Mollie, he opened his mind and began to pray.

God, please help me redirect my thoughts. I'm confused, and I don't know how to stop having inappropriate feelings for Laura. She's important to Mollie and me, but I can't risk losing her by convincing myself I have feelings for her. Please cleanse my thoughts and mind and help me stay focused on being the father Mollie needs. Please also help Rudy learn how to be the man Laura deserves in her life.

"*Dat.*"

Mollie's little voice pulled him from his fervent prayer. He kissed the top of her head as a vision of Savilla's beautiful face filled his mind. His heart seemed to squeeze.

"Your *mamm* would've loved to be here to celebrate your special day," he whispered as he moved the chair back and forth. "Your *mamm* loved you so much. If only you could remember her."

Overwhelming grief lodged in his throat, making it impossible to say more. Pulling in a deep, shuddering breath through his nose, Allen closed his eyes, rested his cheek on Mollie's head, and stemmed the tears that threatened to pour. Mollie would celebrate many more birthdays without her mother by her side, and he had to be strong for her.

Laura's thoughts spun as she sat beside Rudy. She wrung her hands and stared out the window as the streetlights cast eerie shadows inside the dark buggy. The intense interaction with Allen replayed in her mind, and confusion rocked her to her core. Had Allen felt the same unnerving energy flaring between them as they stood so close to each other? She'd never felt that kind of spark with Rudy. Had she imagined it?

Suddenly she remembered how Allen's soft voice had sent shivers down her spine earlier in the day. What was happening between her and Allen? And what would Savilla say? She swallowed a groan.

"I'm truly sorry," Rudy said, breaking through her thoughts. "I've been terrible to you, and you deserve better." He gave her a sideways glance, his expression full of contrition. "I hope you won't give up on me."

Laura cringed as guilt replaced her confusion. "I would never give up on you."

"*Gut.*" He trained his eyes on the road. "After we talked in the bathroom, I walked downstairs and Allen was waiting for me. He said some things that made me realize how awful I've been."

"What did he say?" She braced herself for his response.

"He reminded me that you and Allen are *freinden*, and he also pointed out that I haven't been a *gut freind* to him since Savilla died." He sighed. "He reminded me that he needs your help and it's only temporary. He said your relationship is platonic and he'd never risk your reputation by making your friendship anything more than just that. He also mentioned Savilla has only been gone ten months and he's not ready for a relationship and would never disrespect her memory that way."

"Right." How could she even think about Allen as anything more than a friend when Savilla hadn't been gone a year?

"Then he said I need to be a better boyfriend. I need to cherish you instead of cutting you down, and he's right." He frowned as he turned toward her. "I can't tell you how sorry I am."

Laura's lower lip trembled. Allen had defended her and told Rudy to treat her better. Appreciation flowed through her veins. Allen was such a good man. Savilla was so blessed to call him her husband, even for such a short period of time.

"Are you okay?" Rudy asked.

"*Ya.*" She nodded and sniffed. "I'm just very grateful to hear you say that."

"I should have realized it sooner. You've been trying to get through to me, and I've been too focused on myself to see the truth in what you were saying." He turned back toward the road. "I'll make it up to you. Please just give me a chance." His eyes were hopeful. "Will you give me a chance, Laura?"

"Of course I will."

"*Danki.* I won't let you regret it."

As Rudy guided the horse down the street toward her house, Laura settled back into the bench seat and stared out the window. A vision of Allen staring down at her in Mollie's bedroom filled her mind again, and she rubbed her temple. She had to abandon all her inappropriate thoughts of Allen and focus on being a better girlfriend to Rudy. She couldn't throw away their last four years together, even if her heart seemed to crave Allen and his kind words. Savilla would be so disappointed if she knew Laura was attracted to him.

Laura turned toward Rudy and took in his handsome profile. Perhaps she and Rudy could finally be happy. She turned back toward the windshield and spotted her family's farm ahead of them. Everything would be just fine as long as she had faith.

But as she crossed her arms over her chest, Laura tried her best to dismiss the doubt that remained. In a couple of months, Irma Mae would be well, and Allen and Mollie's life would be back to normal. How would Laura move on with her life without daily visits with Allen and Mollie?

TWENTY-ONE

THE WARM SEPTEMBER BREEZE BOUNCED THE TIES to Laura's prayer covering off her shoulders as she stepped onto the rock driveway at the Smuckers' farm. She searched for Allen's buggy, but then she spotted Allen carrying Mollie and coming toward her. She grinned and waved. *"Gude mariye!"*

"Hi, Laura!" Allen set Mollie on the ground. "Go get Lala."

Mollie squealed and then waddled toward her, her smile wide. "Lala! Lala!"

Laura laughed as she bent down, holding her arms out. During the past four weeks, Mollie had begun walking by herself and tottering all around the house and yard while pushing her corn popper or a small, plastic doll carriage Laura had found for her at a yard sale.

The month had flown by. Mollie had started sleeping through the night, but Laura continued staying at Allen's on weeknights. He'd confessed Mollie cried for her on weekends, and Laura knew he'd never be able to work safely if his daughter kept him from sleeping during the week too. Still, Laura had been careful not to allow herself to have intimate conversations with Allen. Instead, she'd focused on trying to improve her relationship with Rudy. They scheduled one night a week as their date night, eating supper together, and then they saw each other on Saturdays and Sundays. Laura was happy Rudy had been more attentive and kind to her. She'd noticed him talking to Allen more at church too. It seemed Rudy was trying to be a better boyfriend to her as well as a better friend to Allen.

But when she was with Rudy, she still couldn't shake the feeling that things between them would never go back to the way they were before her mother died. It was as if Rudy still distanced himself from her, or maybe she had distanced herself from him.

"Look at you!" Laura scooped Mollie up and kissed her cheek. "You're awfully *schee* in that purple dress."

"It's one of the ones you made for her." Allen joined them. "How are you today?"

"I'm fine." She smiled up at him, taking in his baby-blue eyes. "You look well rested."

"I am. She slept well last night." He touched Mollie's leg.

"That's great. Hopefully that means she's finally stopped crying for me on the weekends. Do you want me to hold her during the church service?"

"No, *danki*. I'll handle her. You have her all week."

"I don't mind. Right, Mollie?" Laura nuzzled her close. "You're my special girl."

"Mollie!" Kayla, flanked by Cindy and Elsie Zook, approached. "Look at you in that *schee* dress. How are you today?"

Mollie moaned and hid her face in the crook of Laura's neck as Laura laughed.

Allen reached for Mollie. "Do you want me to take her?"

"No." Mollie scrunched up her face and glared at Allen. "Lala." Then she snuggled closer to Laura's chest.

Laura's eyes widened as Kayla, Elsie, and Cindy gasped in unison.

"I think she told you," Laura said, trying in vain to suppress a snicker.

"She certainly did." Elsie glanced down at her infant sleeping in her arms. "I wonder if Lily Rose will be that outspoken."

Allen seemed to be at a loss for words. "Well, let me know when you get tired of her, and I'll take her off your hands."

"I will." Laura took the diaper bag from him and hefted it over her shoulder.

"Allen!" Jamie called and then waved.

Allen jammed his thumb toward where the men stood by the barn. "I'm going to go see Jamie."

"Okay." Laura swayed back and forth, rocking Mollie in her arms.

Allen hesitated. "Are you sure you don't want me to take her? She's really heavy."

"I don't mind." Laura nodded toward the men. "Go."

"I'll take her from you when church starts."

"You might have to pry her out of Laura's arms," Kayla quipped.

Allen paused for a moment and then walked over to Jamie. The two men shook hands.

Cindy touched Laura's shoulder. "Let's go visit in the kitchen."

As the women passed the group of men, she met Rudy's gaze and smiled. He reciprocated with a half-smile. That left her wondering if he was upset with her, and a familiar thread of worry coursed through her. She thrust it away as she entered the kitchen and greeted other women in her church district. Mollie rested her head on Laura's shoulder as she spoke to them.

"Is that Mollie Lambert?" Ada Swarey, Rudy's mother, asked as she approached Laura.

"*Ya.*" Laura shifted so Ada could see Mollie's face, but Mollie groaned and turned her face the other way. "She's a little grumpy this morning. She's usually more outgoing."

Ada touched Mollie's head. "Look at those blond curls."

"They're *schee*, aren't they?" Laura gazed down at her. "Her hair is just a little lighter than Savilla's. But she has Savilla's beautiful face and smile. I definitely see her *mamm* when I look at her."

"How long have you been taking care of her now?" Ada asked.

Laura shifted her weight on her feet. Why did that simple question make her so uneasy? "A little more than two months, I think."

Ada nodded. "How is Irma Mae doing?"

"She's getting better. She was able to leave the rehabilitation center and go home last week, but she still has daily physical therapy."

"Oh." Ada nodded. "When you do think she'll be able to take care of Mollie again?"

"It probably won't be for another month or so. She can't lift anything heavy, and she can't be on her feet for very long yet."

Mollie yawned and then buried her face in Laura's shoulder again. Without thinking, Laura leaned down and kissed Mollie's head.

"She's awfully attached to you, isn't she?" Ada touched Mollie's back. "And you're attached to her too."

"*Ya*, I guess we're attached to each other." Laura rested her head on Mollie's. "She's all I have left of Savilla. I cherish her."

"Ada," another woman in the community called. "Come hear about Sylvia's *dochder*."

"I'll see you later." Ada gave her a stiff smile before walking to the other side of the kitchen.

Laura turned to Cindy beside her. "Did you hear that conversation?"

"I did." Cindy nodded.

"Why do you think she asked me so many questions?" Alarm washed over Laura. "Do you think Rudy had her question me?"

"Are you and Rudy having problems?" Cindy asked.

Laura shrugged as if her concerns weren't eating her up inside.

"Not really, but he still seems on edge sometimes. He hasn't said anything, but I can just feel it. I can't put my finger on what's wrong, but sometimes it just doesn't feel right."

Cindy started to respond, but she was interrupted by the chiming clock announcing it was nine. "Time to go," she said when it stopped.

Laura walked to the barn with Cindy, Kayla, and Elsie.

When they stepped inside, Elsie turned to them. "See you after service." Then she went to sit in the section with the other married women.

As she looked at the married women's section, Laura tried to ignore the splinter pricking at her soul. *Mamm* and Savilla used to sit with Elsie, but now Elsie sat between two women Laura didn't know very well. Her heart ached for her mother and best friend. Why did God have to take them both within months of each other?

Dismissing the unsettling thought, Laura shifted Mollie in her arms and moved to the section where the unmarried women sat.

Suddenly Mollie turned and moaned. *"Dat! Dat! Dat!"* She reached toward where Allen sat on the other side of the barn next to *Dat*.

Laura's cheeks heated as she crossed the barn and approached him. "I think she wants you," she said softly, and he stood and took his daughter.

"Your arms need a break anyway." He smiled as Mollie snuggled into his shoulder. *"Danki."*

"Gern gschehne." She walked back to her section, her nerves standing on end and her cheeks still blazing as members of the congregation watched her. She sank onto the bench between Cindy and Kayla and set the diaper bag under the bench before smoothing her hands over her white apron and pink dress.

Cindy leaned over to her. "You okay?"

"*Ya.* Why wouldn't I be?"

"Well, your cheeks are red." Cindy tilted her head. "Are you embarrassed?"

Laura nodded and picked up her hymnal, hoping her sister would let the subject go.

"Why are you embarrassed?"

"Everyone looked at me when I walked back over here." Laura was careful to keep her voice low. "I don't want anyone to get the wrong idea about Allen and me."

"They weren't staring at you, so don't worry about it." Cindy bumped her shoulder against Laura's. "Don't be *gegisch.* Is something else bothering you?"

"No." Laura glanced over to the unmarried young men's section, where Rudy sat between Jamie and Mark. When his gaze sunk into hers, his lips thinned, sending a current of trepidation through her. Was he upset with her again? While they hadn't argued in weeks, that familiar feeling of foreboding took hold. She forced a smile, and he looked away.

The service began, and Laura joined in as the congregation slowly sang the opening hymn. A young man sitting across the barn served as the song leader. He began the first syllable of each line, and then the rest of the congregation joined in to finish the verse.

While the ministers met in another room for thirty minutes to choose who would preach that day, the congregation continued to sing. During the last verse of the second hymn, Laura's gaze moved to the back of the barn just as the ministers returned. They placed their hats on two hay bales, indicating the service was about to begin.

The chosen minister began the first sermon, and Laura tried her best to concentrate on his holy words. She glanced over at Rudy and found him staring down at his lap. Suddenly her thoughts spun with memories of the last four years of their relationship. When they first started dating, their relationship was easy, full of laughter and fun times with their friends. She cherished the memories she and Rudy had made in their youth group, playing volleyball, taking day trips to the lake, and visiting sick members in their community. Back then life was good.

But then her mother passed away. She lost interest in the youth gatherings and couldn't relate to her friends the same way she used to, before her life changed.

While Rudy was there to hold her hand and hug her when she cried, she also felt herself pulling away from him emotionally. He didn't seem to understand her overwhelming grief or her family's turmoil. At times, she sensed he was bored when she shared how her family was lost without her mother. It was as if he couldn't relate to her anymore. If they couldn't relate to each other, then how could they have a future together?

But if they broke up, what would happen to their friendship? He had been a part of her life for so long that she couldn't imagine his absence. Her stomach tightened at the notion of losing Rudy forever.

The first sermon ended, and Laura knelt in silent prayer. She closed her eyes and asked God to guide her heart and her relationship with Rudy. She also prayed for Allen and Mollie, asking him to send healing and comfort to them.

After the prayers, the deacon read from the Scriptures, and then the hour-long main sermon began. Laura willed herself to concentrate as the deacon preached from the book of Romans. As he spoke, a baby began to moan. Laura looked down at her lap as the whining became louder. When Cindy elbowed her in the arm, Laura looked up.

"Look at Allen," Cindy whispered under her breath.

Laura looked over toward Allen and found him adjusting Mollie in his arms as she began to sob.

"Mmmmm. Lala! Lala!" Mollie yelled.

Allen's gaze collided with Laura's, his eyes wide and his expression mortified as Mollie continued to fuss.

Laura nodded, giving him the sign that she would take Mollie from him. Like a married couple, they each stood. With her cheeks flaming anew, she moved to the center of the barn, and he met her there, handing her Mollie.

"*Danki*," he whispered under his breath.

Laura gave him a shy smile, keenly aware of all the eyes burning into her skin as Mollie snuggled into her shoulder. She returned to her seat and sat with Mollie wrapped around her torso. As she rubbed the child's back, she hoped her face would return to a normal temperature.

Her eyes found Allen again, and he smiled at her.

"*Danki*," he mouthed once more as his expression warmed.

She nodded in response and took in his blue eyes and tanned face. His light-brown hair and beard were a sandy hue, thanks to the summer sun. He was handsome—really handsome. And not only was he attractive, but he was a good Christian man. He loved his daughter with his whole heart, and he was a kind, trustworthy confidant. Why hadn't she noticed this before? There was something different about him, but she couldn't put her finger on it—something warm, intimate, and comforting. It was as if she was seeing him in a new light.

Suddenly an unfamiliar heat flooded her. It was intense and overwhelming as it filled her chest, and her heart thudded against her rib cage.

Then it hit her like a thousand hay bales crashing down from the loft in her father's barn. Allen was more than a friend, even more than a new best friend. He was important to her, and she had feelings for him. She was *attracted* to him. She swallowed a gasp as the realization punched her in the stomach.

Oh no. No, no, no!

This was wrong! It *had* to be a sin! She couldn't think of Allen as more than a friend when she was in a serious, long-term relationship with Rudy. But was her relationship with Rudy truly long-term if he'd never even mentioned the word *marriage*?

She mentally shook herself. Any romantic thoughts about Allen were a betrayal to Rudy! After all, this was *Savilla's Allen*! He was off-limits, and he didn't even like her as more than a friend.

Then she recalled the night of the party, when Mollie called her "Lala" for the first time. The fine current of electricity shimming between Allen and her had been palpable. And if she were truly honest with herself, she'd have to admit she saw attraction in Allen's eyes. What would have happened if Rudy hadn't walked in on them?

Laura felt her eyes widen and the temperature in her cheeks rise at the thought of that intimate moment with Allen. She had to stop these insane thoughts! Her job was only to care for Mollie and run the house for Allen. She had to stop treading in this dangerous territory.

Pressing her lips together, Laura took in Allen's handsome face once again and tried to push away her inappropriate thoughts. Across the barn, Allen lifted his eyebrows as if to ask her if she was okay.

Laura looked down at Mollie to avert her eyes from his and break their trance.

Kayla leaned over and touched Mollie's leg. "You're so *gut* with her," she whispered. "She loves you."

"I love her too," Laura whispered, careful to keep her eyes on Mollie.

When she looked up again, she glanced over to Rudy and found him staring at her, his dark eyes narrowed and his face twisted in a frown. She tried to smile, but it felt more like a grimace.

With worry and guilt pressing down on her shoulders, she turned back toward the minister and tried to focus her thoughts on his message.

When the service ended, Cindy touched her arm. "Do you want to help serve the meal?"

"I'm not sure I'll be able to." Laura shifted Mollie in her arms.

"Would you like me to feed her?" Elsie walked over with Lily Rose in her arms. "I'm going to feed Christian in the kitchen, and I can feed her too."

"Are you sure?"

"Of course I am." Elsie nodded toward the barn doors. "When I was in the kitchen earlier, I noticed there were two high chairs. I can put Christian in one and Mollie in the other. I'll feed them while you all serve the men the meal."

"If it gets to be too much for you, then send someone to get me," Laura said.

"Of course."

"I'll walk to the kitchen with you and get Mollie settled." Laura retrieved the diaper bag from beneath the bench and followed Elsie out of the barn.

TWENTY-TWO

"How are you?" Vernon asked as Allen sat beside him at the table during lunch.

"I'm fine." Allen nodded and picked up a pretzel from his plate. "The shop has been keeping me busy. I picked up two more wrecked buggies last week, and I've been rebuilding one of them since then. I have an order for two buggies from a family with twin sons who just turned fifteen, which is great."

"That's *gut*." Vernon patted his shoulder. "I'm *froh* to hear the shop is keeping you busy. If you ever need to talk again, just let me know. I'd be glad to come visit you."

"You just want to get away from the farm and your chores," Mark said, teasing his father from across the table. "You like leaving everything for Jamie and me to do."

"Well, you know I am close to retirement age," Vernon said, teasing his son in return.

"That's true." Mark laughed.

Allen grinned. When Vernon turned to Noah beside him and asked him how work was at his furniture store, Allen glanced across the table to where Rudy was talking with Jamie. Although the conversation was friendly, Allen didn't miss the tightness in Rudy's jaw or the stiffness in his shoulders, as if irritation or frustration plagued him.

As he popped another pretzel into his mouth, Allen's thoughts turned to the service. When Laura handed Mollie off to him before the service began, he'd hoped to keep his daughter content with her pacifier. Mollie, however, had other plans and began to call for Laura during the first sermon. He was grateful Laura agreed to take her.

After Laura sat down with Mollie, he'd done his best to concentrate on the service, but his attention repeatedly gravitated to Laura. He wondered what had happened earlier in the service when she looked nervous, or maybe even stunned.

Later in the service, he glanced over at Rudy and found him scowling at Laura, which concerned Allen. Who was he kidding? Allen always worried about how Rudy treated Laura, even though he'd gathered their relationship had improved during the past few weeks.

Although Rudy had spoken to Allen more during the past month than he had since Savilla died, their conversations during the noon meal after church were superficial and felt forced. Rudy discussed only the weather or work. He was making an effort, but Allen was still aware of an undercurrent of distrust and resentment coming from his friend.

"*Kaffi?*"

Allen craned his neck and glanced over his shoulder. Laura had appeared, holding a carafe. She was radiant in her pink dress and white apron.

"*Ya, danki.*" He handed her his cup, and she filled it. "I can't thank you enough for helping me with Mollie during the service. I had no idea what to do when she started screaming for you. I considered taking her outside, but sometimes that can be even more disruptive."

"You don't need to thank me." She filled her father's cup. "I'm always *froh* to help." She nodded toward the barn doors. "Elsie is feeding Mollie lunch. Lily Rose is asleep in her infant seat, so she's feeding Christian and Mollie at the same time in the two high chairs she found in the kitchen. They were laughing and holding hands when I left."

"That's *wunderbaar. Danki.* I'll go get her when I'm done eating."

"Don't leave before I get a chance to say good-bye to her." Laura gave him a sweet smile and then walked away.

Allen angled his body toward her as she moved down the line, filling cups and chatting with the men. He studied her beautiful profile and admired how her eyes sparkled and her rosy lips curved up as she worked her way toward the end of the long table.

When he realized he'd been staring at her for too long, Allen swiveled around and picked up his coffee cup. He looked across the table and found Mark watching him with his eyebrows lifted and an expression of surprise—or maybe curiosity.

Uh oh!

Mark had caught Allen watching his twin, but Rudy was still engrossed in a conversation with Jamie. A thread of relief filtered through Allen. As he sipped his coffee, Allen braced himself, waiting for Mark to ask him why he was watching Laura. But Mark remained silent for a beat.

"So Allen," Mark finally began, "you mentioned you bought two wrecked buggies this week to rebuild. How often do you come across wrecked buggies to buy?"

Allen blinked, surprised Mark didn't mention Laura. "I normally find maybe one or two a month."

"How do you find them?" Mark picked up a pretzel and ate it.

"Sometimes I see them in advertisements in the paper, and other times people contact me and ask me if I'm interested."

Mark nodded slowly. "I guess each buggy has its own unique issue."

"That's right. Some are more damaged than others."

"Is that how you set the resale price?"

"*Ya*, it depends on how much money I have invested in the buggies." Allen fell into an easy conversation with Mark about his carriage business, but his mind remained stuck on Laura and how beautiful she looked in her pink dress today.

―∞―

"Would you like to go to the youth gathering? It's at the Bontragers'." Rudy stood beside his buggy after lunch.

"I don't think so." Laura shook her head. "I really just want to relax this afternoon and spend some time with my family."

"Mark is going." He pointed to his right, where her brother stood talking with two of the young women in their youth group, Franey and Ruthann. Then he pointed behind her. "I heard Jamie talking to Kayla about going to her *haus* to spend the afternoon with her family. So why exactly do you want to go home to spend time with your family?"

"*Mei dat* will be at the *haus*, and Cindy most likely will too. She hasn't gone to a youth gathering since before *mei mamm* died. Besides, I have to get up early tomorrow to go to Allen's, and I know I won't get much sleep at his *haus* next week." An idea gripped her, and she smiled. "Why don't you join us? We'll have some time to talk one-on-one without a crowd around. We can visit on the porch, and then you can eat with us too. What do you think?"

Rudy's posture stiffened. "You know, Laura, I've been trying to be a better boyfriend. I've had supper with you once a week and visited you every Saturday and Sunday for the past month. I've put you before *mei freinden*, and I've tried to be more patient with you and your job." His face clouded with a frown. "The least you could do is bend a little and put me before Allen and Mollie."

She bristled at his caustic tone. "What makes you think I don't put you before Allen and Mollie?"

"You're refusing to go to a youth gathering with me today because you have to be at his *haus* early tomorrow." He gestured behind her.

She spun to face the barn, where her father stood talking with Allen, Noah, and Jamie. Mollie rested her head on Allen's shoulder, and her heart tugged as she longed to join them before they left to go home. What was her problem? She'd see him and Mollie tomorrow.

"We don't have to stay at the Bontragers' long," Rudy said, his tone warming. "We can leave around suppertime if you'd like."

She swiveled toward him. "I really don't want to go."

His jaw locked. "Just last week you were complaining I don't spend enough time with you, but now you're refusing to spend time with me. You said you want things to be like they used to be, and we used to have a great time at the youth gatherings with our *freinden.* Which is it, Laura? Do you want to spend time with me or not?"

"I don't want to go to the youth gathering."

He opened his mouth to respond, and she held up her hand, silencing him.

"Please let me finish." She took a deep breath. "I want to go home, but I'd love for you to come and visit too. I just want to spend a quiet afternoon at home with you and my family."

And also with Allen and Mollie. She swallowed back the unexpected thought.

Rudy blew out a deep sigh. "Fine, but I think I'll pass. I guess I'll see you soon. Let me know if you want to have supper together one night this week. I'll wait for your call." He opened the door to his buggy and climbed in. "Have a *gut* week."

"What?" She held the door so he couldn't close it. "Don't blame this all on me. You say you want to spend time with me, but

213

you refuse to come to *mei haus* to visit. If you want to see me, why won't you do what I want to do?"

"Because I want to see our *freinden*."

"But that's not what I want. I don't want to play volleyball and listen to the *maed* talk about the *buwe* they like. I want to just relax and talk to *mei dat* before I have to leave to go to Allen's all week. I feel disconnected from my family."

"Do you feel disconnected from me?"

"*Ya*, I do." She leaned back against the door. "I've felt disconnected from you for a while now."

"That's your fault." He pointed at her chest. "That's because you're still staying over at Allen's *haus*."

"That's not true." Her voice trembled. "I've felt that way since before I started working for Allen."

He blanched as if she'd struck him. "Why would you say that?"

She took a step back. "I don't think this is the time to talk about it."

"Oh, no." He climbed out of the buggy and moved toward her. "I think it is time we talked about it. What did you mean by that?"

"I've felt that way since *mei mamm* died." Her eyes welled with tears. "I feel like we've grown apart and we don't relate to each other anymore. We used to have fun, but now I don't remember the last time we laughed together. Sometimes I wonder if we're still together just out of habit. We haven't dated other people, so we have no idea what a healthy relationship is supposed to feel like. Maybe our relationship is falling apart, and we just haven't admitted it to each other."

Rudy's mouth dropped open, but then he recovered to ask, "Why didn't you tell me you felt this way?"

"I don't know. I guess I wasn't sure how to put it into words."

"I've felt you pulling away from me, so maybe the problem isn't just me. Maybe it's you too."

"I think we should talk about this later." She wiped her hand across her eyes. "People are going to stare at us, and then rumors are going to start."

"So you feel like we've grown apart." His words were measured as if he were contemplating their meaning.

"*Ya.*"

His expression relaxed, warming his handsome face and dark eyes. "How can we fix that?"

"I think the only way we can fix that is by spending more time together and talking."

He nodded. "But how can we spend more time together if you're at Allen's *haus* all week and can only have supper with me once a week?"

"You can visit me there. You can come for supper a couple of times a week."

"I don't think so."

"Why not?"

He leaned back against the buggy. "Why would I want to have supper at Allen's *haus*?"

"To see me." She laid a palm on her chest. "And to spend time with Allen and Mollie. I thought you said you want to be a better *freind* to Allen, and this is one of the ways you can be."

Rudy folded his arms over his chest. "I don't know. I'd rather visit with you in private."

"Then come over to *mei haus* this afternoon. We can talk about everything that's bothering us."

Rudy hesitated, and her heart fractured a little. Did he love her at all?

Mollie cried out, and Laura spun toward the barn where Allen was still talking with the men. Allen adjusted Mollie in his arms, and she settled down, resting her cheek on his shoulder.

"It's time for her nap," she whispered.

"Unbelievable," Rudy muttered as he climbed into the buggy.

She turned toward him. "What did you say?"

"I said unbelievable." He slammed the buggy door. "You don't even realize how attached you are to Mollie. It's like I've said before. It's as if you're her *mamm*."

"What do you mean this time?" She stepped over to the buggy.

"During the service, the way he handed Mollie off to you, you and Allen looked like a married couple. Then you held her against your chest like a *mamm* during the rest of the service. I heard someone behind me ask if Savilla had been gone a year yet and if you and Allen were engaged."

"Are you serious?" Her stomach seemed to drop to her knees.

"*Ya*, I am serious." He scowled. "Do you have any idea how it felt to have someone wonder if my girlfriend is engaged to another man?"

"I don't know what to say."

"You're really going to act surprised?"

"I am surprised. I thought people knew I was helping Allen while Irma Mae was healing from her accident. I've held Mollie during church services before."

"Today was the first time you and Allen handed her off during the church service like a married couple." His smile was wry. "Maybe you should have thought about how other people perceive you before you put on that display for the entire congregation to see."

She stared at him, taking in his furious eyes and deep scowl. "You're angry with me because someone else misinterpreted my friendship with Allen?"

"You need to stop acting so naïve, Laura. It's getting old." He grabbed the reins. "I'm going to the youth gathering. I'll see you later."

Before she could respond, Rudy guided the horse down the

driveway toward the road. Her body trembled as her emotional conversation with Rudy echoed through her mind. She needed someone to talk to, someone to help her sort through her confusing feelings, and she could always count on her twin to be honest with her.

She turned toward Mark's buggy and spotted him leaning against it while still talking to Franey and Ruthann. With his arms folded over his chest and a wide grin on his face, he said something and then laughed as the eager young women giggled. Mark was hard at work flirting. He didn't need her to interrupt his fun with her emotional turmoil.

Squaring her shoulders, she took a deep breath to quell her raging emotions and walked over to where her father still stood with Jamie, Noah, and Allen. She plastered a smile on her face as she approached. "Hi."

"Laura." *Dat* smiled. "I thought you were going to the youth gathering with Rudy and Mark."

"No, I decided I'd rather go home with you and relax." Her gaze landed on Allen, and his kind eyes studied her. She found encouragement and possibly even understanding there, and the tension in her shoulders and back released. Could he sense her emotions the way Mark could? No, that was impossible. Allen wasn't her twin or even her brother. But then why did his expression calm her the way Mark's could?

She shoved the thoughts away and turned back to her father. "Did Cindy say she wanted to come home too?"

"*Ya*, I believe she did." *Dat* pivoted toward the house. "I think she was in the kitchen. Would you mind going to find her?"

"No, not at all." She said good-bye to Jamie and Noah and then touched Mollie's arm. "I'll see you tomorrow."

Mollie yawned and rubbed her eyes before burying her face in Allen's shoulder.

"She's ready for her nap," Allen said.

"I see that." She looked up at him. "Bye."

"Have a restful afternoon."

"You too."

As Laura walked toward the house, she tried to redirect her thoughts to her afternoon, but she couldn't stop thinking about what Rudy had said to her. Were he and Mark right when they said she was getting too attached to Mollie? Was this attachment going to damage Mollie when Irma Mae did come back to care for her? She never wanted to hurt Mollie, but she also didn't know how to let her go.

And the real question? How could she let Allen go?

TWENTY-THREE

"*DANKI* FOR COMING BY MY SHOP." ALLEN SHOOK THE customer's hand. "I hope your *sohn* enjoys the buggy."

"I'm certain he will. Have a *gut* day." The man climbed into the flat bed where the buggy was loaded, and then his diesel truck rattled down the rock driveway.

When a horse and buggy came up the driveway, Allen stepped out of the shop and walked over to greet the customer. The morning sun was bright as a warm early October breeze brushed his cheeks.

The driver halted the horse in front of a hitching post, just outside the shop.

"*Gude mariye,*" Allen called as the Amish man climbed out of his buggy.

"*Gude mariye,*" John Smucker, his church district's bishop, responded as he tied his horse to the hitching post. It had been two weeks since Allen attended the service in the Smuckers' barn. At sixty-seven, John had salt-and-pepper hair and a matching beard. He stood several inches shorter than Allen and had a rotund waist and bright, intelligent hazel eyes.

"John." Allen tried to mask his surprise as he shook the bishop's hand. "It's so nice to see you. What brings you out here today?"

"I was wondering if I could speak with you." John's expression was friendly, but worried knots still filled Allen's gut.

"Absolutely." Allen made a sweeping gesture toward his shop. "We can sit in my office. Would you like a bottle of water?"

"Oh, no *danki.*" John followed Allen into the office.

Allen gestured for him to sit in the desk chair while he pulled up a stool. "What can I do for you?"

As John paused and fingered his beard, the knots in Allen's gut fused into heavy balls of lead.

"There have been some concerns in the district," John finally said.

"Okay." Allen rested his work boots on the rung of the stool as his throat dried. "What has been the concern?"

John pressed his lips together. "It has been brought to my attention that Laura Riehl has been spending the night in your *haus* for quite some time. Is that true?"

Allen swallowed. *So this is it.* "*Ya*, that's true. She's been staying to help me with Mollie since August. Mollie started crying out in the middle of the night after Irma Mae had her accident. At times she cried for hours, and it was too much for me to handle along with running my business. Laura sleeps in Mollie's room and soothes her if she wakes up. She's only here to take care of Mollie."

John nodded slowly as if contemplating Allen's words. "I understand you've been through a difficult time, and you're only trying to take care of your *boppli* and run your business. However, you do realize how inappropriate it is for Laura to stay over when you're not married, right?"

Allen's stomach twisted. "I do see how this could be perceived, but Laura is working as my nanny, and I'm paying her. It's strictly platonic, and Irma Mae is doing really well. She's looking forward to returning. I'll need Laura's help for only a couple more weeks." Saying the words aloud made him dread that day.

"I understand, but is there a chance Laura could work for you without staying overnight?"

"*Ya*, but I really don't understand why there's a problem." Allen gestured toward his house. "I have five bedrooms, and there's nothing inappropriate going on between us. She and I have been *freinden* for years. She was *mei fraa's* best *freind*."

John frowned. "I'm aware, but some rumors have been circulating, and I wanted to say something to you before this becomes even more of an issue."

"Rumors?" Allen sat up straight. "What kind of rumors?"

"You know I abhor gossip because of how destructive and sinful it is. Yet sometimes there's a bit of truth buried deep in it." John rested his folded hands on the desk. "A couple of weeks ago, after the church service, a church member expressed concern about your relationship. Then another member told me Laura has been staying over for more than two months. After church on Sunday, the concerns were raised to me again."

"Wait a minute." Allen held up his hand as irritation swept through him. "Why would someone express concern about my relationship with Laura after a church service?"

"There is a perception that your relationship is more than just friendly."

"Why would someone perceive us that way?"

"I suppose it's because of how you interact at church. Mollie is very attached to Laura, and someone commented that you act as if you're married."

Anger shoved Allen off the stool, and he stood in front of the desk. "Why would someone say that? Mollie is attached to Laura because Laura takes *gut* care of her. We don't act like we're married. We're just *gut freinden* who happen to both love *mei dochder*."

John held up his hands as if to tame Allen's ire. "I understand. You don't need to get upset. But you know how people in any community can talk. I'm only here to warn you before the rumors get out of hand."

"I don't understand why members of my church district would talk that way about Laura." Allen's body shook with frustration. "They've known her since she was a *kind*. Why would they assume she's having an inappropriate relationship with me?"

"I agree. I've known Laura since she was born, and she's a *gut maedel* from a *gut* family. However, I think it's in your best interest and Laura's best interest if she only works for you during the day. Like you said, Irma Mae is getting better, and she'll be back soon."

Allen looked out the window toward his house and lifted his straw hat. He pushed his hand through his thick hair and tried in vain to calm his simmering temper. "I still don't understand why anyone would assume the worst about Laura."

"I'm here to stop the rumors. Please sit, Allen."

Allen sat down on the stool.

"I know you, and I know Laura. You would never disrespect Laura or put her reputation in jeopardy."

Allen frowned. "I would never do anything to hurt her."

"That's why I'm suggesting Laura only work for you during the day." John's expression brightened. "I've instructed the people who came to me to stop the rumors from spreading, and I told them I would make sure this situation is resolved. It's best for you and for Laura if you stop giving people the wrong impression."

Allen rubbed his shoulder where a new knot of tension throbbed. "I just don't understand why this is such a big deal. Irma Mae stayed overnight to care for Mollie. Laura is Mollie's nanny."

"But Irma Mae is family, and Laura is not. Plus it would be different if you had hired a grandmotherly nanny to come and stay overnight rather than a young, unmarried woman like Laura."

Allen opened his mouth to protest and say that Laura was, in fact, family to him. But then he closed it.

"Do you agree Laura should not stay overnight?" John asked.

"*Ya.*" Allen nodded, despite his disagreement. "*Danki* for making me aware of the rumors."

"*Gern gschehne.*" John pointed toward the driveway. "Did I see a customer leaving with a buggy?"

"*Ya*, he bought it for his *sohn.*"

"Your business has been booming lately."

"It has." Allen stretched out his legs. "I sold three buggies last week. I've sold two so far this week, and it's only Wednesday."

"That's *wunderbaar.*"

When the bishop had gone, Allen closed up his shop and headed into the mudroom. The house was quiet, and he walked through the first floor. It was empty. He climbed the stairs, and the hum of the sewing machine filled the stairwell and grew louder as he made his way to the top. He glanced into Mollie's bedroom and found her sleeping in her crib. Then he padded past two spare rooms to the sewing room.

When he reached the doorway, he stopped and leaned his shoulder against the doorframe. He drank in Laura's profile as she worked at the sewing table. Her eyes were focused on the gray shirt she was mending. Her pretty brow wrinkled as if she were deep in concentration on her task. He admired her high cheekbones, her long, slender neck, and her slight shoulders. She was beautiful.

And then the bishop's words echoed in his mind.

I suppose it's because of how you interact at church. Mollie is very attached to Laura, and someone commented that you act as if you're married.

And then realization punched him in his gut. Did his overwhelming admiration for and attraction to Laura give their community the wrong idea about their relationship? He had to get his emotions under control. Any inappropriate feelings for her were disrespectful both to her and to Savilla.

"Allen?"

He snapped out of his mental tirade and stepped into the room. "Hi."

She frowned. "Is it lunchtime already?" She looked at the clock on the desk. "Oh, it's only 10:45." She turned back to him. "Is something wrong?"

"I was wondering if we could talk."

"Oh." She spun on the bench, facing him as he pulled a chair over to the table and sat down across from her. "What do you want to talk about?"

"The bishop was just here to see me."

Her eyes widened. "Why?"

"Apparently there has been some gossip about us, and John feels you should stop staying overnight here. He's concerned about the perception of our relationship."

Her mouth twisted into a frown. "Why do people always assume the worst? You need me here, and Mollie needs me. We can't allow what others say to dictate what we do. The members of the community just don't understand our situation. Did you explain you need me to help you so you can get your rest and run your carriage shop?"

A smile overtook Allen's lips, and her dark eyebrows drew together.

"What's so funny?"

He grinned. "I just remembered something Savilla once said to me."

"What did she say?"

"She said all the Riehl *kinner* are stubborn, and she was right."

"You think I'm stubborn?" She sat up straighter and gestured around the room. "I'm just stating the facts. You need me to take care of Mollie until Irma Mae is well enough to do it, and that's what I'm doing. Did you explain that to John?"

He leaned his elbow on the sewing table. "I tried to, but he had some *gut* points. I can't risk your reputation."

Her dark eyebrows drew together again. "My reputation?"

"I can't risk folks thinking you're someone you're not. Irma Mae is getting better every day. She looked great on Sunday when Milton brought her to church. I'm sure she'll be back here soon. I can manage at night until she's back."

"I'm worried about you. You need your rest."

His heart warmed at her words. "I appreciate that, but I can't risk hurting you. I'll be fine. I'll close up my shop at five, and you can eat supper with Mollie and me or go home. It's up to you. I'll pay my driver to pick you up in the morning."

She hesitated. "I don't know."

"You mentioned the other day that Mollie hasn't cried out at night for a month. I think she's been back on her regular schedule for a while now. So, honestly, it isn't necessary for you to stay over anymore."

She nodded. "You're right. I guess I just got used to it. I suppose I'm just as attached to Mollie as she is to me. It's probably better that I go back home at night so she can start adjusting to not having me around. It's going to be tough on her when Irma Mae comes back, and I don't want to hurt her emotionally."

"Exactly. Just tell me what time you want to come over. My driver can take you home at night too."

She shook her head. "I can't let you spend that money. Mark can bring me over in the morning, and I'll have him pick me up."

"No. Mark has enough to do on your *dat*'s farm. I insist on paying for your rides. It's the right thing to do."

She frowned. "Fine."

He suppressed another smile. She was adorable when she was irritated. But she was Rudy's girlfriend. His stomach soured at the memory of Rudy's cruel words the night of Mollie's party.

"Penny for your thoughts." She leaned closer to him.

"How are things with Rudy? Have they gotten better?"

Her expression clouded as she looked down at her lap. "No, not really."

His jaw tightened as he leaned closer to her. "What's going on?"

"I really need to finish repairing this shirt for you." She turned back toward the sewing machine. "I noticed it was ripped when I was doing laundry yesterday." She arranged the shirt under the machine.

"Laura." He rested his hand on her shoulder.

She spun toward him again and took a deep breath. "He said he was going to work at being a better boyfriend. I admitted I wasn't being a *gut* girlfriend, and I've tried to fix things. I've made more time for him, and I've tried to be more attentive when we're together. He's tried to, but I haven't seen him make any real changes." She glanced up at him, and her eyes glittered. "I think things are worse."

"Worse how?" Alarm threaded through his veins. *If Rudy hurt her...*

"He's been angry with me because I refused to go to the youth gatherings with him the past couple of weeks, but I just want to spend time with my family on Sundays." She sniffed. "It's like we've grown apart and we have nothing in common anymore. I don't know how to relate to him, and he doesn't know how to relate to me."

"All your problems with Rudy are because of me, aren't they?"

She hesitated.

"You can be honest with me. I can sense his jealousy when we're at church. I see him frowning when you hold Mollie or when you talk to me." Allen touched his chest. "I don't want to be the reason you break up."

"If we do break up, it won't be because of you." She wiped

away a tear trickling down her cheek. "I think our problems go deeper than just the fact that I work here."

"What do you mean?"

"I've changed since *Mamm* died, and I don't think he understands me anymore. He doesn't understand I've had to take on more responsibilities at home, and I need more than youth groups and singings. Now he doesn't comprehend why I'm so close to Mollie and why I love her so much." Her voice quavered. "He keeps reminding me I'm not Mollie's *mamm*, but I never said I was. I just care about her so deeply because she's all I have left of Savilla." She paused. "No, it's more than that. I love her for herself."

He took a trembling breath as both grief and gratitude rose inside of him. "I know," he whispered.

"I keep wondering if Rudy is right about my relationship with Mollie. Maybe I'm wrong to be so attached to her." She tilted her head as her eyes seemed to search his. "Do you think I've overstepped my bounds with Mollie?"

"No." He shook his head. "But maybe I've overstepped my bounds with you."

"What do you mean?"

"Maybe I've become too dependent on you."

Her gazed locked with his, and his heart thudded as she stared into his eyes. An overwhelming attraction surrounded him. He felt the urge to hold her hand and pull her to him for a hug. Where had this sudden and deep affection come from? And how could he allow himself to feel this way about her after losing Savilla less than a year ago?

Mollie cried out, and Laura popped up from the bench. "I need to go get her. After she's settled I'll start on lunch."

Before he could respond, she was gone.

Allen rubbed his hand down his face and beard. His gaze

moved to the sewing table, where the gray shirt sat awaiting Laura's diligent hands to finish mending it. Laura took such good care of him and Mollie. She was their caregiver, their guardian angel.

Her emotional words about Mollie echoed through his mind.

I just care about her so deeply because she's all I have left of Savilla.

Sorrow coursed through him, squeezing his heart and tightening his throat. He missed Savilla so much that his bones ached for her. Perhaps his feelings for Laura were only misdirected grief for Savilla.

But if that were true, why were the emotions so strong, so overwhelming, so deep?

Dismissing the thoughts, he stood. He had to get hold of himself and rein in his confused emotions. Laura was his friend, and she would never be more than a friend. Any intense affection for her was dangerous, and, most of all, it was sinful.

As he approached Mollie's bedroom door, he silently vowed to reject any affection for Laura. He couldn't risk her reputation or her chances for a renewed relationship with Rudy. He needed to focus on being her friend, and only her friend.

TWENTY-FOUR

"LAURA! YOU'RE HOME!" CINDY EXCLAIMED AS LAURA set her tote bag on a kitchen chair later that evening.

"*Ya*." Laura joined her at the sink and began drying the dishes in the drainboard.

"Why are you home tonight?" Cindy stopped scrubbing a pot and turned toward her.

"Allen doesn't need me overnight anymore because Mollie doesn't wake up at night anymore." It wasn't exactly a fib since Mollie had slept through the night for weeks now. Still, she was too embarrassed to share the details of Allen's visit with the bishop. "Now I can help you with more chores." She scanned the kitchen. "I can mop after the dishes are done tonight, or—"

"I mopped this afternoon." Cindy faced her. "Is everything all right?"

"Oh, *ya*." Laura stacked dishes in the cabinet. "How was your day?"

"It was *gut*." Cindy swiveled back to the sink and returned to scrubbing the pot. "I did a little sewing after chores." Her eyes brightened. "Oh, Kayla's parents, Nathan, Eva, and Junior all came for supper last night. It was so *gut* to see them."

Guilt settled heavily on Laura's chest as she imagined Cindy cleaning the house and then cooking for all those guests. Laura should be helping her sister with the chores at the farm. But at the same time, Allen and Mollie also needed her. Why did she feel so torn between her family and the Lambert family?

"Laura?"

"Huh?" She spun toward her sister, who was studying her. "I'm sorry. What did you say?"

Cindy rested her hand on her small hip. *"Was iss letz?"*

"Nothing is wrong. I'm fine." Laura swallowed. How could she possibly admit to her sister that the bishop had come to Allen's house to let him know community members were gossiping about her relationship with him?

The storm door opened and clicked shut, and after a few moments Mark entered the kitchen.

"Sis!" He crossed the kitchen. "What are you doing home? Isn't it only Wednesday?"

"Ya, it is." Laura leaned against the counter. "Allen doesn't need me overnight anymore."

"That's *gut* news." He sat down in a kitchen chair. "I guess that means Mollie is sleeping better?"

"Ya, she is. Allen is going to pay his driver to pick me up in the mornings and bring me home at suppertime now."

"That's great." Mark smiled.

"What's been going on around here all week?"

"Hmm." Mark rubbed his chin. "I'm not sure anything really interesting is going on. Can you think of anything, Cindy?"

Cindy shrugged and then set the pot on the drainboard. Laura picked it up and began drying it.

Mark snapped his fingers. "Florence Esh and her *sohn* and *dochder* are coming for supper tomorrow night."

"Who?" Laura faced her twin.

"You know. *Dat's* new *freind.*"

Laura froze. "I have no idea what you're talking about." She turned to Cindy. "Who's Florence?"

"His *freind.*" Cindy frowned, her posture rigid. "He met her at the library, and they've been talking for a couple of weeks."

"I don't understand." Laura looked over at her twin again. "His *freind*?"

"You know." Mark gestured. "She's like his girlfriend."

Laura opened her mouth to gasp, but air was trapped in her lungs.

"I'm sure I told you," Mark continued. "They've met for lunch a couple of times, and then he had supper at her *haus* on Monday. She's coming tomorrow night so we can all meet her and two of her *kinner.*"

"No one told me about this." Laura growled the words at him. "Why didn't you tell me?" She divided a look between Mark and Cindy.

Cindy cleared her throat and then shook her head. "I'm going to go take a shower." Then she walked out of the kitchen. After a moment, her footsteps echoed in the stairwell.

"Why didn't you tell me?" Laura repeated, gritting her teeth.

"I thought I did." He shook his head. "I'm sorry. You're not around much."

With her mind rocking unsteadily between irritation and guilt, she turned back to the drainboard. "You're right. I haven't been around much. I'm sorry." She picked up a handful of utensils and began drying them. Then she dropped them into the utensil drawer.

"What's going on with you, Laura?"

"Nothing." She kept working, but she knew she was caught.

He walked over and leaned on the end of the counter. "Once again, you know you can't lie to me, right?"

"I'm not lying." She kept her eyes focused on her task to avoid his stare.

"Look, if there's something you need to discuss, you can always trust—"

"Laura! What a pleasant surprise!" *Dat's* voice filled the kitchen.

Laura blew out a sigh of relief. "Hi, *Dat*." She dropped the last of the utensils into the draw and then spun toward her father and Jamie.

"What are you doing home tonight?" Jamie asked as he sat down at the table.

"Allen doesn't need my help overnight anymore." She hung the dish towels on the oven handle.

"I'm glad to hear it." *Dat's* smile was as bright as she'd ever seen it.

Suspicion crept into her mind. Was he that happy because he'd met someone? Her stomach soured. Did this mean *Dat* was going to get married? Why didn't he tell her he had a girlfriend? Why didn't *anyone* tell her *Dat* was even dating?

Anger and betrayal nearly overcame her. But did she have any right to feel betrayed when she'd put Allen and Mollie's needs before her family's for months now?

Dat sank into the chair across from Jamie. "So what's on your agenda for tomorrow, Jamie?"

"I was thinking about painting my porch railings." Jamie cupped his hand over his mouth to stifle a yawn. "That is, if I have the energy."

Dat grinned. "I think you should go home and get some sleep."

Laura retrieved her tote bag from the chair. "I'm going to go unpack. *Gut nacht.*"

"*Gut nacht,*" *Dat* and Jamie responded in unison.

She glanced back at Mark and found he was still staring at her. Then she hurried up the stairs to her bedroom, where she began to unpack her clothes while trying to comprehend how her father could move on with his life without her mother.

"You can't hide your feelings from me."

Laura's chest tightened as she faced the window, her twin's image reflected in the panes as he leaned on the doorframe. She turned toward him. "Maybe I just don't want to talk."

"Why would anyone not want to talk to me?" He smirked as he entered her room and sat down on the corner of her bed. "You know the *maed* at our youth group can't resist me."

She rolled her eyes. "I know you a lot better than they do. I've known you since before we were born."

His grin dissolved. "Talk to me, sis. I can't stand it when you're hurting." He touched his chest.

Her lower lip trembled at his tenderness. "I'm just so confused."

"About what?"

"Everything." She sank onto the chair across from the bed. "*Dat* is dating. How can he possibly move on when the rest of us are still lost without *Mamm*?"

Mark sighed. "I think it's more complicated than that. He's lonely. Florence is a widow, so they can relate to each other in a way we don't really understand."

"Is Cindy having a hard time with it?"

Mark nodded. "She is, but we'll help her through it."

"Why didn't you tell me?" She sniffed and wiped at her eyes.

"I'm sorry. I honestly thought I did." He pressed his lips together in a thin line. "Can you forgive me?"

"*Ya.*" She nodded.

"What else is bothering you?"

"What do you mean?"

"You were upset before I mentioned Florence Esh."

She fingered the hem of her apron while debating what to share.

"Have I ever given you a reason not to trust me?"

She met his eyes, and they seemed to plead with her, reminding her of a puppy dog's. "I didn't tell you the real reason

I'm home tonight." Then she shared what Allen told her about the bishop's visit. "I wanted to stay there to ensure Allen can get his proper rest before working in the shop, but he insisted I come home."

"Allen was right to send you home. He's protecting you and your reputation."

She frowned. "I can't believe someone went to the bishop and insinuated something inappropriate is going on at Allen's *haus*. He needs me there to help him with Mollie."

"I'm sure he'll do just fine. He's her *dat*. And you said she's been sleeping fine at night, so maybe it's been time for you to come home for a while."

"I know." She sniffed as tears flooded her eyes again. "I feel like I belong at Allen's *haus*, but I also feel like I should be here helping Cindy with the chores." A tear trickled down her cheek, and she wiped it away. "I'm so confused, and I miss *Mamm* and Savilla. I don't know where I belong. I feel like the world is changing at lightning speed, and I need it to slow down so I can catch my breath."

He was silent, and her shoulders tightened with knots.

"Just spit it out," she insisted.

"You're too attached to Allen and Mollie."

She scowled. "Why do you keep saying that to me?"

"Because it's true." He folded his arms over his blue shirt. "Irma Mae will be back in a couple of weeks, and you're going to be devastated. You need to start letting go before you're crushed. And it's going to be hard on Mollie. You need to think about how difficult this adjustment is going to be for her too."

"I know you're right, and earlier today I was even thinking about how Mollie will adjust without me. But I don't have to let go of Mollie. I can still go visit her at least once a week." She gestured around the room. "Cindy and I can make time in our schedules to stop by and see how Allen and Mollie are doing."

He tilted his head. "How are things with Rudy?"

"Not *gut*." She shook her head. "He's been distant."

"You should invite him over tomorrow night to have supper with us so he can meet Florence and her *kinner* too."

"That's a *gut* idea."

"I'm full of *gut* ideas." When he stood, his grin was back. "I'm going to take a shower. I'll see you in the morning." He started for the door.

"Thanks for talking with me."

Laura finished her unpacking and then headed downstairs.

When she entered the mudroom, she pulled on a sweater and picked up a lantern before walking outside to the phone shanty. The crisp evening air tickled her nose as her shoes crunched the rock path. She dialed the number for Rudy's family and waited for their voice mail to pick up.

"You've reached the Swarey family," his mother's voice said. "Please leave us a message. Thank you."

"Hi, Rudy," she said, tapping her fingers on the counter. "This is Laura. I want to invite you over for supper at my family's *haus* tomorrow night since we haven't had supper together yet this week. We're going to eat at six. I'd love for you to join us. I hope you're having a *gut* week. Call me when you can. *Danki.*"

She hung up the phone and then gazed out toward Jamie's house. When she spotted a light burning on the porch, her curiosity propelled her down his path. His silhouette came into view as she approached.

"Laura?" Jamie asked as she climbed the porch steps.

"Hi." When she reached the top of the steps, she set the lantern on the porch floor and leaned against the railing. "I thought you were going to go to bed early."

"I decided to sit outside and enjoy this *schee* night. It's a relief to feel the cool air after the brutal summer we just endured." He paused, his blue eyes assessing her. "Is there something you want to discuss?"

She picked at the wood railing. "Do you have a minute to talk?"

"Of course." He patted the rocking chair beside him.

"Danki." She sat down next to him and then angled her body toward him. "How long have you known about Florence?"

He leaned back in the chair and folded his hands in his lap.

She frowned. "You've known for a long time?"

"Ya. Dat told me about her the day he met her."

"When was that?"

He stared out toward the pasture. "I guess it was about a month ago. He'd gone to the library, and he was standing in line to check out his books when she got in line behind him. She had a large stack of Christian novels, and she dropped a few. He helped her pick them up, and they started talking. I guess they hit it off."

"What do you know about her?"

"Well, she's in her mid-fifties. She lost her husband about eighteen months ago—a massive heart attack."

Laura shook her head. *"Ach.* How *bedauerlich."*

"Ya. She has one *sohn* at home, and he's twenty. His name is Roy. And she has a *dochder* still at home, Sarah Jane. She's nineteen. Her elder *sohn*, Walter, is around my age and married. He has two *kinner."*

"What did her husband do for a living?"

"He was a farmer. Walter has been supporting her since he died. She and her younger *sohn* and *dochder* live in the *daadihaus,* and Walter runs the farm."

"Oh." She moved the rocking chair back and forth. "Why did *Dat* only feel comfortable telling you about her at first?"

"I don't know. Maybe because I'm the oldest." He shook his head. "He was worried about how you, Cindy, and Mark would react."

She shook her head as renewed feelings of betrayal and disappointment filled her chest. "I don't understand why no one told me until tonight."

"Wait a minute." He stopped rocking and leaned toward her. "You didn't know about Florence until tonight?"

"Mark just mentioned off-handedly that they're coming for supper when I asked him what was new."

"I'm sorry. I thought someone told you. *Dat* told Cindy and Mark last week."

She looked out at the darkness separating the houses. She felt like a stranger in her own home. Her heart ached, but she pushed away the hurt and turned toward her brother. "Are you ready to get married in December?"

He blew out a gust of air, and then his expression grew sheepish. "The *haus* is ready, so I suppose I am too."

She chuckled. "You and Kayla are great together. I know it will be *wunderbaar*."

"I just hope I can make her *froh*."

"You will." *I pray I can find that same kind of love someday.* She blinked at the unexpected thought. Then she stood. "Well, I guess I'll let you get to bed. *Gut nacht*."

"*Gut nacht*."

She retrieved the lantern and started down the steps.

When she reached the back porch, she spun and looked toward Jamie's house. Her conversation with him filtered through her mind. While she understood why her siblings had forgotten to tell her about Florence, the oversight still caused her chest to get tight and cold, like a fist of ice was squeezing at her heart.

She suddenly felt as if the world were spinning faster and faster and she might float off into space. When would her world right itself? And how could she cope until it did?

TWENTY-FIVE

"WE MADE YOU A SURPRISE FOR BREAKFAST," ALLEN announced when she entered his kitchen the following morning.

"Lala!" Mollie called from the high chair before scooping food into her mouth.

"Hi, Mollie." Laura set her tote bag on a kitchen chair before kissing Mollie's head. Then she stepped over to the counter where Allen stood. "What's the surprise?"

Allen held up a pan with an exaggerated flourish. "A breakfast casserole!"

A deep belly laugh escaped her lips, and his grin widened.

"It has *brot*, egg, cheese, and bacon it in." His face was filled with pride.

"Why did you do that if you despise casseroles?"

"I never said I despise them." He cut a slice and placed it on a plate as he spoke. "I just grew tired of them. It's like the expected bereavement meal, and at one point my refrigerator and freezer were stocked with all kinds of casseroles. I remember one evening wishing I had steak and potatoes instead of a hamburger casserole." He sliced another piece. "But at the same time, I appreciated the generosity and love baked into every one."

She shook her head. "Love and generosity baked into the casseroles? That's poetic."

He handed her one of the plates. "Here you go. A breakfast casserole to thank you for all your hard work."

"*Danki.*" Her smile dissolved as dread stabbed at her belly. Why had he made her breakfast? Was today her last day? Was Irma Mae ready to take the job back?

"You don't like breakfast casseroles?"

"Oh, it's not that. I was wondering what the occasion is."

"No occasion, really. Mollie and I were up early, and I remembered Savilla had a recipe for a breakfast casserole she used to make for us on Christmas Day."

Her chest constricted at the mention of her best friend's name.

He gave her an embarrassed smile. "I just wanted to do something nice for you."

Her heart warmed. *"Danki."*

"*Gern gschehne.*" He picked up the second plate. "Would you sit and eat with me before I go out to the shop?"

"Of course." She sat down across from him at the table and bowed her head in silent prayer. After a few moments, she dug into the casserole. "This is *appeditlich*. Maybe you should start doing the cooking."

He shook his head. "You're just being nice."

"It really is *gut*." She glanced over at Mollie, who ate while humming to herself. "How did she sleep last night?"

"Fine." He wiped his beard with a paper napkin. "I woke up at one and was convinced I'd heard her. But when I checked on her, she was fast asleep. I guess I was expecting to hear her, but she slept through the night."

"That's great."

"How was your night?"

Laura took a sip of coffee as she recalled her conversations with her brothers. "It was strange."

"Strange?"

"I found out *mei dat* is seeing someone."

"Really?" Allen's eyes widened.

"*Ya*. He's been seeing her for a month, and I was the last person to know." She summarized the whole story.

He placed his fork on his plate and looked at her, his eyes full of what looked like concern. "How do you feel about it?"

"I don't know." She rested her arm on the table. "I was awake for a while last night just staring at the ceiling. My thoughts kept going and going, like a river. I kept thinking about all my favorite memories of my parents together. If *mei dat* marries Florence, she'll sit in *mei mamm*'s chair. She'll cook the meals and try to offer me advice. And she has a *dochder* and *sohn* living at home, so I'll have a new *schweschder* and *bruder*. I don't know how I feel about that. I guess that means Roy would take my room, and I'll move back in with Cindy. Or maybe Sarah Jane would move in with Cindy, and I'd have to take the sewing room."

She pulled a deep breath through her nose as her thoughts turned to her sister. "I don't think Cindy is taking this well. She left the room when Mark started talking about Florence. I went to check on her late last night, but she was asleep. I don't know how she'll adjust to all of this. She took *mei mamm*'s death the worst of all of us because she blamed herself for her accident a long time."

She sniffed and wiped at her eyes. "This is all so strange and scary. I know I should accept it because *mei dat* has a right to be *froh*." She pointed at Allen. "Just like you have a right to be *froh* and move on when the time is right for you."

Something unreadable flashed in his eyes.

"I feel selfish for even doubting *mei dat*'s decision to move on. It's been more than a year, and he has the right to fall in love again. But why was I the last one to know? Why didn't any of my siblings or *mei dat* think to tell me?" Her voice broke, and she covered her face with her hands. *Oh no*. Why did she have to get emotional in front of Allen again? Why couldn't she keep it together until he went out to the shop?

"*Ach*, Laura."

A chair pushed back, and a moment later she heard rustling beside her.

"Laura." His voice was warm and comforting beside her ear. "It's okay to be upset. You've been through so much, and this is yet another change."

"I know." She wiped her eyes with a napkin before looking up at him. "But Florence and her two younger *kinner* are coming to supper tonight." She smiled as an idea formed in her head. "Why don't you join us? I left a message for Rudy too."

He frowned. "*Danki*, but I don't think that's a *gut* idea."

"Why not?" She sniffed again. "You're family, and I want Florence to meet all of the people who are important to me."

His expression warmed. "I appreciate that, but I'm not sure Mollie and I belong there. We'll meet her if she comes to church with your *dat*, right?"

"*Ya*, I guess so." She slouched at the disappointment. She'd hoped Allen would come since he was a source of strength and confidence to her. Allen could help her get through this awkward and emotional supper tonight.

Then Mark's warning echoed through her mind. *You're getting too attached to Allen and Mollie.*

Mark was right. Not only had she become too attached to Mollie, but she'd allowed herself to get too close to Allen as well. Uneasiness flashed through her veins.

"I think it's great that Florence is coming to supper," he continued, oblivious to her inner turmoil. "You'll have to tell me all about her tomorrow."

"Okay." She dismissed the disappointment.

He pushed his chair back and moved to the other side of the

table. "I better finish my breakfast and then go. I have a couple of customers stopping by to look at buggies today."

"That's *wunderbaar*. Your business has been booming for months now."

When Allen headed outside, Laura set to cleaning up the kitchen. Her twin's words intruded as she worked, but she rejected them. She would do her best to let go of her attachment to Allen and Mollie. Instead she would concentrate on just taking good care of Mollie. That was her job.

—∞—

Later that afternoon, Allen sat at his desk and worked on his accounting books. He'd sold two buggies that morning, bringing a grand total of five sold this week, and it was only Thursday. His business was a blessing, and he was grateful his grandparents had left him enough both in real estate and in cash to buy this business when he moved to Bird-in-Hand.

If only he still had a wife with whom to share it.

He tried to concentrate on his accounting books. But then Laura's words from earlier filtered through his mind.

I know I should accept it because mei dat *has a right to be* froh. *Just like you have a right to be* froh *and move on when the time is right for you.*

Her words had punched him in the chest, sending his emotions spinning. But he'd fought to keep his reaction imperceptible, to keep a cover over his heart. The idea of moving on was equal parts terrifying and painful. How could he even consider moving on after losing Savilla less than a year ago?

Eleven months.

Where had the time gone?

The harsh ring of the phone jolted him from his thoughts. He dropped his pen and picked up the receiver.

"Bird-in-Hand Carriage Shop," he said. "How may I help you?"

"Allen. This is Rudy." Rudy's resentment sounded through the line. Or was Allen imagining his former friend's hostility?

"Hi, Rudy." Allen plastered a smile on his face despite his growing dislike for how Rudy treated Laura. "How are you doing today?"

"I'm fine, *danki*." He paused. "Laura left me a message last night. I was wondering if I could speak to her."

"Of course. Let me go get her for you."

"*Danki.*"

Allen set the receiver on his desk and hurried into the house. He found Laura leaning over the kitchen counter while perusing her mother's favorite cookbook, the one she carried to his house daily.

When he came up behind her, she jumped with a start and blew out a deep puff of air.

"You startled me." She placed one hand on her chest as she smiled. "I need to put a bell on you."

"I'm sorry." He grinned, enjoying her smile. "Where's Mollie?"

She pointed toward the ceiling. "She's fast asleep in her crib. It's not so hot up there today, and she passed out shortly after lunch. So I came down here to see if I can find something easy I can put together for your supper."

"You have a special supper tonight at home. I can feed Mollie and me." He pointed toward the door. "Rudy is on the phone for you in the shop."

"He is?"

He followed her out to the shop and then entered the bay while she went into the office. He busied himself with arranging the tools in his large toolbox while he waited for her to come out. He hated the jealousy that swirled in his gut like acid. Rudy was her boyfriend! He had the right to call her.

"Rudy said he's going to pick me up at four."

Allen turned toward the doorway where she stood. "Oh. Okay."

She frowned. "I won't be able to make you supper, then."

He fought his smile. "I promise you Mollie and I won't starve."

"Right." She nodded. "I'd better get back to work. I want to get the bathrooms cleaned before Mollie wakes up from her nap."

She was gone before he could respond.

—◦×◦—

Allen finished his accounting books and then returned to the latest buggy he was set to refurbish. He was tearing down the suspension when he heard the clip-clop of horse hooves heading toward his shop. He grabbed a red shop rag and wiped his hands as he walked to the bay door. His jaw tensed as Rudy climbed out of his buggy.

"*Wie geht's?*" Allen called, hoping the greeting sounded friendly instead of irritated.

"Hi." Rudy gave him a halfhearted smile and sauntered toward the shop.

"I didn't realize it was four o'clock already." Allen gestured toward the clock on the wall in his shop. "The afternoon went quickly."

"*Ya*, it did." Rudy gestured toward the house. "I need to get Laura so we can make it to her parents' *haus* on time." He turned to go.

"Wait," Allen called after him.

Rudy spun around, his brow pinched.

"Can we talk for a minute?" Allen pointed the rag inside the shop. "I have a few things I'd like to say to you."

Rudy paused and then nodded. "Sure."

Allen stepped inside and sat down on a stool next to his buggy project.

Rudy walked over to the buggy and ran his hand over the side of it. "Where did you get this?"

"The man who owned it called me. His teenage *sohn* ran it into a ditch, and he asked me if I wanted to buy it from him."

Rudy looked over his shoulder at Allen. "You aren't fixing it for him?"

Allen shook his head. "No, he just wanted to sell it for parts. He bought his *sohn* a new one."

"Really? That's awfully wasteful."

"I thought so, but it's not my business. I can fix it for a couple hundred dollars and then sell it for more than that." Allen's irritation boiled as Rudy studied the buggy instead of looking at him. "Rudy, you've been *mei freind* since I moved here. I can't stand the distance between us. What can I do to make it better?"

Rudy gave him a dark look. "Stop acting like my girlfriend is your *fraa*."

Allen blanched as if he'd struck him. "We've been through this already. I'm not acting like Laura is *mei fraa*."

Rudy's face flushed as his eyes narrowed. "Really? She's stayed overnight for two and half months while caring for your *kind*."

Allen stood. "She isn't staying overnight anymore. The bishop put an end to that."

"Well, it's about time." His smile was smug. "I was hoping he would."

Anger swirled in Allen's chest like wasps as he stood and walked over to Rudy. "Why do you care about what Laura does?"

"She's *my* girlfriend." Rudy pointed to his chest.

Allen took another step toward Rudy, standing nose to nose as he stared into his dark eyes. "I know that, but why do you care what she does? You're not supportive of her. Why are you dating her?"

"I care about her."

"You care about her, but do you love her?"

Rudy hesitated. "*Ya*, if it's any of your business."

"If you love her, then why have you been stringing her along for four years? Why haven't you married her? I dated Savilla for only two years before I married her. I knew when I first met her that she was the woman I wanted to make *mei fraa*."

"That's none of your business." Rudy's eyes shimmered as he lifted his chin. "Maybe you need to worry about your own life and stay out of mine."

Allen's hands balled into fists. He opened his mouth to spew a biting retort, but then Laura burst into the shop with Mollie in her arms.

"Allen! You have to hear what Mollie just said!" She stopped short and divided a look between Allen and Rudy. Her smile fell, and she cleared her throat as she shifted Mollie on her hip and turned to Rudy. "Rudy, hi. I didn't notice your buggy. Let me get my things."

Rudy glared at Allen and took a step back. "I'll wait in the buggy." Then he walked out of the shop.

Laura looked up at Allen, her eyes wide. "What did I interrupt?"

"*Dat! Dat!*" Mollie exclaimed.

"Nothing." He held his hands out to Mollie, and she reached for him. "You should get going." He pulled Mollie into his arms, and she touched his beard as she started telling him a story of some kind.

"Please tell me what happened."

"Let's walk into the house." Once they were in the kitchen, she spun toward him.

"Please tell me what happened between you and Rudy." Her eyes pleaded with him.

"Don't worry about it. You should just go." He touched her arm. "I'll see you tomorrow."

She bit her lower lip. "Are you upset with me?"

He gave a sarcastic snort. "No. I could never be upset with you." When she continued to hesitate, he added, "You'd better hurry up. Rudy is already angry with me, and I don't want him to take it out on you." She opened her mouth to protest, and he said, "Please, Laura. Just go. I promise we'll talk tomorrow. Enjoy your supper."

"Okay." Her voice was soft and shaky, as if she were holding back tears, and the sound tore at his heart. She gathered up her bag, kissed Mollie's cheek, and headed for the door. "See you tomorrow."

Allen moved to the mudroom window and watched Laura climb into Rudy's buggy. As the horse and buggy started down his driveway, he let out a deep sigh. Perhaps he should have made other arrangements for help with Mollie instead of creating this mess of emotions for Laura.

"*Dat.*" Mollie touched his cheek and smiled up at him. "*Dat.*"

Allen's heart warmed as he took in his baby's beautiful face. "*Ya*, Mollie. We're going to be just fine, right?"

"*Dat.*" She rubbed his beard and then rested her head against his collarbone.

"*Ya*, somehow we'll be just fine." Closing his eyes, he rubbed her back and hoped Rudy wouldn't punish Laura for his caustic words.

TWENTY-SIX

Laura's heart pounded as she climbed into the buggy, and her mind spun with questions. Rudy sat rigid, his eyes trained on the road ahead.

"Hi." She set her tote bag on the floor and smiled at him. "How was your day?"

"*Gut,*" he responded, without taking his eyes off the windshield.

"*Danki* for picking me up."

"*Gern gschehne.*" He guided the horse down the driveway without looking at her.

She folded her hands in her lap and looked out the windshield. Worry consumed her. She couldn't wipe the memory of Allen and Rudy standing nose to nose, their faces twisted in furious glares. Had they been arguing about her?

She turned to Rudy and gnawed her lower lip. A deep frown carved into his handsome face, and the strain radiating off him was palpable.

"Are you okay?" Her voice was timid, sounding more like a child's than a woman's.

He responded with a curt nod.

"Are you angry with me?"

He blew out a deep sigh, but it did nothing to release the tension in his posture.

They rode in silence for a few minutes, and when he halted the horse at a red light, she turned her body toward his.

"Rudy, please talk to me. I can't stand the silence between us."

Finally, he faced her. "Why are you helping Allen?"

"You know the answer to that. He needs help with Mollie."

He gave her an unconvinced smile. "Tell me the truth, Laura. Are you doing it for Mollie or for yourself?"

"I-I don't understand."

"I'm not blind, but you're making me look stupid. I see how Allen looks at you."

Stunned, she flinched. "What are you talking about?"

"At least you're not staying there overnight anymore. I'm glad I could put a stop to that."

She gasped, stunned as his words clicked into place. "You told the bishop?"

He shook his head. "I had *mei mamm* tell him." A coldness had crept into his voice.

Laura's body began to vibrate as fury at the betrayal unfurled in her belly, sliding through her veins like a snake. "How could you do that to me?" she said, seething.

"Do you know how it looked having my girlfriend spend the night with a widower?" His voice held a sharp edge.

"*Ya*, I do." She nearly spat the words at him. "It looked like I was helping Mollie adjust. She lost her *mamm*, and then her *mammi* had an accident. I'm the only one who can console her at times."

"You're not her *mamm*!" he said between gritted teeth, and she cowered. "And you're not his *fraa*!"

A car horn behind them tooted, and Rudy looked up at the green light before guiding the horse through the intersection.

He gave her a sideways glance. "Would you like to be his *fraa*?"

She blinked at him as the words echoed through her mind. "Why would I want to be his *fraa*?"

"I don't know," Rudy snapped. "You were always envious of the relationship he had with Savilla. You told me once you wanted a marriage like that."

"What's wrong with wanting a *froh* marriage? That's what we all want, right?" A tremble of anxiety crept into her voice.

He didn't answer.

"Don't you want to marry me, Rudy?"

His lips formed a thin line as he guided the horse onto Beechdale Road. His silence rang clear in her ears, and then it hit her like a ton of bricks—Rudy was never going to marry her. They would never have a future beyond this complicated, frustrating relationship.

As her farm came into view, tears burned behind her eyelids, and despair scorched her throat. She opened her mouth to speak, but a thick knot of humiliation, disappointment, and hurt began to swell, making words nearly impossible. But she had to know. She had to ask.

"You're not going to marry me, are you?" Her words were thick as tears began to stream down her hot face.

He halted the horse at the top of the drive and then turned toward her, his face lined with regret. "I'm not ready."

"You're not ready to marry at all? Or just not ready to marry me?"

"I don't know." He returned to staring out the windshield. "*Mei mamm* has been pressuring me to marry you for more than a year now, but I'm just not ready to ask you. It doesn't feel like the right time."

"So what are we doing, then?" She pulled a tissue from the pocket of her sweater. "We've been together more than four years. Where do you see our relationship going?"

He looked down and picked at his trousers. "I don't know."

Both anger and confidence surged through her body. "You don't want to marry me, but you don't want me to help Allen. What do you want?"

He looked at her. "If I asked you to marry me, what would you say?"

Stumped by the question, Laura shook her head. "I don't know."

Rudy slumped against the buggy door. "So what does that mean?"

Laura felt as if they were sitting on opposite sides of an electric fence. When she spotted movement out of the corner of her eye, she wiped her cheeks and turned. Mark was coming. "We need to talk about this later," she whispered before pushing the door open. "Hi, Mark."

"Hi." His smile faded. *"Was iss letz?"*

"Nothing." She climbed out of the buggy and hefted her tote bag onto her shoulder. "Is Florence here yet?"

"No, but she should be here soon." Mark studied her.

"I'll see you inside." She made her way up the path toward the house while trying to keep her emotions in check. When she reached the back door, she took a deep breath, squared her shoulders, and stepped into the mudroom. She silently prayed for strength as she prepared to face her family—and meet the woman who might change all their lives.

As Laura set the table and Cindy placed a basket of bread on it, the delicious aroma of chili permeated the room. Laura had managed to keep a smile on her face while she and her sister prepared the meal. She didn't want her asking questions right now.

Rudy's admission that he'd asked his mother to talk to the bishop, coupled with his confession that he didn't want to marry her, weighed heavily on her heart. She longed to run to her bedroom seeking solitude, but she forced herself to keep pushing forward.

When *Dat* entered the kitchen with their guests, his smile could not have been wider. He'd waited for Florence and her children on the front porch, and Laura noticed his change of fresh clothes.

Standing tall, he made a sweeping gesture toward the guests beside him. "Laura and Cindy, I'd like you to meet *mei freind* Florence. And this is Sarah Jane and Roy."

"Hello." Laura approached Florence. "It's so nice to meet you. I'm Laura." She shook Florence's hand.

"It's so nice to meet you, Laura." Florence's chocolaty eyes were warm, and chestnut hair peeked out from under her prayer *kapp*. "Your *dat* has told me so much about you." She held up a pie plate. "We brought two pies—one chocolate and one shoofly."

"*Danki*. That's so generous of you." Laura shook Sarah Jane's hand and noticed she had the same chestnut hair and brown eyes. Both women where slightly taller than Laura, but she was used to most people towering over her petite stature.

"*Wie geht's?*" Laura asked Sarah Jane.

"*Danki* for inviting us over for supper." Sarah Jane's smile was shy.

Cindy welcomed them and shook their hands, but she looked shy as well. It seemed she and Sarah Jane were equally nervous and uncomfortable with the meeting. Cindy took the pie plates from them and set them on the counter.

Roy, who was about as tall as Mark, shook her hand. He had the same coloring as his sister and mother. "It's nice to meet you."

"We're so *froh* you came tonight. I hope you like chili." Laura pointed toward the large pot simmering on the stove. "We thought chili would be the best meal to make for our full table tonight."

"That sounds *wunderbaar.*" Florence clapped her hands together as she approached the stove. "I'll have to get your recipe. It smells *appeditlich.*"

"I'll leave you all to get acquainted while I go pay the van driver. I left my wallet in my bedroom." *Dat* smiled at Florence before disappearing from the kitchen.

Laura's stomach constricted at the love in her father's eyes. Would Florence soon become her stepmother and Roy and Sarah Jane become her stepsiblings? The question sent a pang of grief through her already crippled soul.

Florence moved to the table and rested her hands on the back of the chair where her mother used to sit. "How can we help you prepare for supper?"

"We were just setting out the food." Cindy lifted a large bowl of rice. "Would you like to put this on the table while I get out the shredded cheese?"

"Of course." Florence took the bowl from her.

"What can I do?" Sarah Jane walked over to Laura.

"You can pour our drinks." Laura pointed to the empty glasses on the table. "The pitcher of water is in the refrigerator."

Laura began folding napkins and slipping them under the fork at each place setting. The table was set and ready when *Dat* reappeared. He washed his hands in the sink and then stood by Florence.

"Everything looks lovely." *Dat* smiled at the table and then at Florence. "I'm so glad you're here."

"I am too." Florence beamed at him.

Laura glanced over at Cindy. She was standing by her chair, studying her plate.

"We're ready to eat," Laura said, her voice a little too loud. "I'll call in the *buwe* and see if Kayla has arrived." Before anyone could answer, she went out to the porch and focused her gaze on Mark to avoid Rudy's stare. "Supper is ready." Then she saw Kayla. "Hi, Kayla. It's *gut* to see you."

"Hi!" Kayla rushed over and hugged her as the men filed past them into the house. "I was on my way in to say hello and see if I could help. I'm so glad I could leave the restaurant early to join you tonight. How are you?"

"I'm fine." The overwhelming urge to spill her soul hit her, but she resisted.

Kayla eyed her with something like suspicion.

"Let's get inside." Laura followed Kayla into the kitchen, where those who needed to wash their hands did so at the sink. Cindy and Sarah Jane sat together on one side of the table and *Dat* and Florence sat next to each other on the other side. Laura breathed a sigh of relief that Florence hadn't taken her mother's chair.

Jamie and Kayla sat together and Mark joined Roy, Cindy, and Sarah Jane. Rudy took his usual spot and then met her gaze, his eyes pleading with her to join him. Laura squared her shoulders and sat down beside him.

After the silent prayer, the sound of clinking utensils and the buzz of conversation bounced around the kitchen. Laura filled her bowl with rice and chili and began to eat.

Beside her, Cindy and Sarah Jane fell into a conversation about mutual friends in their youth groups. Roy, Mark, and Jamie discussed Jamie's most recent calls at the fire station.

Laura kept her eyes on her bowl as she felt Rudy's eyes watching her. She silently prayed Mark would pull Rudy into his conversation with Jamie. If only they had a special twin telepathy.

"Laura," Florence suddenly said. "Your *dat* told me you've been working as a nanny for your *freind*."

Laura swallowed and looked up at Florence, who smiled. "*Ya,* I have been."

"How old is the *kind?*"

"She just turned a year."

Florence clicked her tongue. "That's such a fun age. Sarah Jane has been working as a nanny for our neighbor. They have four *kinner,* ranging from one to five years old."

"That's nice." Laura smiled despite sensing Rudy's resentment.

"Do you like to quilt?" Florence asked.

Laura shrugged. "I'm not very *gut* at it, but Cindy is a talented quilter. She makes quilts and sells them."

"Really?" Florence looked over at Cindy, who was still talking to Sarah Jane. "We'll have to get together to quilt sometime."

"*Ya.* I would like that." Laura longed for this supper to end. Why couldn't she just hide in her room and shut out the rest of the world?

"Florence," Kayla began, "I don't quilt much, but *mei mamm* likes to quilt when she has time. What's your favorite pattern to make?"

Laura turned toward Kayla, and Kayla smiled at her. Had Kayla jumped into the conversation to help Laura?

Soon Florence and Kayla were engrossed in a conversation about their favorite quilting patterns. Rudy finally joined Jamie and Mark's discussions, and Laura ate in silence.

When they'd finished with pie and coffee, the women began cleaning up the kitchen and the men moved their conversations to the back porch.

"Are you ready for your wedding?" Florence asked Kayla as she swished a bowl in rinse water.

"Oh, no." Kayla shook her head. "My sister-in-law, Eva, and I have been working on the dresses, but we still have quite a bit to do. We've only completed mine. I still need to finish the others.

I can't believe it's less than two months away. I need to finish them soon."

"Do you want me to help you one day?" Cindy offered. "Maybe you could take a day off from the restaurant, and I could come and help you. Or I could work on two of the dresses here too."

"Really?" Kayla spun toward her. "You would help with the dresses?"

"Why wouldn't I?" Cindy asked.

"I know you offered when Jamie and I were first engaged, but I also know you've been busier than usual while Laura's been helping Allen. So I didn't want to ask."

"I still have time. And I'd really like to help."

"Cindy is a fantastic seamstress," Laura chimed in. "She definitely inherited *Mamm's* talent."

Cindy's eyes sparkled with tears, and Laura immediately regretted the compliment.

"That's so kind of you, Cindy," Kayla said as she dried a handful of utensils. "Maybe I could bring you the material for your dress and Laura's dress."

"I could come and get it from you too," Cindy offered.

"Great. Let's talk about that before I leave."

"Laura." Florence turned toward her as she washed another bowl. "Your *dat* says you and Rudy have been together four years now. Do you think your wedding will be next?"

"Oh, well, uh . . ." Heat crawled up Laura's neck. "I'm not sure about that. We haven't actually talked about it."

"Really?" Florence's dark eyebrows careened toward her hairline. "You've been together four years and you haven't discussed marriage?" She looked at Kayla. "How long have you been with Jamie?"

"A little over a year." Kayla gave Laura a sideways glance that resembled an apology. "But I think Jamie was ready before most men are. And he's also older than Rudy."

Laura lowered her gaze to the counter as she continued drying bowls.

"How old are your grandchildren?" Kayla asked Florence.

"Oh," Florence began, "let's see. Judah is five, and Naaman is three."

A few of the knots in Laura's shoulders released once Florence was distracted from any discussion about her and Rudy. Thank goodness for Kayla's intuition!

"Well, we should get going. I'm sure our driver is already waiting outside," Florence said when the work was done. "We had a lovely time. I hope we can do this again soon."

Laura shook Florence's hand. "It was so nice to meet you."

Florence pulled her into her arms for a hug. "I'm so *froh* to meet you and your family."

Laura swallowed and forced a smile. "Have a safe trip home." Then she turned to Sarah Jane and shook her hand. *"Gut nacht."*

Cindy said good-bye to them and then excused herself before heading up to her room.

Kayla sidled up to Laura after Florence and Sarah Jane disappeared into the mudroom for their sweaters and then out the back door. *"Was iss letz?"*

"Everything is fine." Laura nodded despite her shaky hands.

Before Kayla could ask more questions, Laura walked into the mudroom, her body trembling as she pulled on her own sweater. She knew what she had to do. It was time to let Rudy go.

TWENTY-SEVEN

"WOULD YOU WALK ME TO MY BUGGY?" RUDY ASKED Laura as she stepped onto the porch.

"*Ya*, of course." She buttoned her sweater and shivered in the cool breeze.

"We're heading to the barn." Jamie stood and shook Rudy's hand. "*Gut nacht*, Rudy."

"Gut *nacht*," Rudy echoed.

"See you soon." Mark shook Rudy's hand and then gave Laura a concerned expression.

She ignored her twin and followed Rudy to his waiting horse and buggy. Farther down the driveway, *Dat* leaned into Florence's driver's van, no doubt saying good-bye. Or maybe making plans.

"Look, Laura." Rudy leaned back against his buggy, his expression lined with regret. Or was it contrition? "I'm sorry. I was out of line earlier, and I never meant to hurt you. Lately, it seems like all we do is argue."

"I agree. We can't have a conversation without it ending in a heated discussion or an argument." She folded her arms over her chest.

"I'll try harder."

"No." She shook her head as her hope for their relationship crashed and burned a fiery death. "I don't think that will work."

He swallowed. "What are you saying?"

"I'm confused. I'm not sure what I want anymore. I still feel like we've grown apart."

Rudy leaned against the buggy door. "I do too."

"It hurts." She wiped at more tears. "A part of me doesn't want to let you go. You've been my special *freind* for so long, and I feel as if letting you go means I'm letting part of myself go. It's scary to imagine life without you because you've always been there."

"I know." He rubbed his temple. "But at the same time, it's as if we're together just because we've always been together, not because we want to be."

"Right." And then the truth bubbled to the surface, and she knew she had to be completely honest with him. "I think I'm falling in love with someone else."

"It's Allen, isn't it?" He scowled as if the words tasted bitter.

"*Ya*. And I'm afraid of what that might mean. I didn't plan to fall for him. I had no idea it would happen. It just did." Her voice scraped out of her throat, betraying the emotions she tried to suppress. "I never meant to string you along. It hasn't been fair to you, but I can't ignore how I feel any longer."

"*Danki* for being honest with me." He looked more pained than angry.

Silence hung in the air between them, choking her words for a few long and painful moments.

Finally, he turned to her. "So I guess that's it? It's over?"

"*Ya*, I think so." The finality hit her with a heavy feeling in the pit of her stomach, like an iron bar. "We tried to work it out, didn't we?"

"*Ya*, we did." He sat up straight, his eyes sparkling with tears in the dusky light. "I hate to let you go."

"I know, but we have to face reality."

"Are you sure this is what you want?"

"*Ya*, I'm sure." Her words were strong despite her crumbling heart. "I think it's been over for a long time, but neither of us was ready to admit it."

They stared at each other for a few moments, and then Laura turned toward the house. "I need to go." She hesitated. "Rudy, will you keep what I've told you about Allen to yourself? I don't know what I'm going to do about it."

He looked at her with a kind of pity in his eyes. "I won't say anything to anyone. I promise."

"*Danki.*"

She walked toward the porch, and when she turned toward the driveway, she found it empty. She'd been so engrossed in their conversation that she hadn't heard Florence's van leave.

"Laura!" Rudy called after her.

She spun to face him.

"For what it's worth, I'm sorry." He lifted his hands and then let them drop at his sides.

She nodded as her heart shredded. "I am too."

"Are you going to tell me what happened tonight or do I have to guess?" Mark asked her when she reached the top of the porch steps. His blue eyes searched hers.

The porch was empty except for the two of them. Laura breathed in the crisp October-night air as her mind spun with the events of the evening.

"What did Rudy tell you?" She folded her arms over her waist.

"He said you were arguing on the way over here but everything was fine. At supper, I could tell it wasn't fine."

"We broke up before he left."

Mark cringed. "I'm sorry. What happened?"

She summarized their conversation, both before they arrived at the house and just now, leaving out her admission about Allen. Then she held her breath, waiting for Mark's analysis.

Her brother's face twisted into a deep scowl. "Rudy had his *mamm* go to the bishop about you?"

She nodded.

"What was he thinking?"

"He was trying to make a point, and he made it." She sat down on a porch step, and he sank down beside her. "He never trusted me and Allen."

Mark was silent for a moment, and she could almost feel his thoughts whirling like a cyclone. Then he turned toward her. "Are you in love with Allen?"

She paused, debating how Mark would handle the truth if she shared it with him.

"I'm not blind, sis. I see how you and Allen look at each other and interact at church services." He frowned. "Allen is still in mourning. If you set your heart on him, you'll only wind up hurt."

Laura stared at him, her mind spinning with confusion. Once again, her twin was right. She was falling in love with Allen, but the result could be a disaster.

"You need to try to keep your distance from him emotionally. He's still reeling from losing Savilla and adjusting to being a single parent."

"I know," Laura managed to say. "We've just become very close *freinden*."

"Right." Mark's voice held a thread of sarcasm. "I'm sorry you broke up with Rudy. I was hoping he would finally grow up and start treating you right."

"You don't blame me?"

"Why would I blame you?"

"You kept saying I was going to ruin my relationship with Rudy by spending so much time with Allen."

Mark shook his head. "Rudy was wrong to manipulate the bishop into talking to Allen. That was selfish and thoughtless."

"Danki." She sniffed as grief suddenly dominated all her other emotions. "It was really a mutual breakup, though. We agreed we'd grown apart. But we've been together so long it will feel strange not to have him in my life."

Mark nudged her with his elbow. "I'm sure it hurts now, but everything will be okay. You'll meet someone more mature and who wants the things you want."

So you don't see any future for Allen and me.

"I hope you're right, Mark."

"You know I am." He stood. "We'd better get to bed. It's late."

Laura followed her brother upstairs. When they reached the landing, she stopped at Cindy's door and knocked lightly as Mark slipped inside his room.

"Come in."

Laura stepped inside and found her sister propped up in bed, a Christian novel in her hands. "I want to make sure you're okay."

Cindy set her book on her nightstand and sniffed as her eyes shimmered with tears. "Tonight was tough. Florence, Sarah Jane, and Roy are nice, but I'm not ready for *Dat* to move on."

"I know." Laura climbed into the bed and hugged her. "I'm not ready either." She leaned against the pillows and looped her arms around Cindy's shoulders. "But we'll get through this together."

"It will be so strange if he marries her." Cindy took a deep breath. "I don't want a new *mamm, bruder,* and *schweschder.*" Her tears began to flow, and Laura rubbed her back as her own tears streamed down her cheeks.

Cindy grabbed a box of tissues from her nightstand, and they both wiped their eyes. "I miss *Mamm* so much."

"I do too. Especially tonight." Laura took a ragged breath.

"Is everything all right between you and Rudy?"

Laura shook her head. "We broke up tonight." Then she told Cindy a short version of what happened earlier, again keeping her feelings for Allen to herself.

"I'm so sorry. I could tell something was wrong." Cindy frowned. "But to be completely honest, I never liked how Rudy treated you."

Laura turned toward her sister. "What do you mean?"

"I don't know if I can explain it. I just always felt like he was holding something back. Like he didn't love you enough." She touched Laura's hand. "I know you're *bedauerlich*, but please don't give up on love. God has the perfect man for you, and you'll know when you find him."

"*Danki.*" Laura hugged her sister. She was thankful for her siblings. But she wished one of them thought Allen might be the man God had for her. If he wasn't, what was she going to do with her feelings for him?

TWENTY-EIGHT

"*Gude mariye!*"

Allen greeted Laura as she stepped into the kitchen, but his smile faded as he took in the dark circles under her eyes.

"Hi." She set her tote bag on one of the kitchen chairs next to him and then kissed Mollie's head. "How are you this morning, Mollie?"

"Lala!" Mollie held up a Cheerio.

"*Danki.*" Laura ate the Cheerio. "Yum."

"I made you breakfast." He stood and pointed to the platter of blueberry pancakes. "I hope you're hungry."

"*Danki.*" She studied the food, and now she was not only unsmiling, but frowning. "That was very thoughtful of you, but I'm not hungry." She looked up at him. "Did you eat?"

He nodded slowly as trepidation surged through him. His empty plate was right in front of him, smeared with leftover syrup. "*Was iss letz?*"

"I didn't sleep well last night." She began gathering up the dishes. "I'll clean this up."

"No." He walked over and touched her arm. "Slow down." He pointed to the table. "Sit and talk to me."

"I just have a lot on my mind." She looked down at the table and again began to gather dishes. Then she carried them to the counter next to the sink.

"Did something happen last night with your *dat's* new *freind*?" He searched her eyes, hoping to find the answers there.

She faced him and leaned back against the counter. "Supper was fine, but I'm just feeling a little emotional. I can't stop thinking about *mei mamm*."

"I understand."

She turned to Mollie. "Would you like another pancake?"

Mollie squealed, and when Laura placed one on the high-chair tray, the little girl gleefully tore it apart.

"You should eat. As you've told me, you need your strength." He hoped his comment would elicit a smile, but it failed.

"I'll eat something later. I want to get started on the laundry."

"I'm going out to the shop." Allen started for the door, but he couldn't shake the feeling that she was upset with him. When he reached the doorway to the mudroom, he spun and faced her. "Are you angry with me?"

"What?" She turned toward him, her forehead furrowed. "Why would I be angry with you?"

"I was wondering if I caused problems between you and Rudy yesterday. If I did, I'm sorry."

She hesitated and then shook her head. "I'm not angry with you. It was tough to meet *mei dat's* girlfriend and her *kinner*. This is new territory for my siblings and me. I'm not sure how I'm supposed to feel."

"Do you want to talk about it?" He prayed she would open up to him.

"*Danki*, but I'm not ready. I need to sort through it all first."

"Okay. I'm here if you need me."

"I know." Something flashed in her eyes, and her lip trembled. He paused for a moment, but when she remained silent, he headed out. As he walked to his shop, he sent a silent prayer up to God.

Heal Laura's heart, Lord. I don't know how to help her.

As soon as Allen left, Laura poured herself into housework. She was determined to not break down in front of Allen. After meeting her father's girlfriend and breaking up with Rudy, her emotions were too turbulent and her heart was too fragile to risk crossing a line with him.

She cleaned up the kitchen and then played with Mollie until it was time for her morning nap. While Mollie slept, Laura washed and hung out the laundry.

Laura was careful to keep the conversation mundane during lunch and avoided mentioning Rudy. Instead she told Allen what she knew about the Esh family, hoping it would help her accept them into her family's life.

After lunch, she put Mollie down for her afternoon nap in the family room and then dusted and swept the second floor. She was walking down the stairs when she heard the back door click shut. She stepped into the kitchen and gasped when she found Allen leaning over the kitchen sink and cringing as water streamed over his hand.

She dropped the dustpan and broom and rushed to him. "Are you hurt?"

"*Ya.*" He grimaced. "I cut my hand on a piece of metal. I don't think it's too deep, but it sure stings."

"I'll get first aid supplies." She hurried into the utility room, past the wringer washer to the downstairs bathroom, and rooted around under the sink until she found bandages, tape, salve, and a gauze roll. She hustled back to the kitchen and set the supplies on the counter. "Let me see it."

He turned off the water and lifted his left hand. As soon as he moved it, the long gash began to bleed. She sucked in a breath, retrieved a clean dish towel from the drawer, and wrapped it around his hand.

"Of course this happens after you finished the laundry," he quipped with a smile.

She looked up at his bright, intelligent baby-blue eyes and his electric smile, and her pulse skittered.

She looked down and forced herself to concentrate on bandaging his wound. She dried his skin and then applied the salve. As she touched his warm hand, she tried to ignore the wild thumping of her heart.

"Before you ask, I had a tetanus shot last year when I cut my leg," he said, oblivious to her conflicting emotions. "So I don't need to call your *bruder* and ask him to send an ambulance."

She covered the wound with two gauze pads and then began wrapping it with the gauze roll.

"You must really be in a bad mood if you're not even cracking a smile at my lame attempts at jokes."

"I'm just concentrating on taking care of your wound."

"I can't shake the feeling you're upset with me for overstepping my bounds with Rudy yesterday." He touched her shoulder with his good hand, and she nearly jumped out of her skin at the contact. "Please talk to me."

"What did you say to Rudy?"

He paused. "I asked him why he hadn't married you if he loved you."

She froze and swallowed against her suddenly parched throat. "We broke up last night."

"I'm so sorry." He groaned. "I didn't mean to—"

"It's not your fault." She kept her eyes focused on his hand as she cut the gauze roll and then tied it off. "Our problems have been brewing for a while now."

"But I only made them worse."

"No, you just helped bring them to the surface." She rolled up the extra gauze. "He's the reason the bishop came here."

"What do you mean?"

She looked up at him, and his lips were pressed in a thin line. "He had his *mamm* talk to the bishop about us. I was furious when he admitted that, and that's what started our argument last night." She fingered the gauze as she spoke. "He was worried about how it looked to have me stay overnight here, but he wasn't worried about hurting you and me."

She paused as tears stung her eyes. "When I asked him if he wanted to marry me, he said he didn't know. So I spent four years of my life with a man who never wanted to marry me. But . . . but I couldn't say I knew I'd want to marry him either."

She sniffed and gathered up the wrappers from the gauze pads. She carried them over to the trash can and dropped them in while fighting back her threatening tears.

Allen appeared behind her and touched her arm. "Laura." His voice was low and husky in her ear, sending heat spiraling up her spine and making her knees wobble. "Rudy was the one with the problem, not you."

She looked up at him. "The breakup was mutual in the end, but I was the one who initiated it. In fact, I insisted on it. And then last night I stared at the ceiling for hours, wondering if I should have tried again. What if I made a mistake? What if Rudy is the one God wants me to marry? What if I'm alone for the rest of my life while my siblings all get married and have *kinner*? I don't want to be alone. I want to be a *fraa*, and I want to be a *mamm*."

Her tears broke free, sprinkling down her cheeks and peppering her clothes. "I miss *mei mamm*. If only she were here to offer me advice." She covered her face with her hands as sobs barred any further confession.

"*Ach*, Laura. Please don't cry." He pulled her into his arms and held her against his chest. "You have no idea just how amazing you are."

She rested her cheek against his chest and closed her eyes.

"Rudy was *narrisch* to let you go. If he didn't want to marry you, then he was blind. One day he'll realize he let the best thing in his life go, and he'll regret it." His words rumbled in his chest as he rubbed her back. "The man who marries you will be blessed for the rest of his life." The tenderness in his voice made her limp with gratitude.

Laura took a deep breath as her sobs subsided. She wanted to stay there, feeling safe and cherished in his arms for the rest of her life. A vision of Savilla and Allen smiling at each other filled her mind. The memory came on so fast that it left her spinning. She was caught in a storm of guilt.

She had no right to enjoy Allen's touch. He didn't belong to her.

Mark's words from last night echoed through her mind: *Allen is still in mourning. If you set your heart on him, you'll only wind up hurt.*

Her spine went rigid as she stepped away from him. "I'm sorry."

His forehead furrowed. "Why are you sorry?"

"I shouldn't have—I mean I never meant to—" She gathered up the first aid supplies and fled into the utility room.

"Laura!" Allen took a step after her but then froze. It was clear she wanted to get away from him, and chasing her would only make the situation more awkward.

Groaning, he pushed both hands down his face and beard. Why had he crossed the line with her? He knew why. It was because the sight of her sobbing had shredded his own emotions. His instinct was to protect her, comfort her, and soothe her broken heart. He couldn't stand there and let her sob.

But his growing affection for her was a detriment to their special friendship. She'd become too important to him. And his feelings for her grew stronger every day.

Then the truth slammed through him—he was falling in love with Laura. But it was too soon for him to feel love for another woman. Savilla had been gone for only eleven months, and their community dictated that a spouse must mourn for a year. Were his feelings for her sinful since they had developed too soon? Dread poured into him. He couldn't allow himself to hurt Savilla's memory like this. But how could he deny how he felt?

He leaned against the counter and looked toward the doorway she'd used to escape, hoping she would return and talk to him about what had just happened between them.

After several moments, he stared at his bandaged hand, examining how she'd expertly tended to his wound. Perhaps Jamie wasn't the only Riehl with a gift for helping others. A current like electricity had surged through him as she cleaned his cut and then wrapped it. He'd been grateful when she finally opened up to him, but anger bubbled up when she told him Rudy had been the catalyst for the bishop's visit. And when she told him Rudy admitted he didn't want to marry her, his anger transformed into sympathy, and the urge to comfort and protect her overwhelmed him.

When he held her in his arms, he longed to hold her forever. She felt as if she belonged there with him.

He groaned once again. Yes, he did love her. But did she love him too?

He forced the question away. He had no right to love her or

to even assume she loved him. Laura had just broken up with her boyfriend of four years. Allen was out of line to assume she'd even consider having another relationship so soon, especially with him. He was her friend, and he needed to concentrate on being only her friend—at least for now.

He had to put distance between them and give her time to breathe and sort through her confusing feelings. She admitted she was struggling with not only losing Rudy but with accepting her father's new girlfriend. Adding the pressure of a complicated friendship with him would only alienate her.

Pushing off the counter, he started for the back door. He would give Laura the space she needed. But when the time was right, he would ask her if he was imagining a growing affection between them or if she felt it too.

Deep in his heart, Allen prayed Laura cared for him as much as he cared for her.

TWENTY-NINE

LAURA THANKED ALLEN'S DRIVER AND THEN STARTED
up the path to her house. She frowned as she recalled the events
of the afternoon. She'd hidden like a coward in the utility room
until she heard the storm door click shut, indicating Allen had
returned to his shop.

She spent the remainder of the afternoon cleaning and then
made supper. As soon as Allen came in to eat, she packed up her
things and headed home, thus avoiding another awkward and
emotional discussion with him.

She'd spent the ride home staring out the window and eval-
uating her feelings for Allen. Her body quivered as she recalled
how his arms had felt wrapped around her and how his fingers
had caressed her back. She was falling in love, but she couldn't
allow her heart to feel anything more than friendship for him.

There was only one way to put a stop to this mess, and her sister was the key. She prayed Cindy would agree to help her as she
climbed the back-porch steps and entered the mudroom.

After hanging up her sweater, she walked into the kitchen,
where *Dat*, Mark, and Cindy sat at the table. The aroma of meat
loaf filled her nostrils and caused her stomach to growl, protest-
ing her lack of sustenance all day. Her stomach had been tied up

in an emotional knot, and she'd skipped breakfast and only eaten half of her grilled cheese sandwich at lunch.

"Hi, Laura!" *Dat's* face brightened with a smile. "You made it just in time."

"*Wie geht's*, sis?" Mark asked, and Cindy echoed the greeting.

"Hi, everyone." Laura set her tote bag on the floor and slipped into her usual seat, beside Cindy and across from Mark. "Is Jamie on duty?"

"No," Cindy said. "He went to see Kayla tonight. He's on duty Sunday."

"Oh." She bowed her head in silent prayer along with her family. When the prayer was over, she began filling her plate with meat loaf, mashed potatoes, and string beans. "*Danki* for cooking, Cindy. I was hoping to be home in time to help you."

"I don't mind," Cindy said. "How was your day?"

The question was simple, but it hit Laura square in the chest. She swallowed and held her breath as the back of her eyes burned. She'd already cried too much during the past twenty-four hours.

"Sis?" Mark leaned toward her. "Are you all right?"

"*Ya.*" She sniffed before angling her body toward Cindy. "I need to ask you a favor."

"Okay." Cindy nodded.

"Would you take over caring for Mollie? It will only be a week or two since Irma Mae is doing really well."

"Of course I will." Cindy's eyes widened. "But why do you want me to? I thought you loved taking care of Mollie."

That's the problem. "I do, but it's time for me to move on."

"What happened?" Mark's question was measured and his expression stony.

"You were right." Laura's shoulders wilted. "And I don't want to hear *I told you so.*"

Mark set his fork on his plate. "What are you talking about?"

"I got too close, and I have to step away before I get hurt." Laura stared down at her plate, and her appetite evaporated.

"Laura, I'm lost," *Dat* said. "Would you please tell me what you're talking about?"

She took a deep breath and looked at her father. "I've gotten too attached to Allen and Mollie, and I need to make a change before it tears me apart." She heard the tremble of desperation in her voice. "It would be best if Cindy took over for me until Irma Mae comes back."

Cindy touched her shoulder. "You know I'd do anything for you."

"*Danki.*" Laura smiled at her sister.

"I'll just need you to write out instructions for me. Like, what's Mollie's schedule?"

"I'll do that before the weekend is over."

"Are you all right, Laura?" *Dat* asked.

"*Ya,* I'll be fine." Laura picked up her fork, hoping it would appease her father.

"Do you want to talk about it?" Mark's expression was cautious.

"No, I'd rather not." Laura turned to her father. "I enjoyed meeting Florence, Roy, and Sarah Jane last night. I'm sorry I didn't get a chance to talk to you before I went to bed. Do you have plans to see Florence again soon?"

Dat's expression brightened. "I'm so glad you liked them. They enjoyed meeting all of you as well. We're talking about getting together to have lunch, possibly tomorrow. We'll have to arrange a family supper again soon."

"*Ya,* we will." Laura forced a smile. She was certain her twin could see right through her since she was aware his eyes remained focused on her. "So what does Florence like to do besides quilting?"

"Let's see. Well, she likes to read." He grinned. "After all, we did meet at the library."

Laura relaxed as her father talked about Florence during the rest of the meal. When *Dat* and Mark went out to the barn, she and Cindy began their chores.

"How are you doing with your quilt projects?" Laura asked as she washed the first plate.

"I started on a new one yesterday," Cindy said. "It's going to be a birthday gift."

Laura breathed a sigh of relief as Cindy talked about the quilt. She was determined to avoid a heartfelt conversation about Allen and Mollie.

"What do you want me to tell Allen on Monday?" Cindy suddenly asked as she scrubbed a pot.

"What?" Laura stopped sweeping the floor and faced her.

"He's going to want to know why I'm there, and I'll need to tell him something."

"Would you please tell him I'm concerned about the bishop and feel it would be best if you finished out my time with Mollie? That way he'll understand that I feel like I need to take a step back and prevent more rumors."

Cindy shook her head. "But that's not the truth, and it's a sin to lie."

"You're right." Laura gripped the broom as she considered her response. "Then would you tell him I feel like we need some distance?"

Cindy nodded. "*Ya*, I'll tell him that."

As Laura returned to sweeping, she hoped Allen would understand her choice to stay away, and she prayed her absence wouldn't break Mollie's heart.

And then she stilled as she realized another ramification of her decision. Next week would be the one-year anniversary of Savilla's death. She'd envisioned standing at Allen's side, making sure he knew he wasn't alone, trying to ease his pain by sharing the burden of grief.

But she should have known better. Mourning together would only bring them closer, and she couldn't allow that to happen.

⸺ ❧ ⸺

Allen stepped out onto the porch as the van steered into his driveway on Monday morning. He had spent most of the weekend worrying about Laura and about their friendship. He yearned to talk to her and make sure she was okay.

When Cindy climbed out of the van, his heart sank with disappointment. Then panic rushed through him.

He met her at the bottom of the stairs. "Is Laura *krank*?"

"She's fine, physically." Cindy fingered the strap on her tote bag. "She thinks it would be best if she stayed away."

"Why?" He already knew the answer to that question, but he needed to hear Cindy say it.

"She's concerned she's been getting too attached to you and Mollie."

"She was getting too attached?" He repeated the explanation as he pondered it. Did that mean she'd also felt affection growing between them?

"*Ya.*" Cindy nodded toward her tote bag. "Laura wrote down instructions, so I'm sure I can handle the job just fine. I have experience babysitting for my neighbors."

"*Danki* for coming." He nodded toward the house as his disappointment pummeled him once again. "I made breakfast, if you'd like some."

"I already ate, but *danki.*"

He followed Cindy into the house. She set her bag and sweater on a kitchen chair and walked over to his daughter.

"*Gude mariye*, Mollie." She touched Mollie's head. "*Wie geht's?*"

"Lala?" Mollie looked up at her.

"Lala is at home, but she sends her love." Cindy pointed to the Cheerios on the high chair. "Did you enjoy your breakfast?"

Mollie held up a Cheerio, and Cindy laughed.

Allen leaned forward on a kitchen chair as Cindy interacted with Mollie. His chest ached as he recalled the pain in Laura's eyes when she'd sobbed, and then the shock on her face as she rushed away from him after their hug. Had he driven her away? Had he lost her friendship forever? The thought of not having her in his life nearly broke him in two.

Next week, one year since Savilla left them, would be so much worse than he'd hoped. He'd been counting on Laura's strength, on leaning on the person who most understood what he'd been through.

Cindy spun toward him. "Laura said a couple of pairs of your trousers need to be mended. She left them on the sewing table upstairs. Would it be okay if I mended them today?"

"*Ya*, of course." He stood up straight. "She cleaned the whole house last week, and she finished the laundry too."

"I'm sure I'll find something to do while Mollie naps. Do you want anything special for lunch?"

"No, *danki*." He pointed to the refrigerator. "There's some lunch meat, and we have rolls too."

"*Wunderbaar.*" She gathered up the platters of eggs and bacon. "I'll clean all this up."

Allen bit back a frown. While he appreciated Cindy's help, he would spend the day missing Laura's beautiful smile, sweet laugh, and caring heart. But maybe, just maybe, she was right to stay away from him.

Their relationship would never work. He was still mourning his wife, and he had no business even considering pulling Laura into his turmoil. Grieving the anniversary of Savilla's death together would be the exact wrong thing for them both. He had

Irma Mae and Milton to mourn with him, and that would be enough. It had to be.

But how would he ever recover from his attraction to the beautiful Laura Riehl?

_____ ⌒⌒ _____

Laura set a basket of rolls on the table beside a bowl of tuna fish salad before grabbing a bag of pretzels from the counter. She'd spent all morning doing the laundry and then moved to dusting the downstairs to try to keep her mind off Allen and Mollie.

The more she tried to push thoughts of them out of her mind, though, the more they hijacked her brain. She couldn't help but wonder if Mollie missed her or if Cindy had forgotten to put Mollie down for her morning nap. When her thoughts moved to Allen, her stomach tightened and her chest ached.

Oh, she missed him.

Laura touched her cheek as it warmed. She had to get ahold of her emotions before her father and brothers came in for lunch. She filled four glasses with water and then set them by the place settings. She was adding napkins when the men walked in. She smoothed her hands down her apron and plastered a smile on her face.

When Mark frowned, she looked away. She'd somehow avoided being alone with him all weekend, especially by going to bed early, but she was certain he would find a way to get her alone today. She knew he wanted to know what happened at Allen's.

"Laura." Jamie crossed to the sink and washed his hands. "I didn't expect to see you here today."

"I guess I didn't mention my plans when I saw you over the weekend. Cindy went to Allen's for me." She fetched a head of washed lettuce from the refrigerator and began peeling off leaves.

"Oh. Why?" Jamie leaned back against the counter while drying his hands.

"I wanted to stay home today." She set the lettuce on a plate and then put it in the middle of the table.

Mark looked over at Laura from the sink. His eyes seemed to glitter with questions and concern.

She nodded toward the table. "I think I remembered everything."

"It looks perfect." *Dat* washed and dried his hands and then touched her shoulder. "How are you feeling?"

She forced her lips to curve into the sweetest smile she could muster. "I'm fine. *Danki.*" Then she clapped her hands. "Let's eat."

She sat down in her usual spot at the table, across from her brothers. After a silent prayer, she looked over at Jamie. "How was your shift at the fire station last night?"

"Busy." He piled lunch meat and cheese on his roll. "We had two medical calls and one car accident. I hardly slept at all."

Mark pointed to Jamie. "But notice he's too stubborn to take a nap. He got home and went right to work in the barn."

"You know I don't need a nap." Jamie added mustard and mayonnaise to the sandwich.

Mark cupped his hand to one side of his mouth and pretended to shield his words from Jamie. "He does need a nap."

Laura couldn't stop a laugh as she piled lunch meat and cheese on her own roll.

Jamie rolled his eyes. "You enjoy harassing me, don't you?"

Mark tilted his head mockingly. "Isn't that what younger *bruders* are for?"

"Tell us about the medical calls," Laura said, encouraging Jamie to change the subject.

"The first call was for a little *bu* who had a seizure."

Laura tried to listen to his story, but her thoughts kept drifting to another place.

Laura gathered their plates and carried them to the sink, and her brothers headed outside. *Dat* walked into his first-floor bedroom for a moment. She was washing the dishes when he returned.

She dried her hands on a dish towel. "Are you heading outside now?"

"I am, but I want to talk to you for a moment." His expression grew serious. "I owe you an apology."

"Why would you owe me an apology?"

"Mark pointed out that you were the last one to know about Florence, and I'm sorry. You were over at Allen's the night I told Cindy and Mark, and I should have made a point to tell you the next time I saw you." He rubbed her arm. "I never meant to make you feel left out. You're very important to me."

"*Danki.*" His words warmed her soul, causing her lip to tremble.

He paused for a moment. "Are you okay with my dating Florence?"

"*Ya.* I just want you to be *froh.* You really like her, don't you?"

"I do like her, and I'm enjoying getting to know her. She understands what it's like to suddenly lose your partner. We've been talking about how we're wading through the sea of grief in our souls. We're helping each other, and I appreciate that. We all need to find someone who understands us and offers comfort when we need it. Florence may be that person for me, but I'm still getting to know her." He touched her arm again. "But I don't want to do anything to hurt *mei kinner.* Is Cindy handling this okay?"

"She needs some time to adjust, but I think she'll eventually be okay."

"I'm going to talk to her alone and see how she is."

"I think she'll appreciate that."

He jammed this thumb toward the door. "I'm heading outside."

"I'll see you later." As *Dat* left the house, Laura wondered again if someday soon she would call Florence her stepmother.

———⌒⌒———

"How did it go today?" Laura worried her lower lip as Cindy set her tote bag on a kitchen chair.

"It went well." Cindy sat down in a chair and rested her chin on one palm. "Mollie asked for you all day long. I kept telling her you send your love."

Laura's heart dropped as she sank into the chair across from her sister. "Did she cry?"

Cindy shook her head. "She started to, but I talked her out of it."

Laura frowned. "I'm sorry."

"Don't be. She was fine."

"How was Allen?" Laura held her breath.

"He was disappointed when he saw me."

"What did you tell him?"

"I told him the truth. I said you felt it was best to stay away because you were concerned you were getting too attached to him and Mollie."

"What did he say?"

"He seemed surprised, but he didn't say anything else. He didn't say much at lunch, and he was quiet all day. He kept thanking me for coming, but I could tell he missed you."

Laura swallowed as her throat thickened. *I miss him too.*

But she knew Allen's quiet demeanor was about more than his missing her. The anniversary of Savilla's death would be hard for him this next week. If only she could be there to help him through it, but she couldn't. Being there would only make things worse—for both of them.

Cindy pushed her chair back and stood. "How can I help with supper?"

As Laura joined her at the counter, she tried to push away thoughts of Allen and Mollie, but she couldn't stop imagining Mollie crying for her.

She prayed Mollie would adjust to having Irma Mae back, but a tiny, selfish part of her longed to continue as Mollie's caregiver. She would always cherish the months they spent together.

THIRTY

"WE'RE HERE." ALLEN YAWNED AS HE LIFTED MOLLIE
out of her seat on Sunday morning two weeks later.

Mollie moaned and rubbed her eyes as she settled against his
shoulder. He sighed. She'd kept him up for nearly two hours last
night crying and asking for Laura, but at least that was an hour
less than the night before. She did well with Cindy on weekdays,
but on weekends it was Laura she missed.

When his alarm clock went off this morning, he'd considered rolling over and going back to sleep, but today was a day he
needed church. He had to pray for guidance on how to move on
without Laura in his and Mollie's life.

Mollie squirmed, and he put her down. Taking her hand, he
steered her up the path toward the Glick family's barn, where the
service would be held today. A group of men was gathered by the
entrance, and he immediately spotted the Riehl men.

When his thoughts turned to Laura, he tried to push them
away. She'd made it clear by sending her sister over that she didn't
want to see him.

The weeks since then had flown by at lightning speed, but
his heart grew heavier with each passing day since speaking with
her. He'd hoped to speak to her at church two weeks ago, but she
had stayed home. When he asked Vernon where she was, he'd

frowned and said she'd stayed home with a headache. Allen suspected her headache was caused by the strange emotions that had been brewing between them for months.

And then she'd sent her sister in her place.

His feelings for Laura continued to haunt him. And now he was determined to apologize to her for whatever he did to drive her away. He couldn't bear the distance between them. He prayed she would attend church today and let him talk to her.

He guided Mollie toward the men, and Vernon turned toward him and waved as they approached.

"Allen!" Vernon shook Allen's hand. "*Gude mariye.*"

"Hello. How are you?" Allen greeted Jamie and Mark and shook their hands.

"How are you, Mollie?" Mark squatted down and touched Mollie's arm. "It's great to see you this morning."

Mollie hid behind Allen's leg, and the men laughed.

"She's shy this morning." Allen lifted her into his arms. "It's probably because she didn't sleep much."

"Oh no. Is she *krank*?" Vernon asked.

"No, she just—"

"Lala!" Mollie screeched and leaned away from him. "Lala!"

Allen turned toward the house and spotted Laura standing by the porch, talking to Kayla and Cindy. His heart seemed to turn over in his chest at the sight of her in a bright-blue dress.

"Lala!" Mollie tried to shift out of his arms.

"Calm down, Mollie Faith. You're going to fall." He set her down on the ground and took her hand.

"Lala!" She yelled, tugging at him.

Allen looked at Laura and found her staring at him, her eyes wide. "Excuse me," he said to her family, and then he led Mollie toward the porch.

As they moved up the path, Laura descended the stairs and

met them halfway. Allen released Mollie's hand, and she rushed over to Laura.

Laura lifted Mollie into her arms and hugged her close to her chest. "Hi, Mollie."

"Lala!" Mollie rubbed Laura's cheek and then snuggled into her shoulder.

Laura made a noise in her throat, and her breathtaking blue eyes glimmered with unshed tears. "I've missed you too," she whispered before kissing his daughter's head.

Allen's heartbeat galloped as he watched Laura cuddle with Mollie.

Why can't we be a family?

The question caught him off guard and stole his breath for a moment.

"How is she?" Laura met his gaze and sniffed.

"She misses you."

Laura looked down at Mollie. "Cindy told me Irma Mae will be back tomorrow. That should make you *froh*."

He felt his face cloud with a frown. "You know we both miss you. Is that why you left?"

"What?" Her eyes snapped to his again.

"Did you leave because you didn't want to admit there's something between us?"

She lowered her voice. "Allen, I don't think this is the time or place—"

"But we need to talk about it." He took a step toward her.

"Please don't." She stepped back.

"Laura." Irma Mae walked over to them. "*Danki* for taking care of Mollie for so long."

"Hi, Irma Mae. I enjoyed my time with her very much." Laura gave her a bright smile. "It's so *gut* to see you walking without your cane. How are you feeling?"

"I feel great. *Danki*." Irma Mae held her arms out to Mollie. "May I hold you?"

Mollie blinked up at Irma Mae and then reached for her.

"How are you, sweet girl?" Irma Mae asked Mollie before kissing her cheek. "I'll be back tomorrow to take care of you."

"It's nine." Mark sidled up to Allen and touched his shoulder. "We need to head inside." He glanced at Laura, and an unspoken discussion passed between the twins.

Laura frowned and then looked at Allen. "It was nice seeing you." She touched Mollie's arm and smiled at Irma Mae. "I'll see you after the service." Then she strode back toward the house.

Allen's heart seemed to trip over itself as she walked away. How could he convince her to talk to him about the emotions raging between them?

"May I hold her during the service?" Irma Mae's question wrenched Allen from his thoughts.

"*Ya*, of course." Allen nodded. "Just signal me if you need a break."

"I'm sure I won't." Irma Mae beamed as she gazed down at her granddaughter. Then she looked back at Allen. "I'll see you after the service."

Mark nodded at Irma Mae. "It's great to see you. I'm glad you're feeling better." Then he steered Allen toward the barn. "How have you been doing?" he asked as they made their way to the door.

"I'm fine." Allen held his breath, waiting for Mark to instruct him to stay away from his twin.

"I've spoken to Laura about why she stopped working for you."

Allen halted and turned toward him. "Look, I'm sorry." He was careful to keep his voice quiet. "I didn't mean for everything to get so complicated."

"I know." Mark's expression remained friendly. "I just think you two need a break from each other. Laura is confused about a lot of things. She misses our *mamm* and Savilla, and she's reeling from her breakup with Rudy. I think she needs some time to figure things out. It's probably best if you give her some space to sort through her confusing emotions before you try to figure out what's going on between you two."

"I'll give her all the space she needs."

"*Danki.* I'll see you later." Mark smiled and then walked toward the barn.

As Allen watched him go, he frowned. As much as Mark wanted him to stay away from Laura, he still needed to clarify a few things with her. He had to before he could let her go.

━━━ ༄ ━━━

Laura clasped her hands together and gnawed her lower lip as her nerve endings stood on end. Sitting between Cindy and Kayla, her spine was ramrod straight.

She tried to listen to the minister delivering his sermon, but against her better judgment she allowed her eyes to wander across the barn. Allen sat between her father and Milton. His gaze was intense as it tangled with hers, causing her pulse rate to increase as her body flushed hot. When he finally looked away, she could breathe again.

Again she tried to focus on the minister's holy words, but she was keenly aware of Allen's stare when it found her again.

"Lala!" Mollie suddenly cried from Irma Mae's lap on the opposite side of the barn from Allen. "Lala!"

Laura sucked in a breath and gripped the bench with such force that her knuckles ached. An overwhelming urge to go get Mollie came over her.

Cindy leaned over to her. "Are you all right?"

Laura shook her head and looked down.

"She'll stop," Cindy whispered. "Be strong."

"I miss her so much," Laura whispered as tears blurred her vision.

"I know, and she misses you too." Cindy touched her arm.

Laura squeezed her eyes shut and opened her heart to God.

Please, Lord, give me strength to keep my distance from Allen and Mollie. I never should have allowed myself to get so attached, but now I need your help breaking my tie to them. I feel their pull on my soul, and I'm afraid I'll accidentally break Mollie's heart. She's so important to me, and I don't want to hurt her.

Relief flooded Laura when Mollie stopped fussing and settled down on Irma Mae's lap. She managed to focus on the minister's holy words for the remainder of the service.

As soon as the service was over, Laura went to the Glicks' kitchen with Cindy and Kayla so they could help serve the noon meal. Laura carried a tray with bowls of pretzels to the barn and began setting them on the tables the men had constructed.

When she came to the table where Allen sat with her brothers, father, and Milton, she quickly set out the bowls and gave them a tentative smile before hurrying out of the barn.

As soon as her shoes hit the ground, she heard someone say her name. She spun and almost collided with Allen. Her senses tingled as she looked up at him. The dark purple circles she'd seen rimming his eyes earlier were still there, and now his brow pinched with irritation, or perhaps desperation.

"What do you want?" she asked before craning her neck to see if anyone was watching them.

"I told you. I need to talk to you. If you don't talk to me, I'll stand here and yell your name until you do."

She blew out a frustrated puff of air. "Fine." Then she pointed to a corner of the barn. "I'll give you two minutes."

"*Danki.*" He followed her there and then faced her. "Tell me the truth. What drove you away from Mollie and me? Was it the hug?"

She nodded and crossed her arms over her chest as if to shield her heart.

"I'm sorry."

"It's not your fault." Her voice sounded thin and reedy. "Mark was right when he warned me to avoid getting too close. I got too close and too attached. I guess I just wanted a family, so I latched onto you and Mollie."

He shook his head as his lips thinned. "You really think that's all it was?"

"I can't do this." Her body trembled. She needed to get away from him before he pulled the truth from her. She couldn't admit she had feelings for him, that she might even love him.

She spun on her heel and began to walk away, but he grabbed her hand and pulled her toward him, making her stumble. She glared at him and yanked her hand from his grasp.

"Please don't touch me," she snapped before running toward the house. As she moved up the path, she passed Irma Mae, and she hoped the older woman hadn't seen her awkward exchange with Allen.

Guilt and regret rolled over her. What would Irma Mae think if she knew Laura had developed feelings for her son-in-law?

─ ⌒⌒ ─

The following afternoon Allen knelt on cool ground, and the dampness of the grass seeped through the knees of his trousers.

His eyes stung with tears as he reached over and touched the hard granite that marked the spot where his beloved wife was buried.

He'd told Irma Mae he had to run out for supplies, and after running his errands, he headed straight to the cemetery.

He blew out a deep breath and turned his gaze upward. The sky was clogged with sad-looking gray clouds. It was the same kind of sky above the mourners the day of Savilla's funeral, and the same kind of sky he and her parents stood beneath on the one-year anniversary of her death.

"Hi, Savilla. It's me, Allen. It's been a tough year," he whispered as he traced his fingers over her name etched in the gravestone. "I . . . I wanted to come back to visit you today. I couldn't talk to you like this with your folks here. Mollie and I miss you. She's changed and grown so much. You'd be so proud of her. She's walking, and she talks too." He smiled. "She looks like you. She has your *schee* smile and your gorgeous hair." He chuckled to himself. "She has your stubbornness, but she also has your intelligence. She's already learned how to open doors, and I caught her trying to climb into the linen closet the other night."

He sat back on his heels and pulled his coat tighter around him. "Saying I miss you is a gross understatement. I miss you so much I feel like I can't breathe sometimes. I'll see something that makes me think of us, and I'll want to either laugh or cry. Some days I still can't believe you're gone. And I still don't understand why God took you so soon. I know it's not my place to question his will, but I still think about the plans we'll never see come true. You're on my mind every day. You'll always be a part of me, and you'll always have a piece of my heart."

A car's motor sounded in the distance as he pulled at a brown blade of grass. His thoughts spun. "I didn't think I'd be ready to move on without you for a long, long time, if ever. But something has happened to me. I'm not sure what it all means, but I need to tell you everything. Your *mamm* was hurt in an accident, and while she was healing Laura came over to take care of Mollie."

He ripped out the blade of grass and absently twisted it around his fingers. "I didn't mean for it to happen, but I've fallen in love with Laura. I think she might love me too, but she's resisting. She doesn't even want to talk to me right now. I suspect, like me, she's afraid. Yet she's been my rock as I've tried to figure out how to go on without you, and I think I've helped her through a tough time too."

He closed his eyes. "When I'm with Laura, I feel as if I can go on and be strong again. I've tried to repress my feelings for her, but I can't. They're real and they're strong. And if you could see her with Mollie, you'd realize how much she loves her. She's wonderful with her, and Mollie loves her too."

He sucked in another deep breath through his nostrils and then released it into the chilly air. "I'm just so confused, because being with her feels right, but I'm not sure how you would feel about it. In some ways, I believe I'm disrespecting you, but another part of me believes you would understand. You'd want me to find a new *fraa* who would be a *gut mamm* to Mollie. I believe in my heart you would approve of Laura being that woman, but I can't be sure. And I know she'd want you to approve as well."

He reached out and brushed his fingers over the gravestone again. "Savilla, I need to know what you think of all this. Would you bless a relationship between Laura and me? Would you forgive me for falling in love with your best *freind*? Please send me a sign and tell me it's okay for me to love Laura and move on."

Allen covered his face with his hands as a tear trailed down his face. "I miss you, Savilla. *Ich liebe dich.*"

Pulling himself to his feet, he kissed the tips of his fingers and touched her gravestone one last time. Then he trudged through the grass to his waiting horse and buggy.

THIRTY-ONE

ALLEN CLIMBED THE BACK-PORCH STEPS AS THE CRISP November breeze seeped through his gray shirt, causing him to shiver.

He hung his straw hat on a peg in the mudroom and then stepped into the kitchen. Irma Mae was setting a pot in the middle of the table. The aroma of grilled cheese filled his nostrils and caused his stomach to growl.

"I thought grilled cheese and tomato soup would be *gut* today since the temperature dropped so much last night." Irma Mae carried a frying pan over to the table and set a grilled cheese on each of the two plates.

"*Danki.*" He walked over to Mollie, who was already happily chewing on a piece of her grilled cheese sandwich. He kissed her head, washed his hands at the sink, and sat down at his usual spot at the table.

Irma Mae joined him, and they bowed their heads for a silent prayer.

"How is your day going?" Irma Mae asked as she ladled soup into her bowl.

"*Gut.* How is yours?" He lifted his sandwich but then put it back on his plate.

"Fine."

Allen served himself some soup, and they ate in silence for a few minutes while Mollie grunted with every bite.

Irma wiped her mouth with a napkin and then leveled her gaze at him. "I've been back for a week, and I've noticed a few things."

"What?"

"You don't eat much, and you're very *bedauerlich*." She pointed at him. "*Was iss letz?*"

Stunned by the question, he stared at her for a moment. "The first anniversary of Savilla's death wasn't that long ago, and I guess I'm still taking it hard."

"I understand. It was tough on me too, but there's something else."

He stared down at his bowl of soup and uneaten sandwich.

"You miss Laura."

The words were simple, but they grabbed him by his throat and guilt swept through him. How could he admit to Savilla's mother that he had feelings for Laura? She'd have every right to feel betrayed.

"Have you tried to call her?"

Allen looked up at her. "How did you know I care for Laura?"

To his surprise, she snorted. "I think everyone in our church district is aware of how you and Laura feel about each other. The intensity between you two is palpable." She smiled. "I was young once. I remember what it felt like to fall in love."

He cringed at the word *love*.

"I've noticed how you two stare at each other during the service, and it's obvious how much Mollie misses her too. You've both fallen for Laura, and I don't blame you. She's a *wunderbaar maedel*." She leaned forward. "Why haven't you gone after her? Why have you let her slip through your fingers?"

"It's too soon since we lost Savilla, and I don't want to disrespect her memory."

She sat back in the chair. "If your feelings for Laura are genuine, and I believe they are, then you should see where they lead."

He studied her brown eyes. "You're not upset with me for having feelings for Laura so soon?"

She shook her head. "Savilla would want you and Mollie to be *froh*, and it's clear Laura makes you both *froh*."

Her words settled over him like a warm blanket. Was this the sign he'd asked Savilla to send him a week ago? Did Irma Mae's encouragement indicate Savilla would also approve of his feelings for Laura?

But how would he ever convince Laura to give him a chance when she wouldn't even speak to him at church services? Maybe they didn't belong together. Maybe God didn't bless their relationship and Allen was supposed to wait for another woman to enter his life. But if that were true, why did his heart ache for Laura?

―☙―

"Lala!" Mollie screamed between sobs as Allen rocked her in the middle of the night. "Lala!"

"I know, Mollie," Allen whispered against her head. "I miss her too."

How would he ever console Mollie when her love for Laura was so overwhelming?

He moved the chair back and forth until she fell asleep and then set her back in her crib. He returned to the chair for several more minutes, waiting for her to start screaming again. When she remained asleep, he stood and padded out of her room, down the short hallway, and into his bedroom. The soft yellow light of his lantern lit Savilla's dresser. He walked to it, and his gaze fell on her photo of a rose with that favorite Scripture on it.

He picked up the frame and studied the photo as he recalled

when he'd bought it for her. He'd seen it in a store, and when he read the Scripture verse, he remembered it was her favorite. He'd given her the picture for their first wedding anniversary, and her eyes filled with tears when she opened the gift bag.

He moved his fingers over the frame as he read the verse, 1 Thessalonians 5:16–18: *Rejoice always, pray continually, give thanks in all circumstances; for this is God's will for you in Christ Jesus.*

The words echoed through his mind as he stared at the rose. After several moments, he placed the frame back on the dresser and then sat down on the edge of the bed. His eyes moved to the top drawer of his dresser. Months ago, he'd hidden Savilla's favorite memento in that drawer for safekeeping. He crossed the room, opened the drawer, and pulled out the little metal box where she'd kept her bobby pins. He turned it over in his hand and then looked toward the cardboard box he'd brought in from his shop.

It was time to pack up the rest of Savilla's things.

He retrieved the cardboard container and put the little metal box in first. Then he added the framed photo of the rose along with her comb and brush. He left only the candle. Then he set the box in the corner. He would put it in the attic in the morning.

He climbed into bed, turned off the lantern, and stared at the ceiling as memories of Savilla tumbled through his mind.

He recalled when he first met her. Her face had lit up when she saw him at the bus station, and her brown eyes sparkled as they said hello. And then he remembered how beautiful Savilla looked in her cranberry-colored dress the day of their wedding. He was certain he couldn't love her more than when the bishop declared them married. But he was wrong. His love for her grew exponentially when they moved into their home and then when they welcomed their first child into the world.

But in a flash, Savilla was gone, leaving him to raise Mollie alone. His heart was battered and bruised after losing her, but with God's help, he was able to pick himself up and face each day without her.

And now he found himself lost once again. While his heart still ached for Savilla, his heart also craved Laura. He still longed to talk to her, to protect her, to explore his feelings for her.

If Laura still had a hold on his heart, did that mean the feelings were genuine and true?

Allen rested his arm on his forehead as confusion took hold of him, making his throat tight. Irma Mae's words from earlier in the day sounded in his mind.

If your feelings for Laura are genuine, and I believe they are, then you should see where they lead. Savilla would want you and Mollie to be froh, *and it's clear that Laura makes you both* froh.

He glanced toward the box of Savilla's things and recalled her favorite Scripture passage. Yes, he did need to pray. He needed God to clarify the bewilderment in his heart and mind.

"God, I need your help." He stared at the ceiling as he whispered the words. "I need you to guide my heart and my mind. Irma Mae has told me to follow my heart. She said it's okay to fall in love again, but I don't know if my feelings are real. Am I truly falling in love with Laura? Or am I only confused by all the grief I carry for Savilla? If I love Laura and belong with her, then how can I know Savilla would approve of Laura to care for Mollie? Help me, God. Help me feel your presence and know if my feelings for Laura are pleasing to you."

Then he rolled over on his side and hoped sleep would soon find him.

"Cindy, these dresses are gorgeous!" Kayla held up her blue dress and spun around the kitchen. "*Danki* so much for finishing them for me!"

"*Gern gschehne.*" Cindy's face turned pink.

Kayla pulled Cindy into a hug. "I can't believe we're going to be *schweschdere* in a few weeks!"

Laura smiled as she sat at the kitchen table and fingered her mug of tea.

"Your wedding is coming so fast, Kayla." Florence beamed as she sat across from Laura. "Do you have everything you need?"

"*Ya.*" Kayla draped the dress over the chair at the far end of the table and then sat down beside Laura. "I picked up the table decorations last night, so I just need to put them together."

"We can help with that." Cindy sat beside Florence and looked at her sister. "Right? We can go over to Kayla's tomorrow and work on them with Eva while Kayla is at work at the restaurant."

"That would be fun." Laura nodded and then sipped her tea.

"I can help too," Sarah Jane offered as she sat at the other end of the table. "If you want my help." She looked at her mother. "Right, *Mamm*?"

"*Ya.*" Florence smiled. "I'd love to help too, but it's okay if you don't want me there."

"I'd love to have you there. In fact, I have an idea." Kayla snapped her fingers. "Maybe I can get off work tomorrow. Saturdays are busy, but Nathan isn't volunteering at the fire station until next week. Plus we have two waitresses who are doing a great job. If *mei dat* agrees to let me skip work, then we can all get together at *mei haus* and have a *schweschdere* day!"

Kayla beamed. "My first *schweschdere* day with my Riehl family. Oh my goodness! My name is going to be Kayla Riehl in no time."

Laura looked down at her mug and tried to banish the black cloud of despondency that had settled over her since she'd told Allen she didn't want to talk to him at church. She couldn't get Allen or Mollie out of her thoughts, and her heart broke into tiny, quaking pieces.

She missed Allen and Mollie to the very depth of her marrow. But she didn't know how to even approach him. How could she apologize for pushing him away, and how could she even justify her feelings for her best friend's widower?

"Laura?"

"What?" Laura looked up and found everyone staring at her. "I'm sorry. I was lost in thought."

"Are you okay?" Kayla touched her arm.

"*Ya.* I'm fine." Laura cupped her hand over her mouth to hide a feigned yawn. Then she forced a smile on her lips. "I'm just tired. I'm sorry."

"Oh, Laura." Kayla snapped her fingers. "I've been meaning to ask you something. Did I see you talking to Rudy at church?"

Laura nodded. "I did."

"What did he say to you?" Kayla asked.

"Nothing really." Laura shrugged. "He asked me how I was doing, and we talked a little. He's doing well."

"So he's not upset about the breakup?"

Laura shook her head. "It was a mutual decision. There aren't any hard feelings." She forced a smile. "What were you saying about the table decorations?"

Kayla hesitated and then smiled. "I was thinking we could all get together after breakfast. We can spend the day at *mei haus*, and then Eva and I can make a nice lunch for us too."

"What do the table decorations look like?" Sarah Jane asked.

"They're going to be so nice." Kayla blushed. "I hope that doesn't sound prideful. I found some *schee* cranberry jar candles, and I thought we'd put one on each table with a little red bow on it. We can also put a little holly and pine branch in front of each one. Maybe you can help me tie the bows on the candles and then cut the holly and pine branches. I got all the supplies on sale at that store next to the fire station. I bought them while I was visiting Jamie at work. It was quiet, so he was able to go with me."

As Kayla talked on about the decorations, Laura looked down at her mug of tea again and allowed her thoughts to roam.

Her mind had replayed her last conversation with Allen again and again. She couldn't stop herself from recalling the pain in his eyes when she'd told him not to touch her. She was certain she'd hurt him, maybe even broken his heart. And she longed to apologize. She wanted to tell him how she felt about him, but it was too risky. She couldn't stand the thought of hurting him again, or hurting Mollie if things didn't work between them.

Laura sniffed and cleared her throat before glancing up. When she looked across the table, she found Florence watching her with a kind expression on her face. Laura quickly looked away for fear of raising Florence's suspicions. While she enjoyed the frequent visits with Florence and Sarah Jane, Laura wasn't ready to open her heart to her father's friend. She worried Florence would think Laura was a horrible person if she knew she had feelings for her best friend's widower.

When the clock on the wall read 7:30, Kayla pushed back her chair.

"I guess I'd better get home," she said as she gathered some of the mugs and took them to the counter. "I'll talk to *mei dat* and then call you about tomorrow." She hugged Laura. "*Danki* so much for having me over for supper."

"It was nice to see you too," Laura said. "Hopefully we'll see you tomorrow."

"Why don't I walk you out?" Cindy offered.

"I'll come too." Sarah Jane followed them to the mudroom, where Laura could hear them chatting as they put on their coats.

Laura picked up the last mugs and carried them to the counter. She filled the sink with hot, frothy water and began to wash them while her thoughts spun with memories of her time at Allen's house.

Her thoughts turned to worry. Was Mollie still crying for her at night? Was Allen angry with her for not telling him she was going to send Cindy in her place?

"I realize you don't know me very well, but I'm *froh* to listen if you need someone to talk to."

Laura jumped and gasped as she turned toward Florence. She'd forgotten Florence was still in the kitchen.

"I'm sorry." Florence smiled as she came to stand beside her. "I didn't mean to startle you."

"It's okay. You caught me deep in thought."

"You've been deep in thought most of the evening." Florence picked up a dish towel and began to dry the mugs.

"I have been." She turned back to the sink and washed another mug.

"Do you want to talk about it?"

Laura started to say no, but as she dropped the mug into the water and reached for a towel, a rush of tears overwhelmed her, spilling down her cheeks before she could stop them.

"*Ach, mei liewe.*" Florence pulled Laura into her arms and rubbed her back. "Nothing should make you this upset."

Laura began to fight against the sobs but then succumbed to them, crying on Florence's shoulder.

"Please tell me what's wrong so I can try to help you." Florence's words were warm and comforting in her ear.

After a few moments, Laura regained control of her emotions and stepped away from Florence. She wiped her eyes and nose with a paper towel.

"Please talk to me." Florence touched her arm.

"I'm in love with my best *freind*'s widower." Laura breathed a deep sigh as a weight lifted from her shoulders. Saying the words aloud released some of the tension in her chest.

Florence tilted her head. "Allen?"

"*Ya.*" Laura sniffed. "It's a long and complicated story."

Florence pointed toward the table. "Let's sit and you can tell me."

Laura sat down at the table across from Florence and then poured her heart out to her. She explained how she'd cared for Mollie for three months and then sent her sister to take over when her relationship with Allen grew complicated. She told her just enough about Rudy for the story to make sense. And then she ended with the last time she and Allen had spoken.

"I don't know what to do with all these feelings. I'd hoped being away from him would help me get over them, but they're even stronger now." Laura ran her thumbnail over the wood grain in the table. "I can't stop thinking about him, and I worry about him and Mollie." She peeked up at Florence. "You must think I'm horrible for falling in love with him."

Florence clicked her tongue. "Why would I think that?"

"Because he's Savilla's husband. She was like a *schweschder* to me. I have no right to care about him. She would be so disappointed in me."

"You and Allen both loved Savilla, and she's the one who brought you two together. You and Allen were the most important people in her life, aside from her *dochder*, of course. Why would she be upset that you and Allen fell in love when she loved both of you so much?"

Laura stilled. "I never thought about it that way."

"I believe God leads us to the people we're supposed to love. If you feel in your heart that you and Allen belong together, then you should follow your heart. Let God guide you to Allen and see what happens."

Laura took a ragged breath as a peace settled over her. Was this the answer she'd been craving?

"Laura?" Florence touched her hand. "Did I say something wrong?"

"No." Laura smiled. "You were a tremendous help."

"I'm so glad." Florence looked up at the clock. "I suppose I need to get on the road. Our driver should be here already. I'm surprised Sarah Jane didn't come after me, but she's probably enjoying your family's company out in the barn. I hope to see you again soon."

"I hope to see you too." And Laura meant her words. Florence had been a blessing to her, and she certainly was a blessing to her father.

As Florence walked to the mudroom, Laura hugged her arms to her waist. Florence's words settled over her heart as a tiny glimmer of hope sparked in her chest. Maybe, just maybe, a romantic relationship could work between her and Allen.

That is, if Laura still had a chance after she'd been avoiding him. Or had she lost him forever?

THIRTY-TWO

Allen sat straight up in bed and rubbed his eyes. Something had awakened him, but what was it? He glanced around his bedroom, still cloaked in darkness. The digital clock on his nightstand read 11:50. Had he been dreaming?

Then a wail sounded from down the hall, followed by deep, guttural coughing.

Mollie!

Allen leaped out of bed and ran down the hallway, his feet thumping on the cold linoleum floor as he rushed to her room.

When he stepped into the doorway, he gasped. Mollie knelt in her crib and gagged before vomiting all over her bed.

He rushed over and lifted her. "Mollie?"

Her cheeks felt clammy as she screamed and then gagged once again.

"Shh, Mollie." He touched her forehead and found it was clammy too. "Calm down, *mei liewe*. You'll be fine."

She gagged again, leaned forward, and vomited again.

No, no, no!

Terror gripped him, and his heart felt lodged in his throat like a chunk of ice. No, she couldn't be ill like Savilla was.

No, God, no. Please don't take her too!

He had to get her help. He couldn't waste any time getting her to the hospital.

With his heart slamming against his rib cage, he grabbed the lantern off her dresser, carried Mollie into the bathroom, wrapped her in a towel, and set her on his bed. After pulling on a pair of trousers, a shirt, and socks, he picked her up and rushed down the stairs.

In the mudroom, he pushed his feet into a pair of work boots and grabbed the key for his shop. He ran out the back door and into the shop. Mollie squirmed in his arms and shrieked as he dialed nine-one-one.

Memories of the night Savilla took ill filtered through his mind, and he was determined not to make the same mistakes he made a year ago. He was going to save his baby.

With his entire body trembling, he rubbed Mollie's back and cradled the receiver between his ear and his shoulder.

"Nine-one-one. What's your emergency?" a man's voice responded on the other end of the line.

"I need an ambulance." The words tumbled out of his mouth as he yelled over Mollie's sobs. "My daughter is very ill. She's only fifteen months old. She's vomiting, and I think she has a high fever. Please come quickly." Then he recited his address and held his breath as inwardly he begged God for help.

Please don't take her, God. Please keep her safe. She's all I have left.

"We'll have someone there to help you shortly," the man promised.

Allen hung up the phone and then rushed out to the driveway. Mollie shook in his arms and then began to gag. He held her as she vomited in the driveway and then screeched.

The crisp November air soaked through his clothes as she continued to shake. He walked back into the house and carried her into the downstairs bathroom, where he wet a washcloth and held it to her forehead as she cried.

"Lala!" she moaned. "Lala!"

"I'm sorry, but she's not here." He rocked her back and forth. "Help is coming. Please hold on."

When she began to vomit again, he held her over the commode. He closed his eyes and begged God to send the EMTs soon.

He was cleaning her face when he heard voices sounding in the kitchen.

"Hello! Is anyone here?" someone called.

"Allen?"

Allen rushed into the kitchen and almost ran into Jamie. Leon and Brody were standing behind him.

Allen blew out a deep sigh of relief. "Jamie. I'm so glad you're here."

Jamie's expression was grave. "What's going on?"

"It's Mollie." Allen's voice tried to yell over Mollie's moans and sobs. "She has the same symptoms Savilla did. She has a fever and has been vomiting. I need to get her to the hospital."

"The ambulance is on its way." Jamie held up his hands. "We'll get her there as quickly as possible."

"Please." Tears stung Allen's eyes. "I have to get her there. If I don't get her there in time . . ." His voice trailed off as tendrils of fear curled around his chest and tangled in his throat. Deep down he knew it was unlikely Mollie would have the same condition that took Savilla. But he wasn't taking any chances. He looked down at his daughter, and she squirmed and rubbed her eyes. Her cheeks were bright pink as droplets of sweat shimmered on her forehead.

"Come with me." Brody walked over to him. "Let's walk outside and meet the ambulance."

"Lala!" Mollie hollered. "Lala!"

"Is she calling for Laura?" Jamie asked.

Allen nodded.

"Do you want me to ask her to meet you at the hospital?"

Allen shook his head. "I don't think she'll come."

"I think she will." Jamie started for the door. "Do you want me to call Irma Mae too?"

"*Ya*," Allen called after him. "*Danki.*"

Red lights from outside reflected off the ceiling, and Allen sucked in a deep breath. Help was here.

"Laura!" a voice called as someone banged on her bedroom door. "Laura! Wake up!"

She sat up and yawned as she turned toward her clock. It was 12:30. "*Ya?*"

The door swung open. Jamie stood on the threshold dressed in his uniform and holding a lantern.

"Jamie." She squinted as her eyes adjusted to the light. "What are you doing here?"

"Get dressed," he ordered. "I'm taking you to the hospital."

"What?" She shook her head, trying to make sense of his words. "Why?"

"An ambulance just took Mollie there, and she was screaming for you."

Her blood ran cold as she jumped out of bed. "What happened to her?"

"She's been vomiting, and she has a fever." Jamie's expression was serious. "She was stable when I left his house, but Allen is a mess. They both need you."

She shivered and was suddenly queasy with fear. "I'll be dressed in a minute."

"I'll be downstairs." He started out the door, and then she called him back.

"How did you get here?"

"One of Allen's *Englisher* neighbors came out to see why the rescue vehicles were in his driveway. I asked him if he'd give me a ride to come and get you. He's waiting to take us to the hospital."

"I'll be right down."

"Jamie?" Mark's voice sounded in the hallway. "What's going on?"

Jamie stepped into the hallway and closed the door behind him.

Laura sucked in a deep breath as she pulled on a dress and put up her hair. Panic threatened as tears filled her eyes.

As she finished dressing, she sent up a silent prayer.

Please, God. Please heal sweet Mollie and calm Allen. And let me be a blessing to them.

⎯⎯ ⁓ ⎯⎯

Allen held Mollie's hand as he sat in a chair next to her hospital crib. Thankfully she slept as an IV dripped into her little arm. He glanced over at Irma Mae and Milton, who were sitting together on a small sofa with weary eyes.

"You gave us a scare, little one," he whispered to Mollie. "I'm not sure how I'm going to recover from this one."

A knock sounded on the door and then it opened. Jamie stood in the doorway. "How's she doing?"

"She's going to be okay," Milton responded.

"The doctor thinks it's a stomach virus," Irma Mae chimed in. "But all her labs looked *gut*. They're giving her fluids. *Danki* for sending someone over to get us."

"*Gern gschehne*. I'm glad she's going to be okay." Jamie stepped into the room. He glanced behind him and then over at Allen. "Someone here wants to see you and Mollie." He gestured behind him, and Laura stepped into the room.

Allen's heart seemed to do an unsteady flop as he took in her beautiful face and red puffy eyes. Had she been crying for Mollie? He stood as his heart swelled with love and affection for her.

"Laura." He breathed her name.

Mollie opened her eyes and looked up at Laura. "Lala." Her voice croaked.

"Mollie." Laura came to her and leaned down to touch her hand. "How are you?"

"Lala." Mollie reached for her.

"Oh, I can't pick you up because you have medicine in your arm." She looked at Allen. "But I'll stay if your *dat* says it's okay."

Irma Mae stood. "I think we can go home since Laura is here." She looked at her husband. "Right, Milton?"

"*Ya*." Milton stood and turned toward Jamie. "I wonder if we can find a ride home."

"*Ya*. A couple of the guys from the station are in the waiting room. They'll take you." Jamie touched Laura's arm. "I'm going to go too. Call the station if you need me."

"*Danki*." She smiled at him and then said good night to Irma Mae and Milton.

"I'll call you when Mollie is released," Allen told them as they left.

"*Gut nacht*." Irma Mae blew Mollie a kiss and then followed Milton and Jamie out the door.

"How is she?" Laura asked as Mollie closed her eyes.

"She's going to be okay." Allen's voice sounded strange to his own ears. "Her exam was *gut*, and her lab results didn't show any sign of infection. The doctor said it's a stomach virus. They gave her some Pedialyte and the IV fluid to keep her from becoming dehydrated."

"Oh, praise God!" Her voice sounded thick. "I was so worried when Jamie came to get me."

"I was worried too." He scrubbed one hand down his face and beard. "She woke me up screaming, and then she started vomiting. All I could think about was what happened to Savilla. I just tried to get her here as soon as I could. I keep wondering if I'd gotten Savilla here sooner, then maybe she'd still be—"

His voice broke as tears trickled down his cheeks. He covered his face with his hands as all the fear, anxiety, and frustration of the last year poured out of him. His body quaked as he fought for control of his emotions.

Then he felt arms encircle his waist. Laura pulled him against her, and something inside of him melted—something cold and hard. Was it his fear, his loneliness, or his grief? He knew in a flash that it was all three and more. Laura was here. For the first time since he'd lost Savilla, he felt his ever-present loneliness deflate like a worn-out balloon.

He rested his cheek on her prayer covering and breathed in the flowery scent of her shampoo. His body relaxed as her touch and compassion calmed him. She was the balm his damaged soul needed.

"What happened to Savilla wasn't your fault." Her voice was warm and comforting in his ear, like a gentle caress. "It was God's will, so stop blaming yourself. You took *gut* care of her, just like you take *gut* care of Mollie."

He nodded and sniffed as he worked harder to control his crashing emotions, and then he took a shuddering breath as his tears subsided. "I was so afraid. I kept thinking I was going to lose her and then be all alone."

"She's going to be fine." Laura looked up at him, her eyes fierce. "And you're not alone."

He stared down at her, losing himself for a moment in the depths of her blue eyes. "How long are you going to stay?"

"I'm here for as long as you want me." She cupped her hand to his cheek, and he leaned into her touch. "I'm sorry I pulled away from you after the day you hugged me. I was confused, and I thought staying away was the right solution. But I've realized I was wrong. I miss you and Mollie, and I can't bear to stay away."

"I'm sorry I scared you off, but I can't deny how I feel about you."

"How do you feel about me?"

"You're my best *freind*. You taught me how to love again and how to be a better *dat*." He took her hands in his, enjoying the feel of her skin.

"Laura, you're my first thought in the morning and my last thought before I go to sleep at night. *Ich liebe dich*. I thought maybe I was confused, but I know it for sure now. I kept telling myself I shouldn't love you, not only because you're Savilla's best *freind* but because it's so soon after we lost her. But Irma Mae encouraged me to follow my heart. She said Savilla would want us to be *froh*, and I've concluded that she's right. Why wouldn't Savilla want us to be *froh*?"

"I love you too." She sniffed as her eyes glistened with tears. "And I love Mollie. I felt guilty for falling for you because I believed I was disrespecting Savilla's memory, but last night Florence said something that made me realize it was okay. She said you and I both love Savilla, and it makes sense that we would grieve together. She said it was Savilla who brought us together, and God leads us to the people we're supposed to love. I think she's right."

His chest swelled with happiness. "I think so too. You're everything to me. You make me laugh, and you listen to me when I need a *freind*. You order me around and keep me in line. You've been my strength through the hardest time in my life. I can't imagine my life without you."

She gave him a watery smile. "I feel the same way about you. I can't imagine my life without you or Mollie."

He wiped away her tears with the tip of his finger. Then he leaned down and brushed his lips over hers, sending heat roaring through his veins.

"*Ich liebe dich*, Laura. If your father agrees, will you be my girlfriend?"

She nodded. "*Ya*, I'd love that."

As he pulled her into his arms, he silently thanked God for leading him and Mollie to Laura and giving him a second chance at love.

THIRTY-THREE

"LAURA," DAT SAID AS HE APPROACHED HER IN THE back of the barn. "Could you please come over here for a moment?"

"*Ya*, of course." She nodded at some of the guests who had come to celebrate her brother's wedding, then followed her *dat* to a far corner of Kayla's father's barn. All three of Laura's siblings stood there with Florence, her three children, and her grandchildren. Laura moved to stand next to Mark.

"What's going on?" Mark asked.

"I have an announcement to make." *Dat* glanced at Florence, and they smiled at each other. "Florence and I have been talking, and we've decided we're ready to start a life together. We're going to get married next month, and we couldn't wait to tell you."

Laura's mouth dropped open as she turned to look at her shocked twin.

"That's *wunderbaar*," Jamie said, hugging his father. "We're so *froh* for you."

"Congratulations." Laura hugged her father and then hugged Florence. "Welcome to the family."

Florence rested her hand on Laura's shoulder. "I know this will be an adjustment for everyone, but I promise I'll take *gut* care of your *dat*."

Laura smiled. "I know you will."

Mark tapped her shoulder. "I'm going outside for some air."

"Okay. I'll see you later."

After talking with Florence's children for a few minutes, Laura searched the sea of faces for Allen. She couldn't wait to tell him the news. He'd run to the house to check on Mollie a short while ago. She crossed the barn and then made her way to the doors leading to the outside.

She shivered and hugged her wrap against her body as she stepped out of the barn and breathed in the cold December air. She looked up at the sunset splashing the sky with vivid colors of red and orange.

The day had been perfect. Her older brother had married the love of his life, and Kayla was now her sister. And to make the day even more perfect, her father had announced his engagement. How her life had changed in just a few months!

"Laura." Allen jogged over to her and took her hand. "I was just coming to find you."

"How's Mollie?" She smiled up at him.

"Fast asleep in her play yard in Kayla's parents' room. I think the wedding wore her out."

Laura covered her hand with her mouth to cover a yawn. "I agree. The wedding wore me out too."

He laughed and then pointed to the back porch. "Can we sit and talk for a bit?"

"*Ya*, that would be nice. I have something to tell you." She allowed him to steer her down the path leading to the house and then up the steps to the porch. They sat together on the glider, and she couldn't help but think of their conversations on Allen's front porch. That was where their special friendship had blossomed, and her love for him had started to grow.

There's room on the porch swing for you, he'd said.

"What did you want to tell me?" he asked as he pushed the glider into motion.

"*Mei dat* just announced he's engaged and getting married next month."

"No!" Allen's eyes widened.

"*Ya*, he did."

"How do you feel about it?"

"I'm okay." She hugged her wrap even tighter against her body. "It's going to be challenging as we become a blended family, but we'll get through it. I just want *mei dat* to be *froh*."

He smiled. "That's a *gut* way to look at it."

Laura's gaze moved to the bench near the pasture fence, and she shook her head when she spotted Mark sitting there, surrounded by a group of four young women. He looked as if he were telling a story while they all listened with rapt attention.

"What are you looking at?" Allen's voice was close to her ear.

"*Mei bruder*." She pointed to the bench. "He's the life of the party. All the *maed* love him. When is he going to settle down?"

"Who knows?" He shrugged. "Maybe never?"

"Oh, don't say that. I'd like to see him fall in love. He'd make a *gut* husband and *dat* if he could just pick one *maedel*."

"Speaking of picking one *maedel*, I want to talk to you about something."

She turned toward him, and her pulse zipped at the intensity in his eyes. "Okay."

He angled his body toward hers and took her hands in his. "I've been doing a lot of thinking. You're very important to me. In fact, you're the most important person in my life—other than Mollie, of course."

"You're important to me too."

"I believe God sent you to help me with Mollie for a reason. You quickly became my confidante. You were the only person who would ask me how I was doing and really want to know the truth. You saw me at my worst and encouraged me when I felt like I was falling apart." He paused. "I've thought about what Florence said to you about how Savilla brought us together, and I believe that."

"I do too." She squeezed his hands. "You've been my best *freind* since I first came to work for you in July, but I was too blind to see it. I was so worried about hurting Rudy that I didn't even realize you were a better *freind* to me than he could ever be. You were the one protecting me and encouraging me when I was low. You helped me through my grief for *mei mamm* and Savilla, and you listened to me when I was confused about *mei dat*'s relationship with Florence. You're the person I want to share all my secrets with. When something exciting happens, you're the first person I want to tell. I can't imagine my life without you or Mollie."

"*Danki.*" He swallowed, and something that looked like fear flashed across his face. "We haven't been together officially for very long at all, but I can't stop feeling like God and Savilla want you, Mollie, and me to be together permanently. I think they all want us to be a family."

Her breath stalled in her lungs as her hands quaked.

"I've already spoken to your *dat*, and he's given me his blessing. Now I need to ask you."

Her heart thumped, and now her whole body trembled.

"Laura, I can't wait to spend the rest of my life with you. I'd be honored if you would marry me and adopt Mollie." He held up his hand before she could respond. "I know this is soon, but I can't wait to start a life with you. Would you consider being *mei fraa*?"

"*Ya! Ya!* I'd be honored to be your *fraa* and Mollie's *mamm*."

"I'm so glad." He leaned down, and her breath hitched in her lungs.

When he brushed his lips across hers, the contact sent her stomach fluttering with the wings of a thousand butterflies. She closed her eyes and savored the taste of his mouth against hers. This was how true love was supposed to feel. Allen was the one God had sent to her.

When they parted, his baby-blue eyes were intense once again. "I'm so thankful God brought you into our lives. Mollie and I will cherish you forever. *Ich liebe dich.*"

"I will cherish you and Mollie forever. I can't wait to start my life with you both." She cupped her hand to his cheek. "*Ich liebe dich. Danki* for being *mei* best *freind.*"

As Allen pulled her close for a hug, Laura felt overwhelming gratitude—and silently thanked God for allowing her to love him and Mollie.

DISCUSSION QUESTIONS

1. Laura is certain she's supposed to stay with Rudy even though their relationship has deteriorated over time. She's also worried she'll never find true love or have a family if they break up. What do you think caused her to change her point of view on love throughout the story?
2. Allen is devastated when Savilla dies unexpectedly. Have you faced a difficult loss? What Bible verses helped you? Share this with the group.
3. Toward the end of the story, Florence convinces Laura to allow herself to love Allen. She tells her Savilla would want Laura and Allen to be together, if that's what makes them happy. Do you agree with Florence's assessment of the situation? Share this with the group.
4. Laura feels alienated from her family when she's the last to know her father is dating Florence. Think of a time when you felt lost, alone, forgotten. Where did you find your strength? What Bible verses would help?
5. Laura is shocked when Rudy admits he had his mother tell the bishop Laura was staying overnight at Allen's house to help care for Mollie. Why do you think Rudy did that? Do you think his motive was pride, jealousy, or something else?
6. Vernon is concerned his new relationship with Florence

might upset his children, but he also feels it's time for him to find love again. Can you relate to Vernon and his experience? How?

7. By the end of the book, Allen believes Savilla would approve of his feelings for Laura. What do you think helped him realize it was okay for him to not only love again, but to love Laura?

8. Which character can you identify with the most? Which character seems to carry the most emotional stake in the story? Is it Allen, Laura, Rudy, or someone else?

9. What role did Mollie play in Allen and Laura's relationship? How did she help to reconcile their relationship at the end of the book?

10. What did you know about the Amish before reading this book? What did you learn?

ACKNOWLEDGMENTS

As always, I'm thankful for my loving family, including my mother, Lola Goebelbecker; my husband, Joe; and my sons, Zac and Matt. I'm blessed to have such an awesome and amazing family that puts up with me when I'm stressed out on a book deadline.

Special thanks to my mother and my dear friend Becky Biddy, who graciously read the draft of this book to check for typos. Thank you, Becky, for your daily notes of encouragement. Your friendship is a blessing! Thank you also to Jessica Miller, RN, for her medical research for this book.

Thank you to Janet Jeter for help with the twin research. You're so blessed to not only have a twin brother, but also another set of twins in your family! Thank you for giving me pointers on Laura and Mark's connection. I'm so grateful to have you as one of my work buddies.

I'm also grateful to my special Amish friend, who patiently answers my endless stream of questions.

Thank you to my wonderful church family at Morning Star Lutheran in Matthews, North Carolina, for your encouragement, prayers, love, and friendship. You all mean so much to me and my family.

Thank you to Zac Weikal and the fabulous members of my Bakery Bunch! I'm so thankful for your friendship and your excitement about my books. You all are amazing!

To my agent, Natasha Kern—I can't thank you enough for your guidance, advice, and friendship. You are a tremendous blessing in my life.

Thank you to my amazing editor, Becky Monds, for your friendship and guidance. Thank you also to editor Jocelyn Bailey for your friendship and encouragement.

I'm grateful to editor Jean Bloom, who helped me polish and refine the story. Jean, you are a master at connecting the dots and filling in the gaps. I'm so thankful that we can continue to work together!

I also would like to thank Kristen Golden and Allison Carter for tirelessly working to promote my books. I'm grateful to each and every person at HarperCollins Christian Publishing who helped make this book a reality.

To my readers—thank you for choosing my novels. My books are a blessing in my life for many reasons, including the special friendships I've formed with my readers. Thank you for your email messages, Facebook notes, and letters.

Thank you most of all to God—for giving me the inspiration and the words to glorify You. I'm grateful and humbled You've chosen this path for me.

THE AMISH HOMESTEAD SERIES

AMY CLIPSTON

A PLACE AT OUR
TABLE

— AN AMISH —
HOMESTEAD NOVEL

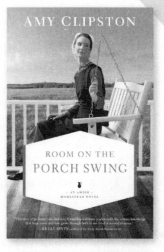

AMY CLIPSTON

ROOM ON THE
PORCH SWING

— AN AMISH —
HOMESTEAD NOVEL

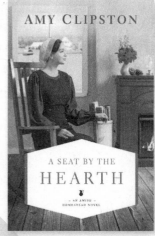

AMY CLIPSTON

A SEAT BY THE
HEARTH

— AN AMISH —
HOMESTEAD NOVEL

BESTSELLING AUTHOR
AMY CLIPSTON

A WELCOME AT
OUR DOOR

— AN AMISH —
HOMESTEAD NOVEL

AVAILABLE IN PRINT AND E-BOOK

ZONDERVAN®

ABOUT THE AUTHOR

Dan Davis Photography

AMY CLIPSTON IS THE AWARD-WINNING and bestselling author of the Kauffman Amish Bakery, Hearts of Lancaster Grand Hotel, Amish Heirloom, Amish Homestead, and Amish Marketplace series. Her novels have hit multiple bestseller lists including CBD, CBA, and ECPA. Amy holds a degree in communication from Virginia Wesleyan University and works full-time for the City of Charlotte, NC. Amy lives in North Carolina with her husband, two sons, and six spoiled-rotten cats.

Visit her online at amyclipston.com
Facebook: @AmyClipstonBooks
Twitter: @AmyClipston
Instagram: @amy_clipston